*T*hey took off into a bright dawn, with the spring air chilly all around them and the sun beginning to rise on their left. Lord Dugannon was much taken with the sunrise. "We don't see them like this on the ground," he said in contentment, watching it for some time with childlike pleasure.

The Halifax was flying like a dream. Although it was heavier and more sluggish than anything Caroline had flown before, it moved with a sort of ponderous grace. Once she got used to the reaction time, she relaxed. The sun had come up nicely and the trip ought to be uneventful.

And then a Messerschmitt came on her from high on her left, right in the sun, just where he was supposed to be. *If* Caroline had been looking. But she wasn't looking. There had not been any radar reports of German activity when she left. The first knowledge she had of the German plane was a spatter of machine-gun fire that riddled the fuselage and caused the Halifax to shudder under her hands.

Lord Dugannon immediately began shouting, and Caroline looked around desperately, seeing for the first time the fighter that had materialized out of nowhere, cursing the fact she wasn't flying the faster, more maneuverable Mosquito and that the plane was unarmed. If she didn't do something fast, they were going to be shot out of the sky because someone in Air Transport had decided that women shouldn't fly armed planes.

Also by Jeannette Angell from Lynx Books:

Wings

FLIGHT

Jeannette Angell

LYNX BOOKS
New York

FLIGHT

ISBN: 1-55802-021-7

First Printing/May 1989

This is a work of fiction. Names, characters, places, and incidents are either the product of the author's imagination or are used fictitiously. Any resemblance to actual events, locales, or persons, living or dead, is entirely coincidental.

This book is published by Lynx Books, a division of Lynx Communications, Inc., 41 Madison Avenue, New York, New York, 10010. The name ''Lynx'' and the logo consisting of a stylized head of a lynx are trademarks of Lynx Communications, Inc.

Printed in the United States of America

0 9 8 7 6 5 4 3 2 1

To Doug, who has taken me flying
more places than I ever dreamed
I could go.

With love and gratitude.

Acknowledgments

Once again, I need to thank Ellis Smith, first and foremost, for helping me understand the world of corporate intrigue, and sketching together this story against that backdrop. Ellis has taught me to look and understand . . . and, perhaps, in some small way, do something about it.

Thanks to Edwin Angell, who once again launched himself into this project with much enthusiasm and tireless efforts to secure material for my research, and whose caring and love mean so much to me. It's been a difficult time. I'm glad that we came through it together.

Thanks also to the National Aerospace Museum in San Diego, California, for use of their facilities and invaluable information on World War II aviation.

My friend Fran Short listened—a lot—and shared her experiences with me. Deborah Wetmore gave me hyacinths for the soul; Andy Nagy provided inspiration and support through his own creative efforts and endeavors. And Michael Manzi took time to explain the intricacies of nuclear mysteries to a very dim pupil.

Daniel Rosenbaum, a writer himself, helped me laugh at myself; he is a faithful friend, and his support over many years has made me both a better writer and a better person.

I cannot fail to acknowledge my editor, Christine Kinser of Cloverdale Press, for putting up with a lot of neediness on my part, and always responding with reassurance and excellent judgment. This book is her work, too.

Barbara Pandolfi and Fred Hammdorff made me feel wanted and needed, and then cared enough about me to let go when this book required that I do so: in their own way, each of them gave me special wings. There aren't enough nice things to say about that. Barbara continues to be a great friend and a great supporter, both of which are bright and shining gifts.

Thanks to Lindsey Torosian, who showed me his own unique view of flight, and enriched my own.

Hardly least, thanks to my family for all of their love and support: Doni and Eric Kronenwetter, John and Bernice Torosian, Edwin Angell and his wife Lydia. And, always, thanks to my mother, Elizabeth, who gave me a great deal more than a name for one of my characters. The world still echoes with her absence.

Finally, and mostly, and always, thanks to Doug. He opened the sky to me, and there will never be enough words to express gratitude for that. He made this story come alive when it seemed to be dying, and his technical critiques have made it far more accurate than I ever could have achieved on my own. He gave me space, strength, courage, and love, and never let me believe that I was a failure, even when I tried very hard to convince him that I was.

Chapter One

*I*t appeared that the war that everybody had said wouldn't happen was closer than anyone cared to think.

Caroline Asheford leaned slightly forward and tapped the altimeter on her instrument panel. The needle swung around wildly for a moment before righting itself, and she smiled. The A.R.M. airplane was still holding together, even though Eric told her that he would replace it any time she chose. "It was built in nineteen twenty-nine, Caroline. Things start to go wrong after ten years."

"Not if it's built as well as you always claim it was!" she had responded, laughing, but the truth was she liked the older model. The new airplanes that Eric's company was turning out on a daily basis were sleeker and safer perhaps, but she liked the uncomplicated systems of her little monoplane. It couldn't go very fast, and it rattled when she banked it too steeply, but it was hers, and it was comfortable, and that was all that really mattered.

She looked down now, watching her shadow flit over the clouds below, an alien shape in this world of white and blue. The clouds were thinning out already in strands of cotton, and somewhere ahead of her she could see the lush green of trees and meadows through gaps in the cloud cover. Any moment now she would be free of it altogether and humming out over Block Island, and the Atlantic Ocean.

The sunlight streamed into the cockpit and lit up her blond hair like a halo. She still wore it short and curly, over the token protestations of her husband and of Eric, both of whom had shown a marked preference for the long wavy tresses she had once had. But Caroline liked it short and tousled—her Amelia Earhart curls, as Steven had once called them—all she had to do was run her fingers through it once or twice to keep it in place. There was a lot more to do in life than fixing one's hair all the time.

Caroline's eyes under the fringe of blond hair were brown: dark, intense, in vivid contrast to the fair complexion and golden hair. Her father's eyes. She had heard that, over and over again, throughout the years, how her eyes looked like his.

The altimeter was behaving itself—it usually did after she tapped it once or twice, just to show it that she was paying attention. She was registering plenty of fuel and the engine was running smoothly. Oil pressure was good. She smiled and unconsciously began to sing softly, her voice barely audible over the roar of the engine mounted at the front of the plane. Someday, Eric had told her, he would make a soundproof cockpit. Someday.

Caroline banked to her right and descended a thousand feet, emerging from the clouds altogether. The sun was sparkling brightly off the water, and the shadow of her airplane skimmed over the waves as gracefully as it had skimmed across the clouds a few minutes before. The whole expanse of the Atlantic Ocean stretched out, endless and taunting. Somewhere, over there, she had been born.

And now over there was a threat, a call to arms. Germany had mobilized, and was threatening Poland. Mussolini had already annexed half of Ethiopia. . . . Her mother was in Ethiopia. Or someplace like that. Caroline narrowed her eyes against the sun, but she could see nothing other than sea gulls which soared and wheeled about, screaming as they flew. Europe was too far away to even imagine, and yet—these days—it was fearfully drawing nearer.

Europe had been her first home: She was born in England to a Frenchman who had already died fighting the Great War—World War I, the war that they had said would end all wars. What nonsense. She wondered, sometimes, what life would have been like if her father had lived. She had never seen him but she did know him through others, and it seemed that he was a person who inspired intense feelings. "The best man who ever lived," Eric said of him, fervently. "He had vision, and he had loyalty, and he had . . . oh, God, Caroline, I don't know. He was unique." Her mother, Amanda, had different things to say about him: "A spoiled aristocrat. He was used to having whatever it was that he wanted." Caroline had laughed at that. "Mother! You just described yourself!" And Amanda's eyes had clouded over as she responded, "Yes. That was the point, don't you see? Neither of us could accept the fact that we couldn't make everything turn out all right."

The sun was shimmering on the water, almost too bright for comfort. Here, up here, Caroline could escape the voices of her past. Here, and here alone, she felt that she could be who she really wanted to be. Between earth and sky, with the air buffeting her about and the clouds her sole companions: Here she could breathe. Down there were too many people who wanted to tell her who she should be, what she should do. Their conflicting voices rose up around her in a cacophony. No wonder that all she had ever wanted to do was escape.

Her father's voice was the only one that wasn't raised, that she couldn't hear, that she had never heard. She thought somehow that he would have approved of her life, of her flying.

She knew the story by heart, knew it from her mother and from the nights—so many nights—when she had lain awake in bed and thought about him, about both of them, weaving her own version of their story in her mind. Her mother, the spoiled debutante from Newport, on her first trip to France, and her father, the aristocratic French count, dazzled by the impetuous American woman. She defied convention, and he had never known anyone who did so with such verve. Except, of course, himself.

They had loved each other, Amanda and Philippe, and had spent a summer of adventure together that stretched into a lingering fall, into winter . . . and eventually into war. Eric, Philippe's friend and partner, had been there and she had his memories to augment her mother's accounts: Eric and Philippe had built airplanes back when no one was building them, and Amanda had come along with her friend Sarah, an aviatrix, to watch them do it. They participated in the first wild days of flight when the airplanes were made out of canvas and wire, with no instruments, no brakes, and precious little other than the daring of the pilots. . . .

In her mind, Caroline could almost see what had happened. She could see them dragging the little contraption out of the hanger, and one of the test pilots—or was it Sarah?—climbing into the cockpit. Sarah had insisted from the first that she wanted to fly Eric's airplanes. The little plane gathering speed as it raced down the dirt runway with peasants from the village running on either side to keep the wings from tipping, and finally the heady wonderful feeling when the nose pointed up and the air caught the wings and provided the lift, and it was actually aloft. . . . And Philippe, later, popping champagne corks, his arm around Amanda, with all of them laughing and celebrating together.

Philippe and Amanda. Eric and Sarah. They had thought that it would last forever.

Caroline shook her head. She, of all people, knew that nothing could last forever. Even if it hadn't been for the war, things would have changed. Philippe, for one thing, was already married, already had a child, a son. No one had ever seriously thought that he would—that he *could*—divorce his wife to marry Amanda. Sarah had married Eric, but she was already wedded to flight—and she died in an airplane. So things would have ended anyway.

And they had, for Eric. Eric had never been the same after his wife's death. Pouring all of his love and energy into the company that he and Philippe had started together, he tried to forget that love could even exist. Then Philippe had died in the war, and Amanda, left alone and pregnant, had married an accommodating Englishman who had given her daughter a name and then had gotten himself killed in the same war that the handsome Frenchman had died in. . . . It sounded, thought Caroline, more like a novel than real life. But it *had* happened: They were her people, and it was her story. Or, in any case, the beginnings of her story.

Hers had not been the world's most secure childhood, growing up as she did without ever knowing her father, or her place in the world. Amanda had returned to the States and had married yet again. Caroline, in the meantime, had been shuttled between her grandmother's houses in Newport and Cornish, New Hampshire—and then out to California, to live with Eric. And there she had learned to fly. . . .

Was that why she was so confused about life? Or did what happen later make her so unsure of herself? Certainly it was not Steven. She had married a man of granite, a gentle giant with flaming red hair and a soul full of goodness and strength—reassurance personified. Steven was steady and dependable and sure of himself, of his place in the world, of how he fitted into the scheme of things. While she, Caroline, knew only that she wanted to fly, and she wanted to be happy, and beyond that she wasn't very sure about anything at all.

In a way the blame could be placed on her father, who had started so much, and finished so little. He had begun that wonderful little airplane company with Eric, and he had begun a life with her mother, and then he had gone off and gotten himself buried under the brilliant red poppy fields in the east of France. He'd left everybody behind to pick up the pieces without him. Her mother had done all right, in the end, flitting from marriage to marriage as she did from town house to estate, leaving Caroline to be raised by whoever would have her. And Eric . . . well, he had transplanted his company to California and it had grown into something very powerful. When she needed a home and stability he had taken her in, raising her through the difficult adolescent years. He had become her only true parent and that must have been difficult for him. But had they, had any of them, suffered the insecurity, the emotional damage that she had? Probably not.

Someone had once said to Caroline, "People generally do the best that they can at any given time within a given situation," and she supposed that that was true. But it seemed sometimes as though it was she who had to pay the price when other people's best wasn't good enough. Once, the price had nearly been her life.

She closed her eyes for a moment. It was all still so fresh, so horrible, so immediate. Caroline's father had made one provision for his unborn child before he died, leaving her his majority shares of stock in the company Aeroméchanique, which later became A.R.M. The company's business was handled by a law firm in Zurich, who would look after its best interests until Caroline was old enough to handle her share herself. But one of the lawyers had become convinced that she would never be capable of handling the responsibility herself, and he didn't even wait to hear that she didn't want the company.

It happened on her wedding day, the day that was supposed to be the most marvelous of all days. Dressed in her wedding gown, and thinking only of the man that she was marrying, of the life that they were going to build together, Caroline had not been prepared for what had happened. The lawyer—de Mornay, his name was, how could she ever forget?—had come crashing into the sacristy of the church, had shot Eric's mother-in-law, the kindly woman who had helped raise Caroline and was more of a mother to her than her own mother had ever known how to be. He had dragged Caroline out with him, meaning to talk with her, to take her hostage—what? God only knew. There was blood on her white wedding dress, but he hadn't gotten far, because Steven had been there. Steven, the gentle giant who had told her that he loved her more than anything in the world, and who had been called upon so soon to prove it. Steven had tackled de

Mornay, had pulled Caroline away from him, and had held her and comforted her and, in the end, had finally married her.

But she had learned a lesson. de Mornay had gone mad because of A.R.M., because of the company's power and what it meant to him. And she didn't want anything else to do with it. She just wanted to be left alone, in peace, to build her own life. She and Steven had made a promise to each other on their wedding night that the company would never intrude on their lives.

She had an excuse for her insecurities, she understood why she was so unsure of herself: She had never been able to control what happened to her. Dragged here and there, her life governed by the needs and best interests of a megalithic, powerful company in which she was not interested . . . It made sense. But, even so, it didn't explain why she was still so confused about what she wanted out of life. Everyone she knew had a strong sense of what he or she aspired to, and how to go about getting it—even her sister-in-law, Justine, meek and kindly Justine, knew that she wanted to make her husband's life good and secure and bear him children. Even Justine had her goals.

Some days, Caroline felt as though she was clearer in her mind about what she didn't want than she was about what she did want. When she was a little girl, she had dreamed of having her own house and her own family. When she was a teenager, she had dreamed of being a great aviatrix. Now that she was twenty-four, an adult, and she had her house and her family and her pilot's license, she didn't know what to dream about anymore.

She had more money than anyone could ever want. She had a loving husband and a healthy child and the dazzling, dizzying heights of the sky as her personal playground. It would have been so easy to settle down, to become part of the comfortable circle of Newport socialites, to belong. But if all the pain and turmoil and destruction in her life had taught Caroline anything at all, it was that settling for the easy life was never the answer. There was something more out there, something that was important enough for her to live for, to strive for . . . to die for, even. She simply had to find out what the something was.

Eric had found his "something": A.R.M. Caroline was tempted to wonder, sometimes, if things might have been different if Sarah hadn't died. . . . If he would have been less obsessed with building the biggest and best airplane company that the world had ever seen . . . Perhaps things would have been different. But life wasn't made up of speculation. The reality was that Eric had never loved another woman since his wife had died. The reality was that the company was his obsession, from which he took time off to care for Caroline. He loved her in his own way: She was the child of his best friend. But the company would come first. The company would always come first. That knowledge was sometimes painful.

Caroline turned back from her contemplation of the sea. Gazing at the vast expanse of waves, the seeming infinity of the water, always made her think too much. . . . There was such a thing as thinking too much. She checked the radio frequency, then touched the transmitter button at her throat and spoke into the microphone on her headset. "Newport Tower, this is November Seventy-seven Kilo, do you read?"

A voice crackled in her headphones. "November Seventy-seven Kilo, I read you, go ahead."

Caroline smiled. It was Eddie in the control tower, his young voice unmistakable even with the distortion of the airwaves. He was the best controller they had. She was also, surreptitiously, teaching him to fly. "Newport Tower, November Seventy-seven Kilo approaching from the southeast. My range is ten miles. I request instructions."

Her headphones crackled again. "Seventy-seven Kilo, you are cleared to join left base for runway two-zero. Surface wind is six knots, zero-six-zero. Caroline?"

She flipped the transmission button. "Who else?"

"I hoped I'd see you today. Can you take me up?"

Caroline settled into the direction that would take her on course for the approach to Newport and descended another thousand feet. Finally she pressed her switch. "I can't, Eddie. Not today. It's Steven's day off and we're—we have other things to do." Belatedly, she stopped herself from telling everything to Eddie, as she was prone to do out of sheer politeness. Somewhere along the line she had been taught that ladies must be nice, that inconveniencing other people was always to be avoided. She had learned it from her grandmother, probably, a stern matriarch who was determined to mold both her daughter and her granddaughter into images of herself. Her personal life wasn't Eddie's concern.

He wouldn't care, anyway. All that he cared about was flying. His absorption had begun when she'd started explaining to him the mechanical workings of an airplane; and before she knew it their casual meetings had blossomed into sub-rosa flying lessons, of which she knew that his family would heartily disapprove. If they had known. They wouldn't have allowed him up in the tower, either, working as a controller, if he had given them any choice in the matter—but he had a way of getting what he wanted. Eddie, like her, was moneyed Newport, and his parents didn't want him to forget it.

"Okay." If he was disappointed, his voice didn't show it. "November Seventy-seven Kilo, call field in sight."

The field was shining in the distance, the hangars catching the gleam of the sun on their glittering metallic walls, the runways crisscrossing one another, the rows of landing lights ready to be lit at dusk. She had impressed their importance on Eddie. "There are colors for a reason, you know." And she taught him the silly rhyme that someone, somewhere, had made up for the benefit of all novice flyers: "White on white, you're high as a kite. Red on red, you're dead. Red on white, you're just right."

She pressed the button down. "Newport Tower, this is Seventy-seven Kilo, field in sight." Banking gently, she lost more altitude and throttled back. There were five runways; and the short squat tower, glassed on the top floor, sat smugly in the midst of them. A few small single-engine planes, not unlike her own, were parked near one of the two hangars on the edges of the tarmac. One was sitting on a runway, presumably awaiting clearance for takeoff, though Caroline hadn't heard any requests being made over her headphones. She circled and lost some more height, lowering her undercarriage—it was extraordinary, really, how many pilots forgot that they were flying with retractable gear and tore off the underbellies of their airplanes when landing—and adjusting her flaps and ailerons, watching her timing as she turned onto her final approach. The runway was gleaming straight and wide ahead of her.

The flaps were down and she was still losing altitude. The plane was buffeting slightly in the air as she played with the controls, sensing rather than calculating how much rudder to give, how quickly to go down, how to come in to her landing without stalling out. Eric's pilots had taught her well. And then the runway was flashing beneath her, closer and closer, as the wheels touched down, bounced up, and then touched again, holding as Caroline applied the brakes. Slowly, the airplane came to a stop. She taxied over to the fuel pumps on the other side of the tower and parked it there, collecting her charts, maps, and leather flying jacket before jumping down from the cockpit.

The mechanic was watching her, ready to refuel the airplane and begin the preparations to get it ready for the next person who took it up. It was Caroline's plane and she had priority when it came to using it, but she had extended the privilege to other pilots as well. Harry took pride in keeping the little monoplane in good condition. "Nice day to be up, Mrs. Asheford," he observed laconically, his eyes already trained beyond her on the plane.

"Lovely day, Harry. Thank you."

The mechanic didn't bother to look at her; his priority had always been, and always would be, the airplane itself. "Wouldn't happen you have any problems with the altimeter, Mrs. Asheford? Craig was complaining about it."

"No problems, Harry," Caroline said cheerfully with an impish grin as she turned to go back to the tower to sign in. She left the maps and charts at the sign-in desk and, slinging her leather jacket over her shoulder, ran up the stairs to the controllers' room.

Eddie was sitting in front of the huge green radar screen, only recently acquired by the airport—and at great expense, too, though well worth it in terms of safety, or so Caroline had argued when Eric first told her about radar. The Newport Airport Council was unconvinced, and she had ended up paying for the screen herself.

Eddie was drinking coffee. Absorbed like that, he looked incredibly young. His sandy hair was cut in the crew cut his father favored, and he had the same piercing blue eyes as the rest of his family. He was tall and a little thin, and might have been very attractive were it not for the acne that marred his complexion. Caroline had heard about that at great length, as well as about all the girls he was too timid to date. There was more to giving flying lessons than met the eye. What she didn't tell him, what he wasn't ready to hear, was that one day the acne would disappear and the power and intensity of his personality would attract girls like a magnet. He wouldn't have believed her anyway.

She watched him over his shoulder for a moment, and then bent to kiss his cheek. "I've got to go, Eddie," she said lightly. "I'll be here on Thursday, if you want to—uh—talk."

Without taking his eyes off the screen, he nodded. "Great, Caroline. See you then." He pushed down his own transmitter button: "Golf November Alpha, you are cleared to take off."

Caroline smiled and left, thinking as she skipped down the stairs and out to the car that the young were more resilient than one thought. At his age, she would have at least thrown a fit of pique over a missed opportunity. Or would she? There were so many things that she hadn't been permitted at his age. Even by herself.

Especially by herself.

The car engine started on the first try, which was somewhat unusual. Steven kept saying that he was going to look at the car himself, but he kept forgetting, and she knew better than to take it to a garage on her own and hurt his pride. Caroline sighed. Marriage had turned out to be much more complicated than she had ever thought. When she first met Steven he had seemed so dependable, so safe, and she thought that he would take care of her, take care of all her problems, make the past go away. She knew, now, that she was looking to Steven to be those things that she could never be for herself. . . . He had seemed so sure of himself.

If there was one thing that Caroline had never been, it was sure of herself.

The green fields flashed by on either side of the road, and she rolled one of her windows down a little to catch the tantalizing fresh earthy smell of spring. Spring, 1939, with a war brewing in Europe and a baby to care for at home. The world never quite seemed to add up.

She had met Steven quite by chance, after she had begun to see a psychologist to help her deal with that other, earlier horror. . . . That was something that she hadn't liked thinking about, hadn't liked discussing, simply wanted to bury back in the darker recesses of her mind, to take out at night, when she had nightmares about it . . . She had been eight years old, and spending her first Christmas with her mother in New York City. Caroline had been so excited. Her mother was so pretty, and smelled of some lush, exotic perfume, and her husband was kind and played music on a wonderful big record player. And then one night her mother went out alone, and her husband raped Caroline.

It had taken her a long time to begin to express anger toward him, and toward her mother for allowing it to happen. No, that wasn't true. She still couldn't express her anger. It had taken her so many years even to know that anger was there, buried along with the horror of the memory. She had thought that it was her fault, that she was a bad person. And she had spent most of the rest of her life trying to be very, very good so that nobody would know that inside she was bad.

Her psychologist made her look at her past and her present, living in a mausoleum of a house—the estate-home out on Ocean Avenue with its huge echoing rooms and long, dark corridors—and he had kindly suggested that she go out into the real world instead of spending all her time brooding and feeling sorry for herself. He had sent her to the rector of her grandmother's church, and he in turn had sent her to the soup kitchen that was run out of the basement. And it was there that she had met Steven.

And Steven didn't think that she was a bad person.

He was a big man with flaming red hair and beard, with strong opinions and an infinite capacity for caring. He had cared for her when she thought that no one could, when she thought that she was unworthy of love, and she had returned his love with enthusiasm and gratitude.

Only later did she begin to discover that her own feelings were more complicated than she thought. She wanted to be taken care of—or did she? She wanted someone to make all the decisions for her—or did she? Some days she was willing to become the child that she must have first seemed to Steven; but, paradoxically, he seemed to have given her the strength that she needed to reach beyond that child and discover whom she could be as a woman. And she was still discovering.

She was rattling into Newport now, and turned automatically into the streets that she knew so well. Strange, in the end, how the wheel goes full circle: She had never planned to settle down in Newport. California, perhaps. California had once been her home, the bright hot summers and the cooler damp winters, the trips to San Francisco and boating around the bay, and the long walks over the orchards of San Jose, the house on Western Avenue where she had spent a good deal of her life. If any place was home, it was surely California. Newport had always meant her grandmother's tea parties, the endless rounds of gossip which held the threads of life together, the summers spent in Cornish on the estate near the old covered bridge, and the small girl who had never quite felt wanted there.

But Newport was where she had met and married Steven, and Newport was where their baby was born, and Newport was her home now, too. Except when she chose to escape from it into the sky.

Caroline frowned. Escape was surely not the word to choose. She loved Steven, and she loved Elizabeth, and she would never want any of that to change. . . . But life in Newport was so clearly defined, so absolutely unchanging, that it was a relief to simply be herself and not act out the role that seemed assigned to her.

For the first time—perhaps the only time—she had begun to understand her mother, understand the childish irresponsibility that had always seemed a part of Amanda. To understand why she had always needed to be away, to be off doing things instead of staying at home with her daughter. She had hated her mother for not being there, but she wondered now how she seemed to Elizabeth, always taking time out to go flying, to escape from Newport. Perhaps that wheel had come full circle as well.

Caroline's street was in the old section of town, with houses dating back to the seventeen-hundreds, each with its little plaque and patch of well-trimmed grass and flower bed. It was only a mile but a world away from the estate houses on the other end of town, the sweeping panoramic views of the ocean where she had lived as a young child with her grandmother. She had slid down gleaming banisters, had played on immaculate lawns and sipped tea in vast drawing rooms . . . And then Eric had taken her away, away from the grandmother who had not been able to keep such a terrible thing from happening to her, away to the sun of California. He had introduced her to airplanes and changed her life forever.

Eric hadn't known what to do with a child any more than her grandmother had, but he wasn't encumbered by her rigid rules of etiquette, and had let Caroline grow in the direction she wanted. He was her father, her confessor, her uncle, her friend. He was both her best friend and her worst enemy, because he gave her love—and he represented A.R.M. And she didn't want to have anything to do with A.R.M.

She pulled into the driveway of her house, and listened to the car engine as it coughed and spluttered and wheezed its way into silence. Then she hopped out, gathering up her charts and jacket in her arms, fumbling with the key to the front door. A world away from her grandmother's estate—but a world away also from the house across the railroad tracks where Steven's brother, William, and his wife, Justine, lived with their baby son, Nicholas. Caroline had wanted to help them. She had, after all, more money than she sometimes liked to think about, but Steven and

William were both adamant. If Caroline wanted to put her money anywhere, she could put it into Asheford Shipbuilding, the company that Steven and William had inherited from their father. But William and Justine could manage on their own. There was to be no charity.

The door swung open to unaccustomed silence. Steven must have taken Elizabeth out for a walk or down to the port. He doted on the baby as any new father would. He had always been especially gentle with weak, or helpless, or hurting people—and Caroline, surprised by her own sense almost of detachment, was grateful for his enthusiasm. Justine was forever wanting to talk about diapers and burpings and milk intake. Caroline had weaned Elizabeth as soon as she decently could and was usually far more interested in talking about flying than she was about babies. Which probably made her a bad mother, too, the dark little voice inside of her said.

She tossed her things on the kitchen table and dashed up the narrow creaking back stairs to run a bath. Her face in the mirror was flushed, her hair windblown, and she grinned at her reflection. Not what the young matron of Newport was supposed to look like, but such was life. She was pleased enough with what she saw.

The water in the tub was almost overflowing. Caroline tossed in a handful of lavender bath crystals and stripped off her flying clothes, khaki trousers and a loose-fitting shirt that had once been Steven's, lowering herself into the hot water and sighing with pleasure as the steam rose up all around her. There may well be a war starting in Europe and there may well be confusion at home, but as long as she could skim over the clouds and ocean as she had done today, as long as she could feel the incredible luxury of clean hot water on her skin, then in the end everything would be all right.

Eric Beaumont had his feet propped up on the desk. Moving the telephone receiver wearily from one ear to the other, he looked out the large plate-glass window beyond his desk to the bustling A.R.M. compound, which was ringed with the latest in security fences and patrolled by men with bristling German shepherd dogs.

The voice on the other end of the telephone continued to crackle in his ear. ''. . . and I said that you could step up production, so you'd better have been right on those figures you gave me. The President is concerned about being caught with our pants down in this whole thing. Um—so to speak, that is.'' The voice coughed discreetly. ''And I said that he could have an update by the end of the month.''

''I can arrange that,'' Eric said calmly. There was only a trace now of a French accent in his voice. He had been an American for too long. He could even drink California wines now. ''I'm flying back east to Washington next week to meet with the secretary. If you'd like to set up something with the President then . . .'' His words trailed off diffidently.

The voice hesitated. ''Well, yes, of course, I'll see what I can arrange. You do realize that the President doesn't wish to be . . . connected too strongly with your company. Not just yet, anyway.''

Eric leaned forward and shook a cigarette loose from the pack on his desk. ''President Roosevelt has never had any problems before with arranging discreet meetings,'' he said, balancing the telephone receiver on his shoulder so that he could use both hands to light the cigarette. He exhaled the smoke quickly, flicking the match into the ceramic ashtray that Caroline had made for him when she was in the sixth grade. ''Just see if he wants to meet. Let him make the arrangements. Leave it up to him.'' What an idiot, he thought. This is absurd: We're getting ready to go to war, and they give me a moron to deal with.

''Fine, Mr. Beaumont. We'll be in touch.''

Eric put down the receiver, shaking his head, and got his secretary on the line. ''Julie, see if those drawings have come in yet from Cal Tech, will you? And bring me some coffee when you have a chance.''

''Yes, Mr. Beaumont.''

His secretary brought the coffee and the information at once: one of the reasons why she had been promoted so swiftly from the typing pool. When one asked Julie Bates for something, one got it. Immediately. Eric had noticed this when she was working for his chief financial officer and had stolen her away on the spot.

Julie put the coffee tray on his desk and poured from the silver English set that Eric liked to use. ''Nothing from Cal Tech today, sir. I asked the front office to give it priority when it comes through. Would you like me to call Dr. Oppenheimer's office?''

Eric leaned back in his chair, running a tired hand through his short dark hair. ''Not yet. I'll give it another week. I have to be in Washington next Tuesday, anyway—no sense in stirring things up until I'm back.'' He didn't ask her if the arrangements for his trip to the capital had been made yet. He knew that they had. Julie was never less than efficient.

She handed him the cup of coffee, black and sweet, stronger than anyone else in the office could ever drink it. "Do you know yet whether you'll be meeting with the President, sir?"

"No," he said shortly, taking a first cautious sip. "No, and I'm not likely to know right away, as long as he has imbeciles like Harrison working as intermediaries. I need a direct line, that's all that there is to it. If I don't get anything else out of this trip, I'm getting a direct line." And the power that goes with it, he thought with satisfaction. He couldn't possibly have a hand in making policy if he didn't have the ear of the President with no scurrying little bureaucrats like Harrison messing up his plans.

He watched Julie leave the room, but his mind wasn't on her. Eric Beaumont was known throughout the business world for his total indifference, his disinterest in women. There was some speculation about this, and only the people who knew him well understood. He didn't need them. He was married to his work, to the company he had brought with him from France to make into such a megalithic force in world industry. Few, if any, remembered the woman he had married, the woman whose photograph stayed on his desk and whose memory had kept him away from others for over twenty-five years.

Few remembered, even, those early barnstorming days of flying, when machines little heavier than the air all around them dared to defy the pull of gravity. And fewer still remembered the daring American woman in the bright flying silks who conquered the skies, and the young French genius who designed the planes that she flew. Sarah Martin Beaumont belonged to a different time, a different place. Only in Eric's heart did her flame burn on.

He looked at her picture now, as he did at least a hundred times a day. She was beautiful—not in any conventional sense perhaps, not in the way that Amanda had been beautiful or that Caroline, now, was beautiful, but in her own way, Sarah had been dazzling. An interesting face, people said when they looked at her. She had died so young, and yet her face showed that she had lived her years well, had learned from them. The mahogany-colored hair, untamed as ever, and her skin porcelain white and smooth, and her eyes dark and bright and holding promises that they never had time to fulfill. She had been the first American woman to hold a pilot's license, and she had been the first woman to fly across the English Channel, and she was the only woman he had ever been able to love. She had come from San Jose, and it was in her memory that he had settled here, had brought his company from France when the lawyers advised him that Europe was too dangerous because of the first war against the Germans. They hadn't known, then, that there would be another.

The company that he had started with dreams in his heart and Philippe's money in his pocket had prospered and grown, expanded and entrenched itself in the U.S. economy. Only the American-based Johnson Industries had the drive, the ambition, the technology to take on the French wonder boy and challenge his right to the skies. Only Johnson had consistently stood in his way, had tried to undermine his efforts. When Eric arrived, they had held a monopoly on the skies of America, and they weren't about to give it up without a struggle. The two companies had become bitter rivals, and the bitterness—on Eric's part—had roots in something far more personal than power. For Eric lay the blame for his wife's death on Johnson's doorstep.

Eric sighed. The struggles had been intense, even in the early days. He had needed boron; Johnson had found out about it, and made A.R.M. pay more than top dollar to haul it out of the desert. Eric had patented ideas, and Johnson had challenged those patents in court. And, when all else failed to dislodge him, they had sent one of their own to seduce Caroline.

He had taken care of that, of course, just as he had taken care of Johnson, time and time again. He was here to stay. This had been Sarah's home once. He had made it his own.

He rubbed his brow and drank some more coffee, reaching automatically for the cigarettes again. No longer a wonder boy now, he thought ruefully. He would turn fifty this year. Fifty. Another—what? Twenty years? Less? He would have to start thinking about the future of the company. The lawyers were always reminding him of that. Think of what you are doing, but also think ahead. Not just in terms of technology; think also in terms of succession.

The line of succession of A.R.M. was only too clear. Upon Eric's death or retirement it would pass directly and nearly completely to Caroline Asheford, who welcomed it about as much as she would welcome the plague. He drew in deeply on his cigarette. It was Philippe who had wanted it that way—Philippe de Montclair, Eric's best friend and Caroline's natural father. Philippe had left the law firm of Beneteau and Giroux in Zurich to safeguard his wishes, and Caroline, or her offspring, would one day—for better or for worse—control one of the most powerful companies in the world. Philippe hadn't known that it would come to that, of course. He never lived to see how A.R.M. developed from a tiny one-office-and-hangar operation, a dream concocted over too many glasses of beer behind the stables, to the megalith that it was today. Philippe hadn't known, but he had left his interest to Caroline, and exacted a promise from Eric that he would do the same.

That Caroline was neither particularly suited to run the company nor interested in doing so mattered little. The will that Philippe had left was perfectly clear. The lawyers would see that it was carried out. And Eric himself, out of respect for the man who had believed in him and supported him and had been his friend, would abide by it.

Caroline was unsuitable, it was true. But Caroline had, last year, produced a child, a daughter named Elizabeth. And, already, Beneteau and Giroux were looking toward the future of that child.

Eric drank his coffee quickly, in gulps. That would have to wait. There was too much to do now to start thinking about Caroline and Elizabeth and what they would mean to A.R.M.'s future. There was far too much to do. There was a war starting in Europe, and it was his job to advise the President's cabinet, the men who supposedly made the decisions. He would tell them that the United States would have to go to war.

It made sense. It would help the economy recover from the Great Depression. It would bring money in to fuel the experiments that Eric had been doing with jet propulsion, with rocketry. An opportunity to put his drawings to the test . . . And then there was that group of scientists that he was sponsoring at Cal Tech. They were working on something that was going to make the world gasp in wonder. Eric was sure of it.

He stubbed out his cigarette and stood up. There was a great deal of work to be done, and time was slipping away from him. He was older now. He didn't move as quickly as he once had. It was time to get back to work.

Chapter Two

Robert Beneteau stood up, his long, thin frame unfolding slowly and carefully. He was feeling the weight of his years. He fumbled in his pocket, and with trembling fingers withdrew the old pince-nez which he stubbornly refused to trade for a pair of new glasses. Placing them on the bridge of his nose, he peered across the room toward the desk occupied by his partner, Marc Giroux.

"Did you," he asked, his voice thickened by years of smoking, "finish reading Monsieur Beaumont's letter?"

Giroux glanced up. He was younger than Beneteau, still in his late fifties, overweight, but possessed of the same indomitable spirit that had carried him through the many crises of his career. He had recently begun wearing glasses himself—round, horn-rimmed affairs—and the topic had fueled more than one argument in the spacious office shared by the two senior partners of the firm.

"Yes," he said. "Did you want to discuss it now?"

Beneteau shrugged. "It was clear, I should think. Beaumont is convinced that the U.S. is eventually going to declare war on Germany, that it's just a matter of time. We need to be prepared for that."

Giroux patted his pockets, searching for the roll of antacid tablets he always kept there. "I don't think," he said slowly, "anyone can be prepared for what is going to happen, Robert. Europe may well be in flames by this time next year."

Beneteau looked at him sharply. "Marc, I personally think that we need to be prepared for any eventuality, but the chances for war are slender. Hitler has what he wanted, doesn't he? Austria and Czechoslovakia—"

"—and Lithuania."

"All right, all right!" Beneteau's voice was irritable. "And

Lithuania. That's not the point. He feels like a king, he's satisfied, and he'll never attempt to put Britain to the test. And as long as Britain is safe, France will be, too.''

"I see." Giroux stood up and stretched behind his desk, then walked slowly over to the window, which was slightly opened to the fresh breezes of spring. An overwhelming scent of lilac came up from the bushes outside the window and he sniffed appreciatively. They always knew when it was spring, from the lilacs. Giroux turned back into the room to face his partner. "I see," he repeated. "All that matters is that France—and presumably Switzerland—stay safe. Is that what you're saying?''

"Our interests," Beneteau said stubbornly, "are in France.''

Giroux shook his head. "Wake up, Robert," he said. "Our interests are hardly as parochial as that. A.R.M. has a manufacturing plant outside of Hamburg. And another near Dresden. And another—"

"They can be closed. We can hardly ask the family to leave—"

"The family! The family! Don't you see, Robert? That's the point. If Beaumont says there's going to be a war, then he's right. We know he's right. We have to work with that. Imagine the worst scenario—Europe overrun, *our* factories used by the Germans, and the family—"

Beneteau shrank back. "The family could be destroyed!''

"The family must not be destroyed. That's the point, isn't it?" Giroux took a deep breath, willing himself to slow down, to be persuasive. He had been thinking about this for days, ever since the letter had come from Eric in California. He had realized at once what must be done, and he had been considering how to put it to the other lawyers in the firm. Especially Beneteau. "Listen, Robert. Pierre de Montclair is of military age. He could easily be killed if this thing escalates. And his son is only two years old. If France were to be occupied—"

"France will never be occupied!" Despite the long years in Switzerland, Beneteau was French to the core. "The Maginot Line—"

"The Maginot Line," Giroux cut in brutally, "is a joke. I think very soon we'll all have to acknowledge that it's a joke. My God, Robert, it doesn't even extend north. What's to keep anybody from simply going *around* it?"

"It can't extend north," Beneteau said primly. "We hardly need to fortify against the Belgians."

Giroux sighed. He was getting sidetracked. "That's not the point, Robert. Maybe the Maginot Line will hold. Maybe Germany will never attack. But, just for one moment, imagine that they do. Imagine that France is taken." He held up his hand as Beneteau made an automatic movement of protest. "Just imagine, Robert! Don't let your nationalism stand in the way of your common sense. Germany is occupying France, Pierre de Montclair is off in the army somewhere. What's going to become of the family then? Of the de Montclair estate? We have to think about these things, Robert. We have to prepare for them as though they were going to happen, and then pray like hell they don't."

There was a moment of silence in the room. From the open window, half-muted, came the sound of car engines from the street beyond the stone walls that enclosed the offices. It was beginning to get very warm.

Beneteau stood up at length, slowly, with difficulty. He went back to his desk and sat down, heavily, behind it. "Sometimes," he said slowly, and with a trace of bitterness in his voice, "I wish that we had never decided to handle the de Montclair affairs."

Giroux said briskly, "Too late for that, Robert. And those affairs have done remarkably well for us over the years, wouldn't you say?"

He was right. When they had first started out together, they had dealt with the estate accounts of venerable titled French families with decaying fortunes. Their offices had been in Paris. The de Montclair account, belonging to an established family living on an estate outside of Angers, was one such. The young count, Philippe, was a bit on the wild side, but that was all in a day's work.

Until the young count decided to finance and support the experiments being carried on in the back stables of the estate by the farrier's son, Eric Beaumont. Farrier's son he might have been, but brilliant, with skill and imagination and dreams. They were friends, Philippe and Eric, which was the really extraordinary thing, and showed just how far the young count was willing to go to defy convention. They started a company together, which the lawyers had not been inclined to take very seriously at first, being much more interested in the marriage that they had arranged that year for Philippe—a brilliant match, really. Marie-Louise had made a fine countess—an ancestor of hers had been made a duke under Henri IV—one couldn't do much better than that.

Giroux pursed his lips. Things had moved very quickly since then. Now, so many years later, it was hard to recall the precise succession of events. Suffice it to say that the company became the foremost French developer and producer of airplanes at a time when the "flying machine" was still little more than a novelty; and the Great War had come along just at the right time, to provide an opportunity to further develop airplanes under government contracts.

There were the women, too . . . Americans, they were. Sarah Martin was already famous then, but she wasn't the one who had caused so many problems for them. A girl pilot who made her living writing articles for magazines and who made history flying airplanes for whoever would let her didn't interfere with their concerns. Even when she ended up marrying young Beaumont, and then getting herself killed in one of those infernal machines before they made enclosed cockpits or even safety belts, Beaumont's reactions had worked in their favor. His belief that Johnson Industries had been involved in his wife's tragic death had spurred on his desire to overtake his rival—to destroy it.

But it was the other one, Amanda Lewis, a ravishing girl, an American society figure from Newport, Rhode Island, who had bollixed their plans. Amanda Lewis had not much of a family name, but more than enough money. She took up with Philippe de Montclair, and God only knows what would have happened if he hadn't gone off and been killed in the Great War. It was bad enough that he had gotten her pregnant. That was quite a problem, especially as Marie-Louise, the countess, had already quite properly produced a son. De Montclair's will left the family estate to Marie-Louise and the baby, but all the count's interest in the airplane company to Amanda and the unborn child. . . .

They hadn't thought much of the company then. But, eventually, it was that very company that carried the day, enabling the law firm—which owned a percentage in A.R.M., as well—to concentrate exclusively on it, to move A.R.M. to California when clouds of war hung over France—and to move them, not incidentally, to neutral Switzerland—in the process becoming very wealthy indeed.

Beaumont had settled in well in California. He had even partially raised Philippe's child there when her mother's many involvements with men had proven unhealthy for the girl. And Caroline had made a suitable marriage.

But it was the other side of the count's lineage that interested them now. Philippe had made it very clear that the de Montclairs were not to know about the illegitimate child, and the law firm had shielded them from it. There were four of them living at the estate outside Angers. Marie-Louise, the old countess, who had never remarried, choosing instead to mourn her husband in the comforts of his family estate. Pierre, the son they had produced before Philippe was killed, was twenty-seven now, but the lawyers knew little of him, as he preferred to conduct his affairs in writing, and was annoyed that he had to do so with a law firm based in Zurich. The annoyance could be read between the lines of every letter he wrote to them.

Pierre himself had married some time ago, a girl from Brittany, Chantale de Kerenec, good family—Philippe's American descendants didn't seem to be interested in dynastic lines, but the lawyers still were. And two winters ago she had given birth to a son, Jean-Louis, so at least the legitimate succession of the de Montclair line was assured.

Giroux raised his eyes and looked at his partner. They had two mandates: to manage the affairs of the company, and to protect the interests of the de Montclair family. Angers, situated on the Loire and Maine rivers, was a perfect conduit to Nantes on the coast and to the English Channel. If the Germans ever were serious about invading Britain, the town would certainly not be spared the trials of occupation. And the de Montclair estate with its acres of pastures, extensive stables, and rambling eighteenth-century château would be ideal for billeting occupying troops. It was even conceivable that the estate might be made the command center for the district.

If there was an invasion. *If* there was to be a command center. All was speculation at this point, but Beaumont believed that such was to be the course of events; and Eric was usually right. If they waited until reality caught up with speculation, it would be too late. And they would have failed young de Montclair—curious how, after all these years, they still thought of Philippe as the young count even though his widow was now well into her fifties! The law firm of Beneteau and Giroux had never yet failed any of its clients.

Giroux said softly, "A.R.M. has been very good to us. We

have done nothing but benefit from Philippe de Montclair's will. And we promised to care for his family, Robert. We have an obligation to them. We must start making plans.''

Beneteau heard the urgency in his partner's voice and nodded. He took off his pince-nez and put them down on the desk in front of him. ''All right,'' he said wearily. ''Where do we begin?''

Eric Beaumont formed a steeple with his fingertips and looked over it at the man sitting across the conference table from him. The deep circles under the eyes that never went away, even when he was rested; the ill-fitting double-breasted suit that couldn't hide the extra weight. Franklin D. Roosevelt didn't look like anyone's idea of a successful businessman, much less a politician. And yet he was President of the United States.

And, at the moment, a stubborn one.

Eric sighed and shifted his position on his chair. ''The situation makes everyone uneasy, Mr. President,'' he said patiently. ''But facts need to be faced.''

''The fact that I am facing, Mr. Beaumont, is that the American people don't want a war. Certainly not a war on foreign territory. I happen to agree with you. I think that our entry into the conflict is inevitable. But it has to be in the long run. I'm going to be facing reelection before too long. I can't afford to do anything unpopular right now.''

Eric smiled a little crookedly and reached into his suit pocket to draw out his package of cigarettes and light one. Slowly inhaling, he thought quickly, planning his strategy as he went. ''Mr. President,'' he said finally, his words carried on a cloud of smoke, ''look at this from my point of view. I know that it's going to happen. I haven't been blind and deaf. I get reports as frequently as you do.''

The other man tried to suppress a smile. ''More frequently, it seems.''

Eric shrugged. ''The point is that we need to be ready. A.R.M. nearly is. Johnson Industries nearly is. We've lined up our subcontractors, and we already have people working on things that the secretary of war hasn't even glimpsed in his wildest nightmares. But we need capital if we're going to continue, and that means government contracts.''

''You make a clear presentation, Mr. Beaumont. I quite understand your point of view, and in your position I would be making the same request, I am sure. But I'm stuck in the same argument as before. I'd be a mighty unpopular President if I went for any more military spending right now."

Eric toyed with his cigarette. "All right. Let's back up a minute and make some suppositions. Let's say that we could get congressional support. Let's say that we could get people—people out there, at the grass-roots level. People in the farms and cities and towns. Would you go for it then?"

"That's a mighty big supposition. But, yes, I might consider it then." He paused delicately. "I might."

Eric left through the back door, as he had promised he would.

The apartment Eric used as an office when he was in Washington was only a few blocks from the White House and was quiet and empty when he unlocked the door and let himself in. He took off his jacket and loosened his tie, walking over to the desk that stood near the window, automatically shaking a cigarette free from the package he had already taken out of his pocket. He frowned at the pile of mail that had been left there. Three leaflets. A letter from Harrison, probably in a huff about being excluded from the meeting with the President. A card from Caroline . . . Eric picked that one up, still in the act of lighting the cigarette.

"Dear Eric, I never know just where to reach you, so I'm mailing off cards to *all* your addresses. Steven and I are having a birthday party for Elizabeth. Do you think that you could come? I know that you're most awfully busy, but it would be so good to see you. It's hard to believe that she's a year old already! How time flies." He smiled and turned it over. Caroline had pasted a picture of her airplane on top of whatever scene had originally graced the card. There was a postscript. "Oh, and Eric, can you find out where my mother is? I haven't heard from her in months and if she's by chance in North Africa, the situation could be quite horrible. I keep hearing the most awful things on the radio. I know you're busy, but . . ." The writing trailed off, but not the concern, and he frowned again. Amanda. Where the hell was Amanda?

It would have to wait. He sat down and reached for the telephone. There were more important calls to make just now.

Caroline finished dressing the baby and smiled ruefully as she looked at her. Elizabeth was starting to look more like a person and less like a bundle of fat and curls, and the person that she had begun to resemble was Caroline's mother, Amanda.

Caroline sighed. There could be worse things, of course. Her mother was beautiful. Eric had told her stories of the men who would have done anything for Amanda. Sometimes Caroline wished that her father had been more willing to do something for Amanda, like divorce his wife and marry her instead. It was a daydream that she had grown up with, closing her eyes to the difficult realities of her life and escaping into a pleasant fantasy where she lived with her parents in a nice house by the river, and her father was kind and gentle, and took her out horseback riding, and her mother was content to stay at home and bake and care for the two of them.

She kissed Elizabeth's cheek, and the baby giggled and reached out to touch Caroline's face. Things would be different for Elizabeth. She had a mother and a father, she had a name and the love that went along with it, and even the shadow of A.R.M. that loomed over them wouldn't be enough to destroy the things that Caroline was able to give her daughter—things that her mother had never been able to give to her.

Justine was waiting downstairs, holding Nicholas on her lap and talking baby talk to him. "Wanna cookie?" she was asking as Caroline came into the kitchen, balancing Elizabeth precariously on her hip. "Baby wanna cookie?"

"Honestly, Justine," Caroline said, sliding Elizabeth down to the floor and settling herself on one of the kitchen chairs, "that child is never going to speak English if you insist on never using it with him."

Justine heard the affection behind her sister-in-law's words and ignored their content. "Baby speak good English," she cooed at Nicholas.

Smiling, Caroline shook her head and poured coffee for both of them. Justine was beautiful and sweet, but . . . sometimes, like now, Caroline found herself wishing that her sister-in-law had some interests other than her husband and her son. She wasn't doing either of them a particular service, either, by concentrating her own life so fiercely and exclusively on theirs. William was bad tempered when his meals were as much as five minutes late, and Nicholas was already showing a stubborn petulance that directly correlated to the way his mother spoiled him.

If only she . . . "Justine," Caroline said suddenly, "would you like to learn to fly?"

"What?" It was a gasp more than a question.

"Learn to fly," Caroline repeated. "I could teach you. I'm teaching Eddie Carruthers, and he's doing so well. . . . Oh, Justine, do say yes! You could get your license in just a few months, and—"

"And what would I do with Nicholas? Caroline, you can't forget that having a family brings on responsibilities."

Caroline closed her eyes. I'll shoot her, she thought, if she says that again. I swear I will. Her eyelids fluttered open and she fixed her eyes on the tortoiseshell comb holding back Justine's luxurious brown hair. "We'll leave Nicholas off with Elizabeth at my grandmother's house. Marie loves children; she'd love to take care of him along with Elizabeth."

"I couldn't." Justine's voice was prim. "I couldn't possibly pay her."

Caroline shook her head. "For heaven's sake, Justine, I don't pay her either. She works for my grandmother, and frankly I think it's a joy for her to do some baby-sitting after spending all her time caring for a dying old woman." She hadn't meant for her words to come out quite as they did, and she was almost as shocked as Justine at what she had said.

Caroline thought about that slip of the tongue all the way out to the rambling estate on Ocean Drive. Justine had gone home to her smaller house across the railroad tracks, murmuring something about Nicholas's nap time; and Caroline had let her go, relieved to be left alone, not to have to listen to Justine's empty chatter anymore. It took her more attempts than usual to start the car, and she was frustrated almost to tears by the time the engine finally caught and held. Damn Steven, she thought, why doesn't he fix his own car for a change, instead of spending all his time working on those blasted all-important ships? But she knew the answer to that one even as she asked it. Steven and William were caught up in the same fever pitch of excitement as Eric was—the excitement of war. They smelled profits in the winds of change that were sweeping across the Atlantic, and they wanted to be ready to reap the dividends when they came rolling in.

Caroline settled Elizabeth into the backseat of the car and drove carefully down the street. She headed out of the old section and into the bustling center of Newport, and beyond that to the long graceful sweeping curve of Ocean Avenue with its carefully spaced mansions, perched discreetly and distantly behind hedgerows and iron fences. She had spent the early years of her childhood here before she went out at age eight to California to live with Eric. The years in Newport were spent with her grandmother in the big house full of servants and genteel lady friends who came to sip tea and play whist or canasta. And now the old lady who had helped to raise her and who had loved her in her own brusque way was dying.

The butler, Jenson, let her in, reaching for Caroline's chamois jacket and the bag that contained a change of clothes for Elizabeth and her diapers. Then he gestured for the maid behind him to take the baby from Caroline. "I'll have Agnes take Miss Elizabeth straight up to Marie, Mrs. Asheford. Will you be staying to tea?"

"I don't know." Caroline surrendered the baby to the maid and ran a hand rapidly through her curls. "How is my grandmother, Jenson?"

His face clouded over, but his words were as correct and noncommittal as ever. "I really couldn't say, Mrs. Asheford."

That sounded bad. She turned and ran up the wide curved marble staircase, her feet tripping lightly through the corridors that led to the suite of rooms where her grandmother was ensconced. She had closed up the house in New Hampshire. The horses and ponies that had been the old lady's pride and joy had been sold, and the Connecticut River continued to flow by the estate impassively as though nothing had happened. And here, in Newport, the ocean pounded the rocks down at the foot of the gardens as ever, but her grandmother never walked there anymore, not as she had in the old days, when she used to look out to sea and worry about the daughter who lived beyond it.

Margaret Lewis was dying, and she was doing so in precisely the same way that she had lived—arrogantly, proudly, and without need of pity.

Caroline approached her grandmother's bed slowly, hesitantly. She knew what the first question would be, and the second. She had answers to neither.

"Hello, Grandmother."

A sound like a snort, and the piercing blue eyes were turned on her. "*Hrumph*. About time you came, gel."

Caroline bent to kiss the dry cheek. "I couldn't come yesterday, Grandmother. I told you. I had to work at the shelter."

This time there was no mistaking the snort. "Waste of time. Always said so, waste of time and effort. People don't have to be poor if they don't want to be." She stopped speaking, struggling for breath after so long a speech. She was wheezing. Caroline placed a placating hand over the thin, blue-veined one on the coverlet. "Don't talk, Grandmother. Just relax. I'm home now. Would you like me to ask Marie to bring up your tonic?"

"Won't do me any good, gel. Can't you—" She broke off to cough for a moment, then struggled to continue. "Can't you see I'm dying?"

"That's no reason to deprive yourself. The doctor said the tonic will help."

"*Hrumph.*" She closed her eyes for a moment, and then said, very clearly, "Did you find Amanda for me?"

Caroline took a deep breath. "Not yet, Grandmother. She's still in Africa. I'm not sure where. I've asked Eric to help me find her."

"Silly notion, that. *Hrumph.* Africa." She said it as though it were a disease rather than a continent. Caroline, who basically agreed with her, didn't say anything, and after a moment the old lady continued. "And what about you, gel? Have you made up your mind yet?"

Caroline swallowed. "No, Grandmother. I've spoken to Steven, but . . ." Her voice trailed off uncertainly, and when she looked again at the bed she saw that her grandmother had opened her eyes and was looking at her intently.

"He's too proud, is that what you're saying?"

"I don't know. I don't know what it is, Grandmother. Maybe he just wants to make a home for Elizabeth and me in the best way he can—"

"Nonsense. The best way that he can is to bring you here to live. Cornish, too. You can put horses back in the stables."

Caroline gestured helplessly. "New Hampshire is too far away, Grandmother. Steven has to go to work." She realized even as she said it that she had touched another sore spot. Her grandmother didn't like the fact that Steven worked at all. She continued quickly, "And I don't know what we'd do here. It's so big, and I'd have to spend all my time just looking after the place."

"That's the idea." There was satisfaction in the old lady's voice.

Caroline looked at her sharply. "Why, Grandmother," she

said slowly, "I'd almost believe that you offered us the house on purpose, just to put me in my place."

"Your proper place, yes. Time you got down to business and stopped gallivanting all over the sky. If God wanted men to fly He'd have seen fit to give us wings."

"If God wanted us to gallop and jump over fences He'd have given us four legs and a tail, too," Caroline said softly. "It works both ways, Grandmother."

"*Hrumph.* You go and find that mother of yours, gel, and bring her here. Time I saw my daughter before I die. And you think about my offer. Can't give the place to Amanda, she'd tire out the help with too many parties. I want it for you. You think about it." She turned her head on the pillow, away from Caroline. "And now you go."

"Grandmother—" Caroline gestured helplessly, but the old woman's eyes were closed and she finally turned and walked to the door. Once there she paused, her hand on the doorjamb, and turned back as though to speak again. Margaret Lewis looked shrunken and strangely defenseless. There was no sense in telling her about the fighting in Africa, no sense in upsetting her if it turned out that Amanda was simply off on safari somewhere and had chosen to stay incommunicado for her own reasons. Best to wait. Caroline turned away again, and this time she really did leave.

The lawyers had all gathered in the large conference room with the huge and hideous scarred oaken table that somebody said had once been at the court of Philippe le Bel in the fourteenth century. For all that anyone knew, it could well be true.

The personnel of the law firm of Beneteau and Giroux had changed substantially over the years—for various reasons, not all of them having strictly to do with the practice of the law. Françoise Duroc and Eugene Rousseau, whom they had hired when the A.R.M. account first became their largest and eventually only work, were still there, but most of the others had gone, replaced by brighter, more energetic young attorneys, all of them either Swiss or French, all of them skilled in business and international law. The partners had learned from their mistakes: There was to be no more specialization. No longer could one of the attorneys work completely independently, follow his or her own intuition without bringing issues to the attention of the entire office. The first mistake—when de Mornay had gone and attempted to kill Caroline Copeland—had very nearly been fatal.

There would be no other.

Marc Giroux was pacing the parameters of the room, too excited to stay still. The prospect of their pending discussion was frightening, but it was exciting, too. Giroux was aware they were going out on a limb, taking a step down a dangerous road, a step that they would never be able to retrace. He smiled inwardly at the platitudes and clichés that he had begun to use, and then continued his train of thought. If the firm hadn't lost its innocence over that affair with de Mornay, then it was surely about to lose it now.

Beneteau entered the room slowly and sat down at the head of the conference table. The firm's head secretary followed him in with a sheaf of folders which she placed on the table in front of him before withdrawing. They wouldn't be needing her. There were to be no notes taken during this particular meeting.

The others, sensing the tension in the room, looked expectant. Rousseau had an idea as to the matter at hand—Rousseau always had an idea—but stayed silent, impassive, waiting. Jean-Claude Trezeres, the lawyer from Lyons, adjusted the cuffs on his elegant custom-made shirt and looked nonchalantly out of the window. The women, Françoise Duroc and Soizic Aubert, sat together as they so often did at office meetings, but they were a study in contrasts: Françoise with her degree from the Sorbonne and her mild intellectual snobbism; Soizic from Brittany with a scholarship law degree from Rennes, the simplicity of her farm background still showing in her clean-scrubbed face. Raphael Marchand, the only Swiss lawyer recruited by the firm, was tapping his pencil impatiently on the edge of the table, his indignantly bristling mustache adding to his appearance of impatience.

Robert Beneteau cleared his throat and looked around the room. Finally, almost hesitantly, he said, "Monsieur Giroux and I would like to share with you some of the things that we have been discussing in private. These matters are for your eyes only, and I must ask you never to speak of them again beyond these walls." He paused, scanning their faces. Evidently he learned nothing there that would keep him from continuing, for he went on. "Once we have had this discussion some of you may decide that you no longer wish to work for this firm as it continues to represent A.R.M. That will be perfectly acceptable, but you must understand in any event that you are bound by your promise of discretion.''

He paused, and tension seemed to mount in the room. Soizic Aubert had drawn in a quick breath, almost a gasp, which she now let out slowly. Jean-Claude Trezeres shifted uncomfortably in his seat, and Raphael Marchand resumed the tapping with his pencil. Only Rousseau remained still. There was nothing but lively interest to be read on his face.

Beneteau shook his head, as though he had been expecting more from them, and gestured wearily toward his partner. ''Marc will explain the situation.''

Marc Giroux had stopped his pacing. Now he pulled out a chair, scarcely containing his eagerness, and sat down on the edge of it. ''We have two commitments,'' he said without preamble. ''To look after the affairs of A.R.M. and to watch over those of the de Montclair family. We are all only too well aware of the fact that changes are taking place in Europe—important and dangerous changes.'' He paused and looked at them all, but they were silent, their attention riveted on him. He moistened his lips. ''We all have our own views of the political situation and I would be willing to wager that none of us feels any affection for Monsieur Hitler, or for his expansionist policies. I know for one, I certainly do not.''

He could no longer contain himself and stood up again, walking theatrically over to the window and then turning to face them again. Beneteau found himself thinking, almost irrelevantly, that Giroux had missed his calling: With that kind of flair, he would have made a fine trial lawyer.

Giroux took a deep breath. ''However, the interests of both A.R.M. and the de Montclair estate dictate that we hold our own opinions and loyalties at bay. Monsieur Beaumont is convinced there is to be a global war—and very soon. Hitler will overrun Europe—including France. Japan may well decide to declare war on the United States. And we already know of Mussolini's plans for North Africa and the Mediterranean Basin.'' He paused again. ''Monsieur Beaumont is in all probability correct, even more so in view of the fact that he has some say in the formation of policy, at least in the United States. So we have to be prepared for some very unwelcome facts.''

He began to pace again. Hardly a breath was taken in the room. ''First, France will probably be at the very least involved in a grueling war, at worst occupied by Germany. Either way,

Pierre de Montclair will be affected. If the second scenario wins out, his family—including his son and thus far sole heir—will be affected. We have seen already that the Germans have demonstrated nothing but contempt for occupied countries. There is no reason to expect they will deal any differently with France. The de Montclair family must therefore be considered at great risk even as we speak.''

Rousseau came to life long enough to drawl, ''I hardly think that we can convince Monsieur Hitler not to invade France because we wish to keep one obscure family healthy and solvent.''

Beneteau frowned. ''Please do not belabor the obvious, Monsieur Rousseau. Pray allow Monsieur Giroux to continue.''

Rousseau gestured ironically toward Giroux, who shook his head. ''Obviously we cannot. But there are other things we *can* do.''

He walked over to where Beneteau sat and tapped the stack of file folders. ''Messieurs, mesdames, I present to you A.R.M. We talk about the company every day. We maintain subsidiary companies whose sole aim is to monitor progress. We live and breathe A.R.M., but I propose to you today that not one of us in this room has any concept of the scope of what we are dealing with here. These are the reports. I urge you all to go through them later this afternoon, at your leisure. I will leave them here. When you do, you will find a company whose assets are greater than those of most governments. You will find a company that is controlling, to a large extent, American and indeed in some cases worldwide production—not only of airplanes, but of rockets, of bombs, of all sorts of military hardware and matériel. You will find a company with a direct line to the President of the United States—and file drawers filled with information to blackmail senators and congressmen. *This* is what we are dealing with, messieurs and mesdames.''

Giroux stopped again, as the whine of a siren came to them from the street. Everyone waited while it screamed by, and then he continued. ''I think that it will not come as any surprise to you that A.R.M. has been supplying Germany with plans for its fighter planes. Yes, the Junkers. Germany paid good money because Hitler wanted the best. And he got it—a German name on an A.R.M. design. A.R.M. has also been supplying France and Britain with similar designs, actual planes and rockets, and— well, the list is long. It's all in there.'' He nodded toward the file folders. ''The point I am making is that Monsieur Beaumont has chosen to ignore political—and, I might dare say, moral—principles in favor of economic ones. His interest is in expanding A.R.M. And so, in fact, should ours be.''

''What you are saying,'' said Soizic Aubert, amazement in her voice, ''is that the company is playing both sides in order to make a profit.''

''Succinctly put, Mademoiselle Aubert. Thank you. That is *precisely* what I am saying. A.R.M. is playing both sides. And very soon so shall we.''

Raphael Marchand had finally stopped tapping his pencil. Now he said, ''Is that a figurative statement? Are you asking us to condone Beaumont's choice or to take an active role ourselves?''

''Monsieur Marchand,'' Giroux said, looking intently at the younger man, ''no one here may simply condone what Monsieur Beaumont is doing. No one. We all have to be committed, or nothing. If any of you—any of you—feels uncomfortable about placing the company's interests first and foremost, then you must leave the firm at once. With good references, of course. That is our promise to you. If you choose to stay, then you will have to take on wholeheartedly what we have decided to do here—to carry out our mandate to protect A.R.M. and the de Montclair family. Nothing else will suffice. Nothing!'' He looked around at all of them. ''Hitler may be reprehensible, but we're going to have to work with him and his people if we plan to keep the de Montclair family safe, and solvent . . . and, not incidentally, keep them from knowing that we are doing so. That will take total commitment on everyone's part.''

''In a sense,'' Marchand said drily, ''it is carrying our fine Swiss principle of neutrality to its logical conclusion. It is refusing to make political judgments.''

''Hardly a neutral position, if we are to be aiding Hitler,'' Rousseau said, with a gleam of sardonic amusement in his eyes.

Giroux stepped in. ''It is what we have decided. And now you will have to make up your minds. I leave it to all of you. By the end of the day, you must come to a decision. Tomorrow we will start making plans. We must know whom we have to work with.'' Giroux walked back to his place at the table and sat down. ''The company—or your political preferences. Let us know by five o'clock.'' He made a great show of opening one of the files and looking at it, and slowly, one at a time, the others stood up. For once they were not chattering among themselves; instead each of them was absorbed in his or her own thoughts. The reality they had been confronted with was too great to be dissipated in idle chatter.

At the door, Françoise Duroc touched Soizic Aubert on the sleeve. "What are you going to do?" she whispered.

Soizic shook her head, her dark eyes wide with fear. "I don't know," she said softly. "I just don't know."

Eric Beaumont reached again for the telephone as it started to ring. "Ah, Congressman," he said, and there was satisfaction in his voice. "Thank you for returning my call."

The voice on the other end of the line was faint. ". . . thought I'd see what was what."

Eric leaned forward. "Here's the situation. We need to have the President appropriate some funding for military spending, something ideally on the order of six hundred million. . . . Just in case," he remembered to add.

"I am not sure, Mr. Beaumont, it's what my constituents want. . . ."

Eric smiled. "Well, you have a point. But here's what I'm willing to do. I have your unemployment figures right here, in front of me." He paused. "Give me your vote, Congressman, and help me lobby one or two other people, and you've got an A.R.M. plant in your district. You name the place, I'll have the construction start by next month."

The congressman cleared his throat nervously. "It's a tempting offer—"

"Well, don't sit on it too long, sir. I have only a finite amount of plants that need to be built, and it would be just too bad if you couldn't pick up one of them. It would do great things for your popularity, sir, if you could lower those unemployment figures a little. . . ."

Eric smiled as he put the receiver back. Then he reached for a list in front of him on the desk and crossed off the congressman's name. A moment later he was dialing again. "Senator Thompkins? Eric Beaumont here . . . Just wanted to ask for your support on a matter with the President. . . ."

They all told him that he spent too much time with his daughter, but Steven was determined not to listen to them. Even Justine was mildly shocked: "After all, that's really Caroline's role, not yours."

He had laughed at his sister-in-law then. "Why on earth

should mothers get to watch their children grow up, and fathers should be excluded? I always want to be there, Justine. I want to be there for her first step and her first tooth and her first dance." He caught himself. Justine was looking at him with a quizzical expression on her face, and probably thinking him foolish. "She's my daughter, Justine. Is there anything wrong with loving her?"

And Steven took an obscure pleasure in doing what he wanted, anyway. He had hardly known his parents: His mother was too ineffectual to be a real personality for him, and his father had always been too busy. Always. Work was all that mattered to him, and he died without Steven ever really feeling that there had been any bond between them. His father had passed on the family business to him, but precious little else.

Steven was determined that things would be different for Elizabeth. She would know her parents; know what they were like, what they thought about, hoped for, feared, dreamed of. They would be real people to her—just as she would be a real person to them. More real, thought Steven, than he had ever been to either of his parents.

He was taking her to the waterfront today, to the little park that looked out over the ocean, with the sun sparkling and shimmering on the water's surface and the wind whipping all around. There were always people there: People walking their dogs, or strolling about with their arms around each other. It was almost possible, then, to forget what was happening in other parts of the world. Newport was at peace, and that was all that mattered.

She was so small, Steven marveled as he dressed her. Like a little doll, but already a person. She smiled a wobbly smile at him and he kissed her cheek. She wasn't talking yet, and he couldn't wait until she did. There had to be amazing things happening inside her head.

She fell down twice on the grass as soon as they reached the park, her skirt getting stained and smeared, and Steven carefully got her up and dusted her off again. Walking was still an experiment in balance. And how different the world must look from that viewpoint, he thought.

His brother William never thought about those things. William was too busy—like their father had been—with Asheford Shipbuilding, to even think that there was wonder to be seen in a child's laughter, or first steps, or simple delight in the world. Those things were reserved for women, as he told Steven time and time again. "This place is important, Steven! Let Caroline take the baby out."

"The baby is important, too," Steven had said mildly.

"For women," William had said. "Leave it to them, Steven. We have better things to do."

Nothing could be better, Steven thought, staring out over the ocean while holding Elizabeth close to him. Nothing could be better than this, than being close to this tiny perfect human being he had helped to create, listening to her small sounds and marveling at how she would, someday, grow up to be a recognizable adult human being. Certainly not poring over designs, holding endless meetings that talked of profit and loss, of gains and expenditures. . . . That was what was important to William. That's what he had always thought had to be important to him. But Elizabeth . . . Elizabeth was something else altogether. One's priorities had to change when one had a child. Yet still in the back of his mind, he acknowledged some of William's words. Asheford Shipbuilding was more than their livelihood; it was a symbol of family as well, and Steven guiltily recognized its needs.

He was feeling torn in so many directions—Caroline wanting things from him, things that he didn't know how to give her, because he didn't really understand what they were. William—and the ghost of his father—clamoring for his time, all of his time, to be spent at Asheford Shipbuilding, to make it into a bigger and better place. And now there was Elizabeth, with her immediate needs and desires, and the odd feeling that she gave him: the feeling of being a father. And the desire to be the best father that he could be.

Nothing that Caroline found, up there in the skies, could equal this feeling. Nothing that William found, peering at his account books or even watching a new ship getting commissioned, could equal this feeling. It was like being drunk without drinking; feeling alive and good and filled with hope and the sparkle of dreams that might come true.

Elizabeth squealed and pointed at a sea gull which had suddenly risen and flew, screaming, to join a flock floating on the water. Steven nodded and followed her gaze. "Birds," he said as distinctly as he could.

It was amazing how such a small word could make one feel so good.

Chapter Three

Chantale de Montclair had taken an egg from the hen coop that morning to use in her hair—the thick, luxuriant red hair that spoke so eloquently of the ancient ties between Brittany and Ireland. Certainly with her red hair and green eyes, she didn't look like anybody else in her husband's family. The de Montclairs had dark eyes and hair and sallow complexions. Her skin was ivory-white, and freckled from staying too long in the sun.

She used the egg as a rinse, and sat outside the kitchen door, soaking up the warm spring sunlight, drying her hair with a towel and thinking of nothing in particular. She liked these solitary early-morning hours when no one in the household was up except the servants—and Jean-Claude, occasionally, waking and crying for her to come and take him out of his crib. He was two years old and would be big enough for a real bed soon. Already he had learned how to climb over the bars when he was very frustrated and his cries had failed to summon her. Chantale smiled as she thought of his face, screwed up in concentration as he negotiated his way out of his bedroom and came in search of comfort. Her mother-in-law invariably got upset, saying that he was surely going to hurt himself one of these days, but Chantale liked these signs of determination and independence in her son.

And now—she couldn't be positive yet—she may well be getting ready to give him a brother or sister. It was too soon to be sure, but the signs were all there, the sudden nausea at unexpected moments, the heavy feeling of sleepiness in the early afternoon . . . She hadn't spoken of it yet to anyone: not her mother-in-law who had been telling her for the past year that it was time she conceived again, not even Pierre, who had been so overcome the last time that he hadn't allowed her to do anything for herself. She sat instead in the early-morning sun and brushed out her long thick red hair and wondered if the miracle was going to happen again.

Annie, the fat cook, waddled out to toss away some dirty dishwater and squinted at Chantale. "Well then, can't sleep?"

Chantale smiled and gestured with her hands, palms up. "No. It's too beautiful outside to be indoors sleeping, Annie."

The older woman snorted. "Stuff and nonsense, if you ask me. Young woman should be in with her husband this time of day." She expertly ran a sponge around the inside of the pot she was carrying. "Be wanting some breakfast, then, Countess?" Marie-Louise was still Madame la Comtesse, but Chantale had inherited the title along with her marriage to Pierre, who was still called "the young count" by those in the district who had known his father, and the servants took note even if Chantale herself didn't.

"Only if you'll let me help you with it."

"What a notion! Come on in, then, Countess, and if you don't mind eating in the kitchen I'll have something ready for you in no time. Fresh croissants, if you'd like." She shook her head as she preceded Chantale into the kitchen, its huge flagstones cool under her feet, the copper pots gleaming over an immense fireplace. The Château de Montclair had been built to accommodate a family that was much more extensive than the one presently living there, but there may be hope yet, thought Annie. Unless she was very much mistaken—and how could she be mistaken in such things, she whose mother had been midwife in this district for nearly fifty years?—the young countess was pregnant again. And high time. She glanced over at Chantale, sitting quietly at the long oaken trestle-table, even as she reached for the coffeepot. Pretty girl she was, though an odd choice for the young count, coming from Brittany as she did. Say what you will, those Bretons, they're different. Even if she lived in a fine castle there, and came from a good family—God only knows what they consider good families, those Bretons. Don't even speak the same language as the rest of us. . . .

Chantale sat silently while Annie put coffee and orange juice, fresh croissants, butter, and marmalade in front of her. She would have liked to take the food out with her and eat outside, feeling the sun dance on her skin and take this horrible dark chill off her, but she knew that that would startle Annie. It was nearly three years since Chantale had come to live in this cold, immense ancestral home, but she knew that she was still a foreigner to these people—the Breton wife of the young count. Chantale shrugged. Fair enough. Anyone coming to live in Saint-Léon-des-Fougères, the coastal village where she had grown up, would have been considered a foreigner, too. Even if he had only come from a village away. But to know that was one thing; to experience it was something else altogether. Chantale sipped her coffee and sighed inwardly. Three years, and she still couldn't stop missing the sharp tanginess of the sea air or the roar of the waves on the rocks under the cliffs. Her bedroom window had overlooked those very cliffs. . . . Three years could be a lifetime.

The young Chantale de Kerenec had so little in common with Chantale, Countess de Montclair.

Soon, upstairs, they would be waking, all of her new family. Marie-Louise, her mother-in-law, the stern widow who had arranged Chantale's marriage to her son. Chantale still winced, even now, to remember her rage when she found out that she was to marry this foreigner, this inlander. Arranged marriages were common at her stratum of society, and she had expected to have hers settled without her having any say in it, but she had always assumed that she would be engaged to someone from Brittany, that she would still have her cliffs and her rocky beaches and her wild salt spray. She had stood all her life on the headland where generations of women had stood, waiting for the fishing boats to come in, waiting and watching on the narrow path worn by their restless feet; and now no daughter of hers would stand on these cliffs and scan this ocean. Her daughter would have fields and meadows, but they were a poor substitute.

Her mother had calmly told her that she would be leaving the following year for Anjou, and Chantale had gone into a rage. She was still embarrassed by the pain she had seen flicker across her mother's face as though she had slapped her. The Countess de Kerenec was doing the best that she could for her daughter, but all that Chantale could see was that she would have to leave Brittany. Leave her home for a foreign, landlocked region where she knew no one, where she would be a stranger to the people and to the customs. Chantale had screamed at her mother, and gone for two weeks without speaking to her. When the betrothal was announced she had worn black. At the time, she had thought it subtle.

Pierre had been proper and correct when she first met him.

He was handsome and elegant in his own way, and her first thought was that her mother could have made a worse choice. She hated being away from Brittany, but Pierre was attentive, listening to her thoughts and opinions and taking her here and there around the countryside to acquaint her with her new home.

They had even, once, gone to one of the *bals populaires,* the street dances that proliferate in the summer when it is hot and where all the common people go. It was in Angers. They had drunk plain red wine and had danced and danced and danced, rubbing elbows with merchants and factory workers, the music spinning around them and the colored lights that had been strung up for the occasion sparkling in Chantale's eyes. She loved her husband that night. And for many nights, she loved him, his impetuous laughter, his daring spirit, his yearning for adventure, for that strange sweet mysterious something that remained elusively beyond his grasp. He would pursue it, and she would pursue it with him. They would be partners in life. She smiled all the time, even when she fell asleep at night she smiled, convinced that she had a good husband.

She did have a good husband—until he tired of her, until he began criticizing her foreign ways, until he started looking for other partners in adventure . . .

Marie-Louise, the countess, on the other hand, was from the very beginning as cold as granite, the original Ice Lady, and Chantale had found herself, more than once, shivering because of more than the drafts in the great château. Poor lady. Chantale reminded herself that she should feel sorry for Marie-Louise. Her husband had been killed in the Great War, with Pierre just a baby at the time. No one could say that she had had an easy life. That accounted for her bitterness, her anger, the edge of unhappiness that lay just below everything she said and did.

And Pierre . . . Chantale sighed again. At least Marie-Louise could console herself with the knowledge that her husband had always been faithful to her—unlike Pierre, who seemed to think that it was perfectly acceptable to have a wife at home and a mistress in town. Chantale had never seen the other woman, but she knew of her. A young widow, pretty and artistic, who ran Angers's most important art gallery. Or so Chantale's maid had informed her one night, when she was coming in from her half day off in town. The maid had seen them together. She had been crying and stammering, afraid of what she was saying, and Chantale had listened to her in silence, with her heart hammering inside of her chest. She had dismissed the girl with dignity, and it wasn't until she was out of the room that Chantale fell apart, sobbing and clutching at the long velvet curtains as she slid down to the floor. It was as though her legs could no longer support the weight of her body, the weight of the knowledge she had just received.

She cried that day, as she cried for many days afterward. But there are just so many tears that can flow, and sometimes even the most horrible of events can eventually be assimilated. Chantale knew that Pierre would always do whatever he wished. He had been raised that way. Marie-Louise had taught him well. He was the Count de Montclair.

He would be getting up soon and announcing his plans for the day—which, on rare occasions, included her. Though more often they did not. He had his life, and she had hers. He was expected to take an interest in his land and house and horses, and in the affairs of his servants. He was expected to be well read and cultured, to make short speeches at public, artistic, and intellectual gatherings, to grace the lives of the people who lived in the neighborhood of the château with the appearance of the young count. She was expected to be the dutiful wife, producing children and appearing publicly at carefully spaced events throughout the year—the hunt, the Easter Festival, the Wassail Cup.

She was doing what she was supposed to do: She had already brought Jean-Claude into the world, and if the signs were right, she would soon be having another child as well. And she dutifully appeared with Pierre and Marie-Louise at all the required social events of the year. But no one had told her what a countess was supposed to do in between those times.

"More coffee, Countess?"

Chantale looked up and gave the cook a tired smile. "No, thank you, Annie. That was a lovely breakfast. Thank you."

The older woman sniffed. "You'll have to do it more justice than that, Countess, if you'll be wanting me to believe your thanks." But she smiled to herself as she waddled away. Despite the fact that she was a foreigner, the young countess was a nicer lady than the old countess, and that was the God's honest truth. Always nice; always seemed so happy. A pleasure to work for her, it was.

Chantale, enveloped in her own misery, sat on in the cold

immense kitchen and wondered if this was what drowning felt like. Tiring and overpowering and, in the end, inevitable.

Soizic Aubert had only recently taken up smoking. It seemed that everyone at the law firm of Beneteau and Giroux smoked, and she was insecure enough to feel that mimicking their habits might help her fit in, somehow make her more acceptable. She didn't really like smoking all that much. It made her throat sore and brought on coughing attacks in the night, but she desperately wanted to feel part of the firm.

Fitting in had become very important to her.

She wondered if the cigarettes she held—still with some awkwardness—might make her more attractive. She had never been concerned with whether or not she was good-looking—she rather thought not, on the whole—but now it had become an issue. She would stand in front of the long cherry-framed flecked mirror in her bedroom and study herself, frowning critically. Too thin. That was the first thing, she was sure, that people noticed. She was fine boned, as were all her people, but there was a drawn look about her, shadows in the hollows of her cheeks, that bespoke a certain . . . unhealthiness.

Her eyes were bright and brilliantly blue, the true Celtic blue, the blue of endless skies over Brittany. Her hair was dark, black almost, with strange reddish lights in it. Against the fashion of the times she wore it long and perfectly straight. Her mouth was full—too full, Soizic told herself—and flanked by dimples on either side.

All in all, it was not a face or a body to make men excited or women envious. Soizic wanted neither. She only wanted, quite simply, to fit into the world of corporate law where she had chosen to carve her niche. And she wasn't convinced that she ever would.

What she couldn't seem to fathom was that she would never have been hired by the firm if she had not been brilliant. Marc Giroux had told her that, the day that he had called her in to a conference and walked around his desk, his hand outstretched. "Congratulations, Mademoiselle Aubert. You are now one of us."

They had spent some time telling her how pleased they were, how dazzling she had demonstrated herself to be in the area of corporate law, and how they were certain that the international law that she would now have to study would be a simple matter for her. She listened to the two senior partners talking to her, their voices lapping over her like waves, and all the while a cold hard knot in her stomach grew and grew. If only they knew . . . They were wrong. She was incompetent, but she had managed somehow to convince them that she was, in fact, brilliant. She was incompetent, and someday they would find her out. But she wanted this job, with all her mind and heart and soul she wanted this job, and so she forced herself to smile brightly and respond to their accolades and ask relevant questions about housing accommodations in Zurich.

She had never believed in herself, and this was hardly the time to begin to do so.

Her fears started in Rennes—or was it before that, in Carnac where she had grown up, the clever child who didn't fit in with the others. All of Soizic's friends had definite ideas about whom they would marry and where they would live and how many children they would have. They played up on the cliffs, high over the headland, where the ancient menhirs, the standing stones, cast their shadows and their legends over the people like a cloak. Jeannine and Marie-Laurence and Aurelie, her friends, would stop and point down below, to the harbor, where the fishing boats came in—the fishing boats that were the lifeline of Brittany. They pointed out the small, dark figures on board and knew their names: Philippe, and Jeannot, and Jean-Louis. I'll marry that one, they would say. Soizic would draw back from them, pulling her shawl closer around her shoulders as though to isolate herself even further, knowing that she could never be part of that laughter, that banter. She wanted . . . more. At that age she didn't know what it was, but she wanted more. Her girlfriends sensed that she was different from them, and they made fun of her because of it.

But the schoolmaster in Carnac, old Monsieur Blehenec, recognized the thing that set Soizic apart from others. He had seen too many pupils absorb only the minimum amount of learning that he had to impart to them before drifting away from him to their fishing boats and their families. And from the moment when she first walked into his classroom he watched with excitement this child who stayed late to read some more, who asked questions with an eagerness he had rarely seen in all his fifty years of teaching. Soizic sought knowledge with an insatiable appetite, like a drunkard desperately demanding more wine. He knew what made her different, but the people of the village didn't understand, and he had applied in secret for her scholarship to the university in Rennes. When it had come as he knew that it would he had gone with Monsieur le Curé, the ancient village priest, to her parents to ask their permission for her to matriculate.

"Of course she can't go. It's nonsense, book learning for a girl." Her father was gruff and tired. He had spent the day as he spent all of his days, hauling in nets from the deck of a fishing trawler. He asked for so little in the evenings, a warm hearth, a hot meal, and peace. Now even that was denied him because of this errant daughter of his. He glared at Soizic and crouched down on the other side of the fireplace.

But after mass the following day, Soizic's mother sought out Monsieur le Curé. She was nervous, rubbing her hands together, constantly adjusting and readjusting the traditional tall white lace Breton cap that she wore. "Is it true, Father, that my Soizic can read and write better than anyone else?"

He looked at her gravely, folding his hands over his midriff. "So I am told, Madame Aubert. And much more than that. A scholarship is given only if the student is exceptional."

She wouldn't meet his eyes. She pulled a lace handkerchief from a pocket in her apron and twisted it helplessly in her hands. "She spends time up at the menhirs," she said.

The curate nodded. "I know. She dreams many things, that daughter of yours. Her mind looks for things to think about."

"Why us?" she wailed. "Why can we not have a daughter that does as she is supposed to do?"

He smiled gently. "You *do* have daughters who are properly married, madame. And sons who go fishing with their father. One is not so much to give up, is it?"

She finally met his eyes. "Is this God's will for us, Father?" she asked. "If it is, then she will go, and I'll not hear no from her father, though it's a fearsome thing that you ask. Is it God's will?"

He smiled again. It was indeed that simple for her. "It is my opinion," he said carefully, "that God does not wish us to waste the gifts that He gives us. He gave your daughter a fine mind, perhaps even a brilliant mind. Not taking this opportunity would be wasting that mind." Not to mention, he added to himself, that trapped in Carnac, Soizic would certainly go mad. A mind like that . . .

Madame Aubert nodded and carefully wiped tears from the

corners of her eyes. A light of resolution had come into them. "You can tell Monsieur Blehenec that she will go to the university, then, Father," she said firmly. "I'll not have it said on Judgment Day that Yves and Sylvie Aubert stood in the way of the will of God."

She had been as good as her word. Soizic had gone to Rennes, where she had taken a room in an ancient pension, and spent all her time and money on her books, and she graduated with honors from the law school.

She loved Rennes; she loved the dusty old library and the way the sun slanted in during the late afternoons when she sat and read—and mostly, she loved the law, so precise and clear and arguable. A society could only work as long as it had laws, proper laws that protected the very fabric of that society.

But even at Rennes, Soizic felt that she did not fit in. She couldn't afford the clothes that the other students wore. She didn't understand some of their discussions, they who had come from the cities, Saint-Malo and Brest. And they did not understand her timidity. She felt, the entire time, that she didn't belong, that her whole academic career was a sham, that she didn't have the right to be there. Even her excellent grades, the ways in which she had distinguished herself to the academy, served only to reinforce her belief that she didn't belong.

And then she graduated, and it was time to make a decision.

She had offers. Offers from Saint-Malo, which her family urged her to accept. She would be close to them, close to Carnac, where she could perhaps marry someone. Certainly there was a priority to be placed upon remaining in Brittany. She was a Breton. She couldn't possibly think of . . .

Soizic had accepted the offer from the Paris firm to practice corporate law.

Paris. She did well at her job, but the city made her feel dazed. So big, so bustling, and always everyone speaking French: At Rennes, some of her classes had actually been in Breton. In fact, she hadn't learned French until she had gone to school, and Monsieur Blehenec had insisted that she do so. Now she was in another world. Your choice, she told herself fiercely, and did her best to make it work. And it did, but she never felt as though she could be totally accepted. She felt as though her aptitude at her work was a cover, and one day they would all find out that she was incompetent, a miserable provincial Breton girl. Go back to your fishing village, they would tell her.

And then, of course, there was François. François with his dark eyes and sandy hair, his laughter and the endless Pernods he bought for her as they sat talking together at the cafés, the chic cafés to which he brought her. François was an architect working on a new building for Soizic's law firm. He asked her to lunch in a moment when she didn't have an excuse ready, and thereafter he could have had anything in the world that he asked of her. But when one night in the narrow bed in his pension he taught her what gave all the married women their secret looks, she wasn't as excited about the sex as she was about the sheaf of new contracts on her desk that Monday. As she became more and more involved in her work she saw less and less of François. She couldn't *not* do the work, Soizic reasoned with herself, and it wasn't her fault that she wasn't able to take time off every evening to walk and laugh and drink and make love with François. But the first time that she saw him on the avenue with his arm around another woman she felt the same horrible knot in her stomach. So she had failed at this, too.

One day an attorney from Switzerland, Marc Giroux, came to the firm and spent the entire morning closeted with the senior partner. The other offices were abuzz with excitement, but Soizic had a case to prepare and was oblivious of what was happening until the senior partner and the man from Zurich appeared at her office door. "Mademoiselle Aubert, a word with you . . . ?" They were impressed with her work, they said. The man from Zurich was prepared to offer the firm a fine settlement if they would excuse her from her contract with them. She was just the sort of person that the law firm of Beneteau and Giroux was looking for. . . .

And so she had gone. To a new challenge. To flee from Paris, where they knew that she was nothing but a girl from a fishing village, to Switzerland, where she could start afresh. To flee from the mocking eyes of François, perhaps into the arms of someone who would understand that her work was, that it had to be, the first priority in her life. And now she lived in Zurich and worked with people whose entire existence was focused on two things: an American company called A.R.M. and a French family called de Montclair.

Françoise Duroc, sitting across from Soizic at the wide conference table, put out her own cigarette and tossed a file folder across to her. "So you decided," she said, her eyes not on

Soizic but on the folder itself. "If the question isn't too impertinent, why are you staying?"

Soizic drew in deeply on her cigarette and fought down an attack of coughing. "I think," she said slowly, "that you probably know that already."

Françoise smiled. "I think," she said, "that they knew already that we all would stay, and why. I think that they chose us precisely for those reasons."

Soizic nodded. "I wouldn't be surprised," she said noncommittally, opening a folder. She was staying. She had lain awake for several nights, wondering why she had so impulsively walked back into the senior partners' office, hours before the deadline, and announced that she was staying. Marc Giroux had not been surprised.

"Thank you, Mademoiselle Aubert," was all that Robert Beneteau had said, and then he put a checkmark next to her name on a list in front of him.

"You knew," she said to Giroux.

He nodded. "We know where your commitments lie," he said.

Soizic was surprised, and a little insulted by their equanimity. "I love France," she said, wondering if it was true. She loved Brittany. She had been brought up to believe that it was not the same thing.

"Of course you do. So do we."

She looked from one of them to the other. "Then . . . how did you know? What—what do you think of my ethics?"

Giroux sat down behind his desk and motioned her to take a place in the chair in front of it. "Mademoiselle Aubert, no one is questioning your allegiance to France. You undoubtedly hope, as we all do, that should this war take place, the French will win. It is our most ardent wish." He folded his hands. "However, I know your commitment to the law, and I know your commitment to a client, once you have taken that client on. We have seen many examples of your loyalty to your clients, both from your days in Rennes and from those in Paris. I know that you feel yourself bound to our clients, and that you will do your best for them. I admire you for that."

"But—"

He raised his hand. "No more, mademoiselle. There is work to do, and we don't have the luxury of philosophizing too much about our lives and our beliefs. Use your private life for that forum if you wish.''

How little he knew of her private life, she thought.

Giroux drew a file folder from his desk. ''I think it's time,'' he said, ''that you get a little better acquainted with the de Montclair family.''

Now Soizic looked across at Françoise. ''I think,'' she said slowly, ''that we're going to have some very hard times ahead of us. But I'm glad that I'm staying.''

What else could you do, Françoise thought silently, looking across the table at the younger woman. How earnest she looked, her blue Celtic eyes sparkling with the challenge ahead, her thick dark hair pulled back from her face as though she couldn't be bothered with it, a glow on her cheeks. What else could she do? There would be no work for attorneys in occupied France, and the fishing town Soizic came from would hardly be able to support her. The thought surprised Françoise, and she paused. Am I such a cynic? But why else am I staying? Economic necessity wins out over political allegiance every time.

''Yes,'' she said briskly. ''I'm glad, too. Now—what of this?'' She gestured toward the folder in front of Soizic.

''We need,'' Soizic said slowly, ''some sort of hold over the Deutsches Bank. We need to control them so that they can look after the financial end of things. And we need some sort of hold over the Army, too, if we're going to keep Pierre de Montclair from being conscripted.''

''Not to mention,'' Françoise said drily, ''the occupying forces, to make sure that the family doesn't get evicted. Let's make a list. Perhaps we can come up with something useful for the meeting this evening.''

''This evening?''

Françoise looked at her sharply. ''Of course. There's going to be a war on soon, Soizic. Nine to five just isn't enough anymore.''

Soizic found herself relaxing for the first time in months. They would all work, and work hard, and in the press of business she would not be expected to have a private life. She could lose herself in the tasks at hand.

Chapter Four

*E*ddie Carruthers was early for his appointment as usual.
In the months that Caroline had been teaching him, he had never
been late for a lesson, had never been less than polite and stu-
dious. He was learning to fly with a single-minded absorption,
an intensity that she herself had never managed to summon up
during her own faraway lessons in California. Caroline was impressed; nevertheless, she wasn't sure that she understood this
young man at all.

He was waiting for her in one of the hangars. With the same
concentration that he demonstrated when he watched her at the
controls of an airplane, he was watching a mechanic take apart
a small monoplane. Caroline had to speak twice before he heard
her.

"Eddie? I'm ready now."

He was so absorbed in what he was looking at that he jumped
up, then turned and answered her eagerly. "Oh, great, Caroline.
I was just watching this guy. . . ."

She followed his gaze and smiled. "Yeah, he's great at what
he does. That's not such a bad idea. But the weather is good,
and I only have a few hours this afternoon. . . ."

Eddie was already on his feet, towering above her, the traces
of acne marring an otherwise pleasant face. "Gee, Caroline,
I'm sorry. Let's get going."

He headed toward the tower, but she touched him gently on
the arm. "It's all right, Eddie. I've already filed the flight plan.
You're listed as a passenger." And from the look of relief on
his face she knew that she had done the right thing. Not for the
first time, she wondered what life was like in the Carruthers
household, what made this otherwise calm and competent young
man so fearful of publicizing the fact that he was learning to fly.

It wasn't a terrible thing, surely. Unusual, perhaps. But nothing to be ashamed of . . .

Eddie knew the basic mechanics of flying already, and it was with assurance that Caroline let him take over the preflight checks, watching him as he examined the outside of the airplane, manually testing the flaps and the rudder, checking the wheels. The airplane was a "tail-dragger," with one small wheel down under the tail of the aircraft which had to be lifted first on take-off; it was one of the only things that Eddie hadn't understood immediately. It didn't make sense, he said.

Caroline told him that Eric was already working on a more efficient design.

The airplane wasn't Caroline's, but a newer, sleeker model—still an A.R.M. plane, though—which permitted pilot and co-pilot to sit side by side in the comfort of the cockpit. Eddie continued his checks inside. This altimeter worked without being tapped, and Caroline smiled to herself. Perhaps she would speak to Eric one day about replacing her own plane with something newer. . . .

Eric had other things on his mind these days. He hadn't even responded yet to her query about Elizabeth's birthday party, which had really only been an excuse to see him, anyway, or about the whereabouts of her mother. She was certain that he was working very hard on production, sending airplanes to Europe. Which was a good thing, of course—for the company, at least—but she missed him and was anxious to know what was happening with the war. Eric's information had always seemed more reliable than what one was printed in the newspapers or broadcast on the radio. . . .

Eddie was talking to her. "I'm ready, Caroline." She pulled herself out of her reverie with a start and put on her headphones, tapping the microphone once, superstitiously, before speaking into it. Eddie was already wearing his headset and was waiting for her approval to start the engine. "Finished with all the checks?" she asked him and saw him nod. He reached for the starter button and the big propeller in front of them started moving, sluggishly at first, then whirling around faster and faster until it was a blur and they were hardly aware of it anymore. Eddie's hand moved back on the throttle, and they taxied away from the hangar and toward the crisscross grid of runways. Caroline saw him check the wind direction from the bright-colored wind sock flying in the middle of the field, and she smiled to herself. Eddie was a careful pilot.

She tapped her microphone again and addressed the controller sitting high above them. "Tower, this is November Alpha Bravo Forty-nine, asking clearance for takeoff." It was a joke, really. Everyone at the airport knew that Caroline was teaching Eddie to fly, but he still refused to ask clearance for anything. Perhaps his own superstitions were showing.

"November Alpha Bravo Forty-nine, you are cleared for takeoff on runway zero-four." Eddie taxied them over to line up for the correct runway, his eyes watching the instruments, watching the airport itself, and the wind sock, rotating calmly from one source of information to another. Caroline flipped her transmit switch. "Tower, Alpha Bravo Forty-nine ready for takeoff."

"You are cleared for takeoff, Alpha Bravo." Above them, the controller would be looking out at the scene around the airport, but keeping an eye, also, on the big radar screen that had been so recently installed to take the place of binoculars. Radar, an acronym for Radio Detecting and Ranging, was an impossibly wonderful device that bounced high-frequency radio waves off objects and returned the images to the sender of the waves. It meant that airplanes could be picked up long before they could be seen; and there was no question that accidents were thus averted. Everyone was a little afraid of it, too, but Eric predicted they would all get used to it in time.

There was no question either that a small airfield such as Newport was an unlikely candidate to have a radar station. The newspapers had recorded huge installations in England, on the cliffs over the English Channel, ready to intercept and identify the shape of incoming German planes, should there be any. No one in London was about to forget the bombings of the last war. But radar was restricted, too. It was only for military use, and still principally in England. Caroline alone, with her connections to A.R.M., had been able to talk Eric into obtaining a radar setup for her. There weren't many things she asked for these days that Eric refused. He seemed to feel as though he owed her something. As though he were trying to make up for having failed her, somehow, somewhere . . .

Her headphones crackled. "Alpha Bravo Forty-nine, you are still cleared for takeoff," said a languid voice from the tower, and Caroline realized that Eddie was looking at her. She pressed her button. "Thank you, Tower."

Caroline nodded to Eddie without speaking, and he gently turned the airplane onto the runway indicated, lining it up precisely. He revved the engine as she had taught him, bringing it up almost to full power before releasing it, letting them start down the runway, faster and faster, the lush green countryside a blur going by them. He pulled back on the stick, gently, feeling rather than calculating the precise moment. And then the tail had bumped off the ground and the nose was pointing upward and they were airborne, with still a quarter of the runway to go flicking out below them and the trees rising up, tall and majestic, at the end of it. Soon they were over those, too, and off.

He didn't take too many chances, Eddie. Calm and unhurried and careful. Someday, Caroline thought, something was going to happen that would demand instantaneous action, action without thinking, without pondering, and then Eddie might die. Probably in a clear blue sky, because he spent too much time thinking.

And then, again, it might never happen.

She instructed him to fly up the coast toward Boston, navigating by sight, because navigation was, predictably, something that Eddie could do effortlessly. Once she had taken him up at night, and he had methodically marked his maps and charts, listening to the homing beacons that they passed, and had predictably brought her back within moments of their estimated time of arrival. Now she watched critically as he flew in and out of bright clouds, blinded from time to time as he turned into the sun, watching carefully around him for other aircraft. Boston had no radar.

They flew back the way they had come, skirting the coastline and seeing, below them, bright shapes of fishing boats and the occasional sailboat as they drew in closer to Newport. Caroline reached for her microphone again. "Newport Tower, this is November Alpha Bravo Forty-nine approaching from northeast, please instruct."

Her headphones crackled to life. "Alpha Bravo Forty-nine, you are cleared to join right base runway three-two, call field in sight."

"Tower, this is Alpha Bravo Forty-nine, requesting permission to perform some touch-and-go exercises, runway three-two." The wind must have shifted while they were out, she thought.

The voice in her headphones was amused. "Touch-and-go exercises, Alpha Bravo Forty-nine? Is that really necessary?"

Eddie's eyes met hers for a brief moment, and Caroline shook her head. "Newport Tower, this is November Alpha Bravo Forty-nine," she said formally. "Respectfully request clearance for touch-and-go exercises, runway three-two."

The voice was still amused. "November Alpha Bravo Forty-nine," it said, placing emphasis on the first syllable of the first word, "you are cleared for touch-and-go exercises, runway three-two, call field in sight." And she could imagine what they were saying down there now. Everyone knew that Caroline Asheford had no need to be doing beginner's exercises. . . . But she had promised Eddie to stay as discreet as she could about his lessons, and she had, after all, once owned the airport.

Eddie was good at this, too. He went into the landing pattern calmly and methodically, arching an eyebrow at Caroline as she picked up the microphone again. "Newport Tower, this is Alpha Bravo Forty-nine, entering the pattern right downwind." A brief acknowledgment in her headphones and Eddie took the airplane down to 1,200 feet, slowly and gradually. They flew over the tower, and Caroline pressed her transmit button again. "Tower, this is Alpha Bravo Forty-nine, one thousand feet and descending, turning into base." Again the acknowledgment, and again Caroline transmitted: "Tower, this is Alpha Bravo Forty-nine, nine hundred feet and turning into final approach for a touch and go."

"Alpha Bravo Forty-nine, you are cleared for a touch and go," drawled the voice in her ears, and Eddie brought the airplane in gently, the wheels touching, bouncing once, and then he was giving it more power for a lift-off, soaring back up to 900 feet and turning right again to reenter the landing pattern.

They tried four more, and then Caroline finally nodded and touched her microphone. "Newport Tower, this is Alpha Bravo Forty-nine, turning right into final approach, requesting permission for final landing."

Eddie taxied to a stop and slowly removed his headphones. Caroline sat looking at him with a quizzical smile. "What is it?" he asked.

She shrugged. "Not much more for me to teach you, Eddie. Time for you to start logging some solo hours so that you can go for your license."

He looked away. "Are you sure I'm ready?"

"You're as ready as anyone I've ever seen. Eddie—what is it?

Why don't you want to go up on your own? You're going to have to, eventually, you know.''

"I know." But he still wouldn't meet her eyes.

She shrugged again. Whatever it was, it was something that Eddie was going to have to work out on his own. She had done her best. "Well, it's up to you. I'm finished here."

She slipped off her safety belt and opened the airplane hatch. Eddie just sat there, not moving, staring straight ahead of him at the instrument panel. Caroline felt an edge of worry tug at her. Whatever the trouble was, it wasn't affecting his flying. Yet such things inevitably did. . . .

She ran up the steps to the tower, two at a time, dumping her charts at the main desk and signing off on the flight plan. "All right," she said calmly, running a hand through her curls, "who was guiding me in?"

There was a rustling in the room, as several of the men standing around grinned and looked away, or whispered something to one another. At length one of them, wearing a flannel checked jacket, standing behind the operation desk, waved his hand. "That would be me, Mrs. Asheford."

"Fine." She walked over to him and said very quickly and very quietly, "Mr. Roberts, if you ever question my judgment again or amuse yourself at my expense over the airwaves, I will see to it that you never find another job in aviation. Anytime. Anywhere. Is that clear?"

The smile had faded from his face, and he looked suddenly very pale. "It's clear, Mrs. Asheford."

"Fine." She raised her voice. "Good afternoon, gentlemen."

There was no one standing around on the tarmac when she went downstairs. For all she knew Eddie was still sitting slumped in the copilot's seat in November Alpha Bravo 49. Caroline realized that her cheeks were flaming. Whatever had possessed her to speak to the controller in such a manner? It wasn't like her to assert herself like that. A strange feeling, but one that, at some level inside her, she liked. Perhaps she was stronger than everyone seemed to think after all.

As she approached her car, a familiar figure opened the door and got out. Tall, broad chested, with the late-afternoon sun catching the red hair and beard and setting them alight. Her husband.

He looked worried, which scared her, and he wordlessly held

out his arms to her, which scared her even more. Steven had always been a great one for talking, and this silent display of affection wasn't like him. She let him pull her to him, felt for a moment the strong, secure thudding of his heart beating inside his chest, and then pushed herself away to search his face. "What is it?" A sudden thought occurred to her and her heart lurched. "Steven—is it Elizabeth? What's happened to Elizabeth?"

"No," he said, his voice as gentle as it had been the first time he had ever spoken to her. "No, sweetheart. She's fine. I left her with Justine, for a while. It's your grandmother."

So it was over. There was a certain undefinable finality in his voice that left no whisper of hope behind it. She reached a hand toward her neck. There was a horrible feeling in her throat, as though a band had encircled her neck and were pulling tighter, closer, harder, depriving her of air. She struggled to breathe. It was over, and she had not even been able to grant her grandmother's last wishes. "When did it happen?" she managed to whisper.

"About two hours ago. I was with her, Caroline, if that helps. I'd gone over to see her, and . . . afterward, I came right out here."

Two hours ago she had been flying out over the ocean, with nothing on her mind but compass headings and the bright brilliant sun above her. Two hours ago she had been doing what she did best and liked the most. She had been *enjoying* herself, and all the while her grandmother lay dying. She had never even said good-bye.

The tears were running hot and useless down her cheeks, and Steven tightened his arms around her. "It's all right, sweetheart," he said, misreading her thoughts. "She wasn't in any pain. Just started coughing—you know, the way she's been doing—and then her eyes rolled up and she was gone."

Now the emptiness begins, she thought dully. Now the encircling guilt and strangeness, the ache for all the words left unsaid and tears left unshed. The season of grief is upon us, and all the sharper because I did not fulfill her last wishes. She wanted so little . . . a word to her daughter, and a promise that Steven and Elizabeth and I would go and live in her house . . . so little. And I couldn't even give her that.

Steven cradled her in his arms and whispered words of comfort that she could not hear. And Caroline wept and wept for the woman to whom she had never even said good-bye.

* * *

"Well, he did it."

"Who did what?" Eric Beaumont looked up from the sheaf of papers on his desk. "Speak up, Julie."

His secretary, standing just inside the door to his office, smiled. "It just came in over the wire, sir. President Roosevelt asked Congress today for five hundred and fifty-two million dollars for defense!"

He leaned back in his chair, reaching automatically for the cigarettes on the desk. "Well, well! You never know until you try."

"Congratulations, sir. All your hard work paid off."

He lit the cigarette. "I think that you'll find, Julie," he said smugly, "that hard work almost invariably pays off. Now go make some telephone calls for me. I need to arrange a few meetings."

Julie's manner immediately became businesslike, even the pleats in her skirt seeming to stiffen to attention, and she readied her pen and omnipresent stenographer's pad. "Yes, sir?"

"First," he said, drawing in on the cigarette, "Jeffrey Kellogg. I want to meet with him as soon as possible. Not at Johnson Industries and not here. We'll choose some neutral territory."

Julie's eyes widened, but she didn't say anything, and Eric smiled. She would work it out on her own, he thought. She wasn't stupid. He stretched his legs out behind the massive mahogany desk that he had used ever since he had first relocated the company in America. It was time to strike a truce with Johnson Industries. Not forever, of course. But one could only fight on so many fronts, and if the industrial complex was going to have any say in making policy throughout the upcoming war, then they were going to have to be united. An uneasy truce, but it might work, if he presented it correctly. Kellogg was no fool. He would see the point.

"Next," Eric continued, "I want a meeting in Washington with the secretary of war and the top generals—you have the names in the files. We can meet at the Pentagon if they'd like. We need to meet as soon as possible—sometime next week would be ideal. Check my calendar." He paused to inhale deeply on his cigarette, and then exhaled again. "Tell them that we need to be planning strategy, and every moment counts. From now on, every moment counts."

"Yes, sir."

He ran a hand through his thinning hair. "Oh, and Julie—I almost forgot." Indeed he had, until this very moment, with Caroline's card sitting in front of him. "Amanda Lewis—or Osbourne or whatever she is calling herself these days—isn't anywhere to be found. Her daughter can't reach her, and apparently Amanda's mother is ill. It's a pain in the neck, but we're going to have to find her. Who can we send?"

"Clark is free at the moment, sir. He does good investigative work."

"Hmm." Eric thought about it for a moment. "The point is, if Amanda doesn't want to be found, then no one's going to find her. But we still need to go through the motions, at least make an attempt." He sighed. "All right. Let's send Clark. Nairobi, I think, for starters. We have some people there, don't we?"

"An airstrip, sir, and a small airplane factory. Mostly engine work."

"Right. They may be able to give him some clues, and provide some native help. Make the arrangements, Julie, will you? And have him report back to me weekly. I want to know if we're being taken on a wild-goose chase."

"Yes, sir."

He passed a hand over his forehead. "And for God's sake, Julie, order me another case of wine. You can have it delivered to my house. I don't have time to pay attention to all of these details myself."

"Yes, sir." The door closed behind her neat figure, and Eric sighed. There were too many things to be taken care of, and he couldn't afford to be sidetracked. A matter as unimportant as stocking his wine cellar—or as ridiculous as finding Amanda. His eyes traveled to Caroline's card. It wasn't unimportant to her, he reminded himself. Caroline was all that he had left, and he would do whatever she wanted him to do.

The telephone at his elbow rang, making him jump. Julie's voice, cool and professional. "I have Caroline Asheford on the line, sir."

Eric raised his eyebrows, thinking whimsically about timing. "Put her through."

A click, and then Caroline's voice. "Eric? Eric, is that you?"

"Most assuredly, my dear. I'm sorry, I haven't been able to get around to—"

"It doesn't matter anymore." Even across the miles that separated them, across a continent, the pain in her voice was strong and real and alive. "Grandmother is dead."

He hesitated, trying to think of what to say. He had met Margaret Lewis only on occasion, most notably when he had demanded that Caroline be sent to him in California, insisting that she wasn't being raised adequately in Newport. Mrs. Lewis was a stubborn old lady, who had produced an equally stubborn daughter. Only Caroline seemed to have a more gentle streak in her. Margaret and Amanda, in their own ways, were tougher and harder to get along with. Perhaps, Eric thought suddenly, in death as much as life.

"I'm sorry, Caroline," he managed to say at last. What else was there to say? You must be in pain? Of course she was.

A muffled sob on the other end of the line. "Eric . . . where is my mother? Grandmother so wanted to see her again . . ."

He swallowed. "Honey, I've been so busy. I've just sent a man to Nairobi; he should be telling me something soon. . . ."

"But I asked you *ages* ago!"

"I know. I know," he said as calmly as he could, stifling his irritation. He had had more important things to do. Couldn't she see that? He wasn't Amanda's keeper, thank God.

"All right." She drew in a long, shuddering breath. "At least come to the funeral, Eric. Please come. . . . It's on Wednesday, with the wake on Tuesday, in the evening. St. John's Church. I'll make sure that they save a place for you."

Wednesday. Goddamn it. With all the other things that he had to do . . . He took a deep breath. "Listen, Caroline, honey—"

"Eric, please."

"All right. All right. I'll do my best to be there. Wednesday at what time?"

"Ten o'clock in the morning. St. John's. And—thank you, Eric."

"No problem," he said, putting as much reassurance as he could into his voice. "I'll see you then, Caroline."

"Bye," she said, her voice sounding small and forlorn and lost.

Eric hung up the telephone and stared at it for a split second, then picked up the receiver again. "Julie?"

"Yes, sir?"

"Julie, arrange for some flowers to be sent to St. John's Church, Newport, Rhode Island. They need to be there on Wednesday morning. Be as extravagant as you'd like. The message to read: 'Condolences from Eric Beaumont and Aviation Research and Mechanics.' Got that?''

"Yes, sir. Condolences from Eric Beaumont and A.R.M. St. John's, Newport, Wednesday morning."

"Right. I'm meeting with that Russian fellow Wednesday, aren't I?''

"Yes, sir. Mr. Sikorsky. He's actually an American citizen, sir, not entirely Russian."

"All right." He took a deep breath. "Call him and tell him—" He hesitated, wavering for a moment, and then went on. "Tell him," he said briskly, "that the meeting's on. Eleven o'clock in my office."

"Yes, sir."

He got up and walked over to the window, staring out over the A.R.M. compound. There was no turning back, he thought, once you started down a particular path. He had promised Philippe long ago in France, on a night when they got drunk together and sat toasting their fledgling company, that he would put the company first. That he would take care of it. And that was what he had to do.

He had promised to look after Caroline, too. But she was married, damn it. He had paid his dues: He had raised her and taught her to fly. He had given her all that he had to give— money, attention, and, in the end, the sky. It was up to her husband now to take care of her. He had to take care of the company.

Turning back to his desk, Eric's gaze fell on the framed photograph of Sarah. Sarah as she had been when he knew her, wearing her bright burgundy silk flying suit, young and strong and laughing—not as the mangled body that they had pulled from the mud flats around Boston Harbor. Not as the absence he had felt during the sleepless nights he had spent since then, aching for her, the ghost that never came. Sarah . . . Things might be different, he realized, if Sarah were still alive. She cared about people, genuinely cared about them, in ways that he never did, never could. She would have taught him gentleness. She would have gone to Margaret Lewis's funeral, and held Caroline's hand, and let the business go to hell while other considerations, human considerations, took precedence. With her, perhaps *he* would never have put the company first.

The longing for his dead wife swept over him then, the wound that would never heal, the feelings as sharp as they had been when it first happened, when he had wanted to die because the world was empty without her. The memories held as much pain as they did joy. . . . The shimmering happy days when he and Philippe were just starting the company, those first airplanes held together by canvas and wire and a prayer, and the long nights spent drinking behind the barn. Was it so long ago, after all? Was it so long ago that the hangar door had opened, and they had stood there, Amanda looking around her with distaste and Sarah looking at him with wonder and the beginnings of love?

Remembering was like rubbing salt on an open sore.

Closing his eyes, he pulled back the chair and slumped into it. Those early days . . . the airplanes barely being able to take off, bumping haphazardly across the field, with the farmhands running on either side of them, balancing the wings, until the propeller finally lifted the light frame into the air . . . Amanda holding her wide-brimmed hat and laughing, her head tipped back in the sunshine, and Sarah running along behind the plane, agile despite her long skirts, teasing him and begging him over and over again to let her fly one of them.

Eric slowly struck a match and watched it burn down, the flame hot and bright, until it singed his thumb and he tossed it into the ashtray. Those had been days of wonder, a summer that never seemed to end. Sarah with her funny American accent and her laughter, her daring at the exhibition shows where she used to fly, the crowd gasping in wonder and the warm feeling spreading around inside of him, knowing that that night she would lie in his arms. Sarah in the old house on the rue de Verdun that they eventually rented together, Philippe and Amanda and he and Sarah. Sarah closing the bedroom door and leaning back against it, watching him, smiling, waiting for him to move closer to her, to unbutton her bodice, to bury his face between her breasts, to kiss her mouth, slowly, filled with need and passion and desire . . .

Stop it, he told himself sharply. Stop it now. He hadn't touched a woman in over five years. There had been some before that. He had tried. Pretty girls, fashionable young ladies looking for a good catch and loose women looking for a good time. He bought them dinner and impressed them with his money and finally took them to bed, which was all that he had ever wanted from them in the first place. And it hadn't worked. With each one he shut his eyes, telling himself: This is Sarah. This is Sarah.

No matter who lay under him, he repeated the same ritual, time and time again. Eventually he gave it up because it took too much imagination. The company had taken her place in his heart.

She had died young, in a cloudless brilliant blue sky with people watching, because some obscure man had decided to use her airplane as his ticket out of existence. And that man who'd committed suicide by jumping out of the airplane had done so because Johnson Industries had ruined him. He was a business-man and Johnson Industries had wiped him out. And so he had jumped from the plane, causing it to tip over and both of them to fall from the sky. Best not to think of that, either . . . not to imagine, as he had so many times before, the man hurtling him-self out of the plane and then the plane itself tipping, tipping over, and then Sarah falling out of it because no one had yet figured out that safety belts would make sense. Falling and fall-ing and falling, as she had fallen so often in his nightmares . . .

Oh, God. If only. If only. The world, Eric thought, was filled with those haunting "if only's." If only she hadn't been killed, things would have been different. If only she hadn't been killed, he might have grown into a different person. She would be here with him now, older, with gray hair and lines on her face, but the laughter, and the determination, and the gentleness would be here with her as well. If only she hadn't been killed, he might have run A.R.M. differently. He would perhaps be flying back east to Newport instead of waiting for a Russian designer to meet him in his office.

But she *had* been killed, and she wasn't there, and he had to do what he thought was best. Not what was right, perhaps. What was best.

The choir was singing Mozart's Requiem Mass. Hauntingly beautiful, the notes floated up in the air, carried on the heavy incense, up and up and up into the lofty heights of the church, and perhaps beyond, to the place where she had gone.

Caroline shivered and slipped her hand into Steven's. There were flowers heaped around the coffin, carnations and lilies with their sickening-sweet smell, and an immense arrangement which she knew had come from California. The place next to her was empty.

Every time she had heard a noise from the back of the church, she had turned to look, hoping against hope that Eric would arrive. Someone was reading something from Scripture, and

Caroline forced herself to listen. ". . . and I shall be their God, and they shall be my people . . ." Margaret Lewis's God had been remote and cold, a deity addressed on Sundays and ignored for the remainder of the week. Were there welcoming arms, Caroline wondered, waiting for her grandmother on the other side of those famous Eternal Gates? And, if there were, would her grandmother find rest there? On the whole, she thought, probably not.

Margaret Lewis had not been a particularly welcoming person herself. Not even when her daughter Amanda had arrived on her doorstep, complete with illegitimate child, asking for refuge—not for herself, Amanda had other things to do and other places to do them in, but for Caroline. Margaret Lewis had taken them in, of course. If her daughter was going to run around, the proper thing for her to do would be to pick up whatever pieces she could. Besides, Caroline secretly thought, there was some admiration behind the old lady's stubborn condemnation of Amanda. Margaret Lewis had been a free spirit in her own time, and if she did not agree with her daughter's choices of men or pastimes or households, at least she respected Amanda's aggressive independence in choosing them.

Caroline, however, was another story. Amanda may well run off and do as she pleased, but her granddaughter would be raised properly. And so Caroline had been schooled by tutors, taught excellent horsemanship before ever being given her own pony, apprenticed to high society at teas and bridge games and outings on the river. She had been brought up to be silent, polite, and proper. For most of her life, Caroline had been terrified of her grandmother, but the old lady had to be given her due: She had done her best.

As an epitaph, that wasn't a bad one.

Steven squeezed Caroline's hand briefly before releasing it so that he could walk to the front of the church and say something about the deceased. The priest had asked Caroline for a eulogy, and it was all that she could do to shake her head. "I know too much about her." The priest had been taken aback, but Steven understood what she meant and volunteered to speak in her place. Caroline now put her hands on the back of the pew in front of her, leaning on it rather than on Steven, and watched him as he prepared to make his statement. He really was quite good-looking, she thought irrelevantly. The black mourning suit

he wore merely accentuated, rather than hid, the rugged mas-
culinity that had attracted her to him in the first place.

His twinkling blue eyes were solemn. "Margaret Lewis's
many contributions to her community are a shining legacy for
us all . . ." His voice went on and on, and Caroline narrowed
her eyes against the tears that were spilling out of them again.
The reality of the situation was beginning to sink in. This woman
whom they were praising and praying for was her grandmother,
and she was dead. The huge house on the Connecticut River was
closed up, and would never again echo with the genteel laughter
of her grandmother's lady friends, sipping tea and gossiping
gently together. And who could predict what would become of
the Newport mansion? Caroline knew that it had been willed to
her, but if Steven continued to refuse to live in it, there weren't
a great number of options. It would have to be sold. And Grandmother would have *hated* that.

She would probably hate Caroline for putting the beloved
mansion on the market, and if it were sold, that would come
back to haunt her.

Steven seemed to be collecting his thoughts. ". . . we have
her to thank for so many things, it seems, but mostly for living
as an example to us . . ." An example? Caroline wondered what
that meant. Was she supposed to live as her grandmother had,
in solitary splendor, surrounded by grandiose mementos of days
long past? Would her grandmother even want her to—she who
could not even grant a dying woman her last wish, an opportunity to see her daughter one more time before she died? Caroline
had tried. But perhaps trying was not always enough.

Thus reminded, Caroline glanced again at the expanse of
empty pew next to her. Eric. She had asked Eric for help. She
had told him that the situation was serious, and she needed his
assistance. He could do the things that she alone could not, find
someone to go to Africa and look for Amanda. Eric could have,
and he hadn't. . . . And now he hadn't even come to the funeral.
Where was he? He had said that he would come. There were so
many reasons that she had needed him here. . . . She had so
counted on seeing him, on getting reassurance from him. He
was the closest thing to a father she had ever had, would ever
know, and he wasn't here when she needed him. She had reached
out to him, and he had left her alone. And *lied* about it.

Immediately in her mind she began making excuses for him.
Perhaps there was bad weather. . . . His flight was held up. . . .

An emergency had arisen, out there in California. . . . But the flowers were there, too many of them, speaking eloquently of his absence. He had known when he ordered those flowers that he wouldn't be coming. Her lower lip began to tremble uncontrollably, and Caroline bit it to keep herself from weeping. She had lost her grandmother: Wasn't that enough? Why didn't Eric care enough to come?

She didn't even see Steven as he slipped back into the pew next to her: A blur of tears was obscuring everything. She clung to him and he slipped his arm around her shoulders, hugging her tightly to him. Damn Eric, he thought savagely. He could have found Amanda. He could have at least shown up for the funeral. Caroline's got enough to live with as it is.

The choir was singing the ''Ave Verum,'' the voices angelic and pure, the music haunting and compelling. Steven's thoughts raced on. Damn Eric. And Steven needed to talk to him. Asheford Shipbuilding was doing well—no, better than well, the orders coming out of Europe and Britain had everybody working overtime to keep up production. His brother, William, had even taken to sleeping in his office more often than not. But there was a great deal more that they could be doing. Expansion. Diversification. And Eric, with the most powerful company in the industrial world behind him, would be just the person to help him. Give them direction. Financial backing. The ideas and concepts that they would need to make them powerful as well. Steven didn't want to ask Eric for help, but the time had come when he felt he no longer had a choice. Things were happening too fast.

Caroline hiccuped and sobbed into his shoulder, and Steven held her tightly. He loved her: her wide-eyed innocence, her laughter, her tenderness. If only she wouldn't spend so much time in those airplanes . . . Still, he loved her.

Chapter Five

"It would work. You know that it would. It would work
for all of us." Eric Beaumont gestured, cigarette in hand, to the
map of Europe on the wall behind him. "For God's sake, man,
that's fractured enough. We can't afford to be fractured, too.
Not at a time like this."

Jeffrey Kellogg narrowed his eyes, still waiting, as he had
been since the beginning of this meeting, for a trick, for a trap.
He didn't trust Beaumont: Never had, never would. It was too
dangerous for starters, trusting one's opponents. What he was
saying might make sense, if only he could be trusted. And that
was the bottom line: Eric wasn't to be trusted.

Kellogg shifted his considerable weight on the chair and
reached for his pipe. The pipe-lighting ritual performed a function for him, allowing him time to think, to weigh options, to
explore possibilities. The biggest mistake that anyone could make
was not to think out all of one's options. As a child in school,
his glasses had performed the same function. When asked a
question, young Jeffrey would carefully remove his glasses, peer
shortsightedly through them as though detecting a spot on their
pristine lenses, remove a handkerchief from his pocket, and proceed to clean them. All the while his mind would be racing.
What *was* the square root of forty, anyway? Was Tennessee north
or south of Kentucky? How many books did Nathaniel Haw-
thorne write? By the time he put the glasses back on, he generally had an answer.

He still wore glasses, thick frames distorting his nondescript
eyes. He had put on the weight since then, too, but other than
that, Jeffrey Kellogg looked much as he had when he was
young—the brown hair still cut into the precise, no-nonsense
crew cut, the absence of facial hair carefully maintained each
morning in front of his bathroom mirror. He no longer cleaned

65

the glasses obsessively, though: He felt vulnerable now when he took them off, even for the briefest period of time.

If there was one thing he didn't want to feel, didn't ever want to feel, it was vulnerable.

So now he smoked a pipe, stoking it slowly, tamping down the tobacco, applying match after match until he had it going satisfactorily. Then, and only then, would he answer a question or make a comment. Once he had had time to think.

He squinted up at Eric again. It was an odd meeting. When he had first been contacted by Beaumont, his inclination had been to turn him down. And then, when Beaumont had insisted that it be just the two of them, no staff, no advisers . . . Hell, that didn't sit all that well, either. Particularly not with his board of directors. "You aren't Johnson Industries," they had argued when he had mentioned the request to them, but the reality was that, to a large extent, he was. It was well known that when Jeffrey Kellogg wanted something, he generally got it from them. Perhaps it was their very resistance to the idea of this secret meeting with Beaumont that had sparked his interest in it. . . .

And, damn it, Eric Beaumont made sense. Not that he wanted particularly to be allied with A.R.M.—they had been sworn enemies for too long—but in fact there was a larger enemy now: the inertia of the American government. There was a great deal of money to be made in military hardware and those new radar systems and God only knew what else, and spies could be used more profitably against other countries than against other industries. . . .

Still, he wanted to be sure that he was getting enough out of the deal. He had to have something to take back to that damned board of directors and make them acknowledge that he was right, once again. That Jeffrey Kellogg knew what was best for Johnson Industries.

Eric stood motionless by the map, waiting. Kellogg had picked the spot for this rendezvous, in an office building in San Francisco owned no doubt by one of Johnson's subsidiaries, and Eric had met him here on territory that Kellogg had chosen. It was important that the man feel he had some control over what was happening, or they would never come to terms. And it was important, it was more important than anything else just now, that Kellogg agree. Congress would be moved only by the concerted efforts of the defense industry, the military-industrial complex, and in order for those efforts to be concerted, A.R.M. and Johnson Industries had to strike a truce. It was primordial. They were, after all, the industry.

Beaumont knew he would probably have to give something up. He lifted his cigarette to his lips and inhaled deeply, wondering what the trade-off would be. Kellogg would demand something, some concession, as a sign of his good faith, and he would have to give it to him. He turned his back deliberately on Kellogg, appearing to inspect the map. He had too high an opinion of the other man's intuition to let him guess at the thoughts racing through his mind. Kellogg hadn't gotten to be chief executive officer of Johnson Industries for nothing.

Eric adjusted his tie, exhaled the smoke from his cigarette, and waited. It wouldn't be money: Johnson had enough of that, if anyone could ever be said to have enough. Power? Prestige? He was already offering them an entrée with Roosevelt, and an equal say—or so they would be led to believe—in directing policy. It could be . . .

"I will agree on one condition," said Kellogg, behind him.

Eric turned slowly to meet the other man's eyes. "What condition?" he asked. It might be . . .

"Give us Sikorsky."

There was a moment of silence in the room. Dimly, the two men could hear the sound of traffic from the street below, and the clanging of the noisy cable car from the tracks on the corner. Eric walked to the conference table and slowly stubbed out his cigarette. Igor Sikorsky. They had already signed papers for him to work exclusively for A.R.M., but how did Kellogg know of that? Sikorsky himself had sworn to keep the alliance secret. . . . Johnson had someone inside A.R.M. That was all there was to it. Another headache for another day. Eric would get Julie to assign someone to ferret out the intruder. And hope to God she didn't choose the spy as her ferret.

Sikorsky had designed something revolutionary, and it was not just on the drawing board but built and fully functional. He called it a helicopter, an amazing flying device that required no runway and no wings. It could be used in a variety of situations and for so many different purposes. Eric had thought of contacting young Steven Asheford to ask about the applications in terms of rescue at sea. It was a good idea to throw the fellow some tidbits from time to time; you never knew when Asheford Shipbuilding might come in handy. Besides, it would keep Caroline happy. . . .

Jeffrey Kellogg was watching him, waiting. Eric sighed. One more dream . . . But it was worth it. The alliance was worth it. And besides, he could always work out some modifications of the helicopter on his own. It might not be so great a loss after all, not when thrown into the balance of things.

Eric cleared his throat and put out his hand. "Mr. Kellogg," he said formally, "you've got yourself a deal."

Marc Giroux nodded approvingly. He had been convinced that hiring Soizic Aubert was the right thing, and now he was justified. Justified before Robert Beneteau, who hadn't been sure that taking another woman in the firm was a good idea, justified before the junior partners, Rousseau and Marchand, who had pressed for another Swiss national to round out the office, justified before them all. The girl was brilliant. He alone had known it before, but now she had proved it to them all.

Soizic had presented him with an excellent plan and in her usual manner had offered the idea to him hesitantly, knocking on his door rather than waiting for the evening conference when she could have dazzled the entire office. As though she didn't believe that the idea had any merit! He had seen that it had right away, and he was more than a little pleased with himself for allowing Soizic to claim it as hers anyway. It would have been so easy to make a few minute changes and claim the concept as his own. Perhaps his ethics were improving after all.

"What we need is leverage," Soizic had told him, looking at the papers she had with her and not at him, her bright blue eyes cast demurely down. "It seems to me that the most discreet way to obtain the kind of leverage we require is to establish ourselves financially in the places where we will see fit to place pressure eventually." She glanced up at him, caught the nod he gave her, and then went on, her voice a little breathless. "I have drawn up a list, Monsieur Giroux, of possible locations and businesses. You see . . ." She spread out her papers on his desk, pointing out the firms and locations as she spoke. "Greece. Three shipping firms: Xanatos, Pyrenie, and Plenhakisis. Situated in Athens and Delos. All of them are fairly shaky financially, and all susceptible to a takeover bid. But they have potential, and their locations are perfect." She took a deep breath. "We would own the Mediterranean shipping lanes that way."

Giroux bent over the papers; he could hardly keep up with her. "Germany. Steel plants in the Ruhr, here and here. We'd

control German military manufacturing. Berlin and Bonn—the
Deutsches Bank is in over its head with the loans it already has
outstanding, and they're susceptible. Sir, if we controlled the
Deutsches Bank . . . !'' Her eyes were shining. ''And here, in
North Africa—oil. Oil again in Persia. We can bribe the sheiks,
or we could simply buy out some of the oil companies. I have
their annual reports all tabulated, and there are two possibilities—Framco and Bay. They're both based in the United States,
which makes sense for us, and they're both doing fairly well and
don't seem to realize that they could be doing better.''

Her excitement was contagious. ''What is this, here?'' he
asked, bending over the papers with her, so close that their
breaths mingled. Hers smelled of peppermint. ''Oh yes, Rome.
Um—actually, sir, it's the Vatican.''

''The Church?''

''Yes, sir. Cash flow, sir—untaxed and available almost immediately in whatever form one might desire. No doubt they'll
stay neutral, sir, and make their usual pronouncements on the
inhumanity of man to man.'' May God have mercy on my soul,
she thought suddenly, remembering kind Monsieur le Curé back
in Carnac, a few hundred miles and a lifetime away.

''If they have the money, then we can't bribe them.''

''No, sir. But we can blackmail them.'' Marc looked up
sharply and met her eyes. She dampened her lips rapidly with
her tongue. ''I have reports, sir, obtained by one of the cardinals
who was susceptible to bribery. He's been monitoring the situation for us for some weeks now. And—well, you can read the
reports.'' She didn't want to discuss them with him; not there,
not alone. She could feel, even now, the blush creep into her
cheeks as she remembered what she had read in those reports.
They were not the sort of things that a woman and a man ought
to discuss together. ''The point is, sir, that they'll work. I'm
quite sure of it. The Church would never want this sort of thing
to get out—especially not now, with war in the air and the uni-
fication of Christendom so important.'' Those reports, she
thought, would rip apart any thought of ecumenical peace for
the duration of the war. The Protestants would never forgive
them.

Giroux wordlessly took the papers she had indicated, and
glanced through them quickly. Well, well, pretty bedtime reading this would be. One thing was clear: The girl was right.
Leverage. They had it, or could obtain it, in all the places where

it would begin to count in the very near future. He cleared his throat. "Mademoiselle Aubert, I cannot begin to tell you what this effort of yours is going to mean to the firm."

She was looking hesitant again. "Oh, Monsieur Giroux, if you really think so . . . I just thought that it might be of some use. . . ."

Was she really as naive as all that? Hard to believe of such a bright girl. She seemed to think that she didn't deserve the credit that came her way. His experience with others in his profession indicated how unusual her attitude was. Most lawyers preferred to snatch other people's credit, as well as parade their own. Unusual girl. And very pretty.

That last thought caught him by surprise. It wasn't a good thing, to start thinking about one's colleagues in that way. Maybe Beneteau was right, having women around the office was no good for concentration. But damn it, the girl had brought them something valuable here, something meaningful. And it didn't hurt that she had those incredible blue eyes and that figure. . . .

Giroux shook his head, as though he could shake the thought away. "Mademoiselle Aubert," he said formally, "you have done extremely good work here. I will spend the afternoon reviewing the details, and, with your permission, we will present it together to the firm this evening."

Soizic was having trouble swallowing. She had done it again— convinced somebody that she knew what she was doing. What would the senior partner think of her when he realized that she wasn't all that smart, that it was just a matter of research, diligence, and hard work? "Thank you, Monsieur Giroux," she managed to say. "Until tonight, then."

"Until tonight." He watched the door close behind her, and then turned back immediately to the papers she had left on the desk for him. If she was right, if this would work . . . But, even as he frowned over her calculations, a part of his mind registered with pleasure the lingering scent of her rich floral perfume.

Caroline wiped her hands on the seat of her overalls and turned to finish packing the cardboard box. She had been crying, but had taken a drink or two from the brandy that hadn't yet been packed and felt better. There was something incredibly sad about leaving this house, this place of new beginnings. This was the first house she had ever really called hers. So many stories, she thought sentimentally, fingering the brandy bottle again. So many stories . . . Her wedding night, and Elizabeth's first cradle, arguments and laughter, tears and love. So many things go into a house, and yet, when one leaves there is nothing but an empty shell, echoing rooms.

She sniffed loudly as though to dispel the thoughts, and closed the box. That was it: That was all. Steven and the moving men had already gotten the rest, but, perhaps to delay the final departure, she had insisted on packing her own things, the small toiletries and photographs that cluttered the top of her dresser. And now she was finished; there was nothing more to do, and the big mansion on Ocean Drive awaited.

Against all of her expectations, Steven had agreed to accept her grandmother's bequest as naturally as though he had been thinking of it all along. "There is no question of selling the house; Caroline and Elizabeth and I will be going to live there," he had told her grandmother's lawyer. She had looked at him sharply, but he had squeezed her hand reassuringly and she had thought how wonderful he was, to put aside his own feelings for hers. He who had said that their house was fine enough, and he'd never take charity from the old lady, was now letting Caroline go back to live in the house of her childhood. The estate in Cornish, he decided, should be rented, and a caretaker found to live in the cottage and look after their interests, but under no circumstances would it be sold. And Caroline had smiled gratefully at him. If he could do this for her then she was happy to make the sacrifice of moving. For if she was leaving ghosts behind, she was to find still more of them awaiting her.

Elizabeth was tearful, as though sensing the change and uncertainty in the air and not knowing the reason for it, and Caroline was grateful to at last reach the mansion and be able to hand her over to Marie, who fussed over the child and took her away to her new nursery. All three rooms of it. The enormity of the house, of the situation, really sank in then and Caroline turned to Steven, trying to pull him closer to her. He was busy, directing servants and movers alike as though he had been born to it.

"What *is* it, Caroline?"

"I'm scared."

"Don't be ridiculous." His voice was brusque.

"I *am*." She was vaguely aware of how petulant she sounded, but she felt unable in that moment to control her feelings. "Steven, just talk to me for a while. It would make me feel better. . . ."

He looked at her, exasperated. "Caroline, darling, it's really going to be all right. Can we talk about all this tonight when we've finished moving in? It's not really a good time just at this moment . . ." He caught sight of someone going by and called out, "No, that box goes upstairs. In the bedroom." He turned back to Caroline. "Honey, this was your house once. You'll feel comfortable in it again. And it's *our* house now, don't forget. Just let's give it some time, all right?"

She felt tired and impatient, like a rebellious child. "You talk as though you know everything! Like you can just—just step in—and make everything all right, just because you want it to be! Like you're taking over this house!"

He sighed. "What do you want from me, Caroline? You're upset when I call it your house. You're upset when I call it our house. What's the point of all this?"

"You're taking over too much," she said, hearing the thin edge of panic creeping into her voice. "You're moving too fast. Grandmother's estate, first . . . and the company. You're too interested in the company, Steven. I don't want to have anything to do with the company."

"What company are you talking about? Asheford Shipbuilding?"

"You know perfectly well what company! A.R.M.! Just because they can give you more business—"

"Caroline." He was annoyed but determined not to show it. Gently taking her by the shoulders, while people moving furniture flowed on either side of them, he kept his voice controlled. "Caroline. You're tired. This isn't a good time—"

"It's never a good time," she said irritably. "I know that you like working with Eric. I know that he can give you a lot of business. But I don't like it. I don't like it!" She tried, with some effort, to quiet herself, to speak evenly. "Steven, are you forgetting that I was almost killed because of that company?"

"I haven't forgotten." His voice was grim. "What I am trying to do is to be practical. The man who tried to kill you will never hurt you again. He's in jail. And you can't blame an entire corporation for something that one unbalanced individual happened to try to do!"

"Yes, I can. It's all tied together, don't you see? If people didn't put the corporation first, if they put people's lives first . . .''

He kissed her forehead. "But I do, Caroline. I do. I put you first, and I put Elizabeth first. I'm just trying to be practical. And you need to be, too.'' He glanced around. "Honey, we've got work to do here. We can talk some more later.'' With a backward glance, he strode away, raising his voice to someone outside.

Caroline walked out to the veranda and stood looking out over the ocean, feeling forlorn and a little lost. Steven was right, of course. Her confusion wasn't because of A.R.M., or because of Steven himself, but because of the restless fear that was growing inside of her—the fear that had something to do with moving back into this house. What was it, then, that she had been expecting to find here? Solace? Peace? Absolution? There could be no peace and no forgiveness in this house. Life here could never be simple. There was too much money, too many restrictions. She should never have come. She should have stayed in the little house on the old side of town and consoled herself with her garden. She should have known better than to have come here.

A breeze was coming up from the ocean and Caroline hugged her arms against her body for warmth. Perhaps, if she really gave it some thought, she would find that she was reading too much into the whole thing. That Steven was right; his involvement with A.R.M. didn't mean that he didn't care about what happened to her—or what *had* happened on that long-ago wedding day. It was just a matter of business. He would always be there; he would always care about her, and A.R.M. would never be able to come between them. Perhaps.

But the other voices were too deeply rooted inside of her, too insistent. Terrible things had happened, and, somehow, somewhere, they were her fault. They were her fault because there had to be some sort of cause and effect in the world, because otherwise none of it made any sense. Because her mother hadn't ever wanted her. Because she had been, had always been, nothing but an inconvenient accident as far as everyone was concerned.

Caroline stopped for a moment. That wasn't true. Steven didn't think so. He had always loved her for who she was, from the very beginning.

But Steven didn't know. He didn't fully understand everything that Eric's company stood for, what it meant. He didn't know what Eric had done for the sake of the company. She had never told her husband of her first love, Andrew, and how Eric had forced them to part. Because Andrew belonged to Johnson Industries. No, Steven couldn't comprehend the kind of power A.R.M. wielded and what that power did to people. He was getting too involved with something that was too scary. But if she kept talking to him about it, he would become impatient and say that it was her fault. Like bothering him when he was trying to concentrate on moving . . . She should have known better. Once again, she thought bitterly, staring out at the breakwater without really seeing it, once again she had done the wrong thing.

Echoes of her childhood drifted back to her . . . her mother's voice, light and laughing, and the perfumed cheek extended to her to be kissed. Caroline standing sadly in the middle of the expensive carpet, holding a crayoned picture, watching her mother's preparations for going out and wondering what she had done wrong. What the magic formula would be that would keep Amanda there with her. What it was that she had said—or hadn't said—that made her mother always want to be away somewhere else. What could she have done to keep her there, looking at Caroline's pictures or reading her a bedtime story or laughing with her over steaming cups of hot cocoa? If she had known what to do, her mother would have stayed.

It was Caroline's fault. Everything was Caroline's fault. Caroline's fault . . .

She collapsed at last onto one of the worn chintz-covered sofas, her shoulders shaking with her sobs, the room swirling around and around and all the voices talking together, her mother and her grandmother, Eric and the psychologist, Andrew and Steven . . .

"As you will see, Mademoiselle Aubert has precisely noted the places where the companies in question are vulnerable. It is my suggestion that we act on this information and these ideas immediately. Monsieur Beaumont was consulted via telephone this afternoon and has already approved all these transactions."

"I'm not sure that I understand fully," drawled Eugene Rousseau. He always spoke slowly, as though he were constantly assessing the situation in which he found himself. As, perhaps, he was. "Are we talking about making each of these companies subsidiaries of A.R.M.?"

"Some of them make sense as subsidiaries. I'm thinking particularly of the Greek shipping companies—or at least of Plenhakisis—and of the Albanian mines. We don't need to have our name tied in too tightly with either of those enterprises. And, of course, the Deutsches Bank issue would have to be entirely sub rosa—a subsidiary of a subsidiary I should think. It will be very delicate." Giroux cleared his throat and glanced over at Soizic for approval, but as usual her eyes were cast down and he couldn't read what was in them. "But in general, what we are proposing is total incorporation. We'd want to change A.R.M.'s name to reflect the new nature of the company, although the original charter and ownership will not change. Monsieur Beaumont has indicated approval of such a move, and has even suggested a name that we could consider. If, of course, the firm chooses to move in this direction."

Françoise Duroc lifted her eyebrows, looking across at Soizic. "Well, well," she murmured, almost inaudibly. "The little country goose has laid the golden egg, after all."

Robert Beneteau stood up and distributed index cards. "I would prefer," he said, "to keep this particular vote as discreet as possible. You have all heard the proposal made by Mademoiselle Aubert and Monsieur Giroux. You know that Monsieur Beaumont approves. You have asked whatever questions you may have had. I suggest that you now vote." He cleared his throat and addressed himself to Marc Giroux. "We will need a clear majority," he warned.

"I accept that," Giroux responded.

Soizic felt the knot in her stomach grow and grow. She had a terrible fear that someone would stand up and poke holes in her plan, tear it to shreds, and point a finger at her incompetence. Or worse, they would remain silent and snicker behind her back. . . .

Beneteau picked up the index cards and cleared his throat again. "There is a clear majority," he said, turning the index cards up for all to see. They were not difficult to count. There was only one "no" written on any of them, and Soizic knew without looking at the handwriting that the dissenting vote was Françoise's.

Beneteau nodded to Giroux, who stood up eagerly. "Very well, mesdames, messieurs. So be it. The company will hence-

forth be known as Intraglobal, Incorporated. Make a note of
that, will you, Jean-Claude, and draft the papers? Now, then''—
and his voice was brisk—''go home, all of you. No late nights
tonight. Get some rest, and come back early, because we have
a lot to do. God knows, we have a lot to do!''

Soizic stayed in her chair as the others filed out, their usual
chatter resuming just beyond the door of the conference room.
Beneteau sneezed twice before hobbling after them.

When they had all departed, Marc Giroux turned to her. ''I
told you! Didn't I tell you?''

Soizic kept her eyes downcast, the elation she was beginning
to feel carefully hidden. ''Françoise is against it.''

''Françoise can leave the firm if she continues to be against
it. It is not she who dictates policy, here or anywhere else. It
was a stroke of genius, Mademoiselle Aubert! And one that will
not hurt your standing in this firm.''

She looked up at him, shocked. ''That wasn't why—''

He held a finger to her lips, silencing her. ''I know. *Shh.* I
know.''

There was an awkward pause, during which both of them
suddenly seemed to notice that he was touching her. He moved
his hand back to his own pocket and made a great display of
producing a handkerchief and mopping his brow.

Soizic nervously ran a hand through her hair and stood up,
gathering her papers in front of her. ''Well, I should be going,''
she said, without looking at him. ''As you said, it's an early day
tomorrow.''

''Right.'' He cleared his throat. ''For me as well. Good work,
mademoiselle. Very good work.''

''Thank you, Monsieur Giroux.'' She walked around the big
conference table to the door. ''Good night, then.''

He met her at the door. ''Good night, Mademoiselle Aubert.''

For one long, interminable moment, neither one of them
moved. Riveted to the floor, as though they were statues, they
stood looking at each other, neither one of them reaching for the
doorknob or for the light switch. Soizic caught her breath suddenly in what was half gasp and half sob, and then Giroux's
arms were suddenly around her and his mouth was pressing on
hers, demanding, opening her lips, and pushing his tongue inside.

There was a fire raging within her that she had never felt
before, and there was no time to think or analyze or prepare,

only to act. Her papers fell to the floor as she encircled him with her arms in turn, allowing him to draw her closer and closer until the length of their bodies melded together.

His mouth was all over her—on her face, her hair, her neck. Reaching up with his hand, he loosened the barrette that she wore so that the long dark hair fell down over her shoulders. She reached for him, too, with an abandon she didn't know, didn't recognize, her fingers fumbling with the buttons on his shirt, pulling his jacket off his shoulders, kissing his neck and his chest. Groaning, he pulled her with him down to the thick carpet beneath them, and then he was taking her sweater off and struggling with the clasps on her bra and she moaned softly and put her lips against his ear, probing the curve of it with her tongue.

Her breasts were released at last, and Marc leaned over and kissed them, first one and then the other, his tongue exploring the hardening nipples, his hands encircling and holding the small firm mounds. Soizic gasped with the wave of pleasure she felt washing over her, and fumbled for his belt, her fingers awkward and clumsy on the buttons of his trousers. He pulled her up against him, her breasts soft against his hairy chest, and their eyes locked once before he bent to kiss her again and again, deeply, for so long that she found herself struggling for air.

She had his trousers off at last, even as he had pulled her skirt from her and was unfastening her stockings, her garter belt, reaching for the thin lace panties and the wetness that they were covering. There was nothing in the room but their labored breathing, their gasps, the moans and exclamations of desire as they fumbled and groped for each other's bodies, their haste making them clumsy, their need making them eager.

Soizic cried out as he entered her, but immediately her body found his rhythm and she clung to him, moving with his thrusts, meeting them with movements of her own. She gasped and moaned again as the feeling spiraled up and up and up, achingly higher, incredibly higher, up and up and up. He was groaning and she opened her eyes and saw his face furrowed as though in agony, and he was groaning and thrusting even harder into her. She felt a hot rush in there, somewhere, even as the spiral inside her exploded into a million sparkling bright lights and she thought that she would surely die of ecstasy.

They lay there for a moment in each other's arms, the perspiration of their bodies mingling, their breathing fast and heavy. And then Soizic looked at him, and her eyes widened, and it was as though she were suddenly conscious of what had happened. She pulled away from him. "No," she whispered, her hand over her mouth. "No, oh, please God, no!"

Marc, too, had recovered, and he reached automatically for his trousers. Slipping them on, he moved over on his knees to where Soizic crouched, against a wall, nothing but horror in her eyes. "It's all right," he said softly, gently, encircling her with his arms. "It's all right, little one. Don't be afraid."

"What did we do?" Her eyes were wide and terrified.

Marc smiled. "Whatever it was, it was wonderful," he said. She shivered in his arms, and he let her go so that she could gather up her clothes. Gently, tenderly, he helped her dress.

She stood up with some difficulty. "Will you want my resignation, Monsieur Giroux?"

He stared at her as though she were mad. What on earth? "No, of course not," he said slowly, wonderingly. "I don't ever want to lose you." He stopped himself. What had he meant by that? He was as startled as she to realize that he meant it. Professionally. And personally.

"This," she said hesitantly, "is going to complicate life quite a bit."

"It is," he agreed gravely, helping her with her coat. "We should talk about it." The wide blue eyes were watching him. "Come home with me," he suggested suddenly, knowing that it was not what he had planned but what he wanted with all of his being. "Come home with me. We can talk about it. We can talk about it all. I don't want to lose you."

She smiled, briefly and vividly. "I don't think there's any risk of that."

"Then you'll come home with me tonight?"

"Tonight, and any other night." She really meant it, too. Who was he? An overweight, middle-aged man whom she had never found attractive, and yet who set such fire to her . . . He made her feel competent. He made her feel desirable and alive. She wanted more of that feeling.

They stepped out into the darkness together, their breath frosty in the night air. In the senior partner's office, Beneteau closed the door, slowly shaking his head.

Chapter Six

The bees were droning lazily over the field, and Chantale felt as sleepy as they sounded. She rolled over on her back, a blade of grass in her mouth, and stared at the sky, dazzlingly blue, with wispy white clouds drifting slowly overhead. August 1939. August 1939, and everything should be well.

She rubbed a hand slowly over her abdomen, large and round now with her pregnancy. The baby was due in October. Annie and the other servants were making a fuss over her these days, not letting her lift a finger on her own. Marie-Louise had received the news of Chantale's pregnancy with her usual detachment and had reacted by going to mass daily for a week to say prayers for a safe delivery.

Chantale felt huge and clumsy, but infinitely better than she had during those first months of sleepiness and nausea. Jean-Claude was taking well to the thought of a little brother or sister, though he insisted that it be the latter. "Already the protective older brother, and him just barely turned three," Annie said, laughing, and Chantale had smiled happily in return.

She ached for the ocean these days. Some afternoons it was possible to have one of the servants drive her out to the Loire, and she would sit for hours on its banks, watching the water rush by headlong on its way to the sea. She imagined herself with it, racing frenetically to be free of the land, to be absorbed into the great heaving swell of the ocean. She had read somewhere that all life had begun underwater, and she was attracted to the theory just as she was attracted to the ocean, the cliffs, and beaches of her childhood. Every summer her parents had let her run wild, turning to their own pursuits, and she had spent many happy hours exploring caves and crevasses, collecting seashells and bits of driftwood that had washed up on the sand. Gazing out at the dim blue horizon, she had wondered what lay beyond. The rhythm of the ocean was a rhythm she knew. She had been lulled to sleep by the eternal pounding below her window for every night of her life until she married Pierre de Montclair and came to live inland. Not far inland, her mother had said, trying to console her. Not far—but far enough.

Especially when she was pregnant she wished that she could be there. When she was expecting Jean-Claude, she had asked Pierre if she couldn't go home for a month or two, and he had been shocked. So had Marie-Louise. "This is your home, Chantale."

"I know," she had said unhappily. "But I miss the ocean."

They both had looked at her as though she were mad, and she had never asked again. They would never understand. Pierre and his mother between them were a powerful force. There was a strong bond there, stronger than the bond between Pierre and Chantale. Chantale knew better than to press her point. They would never understand.

Now she lay on her back and listened to the bees and watched the clouds drift by above her. The sky, she thought, was a little like an ocean in its own way, with air instead of water. Alive and moving. Nurturing and sheltering life, and turning in rage into storms that killed everything. Endless and eternal. Always there, always changing, essentially the same. It was a small comfort.

A small comfort, too, that she was going to freckle in this sun and that Marie-Louise wouldn't like it.

Chantale sighed. What on earth did it matter, what her mother-in-law wanted, or liked, or insisted upon? She shouldn't let it bother her. Pierre was her husband; Pierre was the one she had married.

But that wasn't going so very well either.

He had ignored her for the last few weeks. When she pressed the point, he said merely, in exasperation, "But you're so large, Chantale. I can't even embrace you." And it was her turn to stare at him. What on earth did that have to do with anything?

Jeannine, her maid, let her know soon enough what it had to do with—the mistress in Angers. "It's where he goes, Madame la Comtesse," the girl whispered miserably. Thank God, Chantale thought suddenly, thank God that I had the sense to bring Jeannine with me from Brittany. The Angevine maids would have stayed loyal to the de Montclairs and told her nothing.

"I see," Chantale said, willing herself to be calm. "You've seen them?"

"Oh, Madame," the girl said in obvious distress, "everyone has seen them. They go about the city as though they were supposed to be together." The tears in her eyes were real. She had been raised in the De Kerenec household, had been loyal to the family all of her life. Insulting Chantale was tantamount to insulting her as well.

"I see," Chantale said again. What else was there to say? She could change nothing. Still, she thought, it might be worth seeing if this was an accepted practice.

She walked slowly out of her room and along the dark corridors, down the shiny oak staircase, through the long hall where the dim oil paintings of the ancestral de Montclairs hung. She found Marie-Louise where she knew that she would be, sitting stiffly in the high straight-backed chair in the library, looking out through the mullioned windows at the garden and the stables beyond. That was where she always sat; and that was what she always looked at. Until now Chantale had never particularly wondered why.

Her mother-in-law didn't turn when she came into the room but said, without lifting her gaze from the view, "I think that the gardens look especially beautiful this year, don't you?"

"Pierre has a mistress in Angers," Chantale said directly. "Did you know of this?"

Not a muscle moved in the older woman's body, but by her very stillness Chantale had her answer. She knew. She had known all the time.

Chantale sat down, carefully and heavily. "Why?" she asked suddenly. "It's not the pregnancy. He was seeing her before I got pregnant. Is this something that the de Montclairs—"

"Be quiet!" There was angry energy in the voice. "You have no right to judge the de Montclairs. You're one of them now, or had you forgotten?"

Chantale gazed at her calmly. "Some days, I prefer to forget," she said.

Marie-Louise sighed and turned her chair slightly so that she could look at her daughter-in-law. Marie-Louise was still an attractive woman. Her aristocratic features were blurred but not dimmed by the network of wrinkles that crisscrossed her face and hands. She dressed elegantly for every day, because that was what a countess did. Her gowns were of velvet with lace at the collar and cuffs, gold necklaces encircled her neck, and she wore rings on nearly every finger. Her brown eyes had a quizzical look to them. "Do you really think that men are content to stay with one woman for all of their lives?" she asked.

Chantale was taken aback. "Yes. That's what marriage is for," she responded. "That's why I got married."

The older woman gestured impatiently. "Don't be absurd. You got married because your parents and I decided that you and Pierre would be a suitable match. Sometimes I have regretted that decision, as you seem to make few efforts to fit in here properly. But that is neither here nor there. If Pierre chooses to see another woman, then there is very little that you can do about it." When she saw the look on Chantale's face, she softened. "Do you really think," she asked gently, "that you were his first? Not his first, and surely not his last. But you will be his only wife. Rest assured of that."

Chantale stood up, struggling awkwardly to her feet, and walked to the window. Staring without seeing through its small triangles of glass, she said, "But he's so—so open about it. As though it were normal."

"For him, it *is* normal."

Chantale turned to face her, and Marie-Louise could see the tears glistening in the emerald eyes. "But it's not fair!"

"No, of course it's not. But console yourself. You are his wife. You have the title, and the château, and the children. You are the one he will stay with forever. Women come and women go—and if you ask me, this one won't last much longer—but you will always be his wife."

Chantale took a deep breath. "What about love?"

"What about it?" The other woman looked merely interested.

"He couldn't love me, not if he loves other women, too."

Marie-Louise shook her head. "You are getting confused, Chantale. Love is something for those who are not of the nobility, to console themselves with. We are not expected to love, Chantale; we are expected to behave ourselves properly. And that includes respect, honor, friendship even. Perhaps in time you and Pierre will grow to be friends, who knows? But love? My dear, it has no place here. Do not expect that which he cannot give to you."

"Does he love her, do you think?"

A shrug. "He lusts for her, certainly. Who knows what else goes on in a man's brain? Perhaps he thinks he loves her, perhaps he thinks that he has found the answers to the questions of the universe in her eyes. Later, when he realizes that those answers are not there, he will drift on to another with alluring hips and mysterious eyes. I do not know what it is that men are looking for. Believe me, my dear, you are in the better position by far. You—and perhaps, in the end, you alone—can give him what he is looking for.''

Chantale said softly, "You sound as though you have been through this yourself." It was a shot in the dark, and yet what she said was true. How else would Marie-Louise understand? She spoke as if she had come to these conclusions on her own, through pain and perplexity.

Marie-Louise looked at Chantale sharply, and then shook her head. "You're too perceptive. You will find, in life, that it usually pays to keep your perceptions to yourself." She looked away carefully and added, "For what it's worth, I know the de Montclair men. Philippe was wilder than Pierre has ever been, if that's a consolation to you. He was in Paris more than in Angers—oh, he said that it was for his airplane company, but I knew; I knew all the time, it was for the pretty blue eyes of his little American." She looked up and smiled sadly at Chantale. "But what I told you was true, my dear. He felt more passion for her than he ever did for me. He even lived with her in Paris. But he never considered divorcing me. I was his wife, and I remained his wife. In their own way, the de Montclairs are faithful to us. You simply have to accept that it's in their own way."

"And if I can't?"

The eyebrows rose. "If you can't? Then you will spend your life making yourself very unhappy, for you will be always pursuing something that cannot be caught. Pierre will be yours only as long as you let him go—to Angers or wherever else his fancy leads him. Don't hurt yourself more than you need to be hurt, Chantale. There's enough pain in the world as it is."

"Enough pain in the world as it is." Chantale repeated it to herself, then and in the days that followed, whenever she was tempted to lash out at Pierre because of his inattention to her and the time that he spent away from the château. And she said the words to herself now, lying in the field and watching the sky and listening to the bees drone over the flowers. "Enough pain in the world as it is."

But, she thought, stubbornly resisting acceptance, that still didn't make things fair.

* * *

Pierre de Montclair rolled over onto his side, reaching for the clock on the bedside table and squinting at it. "Damn. I have to get going."

Isabelle, lying next to him, was still breathless. "Now, darling? You do choose the oddest times. I thought most men took advantage of this particular moment to light up a cigarette."

"I'm not most men." She was laughing at him, he knew, and he never knew how to respond to this mocking, bantering tone of hers. Mostly, he realized, he ended up sounding sullen.

After all these months, he still wasn't quite sure how to react to Isabelle herself, and that was probably why he was still so infuriatingly attached to her. Everything else in his life was so well ordered, so predictable: his mother, the château, and the running of the estate, the horses, Jean-Louis, Chantale . . . They all had their place in his life, that was true, and he cherished every one of them. But they were not mercury and fire, ice and quicksilver. They were not Isabelle.

Pierre was aware of her watching him now, as he reached for his clothes and went into the bathroom, and as always he felt awkward. There was something comforting in being able to close the door on those mocking eyes.

He waited for the shower to get hot, and then stepped in, turning the faucet so that the water got hotter still. He always took a shower before leaving Isabelle's house, for whatever reasons: Pierre de Montclair was not given to analyzing his thoughts or feelings or actions.

Isabelle . . . He shut his eyes against the spray of the shower, and immediately could feel her again, the softness of her skin and the wildness of her lovemaking, the screams that echoed through the bedroom when she climaxed and the games that she made him play. Isabelle . . .

He had met her around Christmastime when Marcel Duroc had had an exhibit at Isabelle's gallery and Pierre had come to make a speech. It didn't hurt the town of Angers to have artists of Duroc's stature exhibiting there, even if Duroc himself called it the "provincial tour." It was a splendid evening, really. Pierre was well aware of how good he looked in evening jacket and bow tie. His attire was just the thing to set off his elegant dark looks. He looked like his father, or so he was told, and he had purposely grown a mustache to match the one on Philippe's portrait in the gallery just to emphasize the likeness.

If he looked the quintessential count that evening, then Isabelle looked the perfect artist. She wore red, a flaming red dress encircling a narrow waist that set off her own dark coloring and raven-black thick hair. Her lips and fingernails were painted to match. There was a tiara in her hair and a hollow look below her cheekbones. He remembered thinking afterward that she was a magnificent creature. A lioness. She listened to his speech with her face set in a mask of courtesy, and afterward, as they shared champagne and caviar, she proceeded to tear it to shreds.

"Do you *really* think that art has a place in the modern world, Monsieur le Comte?"

He raised his eyebrows. "But certainly, Madame Vivier. And so must you, or you would not own an art gallery, surely?"

She laughed at him over the rim of her glass and took a deep swallow of champagne. "What nonsense. I own an art gallery because I need to make a living. We were not all born to the life of the château, Monsieur le Comte."

"And yet you are an artist yourself." He didn't know how to respond to the jab about his background. He thought that many people must think the same thing, but no one else had ever been so forthright—or so rude—as to say anything about it to him directly.

"Ah, yes, Monsieur le Comte. I am an artist. But then, one does not have to believe that art has a place in the modern world—or, indeed, anywhere at all—in order to believe in art for its own sake. It is a passion, Monsieur le Comte. Do you know nothing, then, of passion?"

She was putting him on the defensive again, and he didn't like it. He was tempted to drain his glass, excuse himself, and walk away, but something about her held him there, mesmerized, almost against his will. As though she were a black widow spider and he the hapless fly in her web. "Madame certainly has more experience in the artistic realm," he said carefully. "But passion is not a monopoly of those who consider themselves artists."

"Perhaps not." She took another swallow of champagne. She seemed to be a person who did not sip, either at champagne or at life. "What do you consider yourself, Monsieur le Comte?"

"A lonely man." The words were out of his mouth before he even realized that they had been formulated, and he immediately felt his heart thudding in his chest. What on earth had prompted him to say that? What did he mean? He was not lonely: He had family; he had friends; he had everything that anyone could ever hope to possess. And yet, at the same time, he knew that he had spoken words of truth, and he was afraid.

Isabelle Vivier looked at him, a long, assessing, considering gaze, and abruptly put her champagne glass on a nearby tray. "Let's go out," she said.

Pierre followed her wordlessly as she threaded her way through the people and paintings of the exhibition, flashing a smile here, scattering a phrase there. In the vestibule, affecting nonchalance, he helped her into a long fur coat, and slid into his own overcoat and scarf and hat.

The air outside was bitterly cold, and they walked in silence down the rue d'Adam, reputedly the oldest street in Angers, and up to the place du Ralliement. He opened his mouth to speak, to ask if this were simply an aimless walk, but he closed it again. He was more than a little afraid of her. He didn't know how to address her.

Isabelle knew where she was going, however. She stopped at an inconspicuous-looking door on the far side of the great rococo theater, and opened it with a key. The passageway behind was dimly lit by a single bulb, and again in silence Pierre followed her up the stairs, wondering why it was that he couldn't leave, couldn't even find enough energy to speak, only to follow. And then she was opening another door and flicking on a light and standing aside for him to enter before her, and he realized with some shock that he was in her home.

He turned to say something, and she shook her head, anticipating the question. "They are used to me coming and going as I please. And if I am very late, André will lock up for me."

She strode past him, through a narrow foyer and into a living room which glowed from the light of a chandelier overhead. Like Isabelle herself, the apartment was bright and lush, a little overdone, and immensely attractive. One entire wall was taken up by a gilt-edged mirror; the other walls were covered with flocked tapestrylike wallpaper. Louis Quinze furniture, he noted, and as good as that in the library at the château. A motif of large tropical plants covered the walls and furniture alike, and the thick Oriental carpet on the floor was real, too.

Isabelle walked the length of the room and through a door on the far side. Pierre found himself following her into her bedroom. The large double bed was enclosed in a canopy with damask draperies, and diffused light cast shadows all over the room. She was pouring brandy into snifters at a table against the wall, and he took the one that she offered him, drinking it all in one gulp, the fire burning like quicksilver down his throat and into his stomach. Isabelle was watching him.

"Well," Pierre said carefully, putting the glass back on the table, "why am I here?"

She smiled, the silken smile of the lioness who had sheathed her claws. For the time being. "I'll show you."

Pierre turned now and let the hot water of his shower stream onto his back. After that first time, he was helpless. Isabelle had him, and he would do anything for her. Nothing mattered anymore but Isabelle's sensuous mouth, her mocking laughter, her passions, and her desires. He was captivated. The lioness had seized her prey.

Suddenly the shower curtain was drawn aside, and his heart lurched for a second. It was Isabelle, standing naked and splendid on the bath mat, smiling at him. "May I join you?" she purred, slipping in beside him without waiting for his answer. "God, Pierre, you like it hot."

"So do you," he said automatically, drawing the curtain shut again. And then she sank to her knees in front of him and took his penis in her mouth.

"It's all going to work out, you'll see."

Soizic Aubert glanced nervously at Marc sitting behind the desk. "I'm not so sure. They'll wonder why you're sending me instead of Monsieur Rousseau or Monsieur Trezeres."

Marc Giroux stretched out his legs. "I don't have to answer to them, you know. And no one questions your competence."

She bit her lip. "May I ask you a question? Would you have chosen me to go if I wasn't—if we weren't . . ." She floundered for a moment and then lapsed into silence.

Giroux stood up and walked around the desk. She looked so forlorn, sitting there in front of him. Forlorn and adorable. It was all that he could do not to take her in his arms. He leaned back on the desk instead. "Soizic, understand this. You are unquestionably the rising star of this office. You would be under any circumstances. I just characterized you as 'competent,' which hardly does you justice. You are brilliant, m'amie. What do I need to do to make you believe that?"

"I believe it." But her tone said otherwise.

Giroux sighed. The impromptu seduction had led to far more than either of them had expected. They had been careful at first, meeting far away from the office, never leaving a car parked where it should not be seen, cautious about public appearances together. They felt guilty because they thought that they should feel guilty. It was a brief affair, or so both of them had believed, Giroux wondering if he was trying to recover his lost youth in the younger woman and Soizic, who had learned about Freud in school, muttering to herself about oedipal complexes.

The lovemaking was marvelous for both of them, each discovering solace and reassurance, passion and delight, in the arms of the other. And yet, more and more, they realized that the talk they shared was at least as important as the sex, that exploring each other's minds was as essential to their well-being as the exploration of each other's bodies. Eventually it no longer made any sense to either of them to spend time apart. That was when Soizic gave up her lease and moved into Giroux's chalet overlooking the lake outside of Zurich.

She was terrified about the reaction that there would be at the firm, and yet there was none. A ripple, perhaps. Veiled looks, a quick smile as quickly extinguished, but nothing direct.

Marc Giroux loved Soizic. He had taken the months that they had been together to admit it, to acknowledge the fact to himself. He was in love with Soizic, and it felt good and right and needed. For now. Someday, perhaps, her abilities would drive her away from him, and then he knew he would not stand in the way. Someday another voice would beckon, and for the sake of her career she would have to follow it, and he would have to let her go. But every night before going to bed, he whispered to the God he wasn't even sure that he still believed in, "Please don't let it be soon."

Robert Beneteau watched the relationship grow with a quizzical look in his eyes, and Giroux found himself irritated by his partner's reaction. "What is it, Robert?"

"She's very young."

"I know. But she's a first-rate lawyer."

Beneteau raised his eyebrows. "Are we discussing her legal prowess?"

Giroux shrugged. "I don't know. Why not? We might as well be. If she's old enough to practice law—and to practice it superbly, I may add—then isn't she old enough to decide what she wants in her personal life?"

"That," Beneteau said, "is indeed the question."

There was a moment of silence.

"What do you mean?"

"My dear Marc, the girl is filled with insecurities. To seek the stability she needs in an older, established man is not all that uncommon."

"If I wanted a psychologist I would have consulted one!"

"You're getting defensive, Marc. Listen to me: I simply see dangers that you don't. She's a lovely woman and I can understand your attraction to her. But doesn't this . . . relationship . . . set up some questionable situations here at the firm?"

"Such as?" Giroux was still angry.

"Such as a conflict of interest, my good man! Have you never in all your years of practicing law heard of such a thing? You will be accused of nepotism, even if you do not practice it."

Now Marc looked at Soizic, sitting almost huddled in the chair. Was it nepotism? Or was it simply—and this was what he believed, truly and earnestly in his heart of hearts—that he felt she could handle the difficult de Montclair family more tactfully than would Rousseau or Trezeres? Sometimes a woman's touch is more effective, the iron hand covered by a pretty velvet glove.

"Soizic," he said firmly, "you're the right person for this. You will talk to the old countess with sympathy, to the young one with camaraderie—do not forget that she, too, is from Brittany, a compatriot of sorts of yours—and to young Count de Montclair with authority. You can do all these things, Soizic, as no one else in this office ever could. You are the one."

She smiled at him. It was a tentative smile, but better than none. "Thank you, Marc."

He reached forward and ruffled her hair slightly. "It's nothing, *m'amie*. You leave for Angers in three days. And God how I'll miss you!"

The door opened and Beneteau's secretary, Marie-Laure, stood there, papers in hand. She looked from one of them to the other and said hesitantly, "Shall I come back later, Monsieur Giroux?"

He leaned back, away from Soizic. "No, Marie-Laure. Come in. Mademoiselle Aubert and I were just finishing up." Soizic rose and turned to leave, and Giroux continued talking to the secretary. "Marie-Laure, please book Mademoiselle Aubert on a flight to Paris on Thursday, will you? She's going down to the Château de Montclair."

"Very well, sir." But she was looking at the young woman lawyer very oddly.

Soizic was almost glad to escape.

The rainy season had not yet set in, and the hunting was still going on for the great wild beasts that stalked the vast expanses of savannah in the Belgian Congo, the ones whose heads and skins and tusks would bring such a handsome price in London, Brussels, and New York.

Julian Thackery had asked the young native boy to clean and oil his guns, and now he stood with a large gin and tonic in his hand on the house's wide porch, looking out over his property. It seemed to stretch out almost to infinity, the way the land did in that part of Africa, extending right up to the horizon—a horizon that seemed an eternity away. In England there were hills and dales, mountains and mists, intricate little nooks and crannies in the lay of the land that made it feel smaller, more intimate—less intimidating. In England, you felt as if you owned the land. In Africa it was different: The land owned you.

There were plane trees here and there spreading what meager shade they could, with buzzards nesting in their branches. Julian heard the buzzards at night, just as he heard all the other cries of the Congo: the howling laughter of the hyenas and the baying of the jackal, the roar of the lion and the swift fluttering of wings of some unseen creature. The drums, the heartbeat of the Congo, relayed their messages night after night after night. . . . Sometimes Julian just lay in bed, the mosquito netting forming an almost invisible shield between him and the world, and listened to the sounds of the Congo, and was afraid. Afraid because his plantation, immense though it was, was puny compared with the dark continent all around it. Afraid because his defenses against danger, the boys he sent off to guard duty in the night, the locks on the doors, were ridiculous in the face of an elephant or a lion or the great spotted leopard that had terrorized the villagers some months back. He was nothing, really, and the Congo left no doubts about his possibilities of survival in his mind. The Belgian Congo was a merciless, unforgiving land, it was a place where a man could test his strength, and endurance, and resolve. It was now his home.

Nothing that Julian had experienced in his past could have prepared him for the kind of life that he would live here. To be sure, there was danger; but there was breathtaking beauty, as well: from the sudden steep waterfalls on uncharted rivers to the startlingly brilliant plumage of exotic birds in flight. It was a land filled with more questions than answers, with more mysteries than platitudes. It was flat and sullen and enticing and generous, and he had come to love it. Now, he owned several square miles of it.

Julian narrowed his dark eyes against the glare of the sun. The plantation was doing well, the livestock—cattle—reproducing and staying healthy at a really spectacular rate. Everything was running smoothly. It would be all right to place it in the hands of Richards, the overseer, while they were gone on safari.

Inside the house there was an eruption of laughter, and he almost turned away from the view. Almost. Amanda was doing it again, he thought, amusing their guests with her coquetry and her sudden searing remarks, all of which he knew so well. He liked the peace out here. Best not to steal the scene she was creating inside. God knows, there were few enough people around for her to play to.

Kenneth and Brian didn't know her. They were his friends, from his days at Eton and Sandhurst, before this bloody asthma had derailed him from service to His Majesty, and they were experiencing her wit for the first time. She never failed to hold men enthralled, any man, any time. Julian thought that he could do without watching it this time.

Amanda was going on safari with them. When he married her, he realized that this was not the sort of woman who would be content to manage the farm while he was off hunting. Her eyes glittered at the thought of danger, of excitement, of the hunt, and she had actually, to his surprise, become an excellent shot in her own right. Yes, he could be proud of her. But not when she was entertaining his friends.

Kenneth strolled out on the porch behind him. "I say, Julian, old man, stunning wife you have there."

"Thank you," he said, without taking his eyes off the horizon.

His friend came and stood next to him, wearing the smart khaki uniform that Julian himself had longed for and could not now wear. "Right. Time we were off, then?"

"Another few minutes, I should think. The guns aren't ready."

A pause. "I say, Julian, how has it been here for you? We haven't heard from you in so long—didn't even know that you were married, a jolly trick that was to pull—"

Julian interrupted, "Maybe I wanted to disappear. Maybe I didn't want to stay in touch." He was getting a little short of breath already, damn it. What would it be like next year when he turned forty? "No offense, old man. Just wanted my privacy."

"Right, then. Well, it's dashed good to see you now. And I must say I'm terribly enthused about this safari. Great way to spend one's leave. Brian was saying at the club the other night—"

"Taking my name in vain again, are you?" Brian Montfort-Crippen said from behind them. "I say, Julian, *lovely* wife . . ."

"He's already heard that from me," said Kenneth. "I need a refill, men, be right with you." He wandered back into the house.

"Don't ask me if I'm all right, Brian, do me a favor?" asked Julian. "I don't want to be psychoanalyzed."

"Nothing of the sort, then," responded his friend. "And you look fine. So does she. Africa must agree with the two of you."

Julian relented slightly. "I met her here, you know."

"In the Congo? How extraordinary."

"Right. Giving parties and God only knows what else. I couldn't stay away after that. Not from her, and not from Africa. They stay in your blood. . . . At night you can hear the drumbeats, the signals the natives send from village to village. It's eerie, Brian, but in a beautiful, timeless sort of way." He shrugged. "I gave in. I had to marry them both—her and the country, too."

"Surely she wasn't raised here?"

"Oh, God, no. She's an American. Newport. Rhode Island. I gather that she was quite the society debutante in her time. Her first husband was Marcus Copeland—you know, of Copeland steel and iron. He was killed in the war."

"Surely not. That would mean that she is—er—" He coughed delicately.

"Older than I am? Of course she is. Nothing wrong with that."

Brian smiled. "I expect not. Given half a chance, I'd probably have married her myself. Though taking her home to Mummy might have been something different altogether. . . ."

"Right. It's why we stay here. Ah, there he is. We're off, Brian." He turned and called through the screen door behind them.

"Amanda? The boy is here with the guns. We can go now!"

Chapter Seven

Caroline stood on the airport tarmac, looking with some anxiety up into the sky. According to the flight plan, Eddie was supposed to be back already. Had she made a mistake? Had she somehow omitted the one essential, important thing that would cost him his life? What had she missed? Eddie, young and vital, with his puppy-dog eagerness: Had she failed him, too? What could she have—

And then she saw a pinpoint of light, a flash of brightness as the sun reflected off something, and she narrowed her eyes, watching it as it came closer, took shape. The old A.R.M. airplane. Eddie was back.

She had a different plane now, Eric's gift. It had a new shape, it was sleeker, more comfortable, with retractable landing gear and twin engines instead of a single one, the propellers mounted on the wings. The plane itself was called a Butterfly. A shy young pilot had flown it east for her, accepting her thanks with a timid smile and refusing dinner before leaving on the train for New York and a commercial flight back out to San Francisco. Caroline had watched him go, then sped out to the airport to look over her new toy.

Steven hadn't been any too pleased about it.

"What do you want with another airplane, anyway?"

"It's a better one, Steven. Safer, too. And faster." She was looking at the Butterfly with pleased anticipation in her face.

"Well, I don't see the point. It's not as though flying was the only thing in your life."

Automatically, she dampened her enthusiasm. She knew that she had offended him. "Steven, it's all right. It won't take away any time from us—I'll only fly when you're at work."

"And what about your time with Elizabeth? What kind of mother are you becoming, Caroline?"

She stared at him. "I've always flown, Steven. From before you knew me. What's the difference now?"

"The difference is that you have a family. You have responsibilities and obligations."

"Now you sound like Justine."

"Maybe you ought to listen to her. She knows what a wife and mother should be doing with her time. You have obligations, Caroline. You're a respected member of Newport society—no, I take that back. You should be a respected member of Newport society. But you're not, because you're too selfish. You always want to be off gratifying your own needs instead. How do you think that makes me feel?"

She felt as though he had slapped her. "I always thought having money meant that you were able to do what you wanted."

"Well, it doesn't. It carries obligations. And that's not the point, Caroline. Don't try to confuse me. The point is that you should want to be at home with Elizabeth. And me. You should want to be more like Justine."

"If you wanted Justine, you should have married her!" She was really feeling defensive now.

Steven turned his back to her, stuffing his hands in his pockets. For several minutes neither of them spoke. Finally he said, "Did you know that Justine's pregnant?"

So that was it. He wanted her to have another baby. Caroline concentrated on holding back the tears, the stupid tears that always seemed to be just behind her eyes these days, lurking, waiting. She would cry and then Steven would get even more irritated and walk away, but she couldn't help crying. He made her feel so . . . helpless. There was no way to fight his logic. She blinked hard and looked across the narrow strip of grass to where her new Butterfly stood waiting for her. She had been so excited just a few minutes ago. . . . Why did Steven always *ruin* things for her? She took a long, shaky breath and turned to face him. "Is that what you want? Another child?"

Steven looked eager and excited. "Well, yes, among other things. Elizabeth is old enough to accept another sibling. And I'd like a son."

Her temper flared. "Is that the problem, Steven? Do you feel incomplete because you don't have a son?"

"Caroline, you make it sound wrong. Every man wants a son, and every time you're up there in the sky, endangering your life,

I wonder if you'll ever come down again and be a proper mother to Elizabeth and our son, whenever he's born.''

She was angry enough to be sarcastic. ''Maybe that's what you want, Steven. For me to die up there so that you're free. So that you can inherit my money and then marry some amiable person like Justine who will give you lots of pretty babies!''

He looked at her, a long, considering look, and then shook his head. ''You're hysterical, Caroline. It's ridiculous to even suggest such a thing. I am merely asking you to begin thinking about your place in the world.''

''Which is, of course, by your side!''

''Which is where you should be. By my side. By Elizabeth's side.'' Steven's face grew pale, and Caroline could tell that he was trying very hard to sound reasonable. ''You haven't hostessed a single party, Caroline, since we moved to Ocean Drive.''

''My grandmother's only been dead a few months, Steven!''

He shook his head. ''That's not the point, Caroline. The point is that you're acting selfishly. I liked what I used to see in you, your tenderness and your caring. I sometimes wonder what happened to that.''

''And *I* liked what I saw in *you*, Steven. Maybe we've both lost it.''

He shrugged. ''Think about it, Caroline. Just think about it.''

She was thinking about it now, as she watched the old A.R.M. plane enter the landing pattern. Eddie was handling it superbly. She had been silly to doubt him. The Butterfly had proven to be as good—no, better, far better—than she had anticipated, with new instruments on the control panel and a general sense of comfort. And of power! The engines hummed and did precisely as she asked them to do. She had already resolved to give Eddie a flight in it as his reward when he got his license.

And she and Steven had scarcely spoken in the past two weeks.

Eddie touched down lightly and taxied to a stop on the flight apron. She walked slowly over to meet him there, knowing that it would take him some time to get out of the airplane. Eddie Carruthers spent more time in postflight checks than most pilots spent in preflight ones.

''Nice job, Mr. Carruthers. But you're eight minutes late on your estimated time of arrival.'' She was smiling.

He turned to face her, pulling off his goggles and cap. ''Hi, Caroline. I couldn't resist. It was so great up there.'' He sighed, a long, happy sigh. "God, Caroline, sometimes when I'm up there I wish that I never ever had to come down."

"I know the feeling. Sounds like we've caught the same virus. Did you talk to the tower?"

A quick glance. "Yeah. Of course, I had to, didn't I?"

She raised an eyebrow. "I don't know. Seems that it wasn't so long ago when you wouldn't get on the radio at all."

"Well, you do what you have to." He was brusque. "Can I take it up again tomorrow, if no one else has signed for it?"

"Of course you can. But you must have enough solo hours now, don't you, Eddie? Let me look at your log. . . ."

"No." He pulled away from her and then, as though embarrassed by his rudeness, added, "I haven't got an accurate tally. I need to do some work on it. I'll show it to you later."

She didn't press him. "Come on, I'll walk you back to the lounge. I was serious, Eddie. You're looking good up there."

"Yeah." He fell into step with her, pacing his long legs so that he wouldn't outdistance her. "Well, I had a good teacher."

She laughed. "Flattery will get you nowhere."

"I wouldn't count on it." He smiled as he held the door open for her, and she walked inside ahead of him. "I was thinking that maybe with a little more flattery, I might be able to persuade you to let me take up the Butterfly someday."

"Well, try the flattery for a while. We'll see if it works."

An odd assortment of pilots, mechanics, and controllers were grouped around in the airport lounge. There were no passengers: Newport wasn't large enough for passenger service. Small charter businesses, that was all. Over near the counter, a young man was arguing passionately with Bill, the airport manager, about the price of renting an airplane. "But I've got this new girlfriend, see, and I'm out to impress her. But not for that much!"

"Fuel is expensive," Bill said mildly. He saw Caroline and smiled at her over the young man's shoulder. "If you wanted it for more than a few hours, I might be able to cut it back a little, but not much."

"Take all my savings," muttered the young man.

"Well, then, you'd better find a less expensive hobby. Or girlfriend." Bill dismissed him with a glance. "Caroline, what's up?"

"Nothing earth-shattering," she said amicably. "Want some coffee with us?"

"Why not?" He ducked under the counter and strolled across

to where Caroline and Eddie were already lowering themselves into chairs grouped around a small table. "Eddie Carruthers, kid, nice landing out there."

"Thanks, Bill. Um, coffee all around, Margie, please." Eddie had been flirting with the girl who worked in the pilots' lounge for the past two months. As far as Caroline could ascertain, he hadn't yet gotten past asking Margie for refills on his coffee.

"I was thinking that Eddie must have enough solo hours logged to go for his license soon," Caroline said to Bill. "I don't think there's any question he'll get it, either."

"None at all. Hey, thanks, Margie, this actually looks hot!"

The girl was used to him. "Once in a while, once in a while," she said easily. "Here you go, Mrs. Asheford."

"Thanks, Margie." Caroline sipped tentatively at the scalding liquid. "Eddie just wants to be modest about his achievements," she told Bill, as much for Margie's benefit as Eddie's.

Eddie's face turned crimson. "I'm all right," he said. "I just don't want to go for the license yet. I'm not ready."

Bill shrugged. "Up to you, kid," he said. "Pity your parents couldn't see their way to buying you a nice little plane. We could use some class on this airfield." He winked at Caroline.

"As though," she said airily, "there would even be any airfield if it were not for my personal efforts, which I may add were—"

A shout from the other side of the room interrupted her. Someone yelled, "Turn that thing up!" and someone else was talking fast and turning up the volume on the radio at the same time. It was suddenly very quiet in the room as everyone strained to listen to the radio.

". . . German troops marched into Poland this morning a little after dawn. They were preceded by Luftwaffe airplanes which carried out bombings directly in the path of the oncoming Panzer divisions. No statement has yet been issued from the White House. In Great Britain, Prime Minister Neville Chamberlain is said to be extremely concerned about the situation . . . ."

Caroline paled and looked across the table at Bill. "Dear God," she whispered, unconsciously crossing herself, a relic of her childhood at St. John's. "Dear God. It's really true. There's going to be a war."

"It sounds," Bill said, "as though there is one already."

* * *

Returning home from the airport, Caroline had driven faster than she ever had before. All the past difficulties with Steven were far from her mind. She needed reassurance, and all that she wanted now was for her husband to enfold her in his strong arms and hold her there. Make it all better again . . .

As if anyone had ever been able to do that for her.

She left the car parked on the gravel driveway and ran into the front hall of the house, calling for Steven as she went, running through room after room, the panic mounting inside of her and constricting her throat so that she could scarcely breathe, much less cry out. Jenson was in the conservatory, polishing the old grandfather clock that had come from Germany and had been one of Margaret Lewis's most prized possessions. None of the servants was permitted to touch it; Jenson alone could clean and wind it. Irrationally, Caroline was angry with him for even touching German workmanship. "Where is my husband?"

Jenson turned slowly, the polishing cloth still in his hand. "He has left for the docks, Mrs. Asheford," he said. "He said not to expect him for dinner. Perhaps something light would be appropriate, served on the veranda?"

Caroline stared at him. "You haven't heard, then," she breathed. "Germany has invaded Poland, Jenson. The war has started."

"Yes, madame," he said politely. "Mr. Asheford told us just before he left."

"He knew?" Even to her own ears, there was an edge of hysteria in her voice. "He knew, and he left, and you're talking about dinner as though nothing has happened?"

The butler carefully laid down the cloth. "Perhaps Madame would care for some tea? If I might make a suggestion, a bit of brandy—"

"Jenson!" Caroline shrieked his name, and then stopped herself, willing the mounting panic inside of her to subside. "Jenson," she said carefully, "what has happened is terrible. I don't think we can pretend that nothing is going on."

"On the contrary, madame," he said smoothly. "Mr. Asheford is very much encouraged by the news. He spoke rather affably about increased production at the shipyard. And as far as the war is concerned, madame"—he shrugged—"the last one did not disrupt life here. Mrs. Lewis saw to that. It is our assumption that you will encourage the same attitude, particularly among the staff, some of which tend to be excitable."

So. She was being told once again what her role in life was to be. She was to maintain standards, support the staff, ensure that their little corner of Newport did not do anything so incorrect as to think that a faraway war would change their lives in any way. Jenson was right, she realized. Her grandmother would have been affronted by any whisper of rumor. She would have ordered tea and dealt herself a hand of canasta and discussed the evening's menu in measured tones.

But Caroline was not her grandmother. She was different, living in a very different time with its own problems to confront. And yet—and the thought made her angry—and yet here she was, still spending her days in the old lady's shadow. She couldn't even worry. She was being put in her place, as smoothly and perfectly as though Margaret Lewis herself had reached out of the grave to do it. Life had to go on, and it had to go on properly and correctly, for that was what was important. That was all that mattered.

Caroline bit her lip. Was *that*, then, why her mother had done the things that she had? Why she had run away in the first place, to Paris and London and wherever else she could? Was that why she had run away this last time, refused even her inheritance, fled to Africa? Because she hadn't the strength to live in the old lady's shadow? So that she could, in her own chosen time and place, live her life as she wanted to?

In that moment, Caroline both understood and envied the woman who had always been such an enigma to her. Her mother couldn't have lived here any more than she could have ever completely conformed to the expectations of Newport society. She had to leave or die, because she wasn't strong enough to fight.

Caroline took a deep breath. "I'm going out, Jenson. Don't expect me for dinner. See to it that the lights are left on, please."

"Very good, madame." He was already turning back to the clock.

Caroline stared at his back for a moment, helplessly gestured once toward him, and then turned to go. With a cold sinking sensation in her stomach, she realized that unless she accepted this niche that everyone seemingly wanted her in, she would be alone.

Amanda hadn't accepted the niche, but she couldn't accept being alone either, so she'd abdicated altogether. Her mother had gone to a place where there would be no expectations, and she created her own world, became the sort of person that she wanted to be.

Caroline shut her eyes and shook her head. That wasn't for her. Running away was out of the question. She had a family. She had a daughter, and she was determined to give Elizabeth a better childhood than she had had. She couldn't go away; she was going to have to stay here and fight all their expectations.

She couldn't trust anyone—especially not men—because they all tried to turn her into something or someone that she wasn't. Uncle Charles. Eric. That lawyer. Andrew. And, even, Steven, in his own way. They all wanted a little Caroline-doll who would do as they said, think as they wished, become whom they desired.

She wasn't going to do it. She didn't yet know what it was that she wanted, or how to get it. The mists of confusion still swirled around her. She didn't know what she wanted, but she was pretty clear about what she didn't want. Even if it meant, in a sense that her mother would never have understood, being alone.

In the quiet law offices in Zurich the news was received with very little surprise. A raised eyebrow here and there, a decisive nod, a sigh; that was all. Beneteau and Giroux had been expecting the invasion for so long that it felt as though the actors for a well-rehearsed play had finally taken their cue to enter, and were at last on stage.

Most importantly, they were ready for it. Whatever happened, whichever countries Hitler chose to complete his own personal jigsaw puzzle of a united Aryan Europe, they were ready. Their companies and agents were in place. They had spent the last five months pouring out investments on behalf of Intraglobal, Inc. and they were ready.

Eric Beaumont owned or controlled most of the influential businesses and enterprises in Europe, Asia, and North Africa. The Asian connection was a little tenuous still, but the firm would work on that. In the meantime, Europe was in the palm of their collective hands.

Two days later Soizic Aubert was just coming in to work when she read the headlines at the corner newsstand: "Great Britain and France declare war on Germany." She shivered for just a moment and quickened her pace to the office door. Marc was there already, and it was his reassurance that she wanted. After

a year in Switzerland, her heart still beat faster when she realized
that France was really and truly at war.

"They're talking about the Maginot Line holding off invasion," Eugene Rousseau was saying into a telephone in the outer
office when she walked in, her dark hair still damp from her
shower, her eyes unexpectedly smarting. He saw her and held
up a hand to forestall her progress. "Yes, yes, all right. Listen,
hold the line for a moment, will you?" He covered the receiver
with his hand. "Do you know anybody in Strasbourg, Belfort,
anyplace like that?"

Soizic shook her head. "I don't think so."

"That's what I was afraid of." Rousseau returned to his conversation. "I'm here. Yes, I know. It doesn't extend north across
Belgium."

Françoise appeared at Soizic's elbow. "Of course it doesn't
extend north across Belgium. Can't precisely block off an ally,
can they?" Soizic jumped nervously at the sound of her voice,
and Françoise looked at her consideringly. "Concerned, are we?
These are the fruits of our labors, Mademoiselle Aubert, surely
you knew?" She relented then, and added, "Well, come on up
to the conference room. He can join us when he's finished."

"What's he doing?"

Françoise shrugged. "Monsieur Rousseau prefers his own
network of informants to anything that comes off the wire service. He's just lost his man in Alsace. Silly fool got scared and
is halfway across the channel to England, if *my* informants are
correct."

Soizic said slowly, still looking at Rousseau, "The Germans
will take Belgium first and then just walk around the Maginot
Line."

"Yes, that's what we think."

Rousseau hung up the telephone and glared across at them.
"It may be inevitable," he said bitterly, "but one can't help
wishing that they'd at least give an intelligent fight."

Soizic stared at him for a moment, and then turned and walked
up the wide winding staircase that led to the second floor and
the conference room. Sun streamed in through the long windows, reflecting off the white paint of the banister and the yellow
walls. So bright, so pretty: Summer was barely over. And Hitler
was moving already.

She tried uneasily to analyze her feelings. It had been one
thing, last spring and summer, to stand back and determine the

probabilities of this action or that, to think up attacks and coun-
terattacks. It had been amusing, almost like a board game, really. And she had always loved winning at board games. But
now it was real: suddenly, terrifyingly real. For the people in
the Polish villages that had been killed already, on the inexorable
march of the German war machine, it was no game. For them,
it was final.

Soizic hesitated outside the conference room door, wondering
if she shouldn't go into the lavatory first. She was feeling more
than a little sick. But then she heard Françoise and Rousseau on
the stairs behind her talking earnestly together, and she realized
that she couldn't. She had made some decisions about her status
in the firm. She was not going to be characterized as Marc Giroux's mistress. Still less would she be characterized as a spine-
less little nobody who became ill at the least provocation.

As her mother would have said, "You made your bed; it's up
to you to lie in it."

The rest of the lawyers were already there. Marc looked up
and, seeing her framed in the doorway, smiled briefly, before
turning back to his discussion with Jean-Claude Trezeres. Beneteau was dictating something to Marie-Laure. The sun streamed
into this room, and despite the open window the air was already
heavy with smoke from all their cigarettes.

Soizic slipped into the nearest available chair and placed her
briefcase on the table in front of her. Raphael Marchand, the
Swiss lawyer, was seated closest to her, and he automatically
slid an ashtray across the table. His eyes looking at her quizzically from under the thick bushy eyebrows, he inquired, "Are
you all right, Mademoiselle Aubert?"

"Yes, thank you," she said primly, and then, taking a deep
breath, met his eyes. "I'm fine."

Pierre de Montclair was at Isabelle's apartment when he heard
the news. She had left the radio on when she went to take her
shower, and he was puttering around in her modern kitchen,
looking for something to eat—sex always made him ravenous,
somehow—when the news bulletin interrupted the soft classical
music.

Pierre froze. France had declared war on Germany. France
had declared war . . . .

He sat down, heavily, on one of Isabelle's kitchen chairs. He
knew that this put an end to the comfortable existence that he

had constructed for himself. Whatever the declaration meant, his life was going to change, change irrevocably, and he was frightened.

He was still sitting there, not able to move, stunned, when Isabelle emerged from the shower, wrapping herself in a long white towel, the magnificent raven hair wrapped up in a smaller one, Turkish-style, on her head. "What is it, darling?" she asked casually, walking into the kitchen. "Nothing to eat? I told you, the champagne is in the icebox, and there's cold chicken and caviar—"

"France has declared war," he told her, his voice a monotone. Strange how frightened one could feel and still sound normal, he thought. As though he were talking about the price of tomatoes, or his horses' prospects at the October Hunt.

This year, there might be no October Hunt.

Isabelle stared at him, then at the radio, by now emitting music again. "What are you talking about?"

"I told you." He looked at her listlessly. "France has declared war against Germany. So has England."

She sat down across the table from him. "It's all right," she said comfortingly, reaching to take his hand in hers. "The Germans will never invade France. The Maginot Line will hold."

He stared at her as though not seeing her at all. "I'll be called up," he said, his voice hollow.

Isabelle shook her head. "Surely it won't come to that? Pierre, darling, there are too many young men simply lounging around for them to bother with you. You'll see. It will never come to that." She stood up, impatient already with the conversation, and started taking dishes from the icebox. "Let's think about more important things, darling. Here we are—chicken, and strawberries, and caviar. And there's some fresh bread . . ."

Pierre stared at her, going through their normal postcoital routine as though nothing had happened. And perhaps for Isabelle nothing had. She might actually believe what she had said to him.

But the images were flashing through his brain, sharp, as sharp as though he had been there for it all. He had been, of course, but he had been a child, a small child, unable to comprehend what was happening, crying only because he could sense the fear in his mother. He had stood and clutched at her skirts, and she had cried, and that frightened him more than anything else. Something terrible was happening. . . . His father had left one day, and this time he wasn't just going up to Paris, as he did so often. This time he went far, far away and never came back again, and Pierre was alone with Marie-Louise for the rest of his childhood.

It wasn't fair. His father, going gallantly off to take up arms in the Great War, and getting himself killed fighting these same Germans. Philippe had had no business getting involved in the fighting. He could have stayed behind. But through some misplaced sense of noblesse oblige, setting an example for others to follow, he had gone. Over the years Pierre had heard all the platitudes about the role of the aristocracy from his mother, and they still made as little sense to him now as they had then.

All that he knew was that he had grown up with no father, because of these same dirty Germans. Pierre unconsciously balled his hands into fists. He had never known the man in the portrait gallery, the one he looked so much like, the dashing young count who had never had the chance to grow old.

Now it looked as though the same thing was going to happen to his son. He raised his eyes and watched Isabelle for a moment, sitting provocatively across the table from him, dipping a strawberry into the fresh cream she always kept in her icebox. The towel had slipped off her body, and his eyes traveled over the rounded breasts with their dark nipples, sharp and hard because she was chilled after her shower, the narrow waist, the shoulders he so loved to kiss and caress. Suddenly he thought of Chantale as he had seen her this morning, her belly rounded and distended with the child she carried, her long red hair spread out in flames across her pillow, and he realized that he was in the wrong place. Chantale was the mother of his children. If he was going to talk with anyone about this, it should be Chantale.

Pierre stood up abruptly, feeling slightly ridiculous because he was naked. "I have to go." Isabelle's eyes followed him in amusement as he walked out of the room, and it was with surprise that, in the bedroom, he felt Isabelle's arms encircle him from behind when he reached for his underwear. "Do you really want to go now, Pierre?" she purred in his ear, pressing her body against his, and he sighed. Damn her. Why did she do this to him?

Chantale. . . . She was his wife. She would be frightened. His place was at the château at a time like this, taking charge of the situation, calming the fears of his family and his servants. But Isabelle's breasts were pressing into his back, and her hands were traveling lower, down over his stomach, entwining themselves in his pubic hair, and all his resolutions faded. Chantale could wait a little longer. . . . After all, a man needed comfort at a time like this, didn't he? Certainly, he deserved something, too?

Eric Beaumont smiled in satisfaction and tipped back his chair to reread the letter from Paris. For once, he wasn't smoking. His entire attention was riveted on the paper in front of him.

Mon chèr M. Beaumont,

It is with great pleasure and anticipation that I look forward to our meeting in Paris next month. I have followed your career with interest, as has my wife, and I do think that we may be able to do some very important work together. My hope had been to receive financing through an American industrialist, but it is clear to me now that the French academics are more interested in promoting their internal politics than in doing any important work in science. And, after all, you were once French. So it is that I turn to you now.

I will recount to you an event that took place many years ago, when you were still a young lad. The year was 1903. My mother-in-law had just received her doctorate, and her husband had arranged a celebration amongst friends at the house. Rutherford was there, and my understanding is that you have been in correspondence with him as well? In any case, at about eleven o'clock the company retired to the garden, where by that time it was quite dark, with only reflected lights from the house. My parents-in-law had at that time begun their great work with radium, and Pierre brought out to the garden with him a test tube coated with zinc sulphide and containing some radium in solution. Monsieur Beaumont, if I could only convey to you his words, the excitement that they both felt when they saw the effect that it had on their guests! The entire garden glowed with an eerie light. They realized then that no one had yet dreamed of what we could do with the physical universe around us.

But you, Monsieur Beaumont, you are both a dreamer and a realist. And so it is to you that I confide. We have found that the atom can be split. My wife Irene and I have been working both in our own laboratory and at the Radium Institute, and she is prepared to submit the concept to the Academy of Science before the end of the year. This is our first collaborative effort, but it is *her* discovery. What can I say, Monsieur Beaumont, she is not the daughter of Marie Curie for nothing! In any case, I wanted to submit to you first that the possibility exists. I will not reveal the process, for that would be a violation of Irene's work. But I tell you that the possibility exists. The atom can be split, and in splitting can generate heat. Enormous amounts of heat. And heat, as you know, means energy.

We are continuing in our research, which is now involved in separating polonium. I will keep you apprised of further developments. In the meantime, Monsieur Beaumont, please visit the institute next month, and let me know what you think. We are all eager to begin talking about possible applications of this fascinating process.

My mother-in-law, who alas is not well these days, asks to be remembered to you. I believe that you met once in Paris during an air show?

With my most sincere sentiments,

Frédéric Joliot-Curie

Eric tapped the edge of the paper against his hand for a few moments, thinking. All these people doing all these experiments, independently, fiercely protective of their secrets, jealous of any other scientist . . . And, ironically, all of them confiding in him, a neutral but powerful third party. Still, so much effort to keep things quiet . . . what a waste. What would happen if their experiments did not need to be duplicated? What if they all could be gathered in one place and with one goal work together, these great minds? Oppenheimer, the Joliot-Curies, Szilard, Chadwick, even Einstein . . . Eric shook his head. He wasn't able to do that, not yet. It would take more time, a broader power base, the blessing and cooperation of the government and of the military. But it might happen. Once things got moving, with the war and the dangers that it presented—once he had the President and the Congress and the military establishment really listening to him, then it might happen.

It *would* happen.

Eric smiled.

Chapter Eight

*I*n the days that followed the declaration of war there were rumors that the British were sending soldiers into France.

Chantale de Montclair listened attentively to all the rumors, spending more time in the vast kitchen of the château with Annie, who seemed to have her finger on the pulse of public opinion, than in the drawing room or library with Marie-Louise, whose pain at the thought of fighting the Germans again was more than apparent. When her mother-in-law had been told the news, she had closed her eyes for such a long time that Chantale was sure she had fainted. Finally, she had spoken in a voice so soft as to be no more than a murmur: "He needn't have died, after all. We're just doing the same thing all over again."

It was easy to see how she could perceive the turn of events that way.

Pierre was spending more and more time away from the château, in Angers presumably, and was coming back drunk more often than not. One night, when he clumsily tried to get into Chantale's bed instead of his own, and nearly pushed her out in the process, she sat up and angrily snapped on the light. "What's the matter with you?"

Pierre blinked blearily at her. "Sorry. Just . . . tired."

"Then you had better go find your own bed and some sleep," Chantale said coldly, and her husband shook his head.

"Mustn't forget," he mumbled. "Must—n't—forget."

Chantale sighed and heaved herself slowly out of bed. It was getting more and more difficult to move at all these days. She took Pierre by the shoulders. "Come on," she said briskly. "Time for bed."

He let her steer him into the hallway and down the corridor to his suite of rooms, but something in their progress must have awakened Marie-Louise, for her door opened as they passed and she peered out. "What is it?"

"Pierre," Chantale responded shortly. "Apparently his mistress didn't satisfy him tonight, and he showed up in my room looking for more." I must be really angry, she thought, startled. I don't talk like that. I pride myself in not saying such things.

She left him snoring, sprawled out across his bed, and returned slowly to her own room. To her surprise, Marie-Louise was there, waiting for her, sitting stiffly in one of the chairs by the dressing table, a shawl wrapped around her nightdress. Chantale sat down heavily on the bed, readjusting her position until she could find one that was reasonably comfortable. "What is it?" she asked wearily. She was in no mood for lectures about the wifely duties of the Countess de Montclair.

She received none. Marie-Louise sighed, looked slowly around the room, and then back at Chantale. "I'm afraid," she said finally.

Chantale raised her eyebrows in surprise. "Afraid? Of what?"

The older woman shrugged. "The war. What is going to happen. And what will become of him."

"You needn't worry yet. They haven't even mobilized. Annie says that they've just begun calling up the men they have registered for military service, and anyway Pierre will be way down on the list."

"That's not what I meant." Marie-Louise looked down at her hands for a long moment, and then raised her head to meet Chantale's eyes. There were tears running down her cheeks. "I'm afraid of what will happen if he goes, and I'm afraid of what will happen if he doesn't."

Chantale frowned and shook her head. She was too tired to talk in riddles tonight. "I don't understand, Madame. What do you mean?"

The older woman raised a hand and then let it fall again to her lap, a pathetic little gesture. "He isn't his father. He isn't anything like his father. I was so angry, so angry with Philippe for taking his military service when he didn't have to. But I was proud of him, too. He looked so fine in his uniform . . . and he was brave. Blessed Mother, how he was brave." She sniffed loudly. "And Pierre, this one—I have been afraid ever since I heard that we were going to war. And I will tell you the truth. I am not afraid of his dying, or not dying. I am afraid only of his disgracing us."

Chantale bit her lip. As far as she was concerned, Marie-Louise's anxiety came a little late. Pierre, she thought, had already disgraced them all, hundreds of times over, every time he flaunted his mistress in public, every time he came home drunk. Pierre as a disgrace to the family was hardly a novel idea. But it had taken Marie-Louise all the strength that she had to come and confide in her daughter-in-law, and Chantale wanted to reach out to her. Perhaps it was too late for that, as well. Perhaps the lines of communication between the two women had been drawn irrevocably years ago when Chantale had first come to the Château de Montclair. Even as Chantale searched for something empathetic or reassuring to say, Marie-Louise stood up, gathering her shawl around her as though it were a badge of office, and walked to the door.

"You don't understand," she said, her voice low and bitter. "You can't understand."

And then she was gone.

The next day, Annie confirmed the rumor: The British had sent over one hundred thousand men to France. "Are you sure?" Chantale asked.

"Of course I am, Countess. I heard it from the baker's wife in Angers, her what listens to the radio morning, noon, and night, which is a proper thing for a wife to do, I ask you. Still, it serves its purposes for the likes of me, now don't it?" The countess was looking pleased, Annie thought. And a good thing, too, that she finally had something to smile about. It wasn't nice for a woman in her condition to have to be thinking about soldiers and *Boches,* those dirty Germans, instead of thinking about baby clothes and christenings. The more news that they could give her about the war ending soon, the better it would be, both for her *and* the baby.

"I hope it's true," Chantale said. "If we work together, then the war will be over in no time."

"Christmas at the latest, I shouldn't think," Annie said comfortably, rolling out the dough for the little buns she made, of which she was justifiably proud. She didn't realize she was echoing the words spoken of a war twenty-five years earlier. Then, too, they had comforted themselves with the prospect of a short war, over by Christmas. "Christmas, and it will all be like a dream. You'll see, Countess. And you'll have enough to occupy your time around Christmas, too, I shouldn't think."

"I expect so," Chantale said, twirling a lock of her red hair between her fingers, a bad habit she had acquired in grammar school. She had confessed it to Monsieur le Curé every Friday for years until he finally took pity and told her that bad habits weren't necessarily mortal sins. "Annie, do you think that Pierre will be called up?"

"Now, Countess, don't you be worrying yourself about that." Annie thumped the dough with vehemence, and a cloud of flour rose in the air. "The count will have plenty of ways out, don't you worry, not like his father who was hungering to go, you could see it in his eyes. The young count, now, he hasn't got the same hunger. Chances are they won't want him, anyway, him being noble born and all that. Begging the countess's pardon, I'm sure."

Chantale smiled wanly and began to rise from the table. Time to get on with the day. She had heard the car leave when she was still washing her hair. Apparently his excesses of last night had not had any ill effect, nor had they dampened his enthusiasm for renewing his quest—in search of God only knew what— today. She, on the other hand, was feeling terrible.

The pain hit, washing over her like the waves of her native Brittany, the terrible contraction in her pelvic region that felt as though all the bones were tearing apart from one another, and she moaned and bent over double with the pain. Through its haze she heard Annie's startled exclamation, and the sound of running footsteps as others were summoned. Chantale winced and tried hard to hold back her groans. This was it. It was too soon.

Chantale de Montclair was in labor.

To Marie-Louise, summoned by a frightened and stammering maid, the situation was clear. Chantale's physician was in Angers, and it would take him over an hour to reach the château. After ordering that he be called, she proceeded to her daughter-in-law's bedroom, where Annie had brought Chantale after the onset of labor in the kitchen. Over the bed, the two women's eyes met. "I can help, Madame la Comtesse, if you'd like," the cook offered.

Marie-Louise nodded. "Thank you, Annie. That would be most appreciated."

Where was Pierre? The thought flitted through her mind before she dismissed it. It didn't matter: He would be of no help at all. He had cringed when Jean-Claude was born, even though it had happened quite properly in the hospital in Angers.

"Mother, I had no idea that there would be so much blood!" He had retired to a nearby bar to fortify himself for the ordeal, and wasn't sober enough to see his son for at least ten hours thereafter. No, it was just as well that Pierre wasn't here. Nevertheless, she might see if she could make him feel guilty about it anyway.

Marie-Louise set her mouth and rolled up her sleeves. This she could handle. Not the war, the speeches of the politicians, the fear that lived with her almost daily. This was where life was. This was where she needed to be.

"Production quotas are being met in both Düsseldorf and Mannheim, Mr. Beaumont. We've got Intraglobal Sweepers and Junkers both coming off the line daily."

"Hmm." Eric narrowed his eyes to look at the figures on the report in front of him. "What about the English factories?"

A small dark man with a nervous tic leaned forward. "We could be doing better, sir," he said in a thick Lancashire accent. "There's production, I'll not say there's not, but mistakes are being made."

"With the fighters or the bombers?"

The little man shook his head. "Bombers, from the looks of the reports," he said. "That raid on the German warships last week was a joke."

Eric frowned. "I thought the problem was political."

"A little of each, Eric." That was Hawk, his aptly named Production Manager for Aviation. "The Brits didn't want any civilian casualties so they steered clear of any ships within hailing distance of land or port. But there were some mechanical failures, too. They lost over a third of the planes."

Eric shook his head. "What the hell is happening, people?" he demanded of the room at large. "Need I remind you that Intraglobal has a reputation to protect? Need I remind you that our Aviation Division is the foundation of everything else that we do? I don't want to be manufacturing a shoddy product. What's the problem?"

Hawk took a deep breath. "In England, overeagerness. There's a bet on that the war's going to be over by Christmas, and the more birds they can get in the sky the closer they are. Or so they think."

"I don't give a damn what they think. What do you think?"

"I think that given some technical direction the English plants are fully capable of turning out first-class airplanes, both fighters and bombers. They're working on a stealth bomber that might see action by next spring—something light, made out of plywood, to get in through the radar. Your design, Eric." He paused. "But they need that technical assistance. They need somebody to slow them down a little."

"They need somebody," drawled one of the managers on the other side of the table, "to tell them that the war isn't going to be over by bloody Christmas."

"Good point." Eric glanced around the table. "Who wants to go to England?"

There was a moment of silence in the room. California seemed to be infinitely safer than anywhere in England. Everyone at Intraglobal was convinced that things in Europe were going to get much worse before they got any better. Someone cleared his throat. Eric raised an eyebrow toward Hawk. "I'll need a volunteer," he said.

"Fine," the other man responded. "Armstrong."

"Oh, God," moaned the man who had cleared his throat. "Have a heart, guys, I just got married!"

"Give her a look at jolly old England then," Hawk responded, not lifting his gaze from the reports in front of him. He was not known around Intraglobal for his compassion. "We've got good people in the other plants, Eric. I'd leave the rest of it be."

"Fine." Eric reached for his cigarettes and shook one loose from the pack. "That's it, then. I'll need full reports, and somebody ask Julie to come in."

Slowly, silently, the men around the table, the managers of the Aviation Division of Intraglobal, stood up and filed out. The one called Armstrong, who had been volunteered as a consultant to the British Intraglobal subsidiaries, cast one last appealing glance toward Eric and Hawk before leaving. Hawk stood up, his long, lanky frame seeming to unfold as he rose. "Will there be anything else for me?"

"No, thanks. Just stay on top of things, will you? I have a feeling about this."

"What is that?"

Eric inhaled deeply on his cigarette and spoke almost through clenched teeth. "Look at the bombing of Warsaw last week." He exhaled the smoke and continued. "That's the first large-scale bombardment of any major city, ever. And you saw what

happened. The place was leveled. The population had no choice
but to surrender. I'm telling you, Hawk, I have a feeling about
this thing. This war is going to be fought and won and lost in
the air.''

"You could be right.''

Eric looked up at him. "I *could* be right? I'd better not hear
that from you, or from anybody else, not anymore. I didn't get
where I am by being possibly right. I am right, Hawk. I always
will be.''

The other man looked uncomfortable. "Right, Eric. I'll be
going now.''

Eric waved a hand in dismissal, and waited for Julie. Things
were going well, except for those problems in England, but they
could be ironed out. He had met with Roosevelt last week
again—damn the man, he was still more concerned with votes
and U.S. neutrality than with pushing events along.

Eric sighed. If he could get the United States into the war
now, it would be a coup. The military was behind him. He had
spent the last few months closeted with officials from the Pentagon, generals, and admirals, and he had their support. As well
he should, since he was giving them the juiciest matériel that
they'd had in decades. They were ready. He had even been able
to throw a few commissions over to Newport, to Asheford Shipbuilding, which ought to counterbalance his inability to locate
Caroline's mother.

Oh, God. Why dwell on that now? Caroline was angry with
him about it. She seemed to think that he had nothing better to
do than to track down that willful, stubborn woman. . . . But he
loved her. She was his daughter in ways that he couldn't understand and that had nothing to do with biology. She was the teenager who had learned to fly in his airplanes, and would come
running to him afterward, her cheeks flushed and her eyes sparkling: "Oh, Eric, it was marvelous!'' She had lived in his house
in San Jose and argued with him, pouted at him, laughed with
him, talked to him, confided in him. He had tried to give her
the things he would have given his own daughter, had he had
one. Tried, perhaps, to make up to Sarah for not having had
children with her, by being the best father he could to his dead
friend's daughter . . . And now—although he didn't want to admit it, not even to himself—Caroline was the only good and
shining thing left in his life. Caroline had nothing to do with
power, money, prestige.

Except, of course, for the fact that one day she would inherit it all. One day, Intraglobal would be hers. It was a sobering thought.

Julie knocked on the door and let herself into the room, ever the efficient secretary. "You wanted me, Mr. Beaumont?"

Eric tore himself from his reverie and turned to face her. "Yes. Do you have the reports from Asheford Shipbuilding?"

"Yes, sir. Our man has settled in nicely. Middle management, as you suggested. Neither of the Asheford brothers suspects he is there."

"Fine. I want weekly updates, Julie."

"Yes, sir."

He got up and they walked together out of the room and down the corridor to his office. He was feeling a little stiff these days. Probably should be getting more sleep and more exercise. Probably wouldn't. There wasn't time for everything. "What about Amanda?"

"Nothing to report, sir, except that she isn't in Nairobi. That doesn't mean anything. Africa is a large continent, sir."

"All right. Keep the agent there. Keep him looking. No priority, but she's getting on my nerves. It's time we found her."

"Yes, sir."

"All right." He sat down behind his desk. "What's happening with Johnson?"

"Mr. Kellogg has been talking about a stealth bomber, sir. I think he knows that you're working on one already and wants to be in on it. Also, he's been in Tokyo twice during the past two weeks. We were unable to obtain information on his contacts there."

"Why?" That was a major slipup, Eric thought. He trusted Kellogg—and all of Johnson Industries, for that matter—about as far as he could throw him. And the man was overweight. Eric had ordered that he be followed, all the time, no expense spared, no mistakes made. And now it appeared that one had been made.

"Our agent was hit by a truck, sir."

He looked up, interested. "Accidentally?"

"Probably not, sir. He had just telephoned a report here and was leaving the American Express office. His wallet wasn't taken, and none of the money that he was carrying was touched, but his notes on Kellogg and Johnson were missing." She hesitated. "He died before they got him to the hospital, sir."

"Goddamn it," Eric whispered. "Goddamn." So Jeffrey Kellogg was going to play rough, was he? There was a big step between industrial espionage and murder. And he had taken it. Eliminating Eric's people . . . There was the outside chance that it wasn't a Johnson operative that had taken the Intraglobal man out. Relations with Japan were a little touchy these days. It was possible that they thought he was an agent for the U.S. government. But it was improbable, definitely improbable. No, it appeared that the affable fat man who had sat and filled his pipe with such maddening slowness, who had agreed to a tenuous alliance with Eric and Intraglobal, had sealed the bargain with violence.

And what the hell was Kellogg protecting anyway? What was going on in Japan that was so damned important he was willing to kill for it? Didn't he know that the death of an agent would arouse Eric's suspicions—or did he really think that Eric would buy the accident theory?

Johnson Industries had always been his enemy. From the old days, when his company was just starting out in America, and they stole that damned boron patent from him—and he wasn't *ever* going to forget that—they had been his enemy. Trying to get Caroline involved with the boy . . . what was his name? Starkey, that was it: Andrew Starkey. One of their own. They would do anything to destroy him, and it seemed that the peace they had so recently negotiated was merely a signal for the old enmity to go undercover.

Eric compressed his lips. Very well. If that was the way that Johnson wanted to play it, that was all right with him. They had just raised the stakes, and he was more than willing to stay in the game.

"Julie," he said, "I want more people in Tokyo. Now. Give them any cover they want or can work with. I want to know what the hell Jeffrey Kellogg is doing there. I want to know what time he gets up in the morning; I want to know the life history of anyone he talks to; I want to know how many times he belches after dinner. I want everything. Is that clear?"

"Yes, Mr. Beaumont."

"Good." He took a deep breath. He was going to get the bastards.

Caroline listened to the voices around her with disbelief. "What do you mean, you don't want to get involved?"

Bill leaned across the bar in the airport lounge and beckoned to Margie. "Another round, on me." He turned back. "What do you want from us, Caroline? Too many of our fathers got killed over there in nineteen-eighteen. I can't say that I'm over-eager to repeat the performance."

"But Hitler is going to take over Europe!"

"Could be," acknowledged one of the flight instructors, a young ex-farmer from Vermont. "But it's none of our business."

"Besides," said someone else, "if he does, then he'll be satisfied. And he'll leave everybody else alone."

The Vermont-farmer-turned-flight-instructor grinned. "Have to start filing our flight plans in German one of these days," he joked, taking a swig of beer, and everybody laughed. Except for Caroline.

"I don't understand," she said, slowly clenching and un-clenching her fists. "If you all lost somebody in the last war then you should feel more strongly about this one. They'll have died for nothing if you don't take up the same cause!" There were tears behind her eyes again. "My father was killed then, too. In Alsace-Lorraine. I'd like to think that his death meant something."

"Death," pronounced the flight instructor, "is meaningless anyway."

"Besides, Caroline," Bill said appeasingly, "there's no real war going on anyway. You've got to do more than declare it to make it happen, you know."

He had a point. Since the French had declared war and started to mobilize, there had been no attack from Germany. The Ma-ginot Line was silent and peaceful, and the soldiers who had been summoned there posthaste played cards in its subterranean passages. The headlines which a week before had been scream-ing in outrage at the Hun were now talking about how, in France and England, life was going on as usual. Some of the newspa-pers, Caroline knew, were even calling it the "phony war," and predicting an end to it all before Christmas.

"What," she said now in a low voice, "about the subma-rines?"

"What about them?" Bill asked, tilting back his chair. "We haven't heard anything in over a week."

Her temper flared again. "Oh, great. Nothing in over a week. I suppose that's a great comfort to anyone with relatives on the *Athenia*! That's no phony war. Those were civilians, Bill, people like you and me, just peacefully crossing the Atlantic. There's no rule that says people can't start out from Liverpool and hope to make it to Montreal in one piece, is there?''

"Tell that to the *Titanic*,'' someone muttered, and Caroline threw up her hands.

"You are so blind,'' she said, the words coming out thick because of her anger. "You'll all figure out what is happening when it's too late to do anything about it!''

But Caroline's friends at the airport weren't the only ones to think in those terms. When the President told Eric that the American people didn't want to get involved, he was right. Only Steven and William Asheford remained positive about the war effort, and Caroline suspected that was only because of the orders that they were getting for steel ships. Destroyers. Destroyer escorts. They weren't getting the big orders, not yet, the orders for the flattops, the aircraft carriers, but Steven was sure that it was just a matter of time. He had put in a call to Eric at Intraglobal and was waiting for a response. With any luck, this war was going to make them very, very rich indeed.

"You're already rich,'' William had reminded him, and Steven laughed.

"Me? Not a chance. Caroline's rich,'' he said, facing the bitter truth. Once, he hadn't thought that money mattered, but now with a daughter—and he hoped someday soon, a son to raise—he felt uncomfortable living off Caroline's money. "I have nothing.''

Steven was interested in American involvement in the war, but Caroline could not rejoice in his interest, it was for too many of the wrong reasons. Or so she told herself . . .

The truth was that Caroline was confused. Her natural inclination was to support the weak and the helpless, the wronged. She had been wronged so many times herself, had been weak and helpless, and knew what that was like, but that was not enough to account for the vehemence with which in those early days of September she supported France. Rather it was a voice that she did not know, speaking from somewhere deep inside of her that she had never explored, reminding her, over and over again, that she was half-French. That it was her country which had so bravely declared war against the Huns, just as they had in 1914. That it was her blood that might, one day soon, be spilled again on the poppy fields of eastern France.

Caroline didn't know the voice, but she listened to it, and it was speaking a different language than the people around her.

She threw herself into her life with renewed energy, as though by losing herself in daily tasks she could ignore it all: the little voice inside, the poppy fields of Alsace and Lorraine, the German dive-bombers pounding Warsaw into submission . . . and the laughter in the airport lounge, the crude jokes, the unwillingness to become involved.

She spent more time than ever with Elizabeth, taking her daughter for long walks along the breakwater, playing with her in the bath and nursery, but her ears echoed with the cries of the murdered Polish children. She accompanied Justine to church on Sundays, trying to regain the friendship that the two women had once shared, trying to be happy for Justine as she prepared to bring another child into the world, but her prayers were filled with blood. She took the Intraglobal Butterfly up, day after day, seeking solace in the sky, but all that she could imagine were cannons spurting fire from its wingtips. Either she was too obsessed with the situation in Europe, or others around her weren't obsessed enough, but she knew that she couldn't go on this way for much longer.

Steven was anything but helpful. He worked long hours down at the shipyard, and came home to the mansion on Ocean Drive only to closet himself in the library with blueprints and plans. Often William was with him, and Caroline imagined Justine alone at home with Nicholas, mutely accepting her place in the world.

When she tried to talk to Steven about the war, about her feelings, about the little voice that spoke so insistently to her in French, he told her that he had no time for such fanciful notions. If she pressed the point, he told her that he was tired of her whining. Steven was married to her, but his work was becoming his mistress. It hadn't always been that way. When exactly had it changed? she wondered. Asheford Shipbuilding had become his real love, his true love, the object of his most tender devotion. About time you accepted that, kid, Caroline told herself. And fought down the despair that welled up in her at the thought.

She stood out on the terrace overlooking the sea—the same place, did she but know it, where her mother had so often stood so many years ago—and thought about what she could do. France was bleeding, and Caroline was standing idly by. But what was there to do? She was not trained to do anything useful, be anyone helpful. She was not a nurse, or a teacher, or a diplomat. The only thing that she had ever done, and done well, was fly an airplane. Precious little good that would do her.

She was suffocating in Newport. She couldn't breathe, couldn't think, couldn't live. Steven wouldn't even notice if she were gone. . . . And then the thought came to her. There was no sense in staying here with a husband who didn't care for her and friends who mocked the things that she believed in. There was no solace, as she had known there would be none, in this the house of her childhood. Margaret Lewis's ghost may well walk its corridors by night—and several of the servants swore to that— but the mansion was dominated by day with the energetic figure of Steven Asheford.

There was one other place that Caroline had felt secure, sure of herself, at home. There was one place that she would be accepted, no matter what she thought or how she expressed it. There was one place in the world where she could be given unconditional and unequivocal love.

California.

She could go, she realized. Nothing would stand in her way. She could tell Steven that she needed a vacation. He would be pleased enough, she thought, to have her out of the way for a while. And she would take Elizabeth with her. The summer mists would be over, she thought. The sun would revitalize her. The redwood trees would heal her. Eric would care for her.

Shivering from the sea breeze, Caroline turned and walked back into the house. She dialed the telephone there in the drawing room, not stopping to think anymore about what she was doing, not stopping because if she hesitated she might change her mind and she didn't want to change her mind. She called a commercial airline and secured tickets. Boston to San Francisco. She would rent an airplane in San Francisco, she thought, and fly to San Jose.

Fly home.

The very thought brought energy back to her. "Jenson!" she called. "Jenson! Have Martha pack our bags! Elizabeth and I are going on a trip!"

Pierre de Montclair stumbled through the solid, massive oaken front doors a little past midnight. He was tired, he had had more than his share to drink, and his muscles were aching. Sometimes the things that Isabelle demanded of him were more torturous than the workouts he used to subject himself to when he was younger. He smelled of liquor and sex, and didn't particularly care. Everyone would be asleep.

He was wrong.

A figure rose from a chair in the front hallway, the stately, forbidding figure of his mother. Oh, God, he thought. What had he done now? If she wanted to confront him about Isabelle, or about neglecting Chantale, she chose one hell of a time to do it.

She said very little. She looked at him, a slow, assessing gaze, and he felt himself squirming under it just as he had when he was a child and had transgressed against one of her rules. And then, in the same deep voice she had had ever since he could remember, she said, "Congratulations. While you were off fornicating, your daughter was born."

He gaped at her for a moment, and then said, tentatively, "My daughter?"

"Yes." She turned stiffly to go upstairs. "I recommend that you do not disturb your wife. She's been through a great deal this evening."

Pierre shook his head. "It's too soon," he said.

"Apparently not. They're both well. The baby's name is Catherine."

"I wanted to name her Isabelle!" His voice was petulant.

"What you want," she said sharply, "is irrelevant at this moment. Chantale certainly deserves the opportunity to choose her daughter's name. And you will leave her alone until I tell you otherwise, do you hear me?"

He nodded dumbly, feeling the alcohol turning sour in his stomach. "Yes, Mother."

"Very well. Go and be sick, and get it over with."

He stumbled away, and vaguely, in the back of his mind, he thought that he heard her addressing his father's portrait in the large front hall. "If only," she was saying, "he could have been a little more like you. . . ."

Chapter Nine

Robert Beneteau frowned against the wind and turned up the collar of his coat. He and Marc Giroux had walked together in this same park for a half hour every noontime for as long as they had been in Zurich, and the sudden sharp air of late October was not going to deter him now.

Still, it was a sign. Winter was beginning. And what a winter it might yet prove to be. . . .

"So what news do we have concerning French mobilization?" he asked at last.

Marc Giroux was puffing slightly. Beneteau might well have a good ten years on him, but he had thirty pounds on the older man, and his poor physique took its toll at times like this. "It's completed, at least for the first round. They were looking for younger men first, so in any case Pierre de Montclair wasn't affected—mid-twenties is considered old for this particular game." He grimaced at the effort that he was producing. There were days when he would give anything to be in his mid-twenties again. "But of course we've made sure that he won't be conscripted at any future point."

"How?" A gust of wind whipped some dead leaves past them.

"Blackmail. The French secretary of war has been seen frequenting clubs that cater to . . . unusual . . . sexual tastes. I'm afraid he wouldn't remain secretary of war very long if his proclivities were made public. Not to mention that his wife would divorce him, and she has the money in the family. It would be an unhappy retirement all around. He was quite happy to remove the Count de Montclair's name from the secondary lists."

"I see. Was there no other way?" Beneteau's distaste was in his voice.

"If we had had the time, there might have been." Giroux sounded wounded. "I thought that we did well simply to amass the kind of dossier on him we needed to gain control—any kind of control.''

''I see. And what if this particular individual is replaced at some point?''

''Then we do what we need to to gain leverage with his successor. I am convinced, Robert, if one looks hard enough and long enough one will find a point of leverage for everyone. No one is immune.''

Beneteau arched an eyebrow. ''To blackmail?''

''To blackmail, or bribery, or being bought out, or threatened . . . Whatever. What is the problem, Robert? We got what we needed out of it.''

The two men were turning a corner in the park, and a dog darted suddenly in front of them, followed by a small child calling its name. Beneteau waited until the boy was out of earshot. ''It seems that the firm has been taking a much more aggressive attitude toward what you so euphemistically call leverage since Mademoiselle Aubert has begun to have a greater voice in policy.''

Giroux felt himself stiffening. ''What does Soizic have to do with this?''

''I'll be frank with you, Marc—I think that your view of her is subjective and distorted.''

''Give me something concrete. Of course my view of her is subjective. But how has that affected what we have been working on?''

Beneteau sighed. How could he warn Marc of a danger that he only sketchily saw himself? ''She is a good lawyer, Marc. Brilliant, even. And we've been able to accomplish a number of things very quickly because of her clear thinking. I'll not go back on that, and I do not in any way regret hiring her as a junior partner. But I miss you. I miss *your* thinking. You have unique things to contribute as well. And all that I hear from you now is her voice. She's good, Marc, but she's young. She lacks your balance—ballast, if you like. And she is very aggressive.''

Giroux walked in silence for a moment, his head aching. He was feeling angry and defensive, and he didn't want to sound that way; it was the quickest route to assuring Robert that his intimations were correct. Soizic was brilliant, and if he listened to her too much, then perhaps that was for the best. The firm needed a breath of fresh air to wake them all up, especially in these times. The war was unpredictable; they had to think on their feet, make quick decisions. And, no matter what he said, Robert was a lawyer of the old school, just as he himself was. They mustn't forget their roots. Before Eric Beaumont came along, Beneteau and Giroux had specialized in drawing up wills.

And, besides . . . there was a part of him that still wondered if Soizic could really love him. She said that she did. She had even come to live with him. But she was young, and pretty, and he was middle-aged and overweight. If he listened to her, then perhaps it was partly through awe and a desire for her to succeed.

Finally, realizing that Robert was waiting for an answer, he spoke. "Soizic is aggressive, yes. She is young, yes. But ask yourself, Robert: Do not these times require youth and aggressiveness? If the de Montclair château and family are to be preserved throughout whatever befalls, we need to be active, not reactive. And, my old friend, I fear you and I too frequently have a tendency toward the latter. It's in our blood, it's in the law we practiced for so many years before assuming the unique capacity in which we now serve. Surely her youth, and her voice—balanced by ours, and by the voices of the other junior partners—are what is needed now!"

Beneteau stopped, leaning heavily on his cane. "And you do not think that your judgment is clouded by your intimate relationship with her?"

"If it is, that is only to the extent that is natural. I know her better now than I did before, Robert. I know how she thinks under a variety of circumstances. And, with that knowledge, I still tell you: She is what the firm needs now."

"I see." There was a minute of silence, broken only by the raucous cry of a crow somewhere off to the left of them. "Marc, I must ask you: Whose idea was this blackmail scheme?"

"And what has that got to do with anything?" Giroux's temper was rising again, and he had to tell himself, once more, to be quiet. He reached inside his pocket for the omnipresent antacid tablets.

"I think that in the long run, we are tarnishing the reputation and image of our firm if we engage in anything as blatant as blackmail. There are many things that we will need to do in the course of this war that may not be strictly moral or ethical, and I am perfectly prepared for such eventualities. The end justifies the means, in this as in other cases. But blackmail, Marc! It makes us seem like petty hoodlums!"

"And if blackmail is the only course that works?"

"Then for God's sake let it be discreet! Honestly, Marc, following a man to a club!"

Giroux shrugged. He still thought that it had been a good idea.

And they both knew that Beneteau had been correct: It had been Soizic's idea.

They called it "Bundles for Britain," the great amassing of clothing and blankets which were lovingly packaged and carefully sent abroad. It was the most Roosevelt had been able to do overtly, that and make his famous speech about lending a neighbor a fire hose to put out a fire, which had made sense to even the most staunch isolationist. The American people were still overwhelmingly against involvement in a European war, especially as the German attacks on France and Britain seemed isolated and sporadic. The German U-boats were patrolling the Atlantic; silent deadly monsters lurking far under the waves that, like the killer sharks they reminded everybody of, attacked anything that moved on the surface. But, as one politician had said, "We have lived with a Europe dominated by England. Now we may live with a Europe dominated by Germany. What's the difference?"

The general sentiment against American troop involvement did not extend as far as forbidding industrial involvement. Indeed many Americans were becoming quite wealthy as the economy improved, almost overnight, due to the orders from Europe for arms and war equipment.

Caroline Asheford deliberately isolated herself from it all. She and Elizabeth had arrived in California early in October, and had moved back into the big clapboard house on Western Avenue in San Jose where she had lived with Eric. The fortunes of Intraglobal were in no way reflected in his style of living. Whereas others may have opted for opulence and swimming pools, villas and yachts, Eric Beaumont stayed on in the same house that he had inherited when his mother-in-law died, the same house where his wife had grown up, a house haunted by ghosts of happier days. And it was there that Caroline and Elizabeth went to stay with him.

There was no one to care for the baby, and so Caroline found herself discovering that there was more of a bond between herself and Elizabeth than she had previously thought. She took the child everywhere with her, shopping and to the beach, to the airport and out to the vast Intraglobal compound. They even went to San Francisco once in a while and played in the park that was in the shadow of the tremendous Golden Gate Bridge. Caroline found herself, for the first time, enjoying the new intimacy that they were sharing. When Elizabeth exclaimed over the petals of a flower, Caroline exclaimed, too; when Elizabeth cried, Caroline found herself feeling sad as well.

Eric had accepted their presence with calm and little surprise. Caroline cooked for him and cleaned the house when the housekeeper couldn't make it. But she missed the long talks that they had shared when she was a teenager living with him, the philosophy and the light banter. These days, Eric had little time for either.

She was amazed to see how much he had aged. There were wrinkles around his dark eyes now, and deep furrows on his forehead—his whole face seemed to sag in ways that she didn't remember—and he was developing a paunch, no doubt from sitting behind that vast desk of his all the time. She worried, and fed him vegetables and fish instead of the red meat, the tournedos, that he so dearly loved. She fussed and scolded, and he laughed at her. "I'll go in my own good time, Caroline. Don't be so concerned."

"I can't help being concerned," she said. "I love you, Eric."

Because it had been so long since anybody had said that to him, Eric was unable to find anything to say in response.

In her spare time, Caroline wandered around the Intraglobal compound, the parts of it where she was allowed ("Dear Caroline, even I don't go everywhere!" Eric had joked; but she knew that he was teasing her, and she wondered what was behind the steel doors and barbed wire). She looked with interest at the new airplane designs at the Aviation Center on the north side of the compound. The test pilots there were friendly, and took the time to talk with her.

Eventually she asked Eric if she could do some test flights for him as well. Eric sat at the kitchen table and stared at his plate of spaghetti without really seeing it. Hers was too much like that other voice, too familiar, too hard to remember that this was Caroline and that the experiments that they were doing were with jet propulsion and not with single-engine biplanes. Sarah's voice echoed back through the years: "Please, Eric! I'm just as

competent as any of the men that you have trying them out. And
I want to fly!''

"I'm sure that you do," a much younger Eric had responded.
"But if something went wrong, I couldn't bear to lose you."

She had thrown back her head and laughed, that marvelous
pealing laughter, her mahogany-colored hair glinting in the sunlight. "Your designs won't fail, my love!"

And now here was Caroline's voice, taking up where Sarah's
had left off. "If they're safe for them, for those other pilots of
yours, then they're safe for me, Eric! I'm just as good as they
are."

"They're getting paid a great deal of money to risk their lives
up there," he said.

"Well, then, I'm a bargain. You don't have to pay me at all!"

He gestured toward Elizabeth. "And if you did hurt yourself?
If you were killed? How would I explain to her what had happened to her mother?" Don't keep asking, he implored her silently. Let it go. I can't bear another death. I couldn't lose
another loved one out of the sky. Let it go.

Caroline, used to obeying Eric and to the futility of pursuing
her own dreams, did let it go. But she flew his other airplanes,
private models that he had been working on before Intraglobal
began taking up the war effort in earnest. For the most part she
was content with that.

In general she was happy to be away from Newport, from her
husband's expectations and the raucous laughter in the pilots'
lounge, from the endless talk of neutrality—an uneasy neutrality
at best, Caroline thought—and from Justine and her need to bury
herself in her family, like an ostrich, and ignore the state of the
world.

That was the core of her trouble with Steven, she decided as
she walked with Elizabeth on the shore and watched the mighty
Pacific breakers come in and pound the beach. That was the
problem. In his heart of hearts, Steven wanted another Justine,
another ostrich, content to occupy herself with her children and
her home and her parties, and to let him do the serious things.
He said that he loved her, but she believed in truth he could love
any woman. The things about her that made her uniquely Caroline were the very things that he disliked about her. Her
thoughts, her concerns, her ideas were all rejected; her caring,
her nurturing, her passion were all sought after.

And if that was true, she thought, what was the point?

Eric listened to her when he had the time. He took seriously her thoughts about the war, and gravely agreed with her that American involvement was ultimately unavoidable. He told her that Intraglobal was providing military matériel for the British and French troops, and she was glad that someone was doing something positive for the people overseas. "Those poor souls in Poland," she said to him, and he showed her a photograph—God only knew where he had found it—of a little Polish girl crying over the body of her still smaller sister, the victim of German strafing of refugee lines. Caroline cried over the picture. The dead girl was just a little older than Elizabeth.

Eric was doing other things, too, of course, secret things; but she didn't ask him about any of it. It didn't matter. She trusted Eric. He would do only what was good and right. With Intraglobal and Eric Beaumont on the side of right, then the war would be won. Caroline was sure of that.

Christmas, 1939.

Chantale de Montclair had much to thank God for: a robust baby daughter; her own health, tenuous after her premature delivery of Catherine; a place to live; enough to eat. From what she was hearing on the radio out of eastern Europe, these were not blessings to be taken lightly, or for granted.

Marie-Louise was not one to overdo holiday festivities. She hostessed, as she had every year since she had first married Philippe de Montclair, the Christmas celebration for the servants, with mulled hot cider and warm wine, pheasant and apples and new potatoes—the traditional feast of the Château de Montclair. The hunt had taken place that fall, as usual. Marie-Louise's message was clear: life goes on. The nobility had an obligation to demonstrate this to the rest of the people.

Chantale was at her proper place in the midst of these traditional festivities. She rode in the hunt, even though it had been a mere three weeks since Catherine was born, and placed respectably. She poured out the warm wine into goblet after goblet, and smiled endless smiles. She stood beside Pierre when he distributed the Christmas presents to the staff, and she added her wishes for the New Year to his. On Christmas Eve, she sat in the family pew at the Cathédrale de St. Maurice and listened to the old archbishop wheeze his way painfully through a disjointed sermon. Returning to the château, she shared champagne and oysters and the traditional *bûche de Noël* with Pierre and Marie-Louise and Jean-Claude.

And it all felt so empty.

Jean-Claude opened his presents on Christmas morning with all the wide-eyed wonder and delight that any mother could expect, and Chantale laughed her most genuine laugh and hugged him to her. The dinner was special, too, with the Christmas ham, hot chestnuts, and wine; and finally, finally, Chantale began to relax. There may be war raging just beyond their borders, but as long as she could sit here with her family, amid the happiness of her young son and the peaceful presence of her baby daughter, her husband arguing amiably with his mother over methods for roasting chestnuts, then somehow, in the end, everything might be all right. It may be peace in the midst of war, a calm at the vortex of a storm, but for now that was enough. She sighed with contentment.

And then, casting a figurative shadow over the table, Pierre stood up. "I have to go."

Chantale, distressed, said, "Oh, Pierre, must you? We still have the truffles and the cake . . ." Her voice trailed off. She had worked so hard to make this Christmas work, to ensure that it be peaceful and tranquil, and she had thought that he felt it, too—at least a little bit. She thought that her care and her work could make him stay. . . .

Pierre downed the rest of his wine in one gulp. "I can't help it," he said, his voice distant. "I have things to do."

Chantale looked helplessly at Marie-Louise, hoping that the older woman would say something, do something, anything, to keep her son there, but she merely shrugged.

The two women sat and watched him go, both of them realizing that something intangible and important was going with him, that things would never be quite the same again. For Chantale it was a turning point in her marriage, bringing with it a deep sense of despair, but also, she was later to find, a new kind of freedom.

Later, that was what they all would remember of the end of 1939: the declaration of war and Pierre's abdication from the family. The thought of Germans at their doorstep, and Pierre's drunkenness and sorties to his mistress in Angers. The fear of Europe in flames, and Pierre's failure to be part of the life at the Château de Montclair.

Even Pierre, driving too fast on the tree-lined road into Angers, anticipating the warmth of Isabelle's arms and the present that she had promised him for this Christmas, felt a stab of pain. As though something very valuable had somehow passed him by.

For Caroline, Christmas that year was Christmas remembered, Christmas with Eric around a tinsel-bedecked tree, with punch and oatmeal cookies that she had spent most of the day before baking. Steven had even come, flying in at night from Rhode Island on a charter plane and arriving in time to play Santa Claus for Elizabeth on Christmas Eve, his own fiery red beard covered by a cottony white one.

Elizabeth fell asleep on the carpet with her head pillowed on Caroline's lap, and the three adults proceeded to open their presents, a Christmas Eve custom that Eric had always followed. As they laughed and exclaimed over this gift and that, there was peace, an unexpected truce, as Steven leaned over to kiss Caroline, and she smiled happily back at him. It felt so good, so right. . . . She had been silly to write off the marriage so quickly, she thought. Steven had a lot on his mind, pressures because of his work. But he was still the same gentle giant that she had married. Things would work out again.

Eric—the old Eric, not obsessed with his work but relaxed and contented and friendly—brought out champagne and oysters, memories from his own childhood Christmas Eves in France, and they all laughed as the bubbles tickled their nostrils. Eric leaned back on one elbow, almost caressing his glass, finishing his story,

". . . and there was this girl, you see, that both of us had our eye on. Well, there wasn't all that much competition between us, anyway. He was always the handsome count, and women used to *swoon* at his feet, just about. But we'd never been in that bar before, and so she didn't know who we were, and I'll say this for Philippe, he was never one to spread his title around. So he went over to her and bought her a drink, just like that, and said that it was from this other guy, but he was too shy to come and talk to her himself."

"A little like Cyrano de Bergerac," said Caroline.

"Cyrano de who?" Eric said. "Whose story is this, anyway?"

"Yours," she said promptly, laughing.

"Go on, Eric," urged Steven.

"All right, then. So she asked who it was from, naturally, and Philippe gestured over in my direction, and I did my best to look shy, and then next thing I know she's coming across the bar, drink in her hand, just ready to thank me. But she'd misunderstood Philippe, see, and next to me was this big guy from the Auvergne, and she went right up to him and touched his arm and then *he* wanted that girl, too. And so Philippe went over to *him* and said, pardon me, but there's been a mistake here, and the guy pulls his arm away from this girl long enough to make it into a fist, and said, what problem? And Philippe said, indicating me, my friend's bought this young lady a drink. And the big guy turned to me just like that, and punched my chin! I was out like a light—did I tell you that this fellow was *big*?—and Philippe says, oh, no, I'll have to report that to the police. That's when the big guy got scared, I suppose he'd had one or two runins with the police already, because he put down his drink and got out of that bar real fast. And Philippe ended up consoling the girl."

Caroline and Steven were both laughing. "Is this a *true* story?" she demanded, still laughing.

"I swear," Eric said solemnly. "Any story where Philippe ends up getting the girl is a true story." Except for one, he thought in his mind; except for one . . .

Caroline leaned back against Steven, feeling his warmth and steady heartbeat, her own pulse slowing to match his. She was sleepy and full and contented. "He sounds," she said to Eric, "like a nice person."

"He was," Eric said soberly, "crazy." And they all laughed again.

Caroline smiled. That was her father. Every one of Eric's stories, each of his memories, brought her closer to the shadowy figure that was her father, made him more real, a person rather than a figurehead. She had a photograph of him, a faded yellow picture that Eric had given her years ago, of her parents standing together in front of the booksellers on the Seine in Paris. Her mother was overdressed, as appeared to have been her custom, or perhaps it was just the fashion of the times. There was some sort of veil wrapped up around her hat and trailing down her back. Philippe looked perfect, dark and handsome with a well-groomed mustache, and he was smiling into the camera. How dashing, Caroline had thought. *No one* used to smile for the camera; as a rule people in those old pictures looked harsh and angry. Not so her father. All the gay insouciance that had marked his life came through, vividly, in the young man who grinned when his picture was taken.

Caroline imagined that her mother had probably scolded him for it.

Much later, Eric had carried the still-sleeping Elizabeth off to her crib and had excused himself, and still Steven and Caroline sat by the fireplace, picking disinterestedly at the food around them, listening to the crackling of the flames. Caroline closed her eyes and smiled. If life could only be like this all the time, she thought. With Eric and Elizabeth close by, and Steven here with me, not angry but kind, like this, the way he was before.

As though sensing her thoughts, he said gently, in her ear, "It's been a long time since we sat like this."

"I know." She hesitated. "I've missed it."

"I have, too." He leaned forward to kiss her, and she moved gently around until she could face him, putting her arms around him, and kissing him in return. This is it, Caroline thought as she moved closer to her husband, snuggling into his embrace, this is why I married this man. Because he is so strong and so kind and so gentle. Because he cares so much about me. The last few months . . . well, there have been hard times. The war in Europe is taking more of a toll than any of us suspected that it would.

She tightened her arms around him. Her marriage, she thought grimly, was not going to be a casualty of that war. Her mother changed husbands as easily as she changed shoes, but Caroline had meant it when she said, ". . . till death do us part" to Steven in front of the altar at St. John's. They were going to make it work.

Steven helped her up the stairs, into the bedroom that Eric had put aside for them, and he undressed her as he had in the old days, tenderly, carefully, exclaiming over the beauty of her body with each successive layer that he removed. Caroline closed her eyes and shivered with pleasure. This was what she had wanted all this time: this gentleness, this tenderness, this love. He had her naked, then, and leaned over to kiss her breasts, and she held his head to her and realized in sudden surprise that her eyes were filled with tears.

They made love with tenderness, two friends rediscovering each other after a long absence, with laughter and delight. "I love you,'' Caroline whispered into the darkness, and the big hand closed over hers. "I love you, too, Caroline.''

Steven went to sleep at once, as he always had, but Caroline lay awake, smiling happily as the sky lightened gradually in the east. Compromise was possible, wasn't it? She was going to go back to Newport soon and try to be some of the things that Steven wanted her to be. She could spend time with him and still fly from time to time. She might even go see her old psychologist, the man in the tweed jacket with the foul-smelling pipe, who had helped her so much when she was young and frightened. She always felt better after talking with him. He would help her sort things out. Perhaps even Steven could come, and they could all talk together about the things that were problems. It would work.

Elizabeth woke early and Caroline went in to her, and sat on the floor and cuddled and played with her daughter. "Daddy's here,'' she whispered happily into Elizabeth's dark curls. "Daddy's here.''

As they were finishing breakfast Steven announced casually that he was returning to Rhode Island. That afternoon. Caroline looked up from feeding Elizabeth, feeling the disappointment stab deeply into her. "What did you say?''

"I have to leave. The company needs me there.''

"But I need you here!''

"Then come back with me, Caroline,'' he said, putting down his fork. "It was your idea to come running out here in the first place. Whatever it was, you must have gotten it out of your system by now. So come home.'' He did not mean for his words to be as harsh as they sounded. But he felt awkward, unsure as to his footing with this new Caroline.

She bit her lip, fighting back the wave of panic that threatened to engulf her. She wasn't ready yet. Not yet. A little more time, time to stretch and relax and feel better about herself. Surely a little more time wasn't so much to ask? "I'm not ready yet. Oh, Steven—I thought we could go into San Francisco together . . . make a holiday of it. I could show you so many things. . . .''

Steven's face clouded over. "I'm not particularly interested in San Francisco, Caroline. I *am* interested in Asheford Shipbuilding. And I've wasted enough time as it is.''

"Wasted enough time?'' She could feel as well as hear her voice rising, and was glad that Eric was out in the kitchen and not here to witness this scene. For it obviously was going to become a scene. "Spending time with your family is wasting time?"

"Of course not, Caroline." His voice was impatient again. "Holy Christ, you always have to read insults into everything, don't you? I just meant that flying out here, and spending days away from the shipyard, is not good for business."

"What do you think? That they can't function without you while you spend Christmas with your family?"

"I think," Steven said carefully, wiping his mouth on a napkin and getting up, "that my family would find Christmas easier if they were in the right place. Do you think that it's easy for me, running off across the continent just to indulge you?"

"Indulge me? Is that what this is?"

"Well, Caroline, of course." Steven threw up his hands in exasperation. "What did you think? That I yearn for California? That it's not embarrassing telling people that my wife ran away with my daughter because of the war in Europe? Grow up, Caroline."

"If," she said, her lip trembling with the tightness of tears, "it's so embarrassing, then why did you come?"

"To take you back." Steven lowered his voice. "You don't belong here, Caroline. You and Elizabeth belong at home. I'm tired of coming back to an empty house at the end of the day, and servants that gossip about us behind my back."

"I see." She was really fighting now to stay in control. Someone was being unreasonable, and she wasn't sure who it was. She knew only that she wasn't ready to face it all again, the mansion and the airport lounge and Justine. That she needed more time here with Eric, where she still felt the most at home. "And last night?"

"What about last night?" Automatically he glanced at the closed kitchen door, as though afraid that Eric might hear.

Caroline had seen the direction of his glance. "I'm sure," she said loudly, "that Eric knows we make love. At least from time to time. What was last night all about? You said that you loved me."

Steven's voice softened. "I do love you, Caroline. Of course I love you. I just wish that you'd grow up and act the way a wife should."

She stared at him, and then slowly shook her head. They were right back in the same argument, right back to the same hateful things, and she didn't know how to get out of it. They were caught in a hopeless spiral, a never-ending circle of disagreement. Having once entered into it, she didn't know how to step out and change what was happening. Last night had been wonderful. Last night there had been tenderness and love. And now, today, they were at each other again, because each of them wanted the other to change. And neither of them was willing to do so.

Steven left, and Caroline stayed. Eric put his arm around her shoulders and let her cry and cry. But even that wasn't going to change anything, she realized unhappily. It would always be the same: circles of pleasure and circles of pain. Which was all right as long as they were balanced.

But the circles of pain were sharper, more frequent, longer lasting. And the circles of pleasure never seemed to last very long at all. They were tinged with a shadow of pain to come, the certain knowledge that they could not last, a piece of pie with tiny slivers of glass in it. Perhaps that was what marriage was supposed to be.

The people in the yellowed old picture—had they gone through these same storms? Did they love for a while, only to hate all the more vehemently again? Caroline studied their faces, and thought not. Her father, her mother: They had loved, she was sure of it. They had loved until he died.

Perhaps that was the answer, then. Love could only be marvelous for a while. If one of the people died while it was still marvelous, then it would always in retrospect stay magical and untarnished. But if both people had the audacity to go on living, then it disintegrated before one's eyes. Eric would always love his Sarah, she realized with a start, and Sarah had died. And he had never loved again.

He had been lonely all these years. He had lived alone; he had never known the warmth of another woman, another woman's laughter or love. But, in a way, she envied him. His love had been brief, but it had been perfect. Whereas hers . . .

Caroline shook her head. She had always believed that every year a person learns something more, becomes a little wiser. But as 1939 drew to a close, she realized that she would have been a great deal happier without the knowledge she had acquired this particular Christmas.

Chapter Ten

Caroline took a last look at herself in the mirror, her eyes, as always, critical. The rebellious blond curls did as they liked, just as they always had, but the mascara that she had used accentuated her eyes, and the touch of lipstick made her face come alive.

"Are you sure I haven't forgotten anything?" she asked.

The teenage girl beside her shook her head. "It's all right, Mrs. Asheford, I've baby-sat hundreds of times before. Elizabeth will be fine with me."

Caroline smiled. "I suppose that I sound too nervous. Well, all right, I'm off then. If I'm not home by six, then Mr. Beaumont will be here by six-thirty, or did I already tell you that?"

"You already told me that."

Caroline shook her head and bent to kiss Elizabeth. "Bye, pumpkin," she murmured. "Be good."

For all her worries, she felt strangely lighthearted as she left the house on Western Avenue. Eric had given her a plane—an IA-14, even newer than her Butterfly—to use at her convenience, and she was determined to make a day of it, fly into San Francisco, have lunch out, perhaps see a show. She had been feeling so sad lately—ever since Steven had stopped writing to her, actually.

Caroline frowned, and tensed her hands on the steering wheel of the car. He had written after Christmas, and had even called once or twice, but each time she had hesitated, asking for still more time, a little more time.

And then, sometime in February, the letters had stopped coming. Caroline called the mansion on Ocean Drive, but Mr. Asheford was always unavailable. She wrote letter upon letter, sent him photographs of Elizabeth, tried to explain why she needed to be alone, but there was no response. Caroline wasn't ready yet to return to Newport. Nor was she prepared for her husband's silence. The pain, she found, was more intense than she ever would have expected.

And now it was March and she was still in California. Of course he hadn't understood her reasons for staying. She wasn't completely sure that she understood them, either. But now what was going to happen to them?

The IA-14 (Eric didn't make up fancy names for most of his models: IA, of course, stood for Intraglobal Aviation) was waiting for her at the airport, sleek and gleaming in the sunshine, the sight lifting Caroline's spirits. It was, Eric had assured her, a marvelous airplane.

He was right.

Caroline filed her flight plan with the tower and watched the look of interest in their eyes, the slow assessing glance, and she knew that it was because of Eric, not her. No one from her days was left here anymore. The airplane, the old mechanic assured her, was "in tiptop shape, Mrs. Asheford, you couldn't ask better," and indeed the preflight check bore that out. She put on her headphones and, automatically, superstitiously, tapped her microphone once. "San Jose Tower, this is November Bravo Twenty-three, request clearance for takeoff."

Her earphones crackled to life. "November Bravo Twenty-three, you are cleared for takeoff, runway forty-nine."

"Thank you, Tower."

The engines felt strong and steady, and there was a surge of power when she asked for it. For all its strength, it was a light and compact little plane, much like what she imagined a thoroughbred horse to be. Neat and compact and powerful. It seemed to strain against her at the end of the runway, all but urging her to go, go on, be up and off and away and free. . . . With a laugh, Caroline acceded. The tarmac flashed beneath her, faster and faster as she gained speed, and then the nose was pointing up and she was pulling back on the stick. Come on there—yes, perfect, they were lifting off and the end of the runway flicked away behind them and the earth no longer held them prisoners. Caroline smiled. It was better, even, than Eric had said.

She leveled off at 12,000 feet (much higher and she would need oxygen) and put herself on course, and then relaxed. There were hardly any clouds, and none at this altitude. She could see, it seemed, forever. This was how it had been before, when she had first learned to fly. Or was it only her memory that distorted the past? Did she remember an endless string of exquisite days only because she had been so happy then?

Caroline glanced at her airspeed indicator and gave the plane a little more power, bringing her to a cruising speed of 200 knots. The engines responded smoothly and immediately, and again she smiled. She could see the Pacific Ocean now, sparkling and blue, alive in an indefinable way, more alive somehow than the Atlantic. Strange how she seemed to spend all her time flying over one or the other bodies of water, as though she could find peace by looking down on their flat blue surfaces. Hardly flat, but so it seemed, from the air. She could see the differences in depth from here, the deeper blue of the ocean as it pulled away from land, the lighter turquoise of the shallow water as it approached the sands and rocks of the shore.

San Francisco Airport was bustling. Her earphones crackled to life just after she found the radio beacon to bring her in, with heavy air traffic all around her. She initiated contact immediately: "San Francisco Tower, this is November Bravo Twenty-three, request clearance for landing."

A woman's voice answered. "November Bravo Twenty-three, you are cleared for landing, join right base runway zero-four."

"Thank you, Tower," Caroline said, and began to descend into the landing pattern. She moved into the wind and brought the plane down smoothly, applying back pressure on her stick, leaving the elevators in place, as she had so carefully taught Eddie to do, gliding down over the runway. When she was almost down, she moved the elevators back until the wheels had touched and held, and she was slowing down more and more and more. The runway seemed to stretch out forever. It was new, built since she had flown here ten years ago. Longer runways for larger planes.

Caroline wondered precisely what kind of aircraft had been flying in and out of San Francisco that required such long runways.

A flagman was waiting for her as she taxied around, directing her, and that was new, too. She cut the engines and waited until the propellers had stopped spinning around of their own momentum before taking off her headphones and unbuckling her seat belt. Over at the tower, she stopped to talk for a moment with the woman controller, but she was too busy communicating with other airplanes, so Caroline merely waved to her before leaving. The woman had looked somehow familiar, and that was strange, too.

Caroline used the pilots' locker room to change from her flying clothes into a more proper dress and shoes, and then took a taxi into the city. There was a time, she remembered with a sudden ache in her chest, when she had done this with some frequency. When she had traveled to San Francisco to meet Andrew . . .

Caroline shook her head. That was over; that had been over years ago. She wouldn't go to the little restaurant he owned; she wouldn't walk through the park they used to like. It was over. He had disappeared from her life, and she had married Steven Asheford, and one couldn't live one's life in the past. Not even in as agreeable a past as she had once had.

Lunch, she decided briskly, was the first order of business. And she was famished. She deliberately stayed away from the Mission District, where his restaurant was, and went instead to Columbus Avenue on North Beach, selecting an anonymous café which served her shrimp scampi and a wonderful dry white wine. Caroline smiled dreamily. San Francisco had been one of her favorite places in the world once. Delightfully busy, incessantly vital . . . and now a little sad. Perhaps more than just a little sad. It was kind of like losing a tooth, and finding that one's tongue couldn't stay out of the empty socket where the tooth had been. She was drawn here even though she knew that she would find it empty.

Caroline walked around the pier for a while, savoring the smell of the ocean and the shouts of the fishermen. When she had inhaled enough of the salt air she took another taxi up Mason Street to Nob Hill and sat for a while in Grace Cathedral, quietly enjoying its musty shadows and assured peace, drinking in the rich colors of stained glass and altar frontal, breathing air thick with years of incense. Emerging, she strolled slowly through the park, watching the children running shrieking past her, smiling as a sudden breeze lifted her skirts. It was with regret that she realized that she had to leave.

A taxi brought her back out to the airport with time to spare, and she filed her flight plan and changed into her flying clothes— khaki trousers, loose shirt, leather jacket—before walking up the stairs to the tower. Later, when she thought about why she had done so on this particular day, Caroline was hard-pressed for an answer. She wanted to see the woman controller again. She wanted to see the airfield. Dozens of reasons, and no reasons at all.

The tower was crowded with people and thick with cigarette smoke. No radar was in use. Even major airports such as San Francisco didn't have the pull that Caroline had, she noted in amusement. Her jacket slung over her shoulder, she paused to watch the people at work. The woman controller was standing with her profile to Caroline, looking out over the field through a pair of binoculars and talking into her microphone, and there was something about her. . . . Caroline narrowed her eyes. The woman looked familiar, so familiar, and yet Caroline was positive that she had never met her before.

Shrugging, she walked out to the observation platform and stood looking out over the airport. The sun was blazing down beyond, dipping into the ocean off to the west, orange and red and crimson, and the airplanes taxiing about and taking off caught its brightness and glittered like so many jewels strewn out over the field.

Behind her, Caroline heard a group of people come out and stand at the railing, talking and laughing together. She glanced at them, casually, seeing the woman controller among them. The shift must have changed, she thought. And then she turned back to look at the field. The IA-14 was sitting where it should have been after refueling, tied down carefully as were the rest of the airplanes which were not actually flying or in hangars. The crew obviously knew their business, she thought; it was good to know. Gave her a bit of confidence and—

"Caroline?"

The man's voice took her by surprise, interrupting her thoughts, and she turned around quickly to face him. The voice hadn't been particularly familiar, but the face was. After so many years, the face most definitely was.

Andrew Starkey.

Caroline dampened her lips, feeling a lead weight in her stomach, knowing that her cheeks were flaming. Andrew . . . of all people. She had carefully spent the day avoiding him, and now, at the very end, he had somehow found her.

He smiled, the same slow, heart-stopping smile that had so charmed her in the past, and put out his hand. "Caroline! I thought that it was you! What incredible luck!"

Caroline managed to smile, and to shake his hand. The touch

was like electricity, tingling in her fingertips. "Hello, Andrew. This *is* a surprise."

"I'll say." He was beaming, as though having discovered some incredible new species. "Caroline Copeland. Who would have thought?"

"Caroline Asheford now, actually," she said quickly. "I'm married."

"Well, then, congratulations, even if they're belated. I'm getting married myself, next month."

Ridiculous how she could feel jealous at the thought, after all this time, after everything that had happened. "Congratulations to you, then, too. I hope you're very happy."

He smiled again, and then, as though suddenly remembering something, turned and beckoned to the people still talking by the other rails. "Say! Come here and meet an old friend of mine!"

"No, really, I have to be going. . . ." Caroline edged away, but it was too late, they had already walked up, looking politely attentive. The woman controller, it turned out, was Andrew's sister. Caroline had never known that he had one. That was, she realized, the sense of recognition that she had felt; not the woman herself, but her resemblance to her brother. "Laura Starkey," she said, extending a hand. "I talked to you in earlier today, didn't I?"

"I think it was you," Caroline responded, and then Andrew said, "Well, you're still flying, that's great. I thought that you had moved back east." His hand, still on the railing, slid a little closer to her, and she could feel the closer proximity, almost remember what it had been like to hold his hand.

Her cheeks, she knew, were flaming. "I did," she responded automatically, feeling awkward and uncomfortable in front of so many people. "That is, I do. I live in Rhode Island. With my husband." You idiot, she told herself, sounding so prim and proper. It wasn't necessary to add that bit about Steven. And yet, somehow, it was—for her own benefit if not for his.

"I went to New York once," offered one of the girls in the party. "Dirty and dreary place. All soot and tall buildings."

"I'm sure," said Andrew, watching Caroline's face, "that Rhode Island is much nicer."

Laura was checking her watch. "Andrew, I hate to rush you, but if we're going to make that reservation, we'd better be going—"

"Don't let me keep you," Caroline said quickly. "I'm flying out in half an hour myself. It was nice meeting all of you. Nice to see you again, Andrew."

He frowned. "Look, do you really have to leave? We've got an extra place reserved. . . ."

She smiled. "No, thanks. I do need to leave."

Laura laughed. "Andrew thinks that his charms are irresistible. Watch out, or you'll have him thinking that he's been stood up twice."

"Twice?"

He shrugged. "The extra seat we have is for my fiancée. She can't make it tonight."

"I'm sorry." Caroline fought the surge of emotion that was telling her to say yes, anything to be able to continue talking to him, just a little longer . . . She had loved him once. "I have someone taking care of my daughter. I need to get back to her."

Someone said, "Andrew, really, if we're going . . ."

"You'd better go," Caroline told him.

"Yes. Well, it was nice—"

"Yes," she said. "Good-bye, Andrew."

"Nice meeting you," Laura said with a gay wave of her hand. "Andrew, we're off."

He backed away. "Take care of yourself."

"You, too," said Caroline, smiling brightly to cover the emptiness that seemed ready to overwhelm her.

And, as quickly and as suddenly as they had come, they were gone.

Caroline leaned her elbows on the railing and looked back over the field. The feeling of emptiness inside of her grew and grew. It hadn't been good seeing him, not at all. She had lied. He was like an addiction. Best to stay away altogether. Andrew Starkey. God, how she had been in love with him. . . .

He had been her first real love, back in the days of living with Eric in San Jose, before she moved back east. Was sent back east, she reminded herself, by Eric and his company and those beastly lawyers in Switzerland who thought that her personal life was their business. They could have been so happy, and someone else had judged that Andrew wasn't right for her, and so it was all over.

As though meeting her had been some diabolical plot . . . Caroline sighed heavily, remembering. She had been flying her first trip cross-country and she developed engine trouble, throw-

ing a rod. It would have spelled disaster were it not for the
small airfield she had found and where she had landed, and the
friendly young man who had helped her. It was his airfield. His
name was Andrew Starkey, and he loved flying almost as much
as she did.

No one could have engineered that accident. No one could
have predicted (or even followed) her flight plan. And yet later
they all said that Andrew had met up with her on purpose, had
seduced her, so that he—a Johnson—could infiltrate A.R.M. That
was what Eric had said when he explained it all to her. What a
stupid notion. They had taken Andrew away from her, and they
had sent her back east, and the only joy that she had left was
her flying. And then she married someone who seemed to want
to take that away from her, too.

Caroline shook her head and turned with her back to the rail,
leaning on it with her elbows. Andrew Starkey. He had been her
first love. With Andrew she had found that love was enticing,
exciting, an adventure. Caroline bit her lips. It had been an
adventure with Steven, too, at first, she reminded herself.

Eric had been firm, but gentle. The people who had financed
Andrew's restaurant, he had told her, were in competition with
A.R.M. And A.R.M. was, after all, partly hers, or would be
someday. Being with Andrew placed her in too vulnerable a
position, Eric had said. Even if—and it was clear, just the way
that he said it, that he didn't himself believe his own "even if"—
even if Andrew didn't have ulterior motives, then he, too, might
become vulnerable later on to pressures from those people.

Caroline had cried and cried. Andrew had nothing to do with
those people, she told Eric. Nothing to do with anything or anyone bad. He owned a restaurant in San Francisco, and he flew
airplanes, and he loved her. It was all really that simple.

Eric shook his head. He wished that it could be that simple,
really he did. But life was more complicated. Someday, he assured her, she would thank him. Someday she would understand
why things had to be this way. She was going back to Rhode
Island, he said, to take her rightful place at her grandmother's
house. She would meet someone else. Time would heal her.

But Caroline hadn't listened to him, resolving instead to run
away with Andrew. They would take an airplane and fly until no
one could find them, not ever again. They'd even planned on
flying the U.S. mail. Caroline closed her eyes and smiled. How
naive they had been, she thought. How incredibly naive, to think

that they could circumvent the company. What fools they were. . . .

She *had* gone to Andrew, but he had refused to see her. Had left her alone and humiliated outside of his door. He had responded to her telephone call with a cold brush-off, leaving an emptiness in Caroline's heart. He had refused to see her, and so numbly she had packed her bags and had gone to Newport, and Eric had soothed, "You'll see, Caroline, this is all for the best. Really it is."

But Caroline still hated the company that had made her give him up.

Quick footsteps on the observation deck, and she opened her eyes again. Andrew stood in front of her, his short dark hair standing up, his wide green eyes alive and full of questions, his neatly cut jacket flapping open. "Caroline . . . I hope you don't mind . . . I made excuses. I couldn't stay with them for dinner." That quick heart-stopping smile, part little boy, part man. "I haven't waited this many years to see you again to let you slip through my fingers quite this quickly."

Dazed, she found herself smiling. "I still have to go," she reminded him.

"Then let me fly with you."

"You don't even know where I'm going!"

"I don't even care where you're going."

Those were nearly the same words they had spoken together seven years ago when she had been forced into an emergency landing on his field and he had offered to drive her home. And now they were older and yet hardly any more sophisticated, and the words flowed as easily between them as if there had never been any separation at all.

Caroline laughed, and then lowered her eyes in embarrassment. "Just to San Jose. I'm staying with Eric."

"I see." His voice turned cold. "I'm glad to see that you two are getting along again after what he did."

Seeing the expression on Caroline's face, Andrew cleared his throat. "I'm sorry," he said. "It wasn't your fault."

"No, no." Caroline shook her head. "It *was* my fault. I shouldn't have left so quickly. I didn't want to. . . ."

"I know. Oh, God, I know. I let them strong-arm me, too." There was no reason to delve into it all. It wasn't Caroline's fault that Eric's men had bullied him into breaking up with her. They'd both been too young to understand the circumstances that had separated them. He glanced at his watch. "Listen, Caroline, any chance of catching a quick supper together before you leave? Here at the airport, I mean. The canteen food is awful, but maybe the company will make up for it."

She giggled. "I'd be delighted."

"Great." He held the door for her, and they went down the stairs together. "Is this a good time to point out how beautiful you've become?"

"Become?" She smiled teasingly. "What was I before?"

"Oh, you were pretty," Andrew conceded, not losing his composure. "But you seem different now. You've got more compassion in your face than you ever had before."

Caroline felt something catch in her throat. Damn it, this was no time to cry. . . . "I've missed you," she said huskily.

"And I, you." He said it simply and without any hidden meaning. "Ah, here we are. Will it be steak Diane or veal Marsala?"

"Hamburger," said the cook, standing behind the counter.

"Hamburger it is," Caroline said.

They sat at a plastic-topped table and drank coffee that was too strong and ate hamburgers that were too well done. "Are you happy in Rhode Island, with your husband?"

She lowered her eyes. "I'm content, I suppose, most of the time. We have a daughter, Elizabeth—she's wonderful. And I spend a lot of time flying. I have a new plane, a Butterfly, it's—"

"I know," he interrupted. "I've seen them."

"They're great. Eric gave it to me. My grandmother died, and we live in her house now. It's right by the ocean. Very pretty." Why on earth, she wondered, was she babbling so much? To keep from talking about Steven, and her disintegrating marriage? Andrew was getting married, too, soon. . . . "And you? Tell me about your fiancée."

He shrugged, rolling his empty coffee cup around and around between the palms of his hands. "Susan? Not much to tell. She's very pretty and bright. She works for the company now, but plans to quit after we're married. We've already picked out a house up on Nob Hill."

Caroline raised her eyebrows, remembering her afternoon of tranquillity. "Nice place. What company is that?"

"Johnson," Andrew said a bit sheepishly. "I work for them now. Have for a couple of years."

"I see," Caroline said, trying not to show her disappointment. "So in a sense we're still on opposite sides of the fence, aren't we?"

"Even more, I suppose. But not for the duration. They've signed a truce, or haven't you heard? Uncle Jeffrey and Eric Beaumont. We're working together for a while; it's the patriotic thing to do."

"Because of the war?"

"Well," Andrew said slowly, "it's sure as hell not because we decided to be democratic and share the playground on egalitarian principles."

Caroline laughed ruefully. "No, I suppose not. Silly of me. But the U.S. is neutral, hadn't you heard?"

"Not for long, if Uncle Jeffrey is right. And he usually is. He's got me working on something brand new, Caroline. It's very exciting."

"What's that?"

"Helicopters. A fellow called Igor Sikorsky is working for us now, and he's designed this incredible vertical flight machine. Just a couple of rotors instead of wings, they supply the lift. Can't go all that fast, needless to say, but it doesn't need a runway to take off or land, either."

Her eyes widened. "Good heavens, Andrew! The possibilities . . ."

"I know." He grinned. "I know."

There was a small, awkward silence, as each of them digested the enthusiasm they had so immediately and naturally shared, and its implications. "I think," Caroline said carefully, "that I should be going."

"Yes, of course."

"I don't think," she continued, "that either your Uncle Jeffrey or Eric would totally approve of our seeing each other again like this."

"I think you're right." He met her eyes. "But that's not going to stand in our way, is it?"

Caroline smiled. "What they don't know won't hurt them," she suggested.

"I do get down to San Jose occasionally," he said.

"And I really ought to bring Elizabeth to San Francisco from time to time," she added.

Andrew looked at her. "Is this a good idea?"

"No," said Caroline. "But let's do it anyway."

They parted without a wave, without a kiss, with hardly any words. It didn't matter. It wasn't good-bye, and they both knew it.

Chantale was in Angers when the news came.

She had gone into the city as she did once in a while, for errands that she preferred to supervise herself rather than entrust to one of the servants. Today she was ordering Catherine's christening gown, the long white lace garment that the baby would wear next month, in June, when the archbishop would perform the ceremony at the cathedral, but she was also there to get away from the oppressive atmosphere at the château. Marie-Louise had taken to bed with one of her spring colds, Pierre was nowhere to be found, and the rooms had seemed so dark and cold. Outside spring had come, a beautiful bright spring that beckoned her to revel in it. A day spent in Angers was just the antidote she needed.

Perhaps it was because of the spring, the first really warm day after weeks and weeks of cold, but Chantale had taken special care with her dressing this morning. Her long red tresses were neatly coiled in braids around her head, and she was wearing a new dress—a princess-style crepe with a narrow cinched waist, which made her feel younger, prettier, more attractive. She carried her hat and gloves; time to put them on if she needed to be proper, but she was feeling outrageously improper today.

She had driven herself in, against Marie-Louise's wishes, and had parked the car down at the place du Ralliement, across from the theater. She had dutifully performed her errands: had ordered the dress at the de Montclair dressmaker's, had picked up some medicine for Marie-Louise at the pharmacy, had stopped at a toy shop for an impromptu gift for Jean-Claude—a stuffed animal, a little lamb with frothy wool and imploring eyes. Chantale smiled and hummed to herself as she watched the clerk wrap it. Life, she decided, was good. On a day like this, life was very good indeed.

And then she had gone for a walk down by the river, passing the ramparts of the medieval castle which stood guard, and then up the boulevard de Roi René, past the statue, stopping to look in shop windows and to savor the spring air which, even here in town, was soft and light and caressing. The lilacs were out in profusion, spilling over walls and through fences with a heady scent.

When her feet started hurting she was already up near the city hall, so she stopped at the Café de la Mairie for something cool to drink, a peppermint Riqueles. The waiter served her with a smile, his eyes admiring her youth and her beauty, and Chantale found herself smiling in return. Pierre might not find her attractive, she thought, but, damn it, other men did. She hadn't lost her looks after all.

Sipping her carbonated drink, she watched the children playing in the small park across the street, children about Jean-Claude's age, and she found herself smiling. The sun was almost hot on the awning above her. Traffic passed by, with the windows of the cars rolled down for the first time that spring. People were smiling. Young girls walked by in twos and threes, their heavy winter coats shed, parading their new spring clothes and inviting admiration. Young men passing the other way turned to watch them go by. An old man paused near a tree to allow his dog to sniff out past acquaintances. The priest from the small neighborhood church paused to confer with two nuns standing at the corner.

It was, Chantale thought, like a tableau, a picture from one of her schoolbooks back at home, the ones that talked about culture and literature. This is France, it said, and Chantale, who knew only Brittany, had bent over and studied the illustrations. People, she thought, looked the same mostly. In Brittany the women wore lace caps, some of them close fitted, some rising up like a cloud of mist, depending upon the region, but that was the only difference. Children everywhere played and got dirty and priests talked to nuns on street corners and dogs sniffed at trees. This is France.

She smiled at the waiter and was at the point of ordering another Riqueles, and perhaps a sandwich to go with it, ham and Camembert cheese on a slab of fresh bread, when it happened.

The doors of the city hall next to the café opened and a stream of people started out of them. Executives, judges, secretaries, lawyers. The taxi banks in front of the building were quickly depleted as people jostled inside of them. Everyone in the café strained to see what was happening. This was clearly not the usual noontime rush to be free of the office.

One young man, impeccably attired in a double-breasted pin-striped suit and felt hat, came rushing over to the café. "Where is the telephone?" It was not a request, it was a shout.

The waiter gestured toward the back recesses of the café, and the young man rushed in. The girl who had been trailing behind him, dressed smartly as well with dark lipstick and a wool jacket over her arm, hesitated as she looked around her for a place to wait. The waiter pulled out a chair for her and she sat down, giving him a quick, distracted smile. "No, thank you, nothing to drink . . ." Her voice trailed off.

The waiter, seeking a reason for the disruption of his quiet café, asked her something. His back was to Chantale, and she couldn't hear what he was saying to her. The girl's response, however, was perfectly clear.

"Oh . . . we've just heard. It came across the wire just now . . ." She was shaken. Chantale thought that she probably did in fact need a drink very badly, and something stronger than a Riqueles. The girl took a deep breath. "The German Army has moved again . . . into Luxembourg, and Holland, and Belgium."

There was silence in the café, a stunned silence broken only by what now seemed to be the muted droning of traffic out on the boulevard Foch. Chantale found herself thinking, no, it's not possible, there has been nothing for so long, silence from the east; they had all thought that the war would end as quietly as it had begun.

"When?" someone asked, and the girl, with despair in her voice, said, "This morning."

Luxembourg, and Holland, and Belgium, all at once? They were the buffer countries between France and Germany. Chantale felt her throat constricting in panic. No, no, her mind kept repeating, over and over: No. It can't be. This is a nightmare, a horrible, horrible nightmare. "But they are neutral countries!" she managed to say, and the girl turned toward her. "Don't be silly," she said. "For the Germans, there is no such thing."

Chantale shook her head. "And France?" she asked. "The Maginot Line?" Everyone craned to listen to the reply.

"It's under attack," the girl replied, and pandemonium broke loose in the café, with shouting and crying and loud talk. Chantale placed some money—too much money, probably—on her small zinc-topped table and, gathering up her packages, left the café, walking quickly back down to the place du Ralliement where she had parked the car. The brightness had faded from the day.

The Maginot Line was under German attack. Holland to the

north, Belgium, their nearest neighbor, even tiny Luxembourg were being invaded. Chantale tried to remember what she had heard of the invasion of Poland, last fall. Airplanes, they had used airplanes. Fire raining down from the sky.

Before she opened the door of the Renault, Chantale paused, her foot on the running board, and crossed herself. It was beginning, the terrible thing that they had all wondered about was happening. In the place du Ralliement, people were walking about as though nothing had happened; they hadn't yet heard. Just as well, Chantale thought: Let them keep their moments of peace while they still have them. This is France.

As she drove away, she thought that she saw out of the corner of her eye Pierre emerging from a door next to the theater. But when she turned to look, there was no one there at all.

Chapter Eleven

*E*ric frowned at the letter in his hand and read it over again.

My dear M. Beaumont:

As you know, the German Army is nearly at our door. They have already invaded the Netherlands, and it is simply a matter of time before France falls as well. Very soon Irene and I will have to relocate our laboratory. We have plans to go to the United States, and to accept the hospitality and the facilities which you have so kindly offered to us. Indeed, by the end of the week, we shall be leaving on the chartered aircraft which you have left in Paris at our disposal, and we will be profoundly grateful to do so.

But another problem remains. The fall of Belgium into German hands means also that the Belgian territories will now be German controlled, and this includes the Belgian Congo. The Belgian Congo—specifically Shinkolobwe—is where our pitch blende ore is mined. It is sixty-five percent uranium oxide. We will never be able to find a source as pure again, M. Beaumont. Our experiments cannot proceed without a continued supply.

I am reliably informed that mining efforts could be stepped up in the next few weeks so that a significant supply of pitchblende could be available, but this supply would then have to be moved, preferably to the United States. I have no resources and no expertise in this matter. I therefore, once again, must appeal to you for help. You are the only person who can save these important experiments, M. Beaumont. Please advise as quickly as possible, for God only knows when the Germans will be knocking at our door.

With my most sincere sentiments,

                                    Frédéric Joliot-Curie

Eric frowned again and looked out the window of the airplane. Joliot-Curie had not asked the impossible, of course, but this mission was certainly filled with risk. Eric knew that the German Army was already traversing North Africa. Once they discovered what riches were to be found in the mines of the Congo, they would waste no time.

And he knew that there was no one to whom he could entrust this mission.

Young Asheford had finally proven himself useful; he could arrange for a steel ship to be ready and waiting at the mouth of the Congo River to accept a shipment of pitchblende, and of course he could arrange for passage through the southern Atlantic and up the Eastern Seaboard to Staten Island. Steven's tone had implied that Eric should know better than to even ask.

Eric arranged for air cover for the Asheford ship, in case of U-boats. A little overeager, that boy. He had a good head for business, of course. . . . Eric sighed. He was a little too much like himself, that was probably what he was saying. One day, Intraglobal would pass into Caroline's hands—or into Elizabeth's hands—and Steven would be part of more than just Asheford Shipbuilding. Very possibly it was high time to start making sure that Steven had the good corporate sense that he was going to need.

He would encourage the boy, Eric decided. Encourage him to learn, to expand. Through him Steven could learn more about the corporate world than he ever could in that little firm of his. He should come out to California, look over the Intraglobal compound, spend some days with Eric. Yes, as his partner, Edward, would have said in the good old days, that was the ticket. That's what he would do. Encourage Steven.

Below him, the ocean had given way to the plains of East Africa, and Eric regarded the large barren stretches, the sparse vegetation, the herds of animals running in one direction or another, with interest. Leopoldville had an airport, and a small delegation was there to meet him when he stepped off the plane: natives wearing long, flowing brightly colored robes, with small caps on their heads; a few Belgians, sweating in their business suits under the hot sun. One of them, grasping a briefcase in one hand, came panting up to Eric. "Monsieur Beaumont? I am

Hughes Deauville, in charge of the mines. Terrible weather we've been having, terrible. You'll want to rest, I think, and have something cool to drink. . . . This way, please . . ."

Eric followed him toward the terminal building. "Actually, I'd just as soon go directly out to Shinkolobwe if we can. There's a lot to organize, and—"

"Of course, of course," Deauville panted. He was very short and overweight, and would have looked far more at home in a boardroom in Brussels than on the tarmac at Leopoldville. "Just this way, Monsieur Beaumont. A few customs formalities, and we can be on our way. Permit me to offer you some refreshment while we wait. Joseph! Ho! Joseph!" He called after one of the tall black men, who apparently was putting Eric's baggage in the wrong compartment on the bus outside the terminal. "Can't trust him to do anything on his own. Joseph!" He mopped his forehead and turned to Eric with a nervous smile. "Please, Monsieur Beaumont, just a moment, I beg of you," and then he was off to chastise the unhappy Joseph.

Eric removed his hat and looked around at the vast central hall of the airport. As he did, a shadow detached itself from the wall nearby. "I heard that you were coming in person to look at the mines," said a familiar voice in his ear. "Imagine my surprise to see that it is true."

He turned slowly, but he knew already.

It was Amanda.

He wondered later why he had expected her to have changed more than she had. Perhaps because *he* had; perhaps because most people, given twenty years and a number of experiences, do undergo fundamental changes. But not Amanda.

"Eric, darling, isn't it too coincidental that we should meet up like this? I heard rumors, of course, but one plays with rumors, one doesn't take them seriously. And yet here you are, so perhaps I shall have to change my mind about rumors, after all."

"Hello, Amanda," he said slowly.

She had changed in her appearance. Of course even Amanda couldn't keep the years totally at bay. She was fifty, after all, and there were lines around her eyes, her mouth, faint tracings of gray in the fine blond hair. But she was still beautiful; nothing could change that. Her hair, neatly trapped under the hat, was probably still long, he guessed. Her turquoise eyes were startlingly exquisite, alive; they had not been dulled by age. She wore a pale blue dress with a cinched-in waist that emphasized her trim figure; her shoes and hat were of a deeper blue. Always fashionable, always flamboyant. She stood out in that dull airport terminal like a wildflower blooming on a snow-covered hill.

She didn't try to kiss him, but simply stood there and continued to talk. That was Amanda, too. "I heard you were looking for me—really, Eric, dear, you must learn to be more discreet about such things, the communication here is truly excellent and Europeans always seem to bungle things so, or so I'm assured by my staff. And, speaking of which, I thought that you might not have eaten lunch yet. Have you?"

"No," he said, as ever dazed by her stream of conversation. It wasn't yet eleven in the morning.

"Well, then, you simply must give Hughes the slip and come out to the house. He's a dear little man, Hughes is, and has such a reputation with the ladies, don't you know, but he's tiresome. And I do so want you to tell me about Caroline, and I don't want to start any rumors about her, so we'll have to do without him, because he is absolutely the worst person to entrust a secret to."

Eric cleared his throat. "Amanda—it's true that I've been trying to find you. Caroline wanted to be in touch. But I have some business to do, and not much time in which to do it, and—"

"Oh, those silly mines? Don't look so astonished, Eric, darling, it's *hardly* a secret that you're here to cart away all that magical ore before the nasty Germans arrive to take possession. You see, there are no secrets here." Amanda was starting to get impatient. "Hughes can handle that. He's stunningly good at moronic tasks like moving ore. I live an hour out of Leopoldville, darling Eric, and by the time lunch is over you can go out and supervise the rest of the loading to your heart's content. And you see how docile I am being about letting you know where I live, so do accept that as a peace offering and come have lunch with me."

Eric shrugged. "All right, Amanda." And she was right: The loading would take all day. He would have to eat somewhere, and now he would have—finally—an answer for Caroline.

Amanda smiled brightly. "Good. Go tell Hughes to do what he does best, and tell him I'll give you a driver to take you out to Shinkolobwe after lunch, and I'll be waiting outside in the car."

The car, as it transpired, was a Daimler, and Amanda sat in solitary splendor in the backseat, having added several gauze scarves to her outfit in the meantime. The driver, a stoical-looking black man, was silent for the entire journey, and Eric soon saw the point of Amanda's scarves. "Is it always this dusty?" he asked along the way.

"Not during the rainy season," she replied laconically.

Amanda's house was predictably large, built for the place and the climate but with every comfort seen to. Wide porches encircled the house, and large open windows accommodated themselves to any passing breeze. A small army of servants, all of them natives, scurried back and forth as soon as they saw Amanda, and Eric wondered if she terrorized them as much as she had terrorized the servants at the estate in Newport. Certainly they gave every appearance of being frightened of her.

She indicated that he should sit on the front porch. In the back of the house there was a veritable jungle, with cultivated fields and barns on the west side. But the front overlooked the plain—endless, flat land punctuated by the occasional plane tree, its spreading branches affording what little protection there was from the hot sun.

Eric sat in a rush-covered chair and crossed one leg over the other, looking out at the sweeping view. Amanda had disappeared inside, and he fingered the half-empty bottle sitting on the rattan table.

Her voice called out from behind him: "I was going to offer you some wine or beer. But if you would prefer the whiskey, there are glasses next to you." She walked past him, and he could smell her perfume, the same heavy floral scent she had always worn. He hadn't smelled it in years. He closed his eyes for a moment, and was transported back, back to the house on the rue de Verdun, where Sarah and Philippe and Amanda and he had lived, just before the war. . . .

Amanda was sitting across from him, watching him. A shadow of anxiety touched her face. "Are you all right?"

Eric opened his eyes. "Yes. Yes, of course. I'd prefer a beer, if it's all the same to you." He gestured with the bottle. "Too hot for this."

She motioned to the servants behind him. "Some people find the hot weather trying," she agreed. She had changed into white, a dress that was airy and ethereal-looking, loose and yet beguiling. He had been right about her hair. With the hat off, he could see the intricate pattern of curls and braids atop her head. It was still long, and still beautiful.

Amanda clasped her hands in her lap and looked at him. "So. I hear many marvelous things about the company."

Eric shrugged and waited until the black man in the striped robe had placed a glass of beer in front of him, a bottle of champagne and a glass in front of Amanda. "There's a lot of work to be done," he said briefly.

"So I gather." She watched the servant pour the champagne into the glass, and then waved her hand at him. "Thank you, Mmbago," she said. "That is all."

Eric took a swallow of the beer. It was cold and caressed his dry throat. "You knew that I was looking for you. Why didn't you contact me?"

She smiled, the same coquettish smile he remembered. "Why on earth should I, Eric? Just because you wanted to see me? Did that mean that I should want to see you?"

"It wasn't me," he said irritably. "It was Caroline—and your mother."

A shadow crossed her face. "Ah, yes, my mother," she said, and drank half the glass of champagne. Eric found himself wondering, irrelevantly, if she had begun to drink too much. "My mother whose dying wish was to see me one last time. Was that it, Eric?"

"It seems," he said stiffly, "that I have nothing new to tell you."

"So you don't." She drank the rest of her champagne and poured a fresh glass. "My mother," she went on, "who probably spoke of making peace with me after all these years. Who wanted her darling daughter by her side so that she could relinquish life gracefully, having fulfilled all her obligations. And poor, dear Caroline believed her."

"Caroline," Eric said, "was upset."

"Caroline," said Amanda, "has always been, and will always be, hopelessly naive. Let me guess the rest of the scenario, Eric, darling. My mother's dying wishes were to see me, and to have Caroline promise to move into the house on Ocean Drive. And Caroline, distressed that she couldn't find me, decided that the very least she could do for a dying woman was make that promise. And her husband didn't mind one bit, did he? It isn't too hard to settle for an estate and cars and servants. . . . Well? How did I do?"

Eric looked at her steadily over his glass of beer. "Not bad."

"You see?" She sipped her champagne daintily and smiled

at him. "I know Caroline, Eric, I know what she needs. If I had gone to her, she would have wanted me to stay. And Caroline will be much more proper there than I would have been, don't you think?"

"Caroline," Eric said, "is more independent than you give her credit for being."

"Is she? How delightful! Then she may survive. I wouldn't have, Eric. Not there. Not again."

He gestured around him, toward the empty plains. "And how do you survive here, Amanda? I wouldn't have thought it possible."

She drank some champagne, watching him steadily. "Perhaps because no one thought it possible." She smiled then, a secret smile, and gestured dismissively. "Oh, that's silly, of course. But, Eric"—and her eyes became dreamy—"there's something here, something that I can't define . . . the natives *sing*, Eric, when they work the fields for us. They sing . . . and it's the echo of Africa. Not of us, the Europeans who have been here for a few years and have tried so hard to impress them with our machines and our knowledge, but of the heart of Africa. They know something, Eric, that we don't. There's some secret in their songs, and in the drums, at night. They'll be talking about you, tonight, the drums will." She smiled again and sipped some more champagne. "You must be surprised to hear me sounding so—mystical. But can you understand why I couldn't give this up?" She gestured to the scenery around her. "Not to go back to Newport, and all that . . . I couldn't be the person my mother hoped I'd be. And I knew that Caroline could."

"I'm not so sure that she can."

"Well, then, that's her responsibility, isn't it? Not mine. I have my life."

He shook his head. "That's always been your attitude, hasn't it? This is your life, and you can do what you want with it."

Amanda wasn't insulted; she only smiled. "Of course it has, Eric! Is that so very strange?" She leaned forward, across the small table toward him. "Eric, I live in the present, not in the past. You've made a reputation for yourself, for being the man with an eye to the future, and no eye for the ladies. But why? Because you run a company that you promised a dead friend you'd run, and because you love a woman who died before you had time to get tired of her. No, don't interrupt me. I can't live like that. I need to live now, not in some mausoleum in Newport. My life now is here. And I'm happy. Is it so very wrong to be happy?''

Eric shook his head. "But you have obligations."

"To whom?" She smiled. "To myself, Eric. To my husband." She sipped more champagne, watching his face. "Don't worry, darling, you shan't meet him. He's out hunting. I elected for once to stay behind." She took a deep breath. "And if you're talking about Philippe, then no, I have no more obligations. His daughter is an adult, in charge of her own life. I might have been a better mother to her, yes, but now is hardly the time to do penance for that! He's been dead for over *twenty years,* Eric. And I loved him. Differently than you loved Sarah, yes, but I loved him more than I've ever loved, before or since. I loved him, but he's dead, and I'm not. And life, to make use of a dreadful truism, does go on."

"Do you love your husband?"

"Julian?" She leaned back again in her chair, perfectly at ease. "He's a dear, and yes, darling, I do love him. Not as I loved Philippe, but I was a different person then."

Eric finished his beer. "I see. And so you stay here with him. Aren't you even curious to see Caroline—or Elizabeth? Your granddaughter?"

She smiled. "Dear Eric. You're still so concerned about family ties, aren't you? No, frankly, I'm not. Caroline has her life. Presumably Elizabeth will have hers. It's not really my concern. Is that concept so very foreign to you, darling? It's not that I don't care. I wish them both well. But my life is here now."

"Not for much longer." Eric leaned forward. "What will you do when the Germans arrive?"

She shrugged. "They're not interested in the farms. It's the mines they want, all that lovely ore to make their war machines back home. They'll leave us alone."

The same servant was in the doorway. "Please—lunch is ready."

Amanda smiled again, reverting to her old self. "There, darling, we'll have something to eat and you'll feel much better about all this." She stood up, and she was steadier than he thought she would be in view of the amount of alcohol she had consumed. "Do let me take your arm, and we'll have lunch and you can tell me all the gossip, and then you can be off to Shinkolobwe to save the mines. . . ."

* * *

Caroline had been home three days. To her, they had been interminable. She was confused, so confused, and she had been so sure that coming back to Newport would make everything—clearer, somehow. More readily understood . . .

California had been just as she remembered it, only more so. California would always be, in her mind, a little larger than life. Bright and brilliant and filled with promise. In California, it was possible to believe that anything could happen. Anything. Miracles were waiting just around the corner, dreams were meant to happen. And Andrew was inexplicably part of all that. Part of a general feeling that the impossible might actually be possible. That she could turn back time and a fantasy that nothing bad had happened between them, that there had been no anger and no fear and no hurt, just the same easy comfort of each other. Andrew seemed to believe that life was as easy or as difficult as one chose to make it, and, for a while, Caroline had been lulled by his attitude into some similar thoughts of her own.

She had almost believed that their old love could be rekindled. As if the past few years hadn't happened. She had enjoyed it. And felt guilty doing so. All the time spent with Andrew was marvelous, especially after he told her the truth about the end of their relationship, that Eric had made him leave, that until Eric interfered he had really planned on eloping with her, after all. Caroline had relaxed, after that, feeling that perhaps she could trust Andrew again. But it was as if everything was too easy, too comfortable, too fast. There were none of the conflicts that marked her relationship with Steven, none of the doubts, none of the questions. She wanted the laughter, of course, but after all she'd experienced how could she trust it?

She had to go back to Newport, she thought. Go back to Newport, and see if the love she had pledged to Steven couldn't work out in the real world. Because if it didn't work out, then she wasn't quite convinced that she was capable of making anything work.

Now she sat and plucked grapes from a bowl and continued to needle Steven. If he wasn't going to be a fairy-tale prince, then he damned well was going to prove to her just how human he could be; and she felt herself being deliberately provocative.

"Jesus." Steven stood up, ran a hand rapidly through his hair, and strode over to the window, his back to her, hands in his back pockets. "What is it you want from me, Caroline?" Before Caroline could answer, he continued, breathing rapidly, "I told you. I told you that nothing good would come of you running off to California like that! I told you to come home at Christmas! But no! Miss-I'm-Confused needed more time to sort things out!" He turned to face her. "Sort things out! What the hell does that mean, Caroline?"

"I don't know." She knew that she was sounding stubborn and petulant, and she didn't know how to respond to him in a way that wouldn't sound that way. "Maybe we both need to think about divorce," she said in a low voice.

He didn't speak to her for the rest of the evening.

She telephoned Andrew, timing the call so that Steven was out of earshot, surreptitiously talking from the kitchen extension. "I miss you."

"Caroline! Where are you calling from?"

"Newport. I just—" The tears were there, and she blinked hard to keep them out of her eyes and out of her voice. "I just wanted to hear you. I just wanted to talk to you."

"Are you all right?" There was concern in his voice.

"Yes. No." She took a deep breath. "I'm just confused. I'm still so confused. I didn't think that life was going to be like this."

"Why don't you come back out here? If you don't want to stay with Eric, I've got plenty of space."

Move in with Andrew? Caroline hesitated. Was that the answer that she was looking for? But even though in those last wonderful weeks in California when she had seen him almost every day, they had not so much as touched each other. They had talked, they had laughed, they had even gone flying together, soaring over the wild beautiful jagged coast as they had in the old days when they were still in love with each other. . . . But they had never touched. She was married; he was engaged. And that, Caroline told herself fiercely, was that. Whatever her problems with Steven, she was going to have to work them out with Steven. Running away to Andrew wasn't the answer.

Though at this moment, it would feel so good . . .

"No," she said instead. It had been foolish of her to call him. "I have things to do here. I just wanted to say hello."

"It's good to hear your voice. I miss you. Come back soon."

"Yes," she said automatically. "Good-bye."

And she wondered, as she hung up the telephone and weakly sat down, staring blankly out across the vast empty kitchen, where her answer finally would be.

* * *

They made the first flight on the morning that they learned that France was officially occupied by the Germans.

The first flight that worked, Andrew Starkey reminded himself. There had been others. There was a fresh grave and a grieving widow to mark one of the other flights. Test pilots weren't known for their long life spans. But this one had worked; this one at last had worked.

He, Andrew, had flown in a helicopter—an airplane without wings. He had taken off and landed without benefit of a runway. He had flown, like a hummingbird, straight up and straight down. It was a heady sensation.

Afterward, he sat in the lounge at the Johnson test airfield, drinking a beer and smiling, going over the flight in his mind. It had been fantastic. And the possibilities, as Caroline had said, were endless. Most airplane accidents happened when the plane was taking off or landing—those times when the plane was traveling at high speeds close to the ground and the pilot had many things to occupy his mind and hands at once. And now he had an answer—a solution. The helicopter.

Andrew took a mouthful of beer. Of course, there were problems. Speed was one of them. The lift and propulsion were coming from a wing, just as with an airplane, but the helicopter wing wasn't fixed and straight, it rotated. That significantly reduced the speed that it could attain. Still, they would work on it. He was confident they would iron out the kinks somehow.

Into this wave of euphoria walked Jeffrey Kellogg.

"Been looking for you, boy," he said, sitting down heavily across from Andrew and reaching into an inner pocket for his pipe. "Seems you're spending all your time down here these days."

Andrew smiled. "Have a drink," he suggested. "It's on me."

Jeffrey lifted an eyebrow. "Celebrating something?"

"Only a successful flight." Andrew pointed out through the big plate-glass window to where the helicopter stood. Hard to believe that only an hour ago it had risen into the air. . . .

"Great. No, no drink, thanks." Jeffrey filled his pipe with tobacco and carefully tamped it down. "Andrew, I want to transfer you to another department."

"What?" The smile faded. "Why?"

"This helicopter business is great, don't get me wrong. But it seems to me that we can best use your skills elsewhere. Other people can do what you've been doing here." He applied the first match to the pipe. Experience told him that this was the one least likely to succeed. "We'll just put Sikorsky on hold, for now."

"Why? Uncle Jeffrey, I don't understand—"

"Well, the war in Europe is firing up again, and we need to focus all our efforts on fighter planes just now. And I need you."

Andrew sat still. He had been trying so hard not to think about the war. He had thought that by immersing himself in this new project he might care about nothing but this helicopter. As though he could ignore the horror, pretend that it wasn't really happening. The Germans were taking over Europe, and his uncle wanted him to build fighter planes. Well, it made sense. But damn it all, why weren't they doing more? Why weren't they going to help the French? Would they finally wake up when the Germans marched into New York and Washington and Los Angeles?

Jeffrey finally had the pipe going, and he sat back in his chair. "See, I've been hearing things from over at Intraglobal. I think that Beaumont's developed a jet engine for airplanes. He's not saying anything, damn him, but we have our sources. I don't want him getting ahead of us."

Andrew stared at his uncle. "You're more concerned about Eric Beaumont than you are about the war?"

"Well, of course I am. Wars come and go, Andrew, but companies remain. Cooperation or no cooperation, I want Johnson to be on top when this thing is over."

"I see." And he did see. He saw the future spreading out in front of him as futile as the present. This was going to be his life—an endless competition with someone to be ahead, to stay ahead, to be more rich and more powerful and more competitive. An endless series of small and large intrigues, of projects undertaken not for their own sakes but for the company, of important ideas ignored because they didn't fit in with the Grand Plan. And it didn't matter, he realized suddenly, it didn't matter to people like Jeffrey Kellogg and Eric Beaumont whom they hurt in the process. It didn't matter to them whether or not the Germans occupied France, any more than it had mattered whether he and Caroline were happy or not. Nothing mattered but the companies. He was being asked to work on jet fighters not because they should be developed, or because they were needed to keep the cause of freedom alive in Europe, but because Intraglobal was doing it, and Johnson had to be on top of Intraglobal. This is your life, Andrew, he told himself grimly.

Jeffrey was almost finished. "The issue is the combustion chamber. My understanding is that Beaumont's people have designed a new one—more efficient. I'd like you to look into it, Andrew. Find out what he's doing and get our people on it. I'll leave all the material that you need with your secretary."

Andrew nodded, still preoccupied with his own thoughts. Jeffrey knocked his pipe on the ashtray and put it back in his pocket. "Well, I'm glad that we had this talk," he said, standing up. "Don't see enough of each other these days. How is that young lady of yours, anyway? We should get together sometime. Have dinner."

"That would be nice."

"Great. Great. I'll have my girl arrange it with yours." He paused. "I'm counting on you, Andrew. Don't let me down."

Andrew raised his eyes to his uncle. "Whatever you think is right."

Finishing his beer, Andrew walked out of the lounge, his leather flying jacket slung over his shoulder, thinking, and what he thought was that Jeffrey Kellogg was wrong. Eric Beaumont was wrong. They were playing games like children, each of them trying to build his sand castle a little bit higher than the other, ignoring everything else as though it didn't exist. But the world existed. People existed. People fought and loved, laughed and cried, gave birth and wrote songs and baked bread and, sometimes, died: And they were what mattered. The people. Specifically, the people in Europe whose freedom to do all those things was being taken away, even now, and no one seemed to give a damn because they were too busy making money.

He got in his car—a new 1940 Chevrolet—and kept following that train of thought. Susan, his fiancée, would say that Eric Beaumont and Jeffrey Kellogg were right. Susan, Andrew knew, loved him because he was with Johnson Industries, and she had been taught that Johnson Industries was the wave of the future. They had met when he first started working for Johnson, after he had closed the restaurant in the Mission District because it reminded him too much of Caroline and had given in to his family's pressure to bring his college education and his flying skills to Johnson. Susan McCarthy didn't fly, but she was good with numbers and was assigned to the aviation department to oversee their costs, and she was pretty enough to catch his eye. It had made sense to ask her out, from time to time, and things just seemed to progress on their own, from the regular dates to the unstated agreement to make the relationship exclusive to the final—and it seemed inevitable—announcement of their engagement.

Once or twice Andrew had spoken to her about getting out, about going back to running his own small business. Susan had been shocked. "But that's silly, darling," she said, talking to him as she would to a little boy. "You got that out of your system, didn't you? Johnson is much more secure." They had almost gotten married last year, when Susan thought that she was pregnant, and her pressure increased for him to stay. "But, darling, I'll be leaving Johnson once the baby comes, and you'll have to stay there for both of us then." And then her period came, and Andrew thankfully delayed the wedding, but he knew what she needed, what she expected of him. Once he began working with Sikorsky, he didn't mind; the excitement was enough to hook him. He would stay with Johnson, he decided, as long as he could keep doing things like this.

But Jeffrey was letting him know that independence wasn't part of his contract. Nor was creativity. What counted, what mattered most, was loyalty. Loyalty not to progress or to the industry, but to Johnson. To allow himself to do not what *he* wanted, but what Johnson wanted of him. Susan would say that made sense.

And then he remembered something Caroline had said: "The important thing is to feel good about yourself. I seem to spend most of my life trying to feel good about myself—about what I'm doing, what kind of contribution I'm making." Caroline was telling him what was essential—not production, not overcoming a rival company, but feeling good about himself.

If Andrew went to work on jet-propulsion problems with the sole desire to make better jet engines than Intraglobal did, then he wouldn't feel very good about himself. He knew it with absolute certainty, and in knowing that, he knew already that he wasn't going to do it. He was going to disappoint Uncle Jeffrey. And he knew that, in the process, he was going to lose Susan.

He didn't feel terrible about any of it.

Chapter Twelve

Chantale shifted her seat on the kitchen bench and watched Annie as she shelled peas. "But how were they evacuated?" she asked, absently picking up one of the pods and digging out the sweet hard peas inside with her fingernail.

"By boat, Countess. The Royal Navy, or so I hear it's called."

"I see." Chantale tossed the peas into a bowl and brushed off her hands. "So it's really all over now."

The British were gone. Evacuated from Dunkirk in the north in a scant five days. The British Army had given such hope to the French, had made them believe—had made her believe—that they could stand free and strong against the invaders on the coast. Virtually trapped, the British had retreated to England. Now they were on their own, and, already, everyone knew that the Maginot Line hadn't held, that there were Germans in Alsace and Lorraine and that it was only a matter of time before they would occupy Paris. Annie—who was remarkably well informed, even in those early days—said that the government was thinking of relocating.

"Where?"

"Who knows, Countess? Tours, perhaps. Or even somewhere farther south, I've heard talk of Bordeaux. Everyone has an idea."

The French Army was no match for the Germans. The military had been scarcely mobilized when Belgium was invaded: and most of the soldiers had sat underground in the long concrete passages of the Maginot Line, smoking and playing cards and waiting for the assault that had never come. The German fighter planes had simply flown over the blockades, and the line wasn't equipped with antiaircraft artillery. The French had been expecting a repeat of the Great War, assaults on foot and horseback. It was a new war this time, with new weapons, weapons that hissed and flew. They were totally unprepared for the airplanes and the tanks that did come, and the result was inevitable.

Already there were stories of refugees, people leaving their homes with whatever possessions they could carry, running from the Germans. "They're all going to Paris," Annie said, shaking her head over her peas. "It won't do them any good. Paris is what the dirty *Boches* want, not some little village. They'd do best to stay in their villages."

"Don't the Germans want the villages, too?"

"Countess, the Germans want everything."

The trains had stopped. They had heard that, already, from Pierre, who still spent more time in Angers than out at the château. On June eighth, the trains from Paris were on time; on the tenth, they were almost eighteen hours late. By the eleventh, there were no trains running.

Chantale shivered. She knew so little of the Great War; she had been a baby at the time. She knew nothing of these people who were coming, only the rumors that she heard, which were terrible enough. At night she would lie awake thinking about it, about the inexorable march that was coming from the east, knowing that every day was bringing the Germans closer. Sometimes panic would descend on her then, like a smothering dark blanket, and, gasping for breath, she would run from her room to the nursery to see that Jean-Claude and Catherine were all right. They always were, but her imagination painted dark shadows on their walls. One of the rumors affirmed that the Germans ate babies.

Annie shook her head over the people fleeing from the east, but Chantale understood them. Alone at night, she sometimes felt a great urge to simply run: to pack her bags and take her children and run away. Annie said that there was nowhere to run, but Chantale thought about her home in Brittany, the stone château by the ocean. Surely the Germans would not want it. Surely they would be safe there; she had always been safe there from all her childhood fears.

When she was a little girl, Chantale had slept in a heavy four-poster bed with dark tapestries all around it. Her father had fancied himself something of a medievalist, and had decorated his home accordingly. It was a large bed, set well off the floor, and Chantale knew, knew deep in her heart, that monsters lurked under that bed. Sometimes, climbing into it at night, she could almost feel their heavy paws and sharp claws reaching out to

grab her feet and pull her under with them. At night she knew
that it was their heavy breathing she heard, even through the
sounds of the wind and the sea.

The only light switch in the room was beside the door, far
from the bed, and at night she had to turn off her own light, for
her governess lived in the village and was not there in the evenings to care for her. She would carefully turn down the covers,
and then walk softly over to the door, her hand ready to turn the
knob that would extinguish the light. Everyone knew that the
monsters were afraid of the light. She would take a deep, deep
breath, turn the knob, and hurl herself across the room. When
she was good she could do it in three strides. She jumped into
the bed and pulled the covers up over her face and lay very, very
still, so as not to attract them, but she could still hear their
breathing, smell the awful stink of their breath.

Chantale had lived with the monsters for all the years of her
childhood. Now she could feel them coming closer. Every night
they were nearer to her and her children. They were the same,
with their terrible breath and sharp claws. The only difference
was that now they had a name.

Marc Giroux lay down the telephone and stared off into the
middle distance. Robert Beneteau, busily spreading butter and
marmalade on his croissant, finally noticed his colleague's silence. "What is it, Marc?"

Giroux roused himself with an effort. "It's begun," he whispered. "By God, it's begun."

Beneteau put down the croissant, his interest focusing and his
attention sharpening at once. "What of the government?" he
asked.

"Paul Reynaud's gone to Tours for the time being. Route Na-
tionale Twenty is clogged with people leaving the city. The Germans are expected momentarily." Giroux shrugged. "It's what
we expected," he said, more for his own benefit than for Beneteau's.

"Of course it is." Beneteau nodded. "And we're ready. We
ought to contact Beaumont, though. I'll get Marie-Laure to send
a telegram." He rubbed his hands together thoughtfully. "They
won't be in Angers for a few days yet, even if they're in Paris
by tonight."

"No," Giroux agreed. But all that he could see was the road
out of Paris, and the lines of people in their cars and on their

bicycles, leaving before the Germans arrived. His people. His people.

"I am exceedingly distressed, Mr. Beaumont, about this letter. Perhaps you can shed some light on the situation."

Eric leaned forward and took the paper from the hand of the President. "From Dr. Einstein," he said, lifting his eyebrows slightly.

"Yes." Roosevelt nodded. "He thinks that the Germans are going to be able to manufacture an atomic bomb. An atomic bomb! What an ungodly device!"

Eric tossed the letter back on the table. "So they might," he said.

"Well, we can't have it. See here, Beaumont, I can't get involved in that skirmish over there. But we can't have the Nazis with an atomic bomb, either. Can we make one first?"

Eric stifled a desire to smile. "Well," he said, "we might. But we'd need some money."

"Seems to me that you're always needing money."

"There's never enough of it, Mr. President."

"Hmm. And how are we going to go about doing this?"

Eric coughed delicately. "Well, sir, what I would propose would be to set up a laboratory, somewhere isolated, and gather some of the scientists in this country and in Europe who have been thinking about this, independently, for some time. I've been in correspondence with several of them already, sir. And we have some of the raw materials ready, too. I went to Africa recently to—"

The President held up his hand. "Enough. I don't want any details. Not yet. You think that you can get these people, Beaumont?"

"I think so, Mr. President," Eric said modestly.

"All right. I like the idea of a laboratory. But top secret, Beaumont! We can't have it getting about that we're working on an atomic bomb."

"No, sir."

"And we can't have the Germans doing it first. It would be the end of civilization as we know it. Carry on, Beaumont."

"Yes, sir."

Roosevelt turned his back to Eric. "I'm signing an executive order," he said, "to establish a National Defense Research Committee. It only makes sense now that Paris is occupied. I don't think that we're going to be able to stay out of the war much longer, though God knows I'll hold out as long as I can.'' He turned around, a wry smile on his face. ''It's an election year, Mr. Beaumont. I have to stay popular.''

Eric stretched out his legs. ''Are you sure that the war won't become popular?'' he asked softly.

''On the contrary, as you yourself might say, I think that it will. But not yet.'' He shook his head. ''Anyway, it's time we started getting ready. I think that Congress is already talking about mobilization, so it may well be out of my hands soon in any case. But the point is, I'm making some of that money you want available. You can't have the whole pot, of course. I want all sorts of weapons research, not just this infernal bomb idea. But I suppose that you're on to other things, anyway, aren't you?''

Eric allowed himself a smile. ''I expect,'' he said carefully, ''that Intraglobal will be in competition for most phases of weapons research.''

''I thought so.'' Roosevelt sighed. ''Aren't you monopolizing things a little?''

''Hardly. There is room for everyone to compete.'' Eric's tone was bland.

''Hmm. Well, as it stands, the NDRC will be starting up in the next few weeks, so get your proposals ready. We've got to apply our minds to winning this war, once we're in it.''

''Of course, Mr. President.''

Eric was humming when he left the White House. He had been applying himself to it for some time.

''I'd like to know exactly what happened.''

Robert Beneteau looked expectantly around the conference table on the second floor of the law offices. They were all there— his people. The junior partners that he and Marc Giroux had so painstakingly assembled to advance the fortunes of Intraglobal and protect the interests of the de Montclair family.

And now he was asking them for an accounting.

Beneteau cleared his throat. ''The German Fifth Army entered Paris on Saturday,'' he said. ''The government was already gone. The swastika was immediately placed on the Arc de Triomphe and the Eiffel Tower.'' There was a movement in the room when he said that: not a sound, not a rustle, more like a common thought uniting all the minds present. Françoise Duroc found herself shivering, as though taken by surprise by a sudden wind or an old ghost. But there was no wind.

"The provisional government is in Tours, but they expect to be moving on to Bordeaux if the German movement out of Paris goes that way," said Jean-Claude Trezeres. "I'm in contact with one of Reynaud's cabinet members. I'll stay on top of the situation."

"Of course they'll go that way," said Rousseau.

"What about the army?" asked Giroux.

"They're still behind the Germans—there was a concentration of troops at the Maginot Line; they're still retrenching from that," said Françoise Duroc. "The British evacuation from Dunkirk was a tremendous affair, and a number of Frenchmen went with them. It was felt best to get to England and continue fighting from there." She looked up from her papers. "Morale is extremely low. Everybody's saying patriotic things, but no one really believes that the war can be won. Not now. Not with Paris occupied."

"The losses are tremendous, too. The French," said Jean-Claude, "have lost over four hundred airplanes in the past two weeks."

"Intraglobal airplanes?" asked Giroux.

"Indirectly. Through the French subsidiaries." Jean-Claude cleared his throat. "Shot down by the German Intraglobal subsidiary airplanes."

Françoise Duroc raised her eyebrows. "Playing both sides," she murmured, but when Giroux looked at her sharply, she shook her head. "Nothing."

"What about the family?" asked Beneteau, and everyone turned to look at Soizic.

She dampened her lips nervously, as she did every time that she needed to speak in front of more than two people. "Pierre de Montclair is spending most of his free time with his mistress in Angers," she said without looking at her notes. "He is extremely fearful that he will be conscripted to military service and seems to feel that the less time spent at the château, the better for him."

"He doesn't know, then, that we've arranged for him to be exempted?" asked Jean-Claude Trezeres.

Soizic shook her head. "He doesn't know that we're involved at all."

Giroux cleared his throat. "That was my idea," he said. "Best for the family to think they're on their own. When Soizic went to see them last year, she said she was an insurance adjuster. If we're to keep them in the dark about Intraglobal—and Monsieur Beaumont is adamant on that point—then it's better for us to maintain as low a profile with them as possible.''

Soizic continued, ''It's not yet clear what position Marie-Louise de Montclair will take. Her sentiments are clearly anti-German, mostly because of the death of her husband during the Great War. I don't know how far she will go.''

Rousseau raised his eyebrows. ''How far she will go? Meaning exactly what?''

Soizic shrugged. ''We have to assume,'' she said, ''that with German occupation there will be some sort of resistance movement. We're already seeing it in Poland and Belgium; France will be no exception. It would be extremely dangerous for anyone in the de Montclair family to participate, but we have to be aware of the potential.''

''And is there one?''

''Possibly. Not from the family, directly, but from the household. The family cook, Annie Savoyard, is already part of a network in Angers and the immediate area. Their current goal is communication, but I don't think that we need to maintain any illusions that it will stop there. Like Marie-Louise, her husband was killed in the last war.''

''Would there be reprisals if her actions were discovered?''

Giroux cleared his throat. ''Not for the family, I think. And in any case, we have the family covered, don't we?''

Jean-Claude Trezeres nodded. ''Right. There won't be any occupation of the château by the Wehrmacht—they're government, and the government is answering to the Deutsches Bank these days. The Gestapo—we've got that covered, too. I don't think that there will be a problem. If there is, we know where to place pressure.''

''Fine. We know what is going to happen, ladies, gentlemen. Let's not be unprepared.'' Giroux looked at Beneteau. ''Anything else for now?''

Françoise turned to Soizic. ''You don't mention Chantale de Montclair. Is she so insignificant?''

''She spends time with the servants at the château. She may or may not be aware of the cook's activities.''

''And where would she stand?'' Françoise's tone was catty.

"She's a Breton, don't forget. As a Breton, you must understand her mind. How will she respond to occupation?"

Soizic closed her folder. "As far as the Bretons are concerned, we are occupied already and have been for several centuries. I wouldn't make the mistake of thinking, Françoise, that any Breton considers himself a Frenchman first."

"Yes," Françoise said, still watching Soizic. "I'll remember that."

The first refugees arrived in Angers three days after the Germans marched into Paris.

Chantale de Montclair had trouble sleeping that night. She was dreaming again, dreaming of the monsters in their dark uniforms, dreaming that they were taking her children away from her. She woke up, her linen sheets drenched with sweat, and lay for a few minutes watching the shadows on the wall and telling herself that it was a dream, a mirage, nothing, trying to still the hammering of her heart in her chest. After a while she got up, her long red hair uncombed and tousled, and went along to the nursery, not bothering to put a robe on over her long white nightgown. It was June and warm already. The window was open, and she reached to close it against the rain. It had finally begun to rain, the rain that they had wanted for so long, for the crops.

The children were all right. She took several deep, thankful breaths, and then went downstairs for a glass of wine, a space of time to banish the nightmares before going back to sleep.

There were voices in the kitchen.

Chantale opened the door slowly and crept into the enormous room, shielding her eyes against the light. The flagstones were cold against her bare feet.

The lights were blazing, and she inhaled an aroma of onion soup and freshly baked bread. Annie was dressed, her blue apron over her immense breasts and stomach, a kerchief over her hair. There were six or seven people sitting at the long refectory table, men and women and several small children, dressed in odd assortments of clothing. Annie was serving them food.

Annie looked up then, sensing movement, and saw Chantale. "Good evening, Countess," she said calmly, and went back to ladling soup into the tureens on the table.

Chantale came closer. "Annie, what is going on here? Who are these people?"

"Sit down, Countess. You'll be wanting a glass of wine, I'll warrant." Annie was familiar with Chantale's sleeplessness. "I'll have it for you in just a moment. Poor folks haven't eaten in days."

Chantale sat warily at one end of the table. "Who are they, Annie?"

"Well, now, Countess, I couldn't say. Folks from Paris."

Chantale's eyes widened. "From Paris?" she asked, her voice faint. A woman sitting near her lifted her head from the soup. "Yes, until the dirty Germans came. We lived on the boulevard St. Michel."

"They threw you out of your homes?"

The man sitting across from her tore a piece of bread savagely from the loaf Annie had set on the table. "Didn't wait for them to do it," he said, anger in his voice. "We won't be there to watch them take over. And there won't be much left for them to take, either."

"We smashed all the china," the woman confided. "All Grandmother's Limoges. And left the faucets running. The apartment is probably waterlogged by now."

"You destroyed your own apartment?" Chantale was amazed.

"Better at our hands than theirs." The woman nodded vigorously. "It's what everybody's been doing. All along the roads we traveled, people were smashing furniture, killing their own chickens. The *sales Boches* won't get much satisfaction from us!"

Chantale shook her head. "How long have you been on the road?"

Another woman, sitting farther down the table with a child asleep in her arms, spoke up. "Almost two weeks. We've had to hide, and that wasted time."

"Hide?"

"From the planes." The man's voice was contemptuous. "The German planes. They've been strafing the roads."

"Strafing . . ." Chantale's voice trailed off in horror.

"Aye, that's right." He winced at the memory, his face as bleak as his voice. "Killing everybody regardless. Men, women, children . . . I saw an old priest standing in the center of the road, crossing himself and holding his rosary. They mowed him down, too. People just step aside and bury the bodies and then move on. There are crosses all along the roads."

The woman with the child in her lap said, her voice blurred

with her tears, "I saw crosses with teddy bears and stuffed animals on them. Graves of children."

Chantale and Annie exchanged glances, and Chantale felt her heart beating faster. Teddy bears. Children, children like her own, out on the roads. And perhaps soon, her family might be there with the rest of them. If the Germans came to Angers . . .

The man was continuing. "Got so we could hear them coming, we could hear the engines. So we'd all run off and jump in the ditches by the sides of the road—hide in the trees, behind a wall, whatever was available. The people who had automobiles stayed in them, but sometimes the guns would hit them just right and they'd explode." There was a moment of silence as the room seemed to reverberate with the explosions he spoke of.

The woman next to Chantale broke the silence. "Not too many automobiles," she said, frowning as she remembered. "They'd run out of gas, and there's no place that has gas anymore."

"Funny kind of war," the man said, shaking his head, using his crust of bread to wipe out and eat the remaining soup in his bowl, "where it's the civilians that get killed."

Annie set a glass of wine in front of Chantale, who took it without looking and drank half in one swallow. "Where are you heading now?" she asked.

"The coast," he replied. "Government's going to Bordeaux. So are we. Safest place around, it seems."

"We thought Nantes first," the woman next to Chantale said. "Then just follow the coastline down. If the government gets evacuated to England, we'll stand a chance of going, too."

The woman with the child said, her voice dull, "I haven't thought about where to go. I just had to get out of Paris. I just had to get away from the Germans."

There were grunts and nods of assent from the others present, and Annie passed the decanter of wine around the table. "I'll pack you up some food for the road," she said.

Chantale looked at her, shocked. "They're not leaving now!" she said. "They're exhausted." She looked at the group. "You'll stay here tonight," she said. "You can continue tomorrow. And I'll give you some clothes."

Annie made a movement of protest. "Countess, perhaps that's not such a good idea," she said. "Monsieur your husband doesn't know that folks stop off here, and neither does his mother. If they stay—"

"They will stay," Chantale said firmly. "It's all right, Annie. I'll take responsibility for it."

Annie still looked uncomfortable. "In the stables, perhaps, Countess . . ."

Chantale shook her head, but the man spoke up. "It's all right," he said. "We'd be most grateful for the stables, and you don't need to worry. We've been sleeping in much worse places."

The woman next to Chantale said, wonderingly, "If you had told me three months ago—or even one month ago—that I would be sleeping on anything but silk sheets, I'd have laughed. And now I'm grateful for straw." She smiled at Chantale. "How war changes us."

Chantale sat and waited while Annie settled the people out in the stable loft. The rain was still falling outside, and she could feel the dampness penetrating her muscles and joints. Imagining life on the road in this weather—no place to stay and the fear constantly at one's back—Chantale shivered. "How war changes us," the woman from Paris had said. What had been their life before they fled from the Germans? The boulevard St. Michel was not an inexpensive place to live.

It seemed hours before Annie was back, clutching her shawl about her and taking off her wooden shoes—the heavy peasant shoes best suited for rain and mud—at the door. She was shaking her head and clucking to herself. "Little ones don't even stand a chance. If they don't catch a fever in this dampness it will be a miracle. Countess, you still awake? I thought you might have gone off to bed, seeing as it's late. Will you have some more wine? I could do with a bit myself, and that's no lie."

"No," Chantale said. "Sit down, Annie."

The older woman heaved herself onto the bench across the table from Chantale. "Aye, and it feels good to sit." She reached for the wine decanter and poured some in a glass for herself.

"Tell me why you are so worried that my husband or mother-in-law might find out that you've been feeding refugees," Chantale said.

Annie shook her head. "Doesn't do to worry folks," she said easily. "What they don't know, they can't tell me not to do, now can they?"

"There's more to it than that," Chantale said. She leaned forward, and some of her hair fell over in front of her shoulder.

"What else have you been doing, Annie? And why do you trust me? I might go and tell Pierre in the morning."

"Well, now, Countess, and there's a lot of questions. But I don't think that you'll be going to tell Monsieur the Count, and that's a fact. You've got more sense than he has, and more courage. I don't think that Monsieur the Count will be any too brave over this whole question."

"That's not the way that you should speak of your employer." There was no anger in Chantale's words.

"Well, then, Countess, you shouldn't ask me questions if you don't want the answers. Don't get me wrong: He's all right in his own way, Monsieur the Count. Nothing like his father, though. He'd have been out here serving up the soup himself, Count Philippe would have been. Count Pierre now, he does his best. But he hasn't got the brains or the imagination."

"The imagination? What do you mean?"

"He can't feel for other people, Countess. Look at the way he treats you. Doesn't know he's hurting you all the time, doesn't care. If he doesn't care for his own wife, then how's he going to care for all those poor folks, what he doesn't even know?" Annie shook her head. "And you don't need me telling you this, you know it already. That's why you won't talk about this to him."

"You seem to see a lot, Annie." Chantale closed her eyes. The cook was right: Pierre would have turned the people out—and shouted at her for even thinking of risking anything to help them. "What else?"

Annie took a drink of wine. "I don't know what you're talking about, Countess," she said carefully.

Chantale opened her eyes again. "I think you do," she said steadily. "How did those people know to come here—and at night? How is it that you know what is happening elsewhere—in Paris, in the other districts? What exactly is it you do, Annie?"

"I cook," Annie said proudly, drawing herself up to her full height. "I cook, and I'll carry on cooking for as long as I've got an employer what speaks French. But I'll not be working for any *sale Boche*, you can be sure of that." She paused. "And I'll not make life any easier for them when they come."

When they come. Chantale wasn't sure when it was that the "if" in all their minds had changed to "when." She shivered. "Annie, they'll take the château. You know it, and I know it.

It's the largest house for miles around. What will happen then?
Will you leave?''

"That depends," said the cook, "on whether I can do them
more damage by going or by staying."

Chantale nodded in complete understanding. She drained her
glass and stood up. "I'm going to bed. Make sure those people
eat and are given some blankets before they leave in the morning."

"Yes, Countess."

Chantale walked to the door, and then paused, looking back.
"If I can help in any way, Annie . . ."

"Don't say that, Countess. You'll want to stay safe when they
come. You've got people to look out for."

"I mean it, Annie. What good am I to my children if they
can't look up to me?"

Which left the one obvious question unanswered. What good
was Pierre to his children if they couldn't look up to him?

Caroline ran a hand through her tousled hair. "Are you sure?"
she asked for the third time, and Steven finally lost patience with
her.

"Of course I'm sure," he snapped. "The Germans are occupying Paris. It was on the radio this morning, for God's sake.
The French have lost the war."

She turned away from him and sat down on the chintz-covered
sofa. "The French have lost the war," she whispered. "Oh,
God, how horrible."

"It could be worse," Steven said briskly. "Maybe now they'll
ask for some help and we can get involved."

She didn't turn to look at him. "You want America involved
in the war? Since when did you change your mind? You didn't
sound so patriotic a few months ago."

"It's not an issue of patriotism. It's an issue of economics.
The faster we get involved, the more work there'll be for Asheford Shipbuilding."

There were tears in her eyes. "That's all that you care about,
isn't it?"

"Of course not, Caroline. Our involvement is inevitable
now—sooner or later. And in terms of economics it would be
better if it were sooner."

While Steven went around whistling, watching the newspapers and his production figures with the same cheerfulness, Car-

oline cried and raged and felt the dim dark curtain of depression hovering over her again.

She wrote long letters to Eric, asking him over and over again to use his influence with Roosevelt to get the United States in the war. "We can't just stand by and do nothing!" she wrote, the despair flowing from her body onto the page. "They're your people, Eric! Don't let them die. . . . We have to help. The Nazis are monsters." But even she didn't know yet how monstrous they would become.

She wrote letters filled with anguish to her mother, Eric having given her the address of the estate outside of Leopoldville. "I never saw the places you and my father used to go," she wrote. "Now it may never happen. They may be destroyed or occupied forever by the people who killed him. I can't stand the thought. What do you think about there in Africa?"

Caroline wrote letters and paced the terrace outside of the mansion on Ocean Avenue, hugging herself fiercely in the early-summer sunshine, shaking with her anger and her fear and her impotence. There was talk of German submarines being sighted off the coast, and Caroline flew low over the ocean in her light Butterfly, scanning the waves yet seeing nothing. She wondered what she would do if she saw one. If the Butterfly only came equipped with bombs . . .

The news continued to filter out of Europe. The French prime minister had resigned, to be replaced by an old man, Henri Pétain. The Germans were all over France. The French surrendered officially on June 22 and signed an armistice with Hitler, giving up the north of France and all of the Atlantic coast. The new French Vichy government was a pawn in the south. For the French the war was over.

Caroline wore black when she heard the news.

And then she received a letter from Andrew.

My dear Caroline,

This will probably come as a shock to you, but I think that you will understand. Maybe you are the only one who can understand. Remember when you told me that the most important thing in life is respecting yourself? I think about that a lot. Lately, especially, and it's helped me make some important decisions.

God, I wish that I could see you in person to tell you about this. So many things have happened. I've resigned my position at Johnson Industries, and Susan and I have broken up. I just kept thinking and thinking about what is happening in Europe, and about *you,* and realized that I couldn't keep playing this game anymore. It just doesn't make sense to me.

Caroline—I'm in England. There's a group of American pilots who feel the same way that I do, that we can't wait for the ponderous political mechanism in the U.S. to decide that this is something that we have to do. It's called the Eagle Squadron, and it's part of the RAF. And God, it feels good to be doing this—I know it's the right thing. These people need us. I'm flying for them, and doing what I can to help.

I wish that things were different—especially now that Susan and I have broken our engagement. Is it just wishful thinking to fantasize about you divorcing your husband and marrying me instead? I suppose so. But I've always loved you, Caroline. I always will.

                                            Andrew

Caroline read the letter over and over again. Andrew was doing something, not sitting around thinking about profits and losses, but caring about people. Doing something to help. "These people need us," he had written, and Caroline's eyes filled with tears. Yes. He was right; there was no sense in waiting. The American people would eventually come to their senses and Congress would declare war, but at what cost? In the meantime, how many other lives would be lost? How many people deprived of their freedom? Andrew was doing the right thing, the brave thing, and Caroline felt a thrill of pride and excitement at the thought.

Chapter Thirteen

Pierre de Montclair was celebrating.

He had good reason to do so. They had signed an armistice. The war was over. Whatever happened now, he wasn't going to be called up, wasn't going to have to uselessly give his life as his father had on some desolate battlefield that he didn't even care about. The war was over.

Chantale didn't understand him. All that she wanted to do was talk about what terrible monsters the Germans were. She obviously didn't understand the situation; she didn't realize that occupation might not be so bad, and it was useless trying to explain things to her. The Germans spoke of cooperation and peace. None of that sounded so very bad. Chantale was growing hysterical; he had always thought that she was a little unbalanced.

Isabelle, on the other hand, was quite willing to celebrate with him. Pierre smiled at the thought as he straightened his tie in front of the mirror in his bedroom. Isabelle had been as desperately afraid as he had been, afraid that he would have to go and fight, perhaps be killed. Isabelle had lain awake in his arms, night after night, begging him to flee or to hide, not to leave her, never to leave her. If the war had proven one thing, Pierre thought, it had proven who really loved him. Not that he needed any justification for his affair with Isabelle, but if he did, he had it now. Isabelle cared about him. Chantale cared about herself. It was obvious.

He hummed to himself as he drove into Angers. June 27, 1940, and all was well. The air was warm and alive, and he found himself smiling at the pretty girls on the streets. There was nothing wrong with the world that a little celebration couldn't cure.

He parked the car at the place du Ralliement and stopped at

a florist's shop on the way up to Isabelle's apartment. She opened the door at once, as though she had been expecting him at exactly that moment, and when she saw the flowers she smiled, that wide, mysterious, inviting smile that had entranced him for so long. The evening, Pierre knew then, was going to be perfect.

And it was. Isabelle was dazzling, breathtakingly beautiful, her raven-black hair loosened and falling down her back, her dark violet eyes promising, her throat uncovered by the low-cut black gown she wore. Seeing her neck uncovered, Pierre was moved by a sudden impulse to go by a jeweler's shop, Isabelle smiling and offering token protestations. He bought her a gold necklace with three diamonds framing a single gold teardrop, and clasped it around her neck with a wonderful feeling of extravagance and possessiveness. This was his mistress, his woman. He wanted all the world to know.

They had dinner at a small *recherché* restaurant down by the river, almost in the shadow of the old medieval fortress, watching the lights reflecting off the water. Isabelle's eyes were brilliant in the candlelight. "So now, Monsieur le Comte," she said, smiling at him over her wineglass, "what do you do? What place will you have in the new German society?"

Pierre smiled back, too contented to hear the barbs, the mockery behind her words. "They have nobility in Germany, counts and dukes and princes," he answered easily. "I am sure that I will receive the same respect. Perhaps more, since I did not myself fight them off."

She sipped the ruby wine. "And what of me? Will they respect my gallery, my independence?"

"But I shall see to it that they do!" he protested at once. "Isabelle, my love, surely you realize by now how important your happiness is to me! I shall insist that you be respected, that you and your gallery be left in peace."

She disengaged her hand from his and looked out the window, watching the lights on the river. "And yet," she said, almost musingly, "perhaps you will not be able to take care of me. You have so many obligations—your name, your château, your family . . ." Her voice trailed off.

Pierre frowned. He was too unsure of himself and of what would be happening to their lives in the next few months to be able to give a concrete air to his assurances. What was she saying? Would she look for someone else to take care of her? Surely not! "You," he said intensely, leaning forward to her, "come first. You will always come first, my darling."

Isabelle met his eyes. "Be sure of that," she said, her voice low. "If I do not, I want to know now."

"I swear it," Pierre responded. "I will take care of you, Isabelle. No matter what happens."

She smiled again then, brightly, as if the subject was closed. "In any case," she said, "there may be no need. Perhaps we shall like learning to speak German, after all."

"I am sure," he said, trying hard to keep the relief out of his voice, "that it will be positive. Oh, there will be changes, of course, but positive changes. I don't think that our lives will be affected, not in what matters." He took her hand in his. "Not in this, my darling. Not our love."

"No," she said, smiling. "Of course not."

Later, they stopped at a bar for a few drinks, and they listened to people talking about the armistice. "I'd have fought on," said one old man aggressively, cradling his whiskey and water in his hand. "I fought them the first time, and we never gave in. Shouldn't have given in this time either."

Pierre could sense Isabelle's eyes on him, and felt obliged to respond. "Listen, old man," he said, "we wouldn't have had to fight this time if your generation hadn't been so stubborn. Maybe German dominance was meant to be!"

The old man swiveled to look at him. "You gave up too easily," he said thickly, but Isabelle was squeezing Pierre's arm and smiling at him. "You're right," she whispered. "You're the one who's right."

In the darkness, miles away, Chantale de Montclair sat at the window of her bedroom, looking out toward the stables. Another night when Pierre wouldn't come home. Another night when she would sit here alone, finally falling asleep after drinking several glasses of wine, knowing as she did that at this very moment her husband was making love with another woman.

She sighed and sipped from the glass in her hand. Despair was waiting in the recesses of her mind, a horrible throat-catching feeling that welled up sometimes when she thought of Pierre. He had tried to make love to her the other night, and she had submitted to him, lying still and passive beneath his body, willing herself to stay silent, not to cry, because all that she could think of was that other skin that his hands had caressed, those other lips that his mouth had touched, that other body that his had penetrated. And when he was finished, Pierre looked down at her in disgust. "You're like a cold fish," he said, contempt in his voice. "You can't blame me when I don't come home."

There was a light in the stables. That would be Annie, seeing that the people there were settled in. Chantale would have to remind her in the morning to cover the windows. More people, more refugees. Still more in the thin straggle of people heading for the coast. They came more infrequently these days than they had when the Germans first invaded Paris, but somehow they all knew to come to the Château de Montclair, that there would be a hot meal and a safe place to stay. Chantale didn't know how they knew, but they did, and they came.

And now she knew where to send them.

Her husband and mother-in-law weren't aware of her activities. But her own mother had written, had talked in veiled terms about the fishing boats that she could see from her window, the ones that left and drifted off toward Penzance, returning with fewer people aboard and no fish. And Chantale has started telling the people that a safe place could be found at the Château de Kerenec. Her home. Her only real home. Her mother had taken them in and, like her, sent them safely on their way. She never mentioned it in her letters. But Chantale knew.

Chantale put down her empty glass and stood up, stretching for a moment, before slipping out her door and down the corridor to the nursery. Catherine was sick; she had had a fever earlier in the evening, and Jeannine was sitting up with her to hold the cold compresses on the tiny forehead and keep the little girl's temperature down. "How is she?"

The maid looked up, startled. "Oh, Countess! I didn't hear you come in. . . . She seems to be resting well."

Chantale reached down into the cradle and lifted the baby into her arms. Ten months old, and already she was making noises that sounded like words, already she was trying to stand up on her plump and wobbly legs, and showing signs of a definite personality. Jean-Claude was pure de Montclair; he had the dark looks and thin nose of his father's family, but Catherine was Celtic. One could tell. Already Chantale felt closer to her daughter than she did to her son.

Jeannine was right. The breath was measured, though light. The fever seemed lower. "If she is ill in the morning," Chantale said, "we will send for the doctor. It is very good of you to watch her, Jeannine."

"Oh, Countess, it is nothing. For you, I would do anything."

Chantale smiled. "I know. I know, Jeannine, but thank you anyway. You're a good girl."

She wondered, as she went back down the passage to her own room, precisely what that meant. A good girl. Virtue must indeed be its own reward, she decided. She had been a good girl, too, and see what it got her. A philandering husband and a cowardly country. Surely a good girl deserved more than that.

Caroline flew almost daily now, scanning the ocean for the submarines that were believed to be off the coast, restless unless she was actually in the air. She took Elizabeth with her more often than not, and the child sat strapped into the copilot's seat, smiling and gurgling, unaware that she was winging her way thousands of feet in the air. Caroline found her presence comforting. She could talk to Elizabeth, and not be afraid of judgments or criticisms. "Look over there, honey! See those clouds!" And mother and daughter would smile together in shared delight. Those times, Caroline thought, more than made up for the occasions when Elizabeth, for no apparent reason, would become stubborn and petulant, crying and screaming to get her own way. Marie assured Caroline that this was normal behavior for a two-year-old, but Caroline didn't know how to handle her daughter at these times.

Justine's baby had been born, another boy that she named William, after his father. Justine spent all her time now with Nicholas and William. The baby had been born prematurely, and was sick and weak most of the time. Justine was constantly worrying about him. "No, Caroline, I'm sorry, I really can't come. I have to take care of the children."

"Bring them over to Ocean Avenue, then. Marie will watch after them for you."

"Oh, Caroline. I couldn't. I really couldn't. I'm sure that she's competent and all that, but she's not their mother. . . ."

What, Caroline wondered, was all this saintliness about motherhood? When Elizabeth was tearful, she was delighted to leave her with Marie, who was far more patient with the child than she herself ever could be.

There was a time not too distant, Caroline realized, when she had longed for just those things—a settled life with the gentle giant she had married, children, a house to tend. When had she changed? When had she outgrown those dreams? Why weren't they enough anymore?

Or had they ever really been her dreams? More and more, Caroline was wondering if her longing for a settled, predictable life was nothing more than a reaction against her erratic, confusing childhood. She didn't want that kind of insecurity, not for herself or her daughter, and she had seen only one way of getting away from it.

Perhaps, more than she even knew, she had formulated her dreams in her mother's shadow. Perhaps it was Amanda who dictated Caroline's restraint, her inability—or unwillingness—to take risks. And perhaps it was that part of her that *was* Amanda that now questioned what she wanted from life.

Maybe Steven was right. Perhaps she had changed when she had started flying again, just after Elizabeth was born. Was it possible, after all, that there was something to what he said, that flying changed things? It certainly offered a different perspective on life.

And yet it was a perspective that made sense to her. When she was out in California one afternoon—a Sunday, it was— Andrew had taken her for a ride in his car, a long aimless trek down the coastal road in search of lunch. They had passed a tiny airfield, two hangars, one runway, no tower, only a wind sock flying bravely in the breeze. Near one of the hangars was an old junk heap, rusted pieces of metal, the cab of a truck, discarded automobiles, and in it the wreckage of two airplanes. Caroline had made Andrew stop the car, and they made their way through the overgrown weeds to the junk heap.

One of the airplanes had flipped over: the fuselage was dented, the propeller twisted out of shape, and the cockpit caved in. Caroline climbed into the stripped interior, looking at the places where the instruments once had been, peering out through the cracked glass of the windshield. She wondered, sitting there, what it felt like to crash, to be going down and turning over, seeing her fate spinning out in front of her eyes and being incapable of doing anything about it. Sometimes her own life felt that way—spinning out of control while she sat, powerless, and watched it happen.

Andrew was examining the other airplane, which was in even worse shape. The elements and time had wreaked havoc with the canvas and wood and wires, but it was recognizable, nevertheless, as an old biplane. "Look, Caroline," said Andrew, enthusiasm in his voice. "It's a nice old one. God, imagine what it was like to fly one of these things!"

Caroline climbed down from her perch and joined him. "Whose design?" she asked automatically, but he shook his head. "Who can tell? There's not enough of it left."

The propeller was still there, rusted through in places, and the steering stick, which for some reason was made of metal. No brakes; they hadn't had brakes in the old days. "Eric said that Sarah used to stop by turning into hay bales. Sometimes, if the plane was going too fast or the balance was off, they'd tip right over them."

"Those were the days," Andrew said reverently, running his hand over the old biplane. "Imagine, Caroline! Imagine being one of the first people ever to fly!"

She smiled. "I know. But those people were crazy, too. Think of flying with no brakes!"

"Imagine flying with no instruments! Or no safety belts! Or no parachutes . . . I can hardly conceive of it." He shook his head. "They were crazy days, maybe, but I envy them. Everything was fresh and new then . . . you could do what you wanted. Really carve out your own destiny."

If it wasn't carved out for you, Caroline thought, by circumstance. As it had been for Eric's wife, Sarah. She wondered about his comment now that Andrew had gone to fly fighter planes in England: Was that what he was trying to do? Carve out his own destiny? If so, he wasn't doing a bad job of it. And, Caroline thought, perhaps Andrew was more realistic than she'd originally assumed. When she'd been with him in California she'd wondered if he wasn't a fairy-tale prince living in a land of make-believe. He was proving her wrong.

Caroline's restlessness took her day after day out to the airport, even when the weather was bad, even when she wasn't flying. Eddie Carruthers kept her company, sharing his cigarettes and talking with longing about Margie, the waitress in the pilot's lounge, who he had not yet asked out for a date. One afternoon as they sat side by side next to a hangar, watching a mechanic take apart an engine, Eddie passed Caroline his pack of cigarettes. "I could ask her to the movies," he suggested. "*Gaslight* is playing down at the Strand."

"Hardly original," Caroline said, accepting the cigarette and the light he held for her. "But it's bound to work. When were you up flying last?"

"Yesterday. It was great." A smile broke out across his face.

"Hmm." She leaned back against the hangar and shut her eyes. "And when do you go for your license?"

"Not yet. Do you think she'd like *Gaslight*? Maybe Hitchcock is a little too scary. I think I heard that *Fantasia* is coming next week, and that's supposed to be great. . . ."

Caroline opened her eyes to look at him. "Eddie, what's wrong? A pilot's license isn't that hard to get. You've got the expertise and the hours. What is it that's stopping you?"

He didn't meet her eyes. "I'm not ready."

"That's nonsense."

"Just leave me alone, Caroline, okay? You wouldn't understand. No one understands." He squinted at the horizon, where a plane could be faintly discerned entering the landing pattern.

Caroline shrugged and ground out her cigarette on the tarmac. "I have a friend," she said to change the subject, "a pilot who's gone to England to fly with the RAF."

"The Royal Air Force?" Eddie's eyes were bright with interest. "Oh, wow! Is he English?"

"No. He lives in California. There's an American squadron of fighter pilots that's been formed as part of the RAF. When America enters the war they'll probably all fly for the Air Force."

"Wow!" Eddie sighed in contentment. "That's the thing to do. You can't be a hero by sitting around control towers all your life. God, Caroline, the RAF! You must be proud of him."

"I am." Caroline gave him a sidelong glance. "Is that what you want, Eddie? To be a hero?"

"Who doesn't? Margie would sure notice me then, wouldn't she?"

"Margie will notice you," Caroline said firmly, "when you get up your courage to ask her out. That's your heroism for today."

"Yeah. Yeah, I guess that I should." The plane was on final now, and they both watched it critically. "He's a little high."

"He'll have to go around again," Caroline agreed. "I wonder where he learned to fly."

"Not from you," Eddie said, immediately and loyally. "You're the best teacher, Caroline."

"Thank you." She smiled. Compliments were few and far between these days. She would take them when she could.

They watched the plane abort its landing and circle around the field again. "Tell me about your friend," Eddie suggested.

"Andrew? He's a little older than I am. I've known him for years and years." Well, that was almost true. She had known him very intensely several years ago. It almost amounted to the same thing. "He's an excellent pilot," she added, wondering whether Eddie would be able to read anything in her voice.

Eddie had his own thoughts. "What's his name? Andrew what?"

"Starkey. Why?"

"Nothing." He caught her glance and smiled. "Nothing, Caroline. Just wanted to know the name of a real war hero."

A few days later, when she hadn't run into Eddie at all—an unusual occurrence, since he normally haunted the airport—she asked Bill about his absence with trepidation and a prescient sense of disaster.

Bill, busily filling out forms, didn't look up from them as he answered. "He resigned last week. I'm surprised he didn't tell you."

"He resigned? That's not possible!"

The airport manager shrugged. "Well, that's what he did, Caroline. He quit, and I can tell you I'm hard-pressed to replace him. He was good, even though he was so young."

"Where did he go?" Caroline's voice was faint. No, please no, she prayed silently, dreading the answer. Not that. Please not that on my conscience.

"Jesus, Caroline, what do I know? Ask Margie. He spent all of his last afternoon here talking to her."

Margie looked up from polishing glasses and smiled as Caroline approached. "Hi, Mrs. Asheford. Coffee?"

Caroline slid onto one of the plastic-covered stools by the counter. "No, thanks. Margie, I want to ask you something."

"Sure. What is it?"

Caroline drew in a deep breath. "Bill tells me that Eddie Carruthers resigned. Do you know where he went?"

The girl's face abruptly turned bright pink. She made a show of finishing the glass she was polishing and putting it on a shelf. By the time she turned back, she was composed again. "I'm not sure, Mrs. Asheford."

"He told you not to tell?"

A sidelong glance from under the dark lashes, and a quick nod.

Caroline dampened her lips. "All right, Margie. I think that I know. It wouldn't be so bad if you just told me if I'm right or wrong, would it?"

She looked genuinely distressed. "I don't know, Mrs. Asheford. I promised Eddie. . . ."

"You see," Caroline continued in a conversational tone, "Eddie and I had a talk a few days ago about a friend of mine who went to fly for the RAF. Eddie seemed interested at the time, and I wondered if . . ."

Margie's eyes were bright. "Oh, Mrs. Asheford," she said eagerly, "that's it! I don't suppose it matters now there's nothing that anyone can do to stop him, and you guessed it, after all, so it's not as though I told you. . . ." She wiped her hands on her apron and leaned forward. "I'm so proud of him, Mrs. Asheford, you have no idea! All this time I thought he was nice, of course, but too shy, you know? And now he's gone off to be a hero! He gave me his ring." Another shy smile. "When the war is over, he says that we'll get married."

"That's a long way off still," Caroline reminded her. "When did he leave, Margie?"

"Oh, Mrs. Asheford, you wouldn't do anything like try to get him back, would you? I mean, I know that he's a little young, but he can fly! You know that! You taught him yourself. He's a good pilot."

"He's a pilot without a license," Caroline said grimly. "It seems that maybe the RAF would take that into account."

"Well, he was going to lie to them. Just like he did here . . ." Her voice trailed off in dismay, and she immediately reached for another glass. Caroline leaned forward and grasped the girl's wrist in her hand. "What did you say, Margie?"

"I promised not to tell."

"You have to tell me, Margie. Eddie may be in danger there. I can help. I know someone flying with that squadron. Tell me, Margie."

There were tears in her eyes. "That's the reason he couldn't go for his license," she said. "Couldn't you guess? He's too young. He's too young for a license and he's too young for military service, but he looks older, and so he lies about his age. And that's why he had to run away, and couldn't say good-bye because his parents would have stopped him. But they don't know where he is, so they can't do anything. He had just enough money in his own bank account to get to London—"

"How old is he, Margie?"

"Old enough to want to be a hero," she said stoutly. "Old enough to be the best pilot around here, and the best controller."

"How old?"

"And I'm so proud of him, and we *will* get married when the war is over, you'll see—"

"Margie!"

There was an uncomfortable silence. Margie picked at a nonexistent spot on the countertop. Finally, in a voice that was barely a whisper, she said, "Fifteen."

"Fifteen!"

"Almost sixteen," Margie added defensively.

"Oh, my God," said Caroline. She sat back, shaking her head, feeling stunned. It was all her fault. She had sent a child into battle. He was good, and that had been his cover and his downfall, but he couldn't be expected to be good in combat situations. He knew nothing of any of that, and at fifteen his judgment couldn't be . . . "Oh, my God," she said again. She would have to contact Andrew. She would have to tell him . . . what? Get Eddie off the squadron? That was assuming he'd even been accepted. Perhaps she should wait a few weeks and see if he came home on his own. But in two weeks he might be dead. It's possible they would accept him. Margie was right: he was the best pilot around. Careful, meticulous, punctual. They would be impressed. And at the rate that they had been losing planes out over the channel to the Germans . . .

Margie was watching her, worried. "You won't tell him, will you?" she asked anxiously. "You won't tell him I told?"

Caroline slid off the stool. "No, Margie," she said wearily. "I won't tell."

She drove home with her heart thudding in her chest, and immediately got on the telephone. "I need a flight to London," she said, trying to keep the panic and the urgency out of her voice. She would have to see Andrew. She would have to tell him— "I'm sorry, madame. We have no connecting flights in the next three weeks."

"What? Why?"

"It's not currently considered safe, madame. If you have military or diplomatic clearance . . ."

"Never mind. Thank you." Caroline hung up the phone and stared at it for a moment, thinking. She had to get to England.

She could ask Eric to help her, but if he knew that Andrew was there—and of course he knew that Andrew was there, he had a way of finding out everything—then he would not only refuse, but put as many obstacles in her way as he could. And Eric Beaumont's obstacles could be formidable.

Finally she picked up the telephone again and called the airport. "Bill? It's Caroline. Would you see to it that the Butterfly is serviced? I'm going to need it tomorrow."

"Sure thing, kid. Going far?"

"Yes," she said. "I'll need auxiliary fuel tanks."

"Why the hell you need those?"

"I'm going to California," she lied. "And I don't want to stop on the way. Just do it, Bill, please?"

"Okay, kid. It'll be ready and waiting."

"Thanks." She hung up and stared at the telephone for a while longer, and then went looking for Elizabeth. If her feelings were right, it might be a while before she saw her daughter again.

"There are some American pilots flying with the RAF." Soizic Aubert spoke hesitantly, as though not sure of herself. But she knew her facts were correct.

Marc looked up from the papers on his desk. "Yes? And what about it?"

"One of the pilots is Andrew Starkey," she answered, moving into his office and closing the door behind her. "He was engaged to Caroline Asheford before her marriage to Steven Asheford."

He leaned back and ran a hand through his thinning hair. "Yes. We took care of separating them at Beaumont's request."

"Right. He's been working for Johnson Industries since then. I have a full report on his activities. He's been working with Igor Sikorsky on helicopters." She glanced at him. "That's a flying machine that uses propellers instead of wings to—"

"I know what a helicopter is." Marc knew that there was irritation in his voice, but he wasn't any too pleased with the discussion he had just had with Beneteau, and what he had to tell Soizic. Funny how you can want something and want it passionately, and then when it happens you don't want it anymore. "Please go on."

She was looking frightened, afraid of intruding, of offending. "I can come back later, Marc, if . . ."

"It's all right." He gestured toward the chair in front of his desk. "Robert is out for the afternoon. Sit down, Soizic, and tell me."

She perched on the edge of it like a bird ready to fly away. "Monsieur Starkey recently left his position at Johnson Industries, called off his engagement to a Mademoiselle McCarthy, and left for England to fly with this Eagle Squadron." She hesitated. "He did so not long after spending time in California with Madame Asheford."

"Caroline saw Andrew Starkey in California? Who planned that?"

"Marc, no one did. It was apparently a matter of bad luck. They ran into each other in San Francisco—accidentally, I am told—and saw each other several times before she returned to Rhode Island. And then he left Johnson and went to England."

"It's a little too coincidental."

"That's what I thought. Anyway, the feeling at Johnson Industries is that it's simply a youthful impulse and that he'll be back. But we have reports on Madame Asheford, and frankly, Marc, I don't like what it's adding up to. She's intensely unhappy in her marriage. She is bored and is expressing a great deal of patriotism—uncovering her French roots if you will. She's been urging Monsieur Beaumont to use his influence in Washington to get America involved in the war. Also, she's been in touch with her mother."

"I can't see what Amanda Thackery has to do with this."

"I can't, either, except that it completes a picture of restlessness and discontent. She has been corresponding with Monsieur Starkey. She has encouraged a young man of her acquaintance, a Monsieur Carruthers, to go to England and join this Eagle Squadron." Soizic took a deep breath. "I am asking, Marc: What would happen if Caroline divorced her husband and married Andrew Starkey, and he went back to Johnson Industries?"

"This isn't good," he said slowly.

"No," she agreed. "But there is a solution."

He looked at her but remained silent.

She took another deep breath. "The air over England is cluttered these days. Ninety German bombers have been shot down over Britain so far this year, and the British have begun to bomb Germany in retaliation. Fighter planes are having dogfights over the Channel. Barrage balloons are up everywhere. It's not a very safe place to be."

He nodded, instantly aware of what she was proposing. "An unfortunate accident could be arranged."

"It would certainly take care of the situation at hand."

"All right," Giroux said heavily. "We'll consult with Monsieur Beaumont, of course. And I'll mention it to Robert." It was the only solution, damn it. But he was sorry that it was Soizic who had come up with it. He hesitated. "I wasn't going to bring this up yet, Soizic, but now is as good a time as any."

"Yes?"

He sighed. "You're doing good work. In the past few months, Robert has noticed it—how could he fail to notice it? I'll be honest: He was against you at first, but your work has won him over. We've had a discussion. He is very anxious to keep you with the firm."

"I'm very anxious to stay. I don't understand, Marc."

"We've decided to offer you a full partnership, Soizic: Beneteau, Giroux, and Aubert. I know that you haven't got the money for that kind of investment, not now, but we've arranged a loan. I think that with your new salary you'll find it quite manageable."

Soizic felt her stomach contract, and for the first time in a long time she realized that there was no fear, only pleasure. She was being offered a partnership in one of the most prestigious law firms in the world, and she fully believed she was going to be able to handle it. They wanted her. She was good; she had proven it. Oh, God, Soizic thought, if only for a while I can keep the doubts at bay. If only I can just go on, savoring this triumph, this power . . .

"Are you sure, Marc?" she asked, but deep in her heart she knew that he was. And so was she.

"Sure that you'll be able to repay the loan? Or sure about the partnership? Of course we're sure. You're the rising star in the law world, Soizic, even though you don't believe it." But now you'll start to believe it, he thought. Now you'll realize how good you really are. When you were insecure, I could keep you. You were bound to me by awe and admiration. But now, you'll know. And you'll leave me.

She stood up, unsure of how to end the conversation. He stood up, too, and formally shook her hand. "Congratulations, Mademoiselle Aubert."

Chapter Fourteen

Chantale de Montclair found herself looking back over her shoulder as she hurried down the street. It was a habit she'd developed as though anyone seeing her could read the thoughts that were in her mind. She wasn't particularly comfortable with that idea. Her thoughts were private, furtive, careful. She hoped that her actions could match them.

Annie had given her the address on the rue des Lices in Angers; now it was up to her to do the rest. Annie couldn't spend all her days in Angers, not like Chantale. The cook didn't have the time; Chantale, on the other hand, was free to come and go as she pleased. She had committed herself and she was fearful. She had had no idea at all how difficult it would be.

She looked around once more before knocking on the door. They let her in at once, up the musty-smelling narrow staircase to the apartment within. It was an artist's apartment with most of the space devoted to a studio with tremendous windows and skylights, benches spattered with paint, and easels upon which sat paintings covered with drop cloths. It was obviously inappropriate for the business at hand.

"He's in here, Countess." The woman in the faded apron who had opened the door to her indicated a room she hadn't yet noticed, small and dark, with a double bed built into a cupboard in the wall. On the bed sat a man.

He hadn't shaved in days. There was a blue tint to his chin, and his eyes were wary. He was wearing peasant clothes, a loose blue smock and trousers, which were inappropriate in the city. They had done well to keep him hidden here. He couldn't have been more than twenty or twenty-one years old, and when he looked at her, the fear obvious in his face, Chantale felt her heart contract. No one should have to look like that, she thought—not ever.

She wondered briefly what he saw, why he looked so frightened. She couldn't be all that intimidating. He saw a woman in her mid-twenties, with long red hair clasped behind her neck in a ponytail, and cascading down her back in curls. He saw high cheekbones and green eyes, and perhaps his fear only reflected what he could read there. He saw a woman too tall, too thin, with a fine tracing of lines around her eyes from too much time in the sun. He saw a woman who wore her dignity like a cloak, and her title not at all.

She swallowed. "Good morning," she said formally, in the schoolgirl English she had learned from her tutor in the castle by the sea. "I am Chantale de Montclair. I speak a little English."

A brief smile crossed his face. "It's all right," he said easily, in heavily accented French. "I speak French."

She raised her eyebrows. "So? I understand you want to go home. To England." Even though he had said he spoke French, she kept her sentences short and careful. She had never spoken to a foreigner before.

The Englishman glanced quickly around the room. "Not so loud," he advised. "Won't you sit down? This chair isn't much, but it serves the purpose."

"Thank you." She sat down on the plain wooden chair, holding her purse in her lap, in front of her, almost like a shield. "I'm here to help you."

"So I gathered." The eyes looked at her, consideringly, and she found herself wondering how long it had been since he had slept. "I need to get to the coast. Can you help with that?"

"We've been sheltering people on their way to the coast for many weeks now. And we know where to send them, whom they can trust. It has worked for the French people. I should think it would work for you."

He smiled again briefly. "And—forgive my impudence—how do I know I can trust you?"

Chantale's eyes widened. "Because I hate the Germans," she said simply.

"It's easy enough to say."

"It's easy enough to do."

He looked at her for a moment and then nodded. "Right. You'll do. What happens now?"

Chantale gestured. "Your clothes. You cannot walk through

Angers in those clothes.'' She raised her voice to the woman that she knew was listening at the door. ''Madame Leclerc!''

Behind her, there was a rustle of skirts. ''Yes, Countess?''

Chantale was rooting around in her purse. ''Here. Take this money. Go and purchase a decent shirt and some pants for Monsieur here. And a jacket. And a razor. Go and do it now, please.''

''Of course, Countess.'' The door closed.

There was a moment of silence, and then he spoke. ''Countess? Is that a nickname or are you one?''

She met his eyes, holding her chin high. ''I am the Countess de Montclair.''

''And Chantale? That's your real name?''

''Of course it is.''

He shook his head. ''You haven't been doing this for very long, have you?''

Chantale said slowly, ''You are the first Englishman. The first time I have come into Angers. Usually the people come to us— out to the château. My cook makes the arrangements. Why do you ask, monsieur?''

He ran a tired hand through his hair. ''Oh, God. A bloody amateur. Just what I needed. I don't suppose you have a cigarette?''

''I'm sorry. I don't smoke.''

He smiled. ''Just as well. I was thinking of giving it up anyway.'' He stood up, stretching to his full height, and walked to the door of the studio, looking at the paintings that were on display there. ''I used to paint a bit myself, in the old days.'' He turned to look at her, leaning against the doorframe. ''Ready for a lesson, Countess?''

''A lesson?'' She was nonplussed.

''In the fine art of espionage. Rule number one—don't give out your real name. Not ever. Not to anybody. It's the best way to stay safe.''

''What is your name?'' she asked, looking at him steadily.

''Depends on who you ask.'' He grinned, seeing the expression on her face. ''I've got an official name for the RAF, but since I've been in France I've found a few others useful. John will do, for now.''

''For now?'' Her smile was faintly flirtatious.

''For now.'' He nodded and continued solemnly, ''Rule number two—don't bring people to your house. Not if it's a big one.

Big houses have servants, and servants talk. Hide people somewhere else whenever possible."

"I see." So that was why Annie had always insisted on the
stables. To keep the refugees hidden from everyone. But who at
the Château de Montclair would talk? And to whom?

"Rule number three . . . Ah, but here is my new attire. Rule
number three can wait. God knows I can't." Juliette Leclerc
stood on the landing behind him, packages in her arms. "I went
just down the street, Countess, where they know me. I said that
it was for my husband."

"Thank you, madame." Chantale stood up. "I will leave you
to your toilette, Monsieur John."

His mocking eyes followed her as she shut the door.

Outside in the passageway, she leaned against the wall and
closed her eyes. Her heart was pounding in her chest. She was
not good at this—what was it that the Englishman had called
her? An amateur? If she was this nervous now, what would it be
like when the Germans came to Angers? Perhaps she should stop
this charade before anybody got hurt because of her.

But if she did not do it, who would? The faces and voices of
the refugees from Paris haunted her: There were teddy bears on
some of the crosses. . . . The planes just fired on the people as
they walked down the road. . . . They shot the old priest. . . .
There was mud, always mud, because of the rains that had finally come. . . . Chantale drew in a deep breath. She had to do
it. She couldn't count on other people to take a stand.

The Englishman was quiet enough as they walked together
back to the place du Ralliement. Seen in the daylight and in
proper clothing, he was more presentable, though still achingly
young. "Do not speak," she had warned him as they left the
house on the rue des Lices. "People will hear your accent."
And he had smiled at her as though she were a child telling a
grown-up about the ways of the world.

He didn't speak again, in point of fact, until they were on the
road out of Angers. Inside the car, away from the ears of passers-
by, he seemed to relax a little. "Very good, Countess. I expect
that we can skip rule number three, after all."

"Do I pass the test, then?" She glanced at him for a moment,
then looked back to the road ahead. It would not do to be in an
accident today.

He was looking out the window. "It's pleasant around here."

"Angers is known as the city of flowers," she said automatically. "It's not as pretty as my home. I am from Brittany."

"Ah, yes. A fellow Celt. I'm Welsh myself."

She smiled and, warmed by this small confidence, risked another question. "How is it that you are still in France? My cook told me that there are many Englishmen stranded here. What happened?"

"Dunkirk was a bloody miracle," he said. "Over three hundred fifty thousand evacuated in four days. A miracle, Countess. The only problem was there were about another ten thousand of us in France." He sighed and settled back into his seat. "Mostly in the north. Hiding out in caves, in the forests, like bloody animals. And being hunted like animals, too. Did your cook tell you that a special elite German motorcycle unit was formed just to look for us?"

"No," Chantale said faintly. Like animals, he had said . . . "What do they do when they find someone?"

He laughed, but there was no mirth in his voice. "What do you think they do?"

She said nothing, only compressed her lips and tightened her hands on the steering wheel. She might not be good at this yet. But she would get better.

The Englishman was watching her reaction. "Not a pretty thought," he agreed. "I decided to set out inland aways, and come a bit farther south. The routes here aren't being watched yet. I traveled at night through fields. I thought that I had a contact in Angers."

"What happened?"

He shrugged. "Who knows? Maybe he cleared out when he heard the Germans were coming."

Her heartbeat quickened. "How soon?"

"How soon? Don't tell me you don't know, Countess. A day away at the most."

A day away . . . Chantale bit her lip, thinking of Jean-Claude and Catherine. A day away. A day away . . .

"You'll be gone by then," she said, and they both recognized the new air of resolution in her voice.

"Got your flight plan for me, angel?"

Caroline glanced up from the form she was filling out. "Just a second, Bill," she responded, signing her name on the bottom of it. There she was. Committed.

He took it from her and gave it a cursory glance. "California again, huh? What's the matter? We're not interesting enough for you around here?"

"I get homesick sometimes," she said. "Do you have a weather report?"

"Yeah. I'll get you one. Be gone long this time?"

She shrugged. "I don't know, Bill. A few weeks maybe. Have to spend some time with Eric in San Jose. Why so many questions?"

"Why so touchy? Here you go. Looks like some turbulence a little west of here."

"It's all right." She took the paper from him. "I can handle it. Is the Butterfly ready?"

"Should be. Extra fuel tanks and all. Though why you don't want to stop is—"

"Bye, Bill," Caroline interrupted. "Have to be going. See you in a few weeks."

"Right." He shook his head as he watched her go.

The airplane was at its usual place on the field, pegged securely down against the wind and rain. Caroline tossed her suitcase and flying gear inside and started her preflight check. And, all the time that her hands were expertly checking out the airplane, her mind was racing. Was this really the right thing to do? Filing an erroneous flight plan carried penalties with it. And the airlines she had called had said it was too dangerous to fly into London.

Caroline shook her head and made herself concentrate as she climbed into the cockpit. The engines whirred to life instantaneously, the propellers spinning cleanly. All the instruments seemed to be in order: full fuel tanks, good oil pressure. Eddie was her responsibility. He was only a child, and she had been the one to fill his head with dreams of being a hero. Were it not for her, he would still be in the control tower, talking her up into the sky . . .

She was ready. Taking a deep breath, she slipped into the leather flying jacket and pulled her cap on over her rebellious curls, checked her parachute one last time, slipped on her safety belt. The radio was working, and she sent out her first call signal to the tower.

Eddie was only fifteen. That was what she had to remember. He was not a man, making a man's decision. He was a boy, a child filled with hope and wonder at the thought of glory: bored in Newport with his stuffy family and his position in society and wanting to impress a pretty waitress with his feats. He would do something stupid. Most heroes did, and if they lived through the stupidity, they were given a medal. If they didn't, people called them foolish.

Caroline took off, flying toward the west. It wasn't until she was ten miles out that she changed course. She took the headphones off and turned off the radio. She didn't want to hear what anybody had to say once they realized that she'd turned back.

And Andrew . . . soon she would be seeing Andrew. Her stomach muscles tensed as she thought of Andrew. He was different. He was in England because of an intense conviction. He wouldn't do anything stupid. He would outlive the war and come home with stories to tell. She wanted—she had—to believe that.

The coastline flashed below her, the white line of breakers on the beach receding as she flew out and over the ocean, still dotted here and there with gay fishing boats and the occasional sailboat. It seemed everyone in Newport had a sailing boat. Eddie Carruthers's father did little but talk about the America's Cup, some sort of trophy for racing. Caroline had hardly listened to him, on the one occasion when they had met at a formal luncheon party. If the conversation didn't have to do with airplanes and flying, she wasn't particularly interested. Now she wished she had listened. It would give her something to think about during this long flight.

She knew that she could do it. She had flown across the continent several times, and she was sure that she had the endurance. And others flew across the ocean all the time. Even women. Hadn't Amelia Earhart done the exact same thing years ago? Of course, she had also disappeared at sea, but it was best not to think of that. No, that wasn't the problem. What she had to do was calm herself and her heart and all the strident voices inside her head that told her everything was her fault. If she didn't, Eddie Carruthers was going to get shot out of the sky and she would be at fault.

Mostly, the trip was boring. There was no radio contact at all, and the weather was almost uniformly good, somewhat to Caroline's surprise. She had heard of the terrible storms that sometimes brewed over the Atlantic. The most danger she faced was the sun slanting into the cockpit which made her feel warm and drowsy, and the monotonous view of ocean and sky which added its soporific effect. She flew at twelve thousand feet to stay well within the zone where she could breathe, and at that height could see the whitecaps dancing on the waves, the occasional whale surfacing to spout into the sky. Caroline found herself smiling in appreciation of these small things. Perhaps someday when the war was over, she would learn to sail. It would be nice to be closer to everything that was happening below her now.

Twice she saw ships, gray hulking monsters. Battleships, she realized, recognizing them from their lines. Steven was trying to get a contract for battleships. He had been talking about it all last week, complaining that so far he had been able to build only the smaller vessels, the destroyers and the escorts and, recently, the submarines. He wanted more; he always wanted more. Clustered around the battleships was a small flotilla of craft, and these were more familiar. The destroyers and their escorts that Steven manufactured in Newport crisscrossed in front of the battleships, scanning the ocean for enemy submarines. She altered course drastically both times when she saw the ships, not knowing whom they belonged to, but knowing that it would be exceptionally ironic if it were she who was shot out of the sky. She flew around them each time in a wide circle, not coming back to her original course until they were many miles behind her. And she couldn't help wondering, each time, what battleships were doing out in the North Atlantic. Much later she would find out they were part of Roosevelt's destroyers-for-bases trade with England.

She ate the sandwiches that she had prepared herself: ham with Swiss cheese and tangy mustard and thick fresh lettuce, and she sipped coffee from the Thermos flask she had brought. Not too much coffee, though. She had no toilet facilities for the ten hours on the Butterfly. The sun slanted down behind her, and the clouds all around lit up with shades of fire from its setting rays: pinks, and oranges, and scarlets. Caroline smiled, appreciating the show that was being put on for her alone.

With another four hours to go, she switched to the auxiliary fuel tanks. Everything was running smoothly. Nothing had overheated; all the gauges looked good; the engines were purring along contentedly, and she blessed Eric for his competence in airplane design. From time to time, she reached an arm in the air, flexing her fingers, stretching her body as much as she could in the cramped cockpit.

The sun had gone down, and the sky behind her flamed for a

while before subsiding into a deep blue-gray. Caroline switched on her navigation lights out of habit, and flew on into the darkness. There was a blackout in England, she knew, but Heathrow would surely have a runway lit. The Germans wanted to bomb London itself, not the airport, she reasoned. She would be able to land safely.

As long as she found Heathrow.

Caroline flipped on the cockpit light and frowned at her charts. She should be approaching land by now, but there were no variations in the darkness below her, no welcoming lighthouses discernible in the distance. She could have gone off course. It wasn't probable, but it was always possible, especially as she felt so tired.

There was the other problem, too, lurking in the back of her mind. She was coming in, low on fuel, and with no way to identify herself. What if she was picked up on radar and thought to be an enemy aircraft? What if they decided to shoot first and ask questions later? What if, what if, what if . . .

She frowned and shook her head. It was all right. She was getting nervous and beginning to imagine things because it was dark and she was tired and hungry. She would see the coastline soon. And then, just as she was persuading herself that everything really was all right, she heard a clanging sound, off to port in the engine. Horrible and wrenching, the sound of metal on metal, screeching into the darkness. Oh, God, she thought desperately. No. Nothing can go wrong. Not now. Not when it is so important that I get to England. . . .

And the unwelcome thought, rising unbidden in her mind: If she went down now, no one would ever know what had happened to her. She had filed a flight plan for California. No one knew that she was here. No one.

The clanging sound continued, and she scanned her instruments. Nothing. Nothing looked amiss, but something horrible was happening in that engine. Think, Caroline. What did it sound like? The flywheel, perhaps? If it were loose, it could make that noise. Maybe.

She wasn't going to take any chances. Better to feather the engine now, and hope that it would come back to life later when she needed it to land the Butterfly. The plane could fly on one engine. She had never done it for any length of time, but this was supposed to be an advanced airplane design. She would have to see. Compressing her lips, she reached out to turn off the port engine.

The comparative silence, with only the normal engine roar after that horrible noise, was almost ominous. The Butterfly, deprived of one of its engines, swerved immediately to the left, and Caroline wrenched it back, making the corrections that would keep her on course. Airspeed was down . . . well, that made sense, she was flying at half power. Theoretically, she could do this. Theoretically, it wasn't a problem to fly on one engine. Practically, it was something else altogether.

And if the reserve fuel tank on her starboard engine ran out, she was going down anyway.

It was cold at this altitude, but there were beads of sweat on her forehead. This was trickier than she had thought it was going to be, but if she had it to do over, she would still do the same thing. Eddie was her responsibility.

She thought that it was her imagination at first, but it seemed that the darkness below her was suddenly more tangible, more bulky. And then, here and there flashed a pinpoint of light from blackout curtains poorly drawn, candles in the darkness. With relief, she knew she was flying over England.

Caroline thought desperately of the charts she had looked at before taking off. She had to be sure of her altitudes, sure that she wasn't flying too low. She had lost some height when she feathered the port engine, and the last thing that she wanted now, was to run into the side of a mountain. The Butterfly flew on on its one engine, a little crookedly, like a horse doing a half pass in a dressage competition, but bravely and steadily nevertheless.

Ten minutes out of London, Caroline pressed the starter button for the port engine. It didn't catch, and she tried again, her mind spinning as quickly as the feathered propeller outside her window. Please God, please God, please . . . And then on the third try it caught, and immediately the horrible screeching sound was back. Caroline bit her lip and left it on. Whatever was getting torn up in there, she needed that engine to land. She would worry about the damage later.

Five minutes out of London there was a flicker on her instrument panel, and the port engine blanked out for a moment. It fired again, almost immediately, and then there was a final wrenching scream and the engine whirred on. Caroline frowned. Something had gone, obviously. And if it *was* the flywheel, then the engine was going to start overheating, very fast. She thought back to the diagrams she had studied. What was next to the flywheel? Something was going already, or the engine wouldn't have blanked out like that. . . .

She had the radio on, but none of her call signals were getting any response from the ground. Very well. She could go in silently, and pray that no other plane was doing the same thing at the same time. . . . She was over London now, but there was still nothing but darkness below. It was a strange feeling to fly over a blacked-out city.

And then the port engine misfired again.

She followed her compass heading and turned into Heathrow's landing pattern. Yes, she was right, there were lights on one runway, dim and barely visible through the rain that was falling, but there nonetheless. To Caroline, flying through the night with fear on her left, they were as cheerful and cozy as a welcoming fireplace. She took a deep breath and turned into her final approach.

After all that, landing was easy. The wheels touched down lightly once and then bit and held on the wet tarmac. Finally, she glided to a stop with eight hundred feet of runway to spare.

Outside in the rain, a spotlight directed her way suddenly turned on. Caroline blinked in the bright light and switched off her engines, pulling off her cap and shaking out her curls. She was exhausted and relieved, but a small edge of fear clutched at her stomach. She hoped she wasn't too late.

Only when she opened the cockpit did she realize that the ring of men standing around her wore the uniforms of the British Royal Army, and that all their guns were leveled at her. From somewhere off behind the spotlight, a British voice drawled, "And what, pray tell, have we here?"

Chantale's English pilot had been right. Two days later the German Army arrived in Angers.

Pierre de Montclair was first aware of the Germans' presence early in the morning when he awoke in Isabelle's apartment. He got up carefully so that he wouldn't wake her and slipped into the maroon dressing gown that she kept in her bedroom for him. He would make breakfast, he decided: café au lait and croissants and that wonderful English marmalade that Isabelle loved so dearly. He crossed through the luxurious living room into the kitchen and went to open the window to the morning. Another perfect summer day, now that the rains had stopped.

The place du Ralliement, spread out below him, was filled with people.

Pierre frowned. It wasn't market day; there was no reason for such a crowd. He opened the window wider still and leaned out, trying to catch a glimpse of something, anything, that would tell him what was happening.

From the rue des Arènes came the muffled roar of engines. Not the usual automobiles that had driven around when gasoline was plentiful, but vehicles with larger motors, and many of them. As Pierre watched, a cavalcade of trucks and motorcycles and one armored tank swept out of the street and into the square, going around it once before braking in the middle, facing the theater.

Facing him.

Behind him, there was a whisper of silk and a hint of lush perfume. Isabelle's arms encircled him from behind. "What is all the noise, Pierre?"

"It's the Germans," he replied, not turning from the spectacle. "The Germans are here."

She moved around him to look at them, her eyes dancing. "Oh, good!" she exclaimed. "Finally! Now we can all have some peace and quiet. Were you making breakfast, darling?"

"Yes," he said tonelessly, not moving from the window. This was the first time he had actually seen any of them—the conquerors. They were very dapper, he had to admit that, in their gray-green uniforms and their shining boots. The formation that they were making below him was perfect. The point of this particular formation, he saw, was to unfurl a vast flag displaying an enormous swastika which they were putting up across the front of the theater. The scene was all very impressive, from the soldiers standing at ramrod attention to the sweeping statements of their commanding officer, now standing in front of the theater and addressing the people through a microphone. "People of the city of Angers! We come to bring you peace. You have nothing to fear from us. All that we ask is cooperation, and everything will be fine. We are your friends! Do nothing to offend us, and we will do nothing to offend you. Peaceful coexistence is possible!"

"Sounds reasonable to me," said Isabelle, still looking at the soldiers below. "They're terribly handsome, aren't they?"

" 'Terribly handsome'?" echoed Pierre, diverted for a moment from his dark thoughts. These were the people who had killed his father. "Should I be jealous, Isabelle?"

"Oh, darling, not at all," she said carelessly, but he saw how she was looking at them, and her glances struck fear in his heart.

Annie had the news almost immediately, and went rushing out to the stables. "Countess! Countess, are you here?"

Chantale, dressed in jodhpurs, riding boots, and a white shirt, emerged from the gloom of one of the horse stalls. "Annie? What is all this noise?"

The cook's round face was red with the heat and strain of running. "Oh, Countess, I've just heard! They're here!"

"Who?"

"The Germans! The *sales Boches*!"

"Here?" Chantale looked out into the stable yard.

"No, no, Countess, not here at the estate. But in Angers. They've just taken over the Hôtel de France and the railway station, and they've put a swastika on the theater." She paused a moment, breathless. "They're giving speeches about cooperation, Countess."

"So." Chantale felt her legs grow weak and sat down on a nearby bale of hay. "It's happened at last." She felt suddenly old and exhausted. She brushed a lock of red hair off her forehead. "So what happens next?"

The older woman shrugged. "Who knows, Countess? We are occupied."

We are occupied. And who knew anything else? Who knew how long it would be before the Germans found the Château de Montclair and decided to make it their home? Soon there would be German officers riding their horses, eating the fruits from their orchards, sitting down at their table . . . Chantale shivered at the thought. The refugees would no longer have a safe place to come.

Who was she fooling? She would probably be a refugee herself before very long.

She stood up abruptly. "I'm going out riding, Annie," she said. "Thank you for telling me."

"But, Countess—"

"Thank you, Annie." Chantale led her gelding out of his stall and into the sunshine of the stable yard. The day was, indeed, starting to get hot. She mounted quickly, and, picking up the braided leather reins, turned the head of the horse out of the gates toward the forest.

At first, she walked him quietly among the dappled shadows of the trees, down the familiar paths, worn by generations of de Montclairs who had ridden their horses on days such as this one. And yet no day could ever be like this one. Where the trail opened up she urged him on into a canter, the rhythm smooth and pulsating, and as they emerged back into the sunshine of an open field the canter became a reckless gallop, on and on and on, as though they could escape anything and everything by running, running, running . . .

They came back, both of them sweating, two hours later. Chantale hosed the horse down out in the stable yard before giving his care over to Etienne, the stableboy who watched over the people as well as the horses who spent their nights in his stables. She went back to the house and showered quickly, and played with the children in the nursery until it was time for their supper. She was laughing and giggling and singing with them as though nothing in the world could be wrong. I want them to remember this, she thought suddenly, fiercely: I want these to be their memories of their home, not their father storming out, not the *Boches* marching in. These times.

She dressed for dinner, selecting an emerald-green dress that matched her eyes, putting on the diamond necklace that Pierre had given her many years ago as an engagement present, plaiting her long tresses into braids, which she wound around her head.

Surprisingly, Pierre was there for dinner.

They sat in the vast dining room, at the long mahogany table that had fed generations of de Montclairs before them. Marie-Louise presided, dressed in her eternal black, with Pierre in his elegant dinner jacket sitting on one side of her and Chantale on the other. Antoinette served them the potato-and-leek soup, and Pierre poured out the wine, one from their own small vineyard. It was almost too cold in the big room.

Marie-Louise cleared her throat. "There have been rumors about today," she said carefully. "It appears that the Germans may be in Angers very soon."

Pierre blew on his soup, the same annoying habit his father had had before him. "It's not a rumor," he said comfortably. "They're in the city. They've made the Hôtel de France their headquarters. Most of the enlisted men are staying at the railway station for now."

Marie-Louise did not show her surprise.

"For now? Meaning exactly what?"

He shrugged. "Until they find something more suitable, I suppose. They will have to requisition some space, Mother, it only makes sense. You can't hold that against them."

"I see." Marie-Louise's voice was icy. "And if they have to requisition the Château de Montclair? Will that make sense to you, Pierre? Will you not hold that against them?"

Pierre's hand jerked for a moment, but then he said smoothly, "I'm sure that they want to stay in the city, Mother. They won't be interested in us out here."

Antoinette appeared and removed the soup plates, moving swiftly and silently between table and sideboard. She replaced them with the trout and withdrew. Pierre frowned at his plate, and frowned still more as he tasted the fish. "Ugh! What happened to the butter sauce?"

"There is no butter," Chantale said evenly. "Annie says that it hasn't been on the market for weeks. She's had to make do with what she can get."

"Well, it's not good enough. I had butter just last night at a restaurant," Pierre rejoined.

"Then perhaps you should go on eating at restaurants," his mother replied. "If you wish to eat at home, we would appreciate fewer complaints. I have no quarrels with the way my kitchen is being run."

Chantale took a drink of her wine. Was it her imagination, or had that last comment been intended for her ears? She had no idea how much her mother-in-law knew, or didn't know, about her activities. They didn't talk; they never talked. Perhaps there was no meaning behind Marie-Louise's words. Or perhaps there was.

Pierre pushed away his plate and poured himself more wine. "The problem with both of you," he said, "is that you always think you're right. Whatever you think, whatever you do, that's right. But you don't stop to consider that there might be other points of view. What? Oh, yes, Antoinette, I'm finished."

"Thank you," Chantale said to Antoinette as the girl took away her plate and replaced it with the chicken and asparagus and new potatoes. To her husband, she added, "What other points of view are you talking about?"

"Other points of view on trout?" Marie-Louise asked with a twinkle in her eye.

"Don't be ridiculous," he said, savagely cutting into the chicken on his plate. "I mean about the Germans, of course. Can't you see that we would benefit more from just accepting the fact that they are here? All right, so we didn't ask for this. But maybe it was inevitable. After the last war—"

"You will not," said Marie-Louise coldly, "speak of the last war. Not at this table."

"All right, all right." He washed down the chicken with a swallow of wine. "But, Mother, they're here. We might as well make the best of it."

"And what exactly does that mean?" she asked him.

Pierre shrugged. "Try to get along with them. Don't always be so damned negative. They're not monsters, you know. They're just human beings like you and me."

Chantale stared at him. "Human beings perhaps," she said softly. "But not like me."

"There you go again." Pierre fairly shrieked. "Being so damned judgmental. Who gave you the right? You don't even know them!"

Chantale threw down her fork. "And you do?"

"Not yet, no! But, given the chance, I will! It's the best thing to do—cooperate. They'll be reasonable as long as we cooperate!"

"Somehow," Chantale said, pushing away her plate, leaving most of the food untouched, "that thought doesn't give me much comfort."

Pierre poured himself another glass of wine. "It's hopeless talking with you," he said. "Hopeless. You're too naive. You can't possibly understand."

Chantale almost said something, and then bit it back. There was no sense in getting angry with him.

As though to change the subject, Marie-Louise said to Chantale, "I see that you are spending a great deal of time in the stables these days. It's good to see you so interested at last in horses."

There *was* something behind that, Chantale was sure. "I have felt more interested lately," she replied carefully.

Pierre looked at them both, shaking his head. "You see?" he asked. "Something politically important is happening to us, and all that you two can find to talk about is horses. You see why I don't enjoy talking with you!''

Later, as Chantale was starting up the stairs to her bedroom, Marie-Louise stopped her with a hand on her arm. ''I have been wrong about you,'' the older woman said softly. ''You are a good girl, Chantale.''

Chantale searched her mother-in-law's face. It was impossible to tell how much she knew, what she approved, how far she would be willing to go. But for now, perhaps, this was enough. Only time would tell if more would be needed.

Chapter Fifteen

Caroline leaned her head back against the wall and closed her eyes. She had been sitting on the same bench, in the same place, for over two hours, and to say that she was feeling exhausted would be a gross understatement.

It was a drab room, furnished with only a large table and a few chairs, a filing cabinet in one corner, and this bench against the wall. No windows. She had already, in the time she had been there, explored all that there was to explore; the filing cabinet was locked. They had let her out once, when she had asked to go to the bathroom. That was all.

They had been polite. Her airplane had been politely confiscated; she had been politely brought here—wherever here was—and politely escorted, when she had requested it, to the washroom. Everyone was correct and courteous in their expressions. After listening to her story, or what she was permitted to tell of it, they had scratched their heads and gone off to consult. Presumably they were still consulting.

Caroline took a deep breath and tried to calm herself. In another few minutes she was going to start taking this room apart. Precious time was being wasted. While she sat here and the British Army did whatever they did with foreigners who set down at their airport, unannounced in wartime, Eddie could be dying. It would be the height of absurdity, she thought, if he were to be shot down somewhere over the Channel while she waited here for someone in authority to let her go.

There were footsteps in the corridor, the jangle of keys, and finally the door was opened. Caroline raised her eyes. It was the same jailer who had locked her there before. "Mrs. Asheford? The colonel will see you now."

Decent of him, she thought grimly, following him out into the corridor. "This way, please." They went down another corridor, up a flight of stairs, to a large mahogany door on which her escort rapped smartly. Hearing something from within that she couldn't, he opened the door, stood aside, and said, "Mrs. Asheford," in the same manner as he might have announced the King of England. Caroline walked into the room.

The first person she saw was a middle-aged man with gray hair and a gray mustache standing behind the vast oaken desk which was directly across from the door. And then, scanning the room quickly, she saw Andrew.

He was half sitting, half standing, leaning against what was some sort of operations table, and he looked dazzling. Perhaps it was the RAF uniform, or perhaps it was her relief at finally seeing a familiar face; but she smiled quickly, spontaneously, and ignored the middle-aged colonel behind the desk. "Andrew!"

He smiled before glancing quickly at the other man. "I'm glad to see you're all right," he said to her.

The colonel cleared his throat. "Ahem. Er—Captain Starkey—I assume that you are prepared to vouch for this woman and her story?"

Andrew pushed himself off the table. "*Are* you all right?" he asked.

Caroline nodded. "Just tired."

The Englishman was not to be deterred. "Captain Starkey, do you identify this woman as Caroline Copeland Asheford?"

"Yes," said Andrew, not looking at him, still watching Caroline. "This is Mrs. Asheford."

"Well, then, that's that. I don't mind telling you, Mrs. Asheford, that you've caused quite a few difficulties around here."

Caroline forced herself to look at him. "I'm sorry," she said. "I tried to make radio contact when I came in. I didn't mean to do anything quite so irregular." She looked back at Andrew. "I just had to get to England."

"I understand," he said.

"Yes, well, that's all well and good, but there are certain formalities," the colonel pointed out. "It's wartime, and any airplane coming in unannounced like that is suspect." He shook his head. "You are extremely fortunate, Mrs. Asheford, that you did not come up against a barrage balloon, or, worse, a German bombing unit. We've had quite a few of those over London these last few weeks."

"Mrs. Asheford," Andrew said, still looking at her, "is a superlative pilot."

"Mrs. Asheford," rejoined the Englishman, "is a very lucky woman." He walked around his desk and over to a small table, up against a bookcase, on which stood a decanter and some glasses. "May I offer you a drink, Mrs. Asheford?"

Caroline wrenched her eyes away from Andrew again. "Yes, please," she said, walking over to accept the snifter of brandy he offered her.

"There you are. Just sit there, Mrs. Asheford, it's the most comfortable chair. Drink, old chap?"

"Thank you," said Andrew, crossing over and sitting in an armchair across from Caroline. "I'm sorry this all took so long. I'm afraid they had a hard time finding me."

"It's all right," Caroline said. "I was just beginning to be afraid that you wouldn't come. Andrew, it's about Eddie Carruthers—"

He held up his hand. "It's all right, Caroline, everything's all right. Don't worry about him. Just try to relax." He smiled at the colonel, who was seating himself in the remaining plush armchair. "Mrs. Asheford will need a hotel room and a meal. Can your people make those arrangements for tonight? I'll find her a place tomorrow for the remainder of her stay in England."

"Quite right," he said. "Not a problem at all. We'll see to it at once." He looked over at Caroline and smiled benevolently, raising his glass. "Permit me, my dear Mrs. Asheford. I knew your father slightly. I always thought highly of him."

Caroline felt bemused. The brandy was warming her insides, and she cradled the glass in her hands. "My father?"

"Yes, yes, of course. Marcus Copeland and I were business associates for a short time, just before the war. A minor enterprise, I was only a young man then, just starting out. But I respected Marcus enormously."

She forced herself to smile. "How gracious of you," she murmured. To all of England, she was Marcus Copeland's daughter. That had been the purpose of her mother's hasty marriage to him—to give Caroline a name. "I never knew him myself, of course," she said, enjoying the irony.

"Of course not. Dreadful luck. I daresay you would have liked him. And what, if I may ask, has become of your mother? I met her just once, at a dance I believe. Stunning woman. You have her looks, Mrs. Asheford."

"Thank you. She's remarried. She's living in Africa."

He raised his eyebrows. "Africa, eh? Dicey place these days. Dicey place. Well, Starkey, you'll be wanting to be off. I'll have one of my men escort Mrs. Asheford to her hotel . . ."

"Not at all," said Andrew amiably. "I'll see that she gets some supper and take her to the hotel myself. It's the least that I can do, seeing that she flew all this way to talk to me."

"Eh? Oh, right you are, then. Right you are." The colonel stood up. "A pleasure, Mrs. Asheford. Do us a favor, though, and the next time you visit, do so in a more conventional manner. . . ."

"Thank you, Colonel." She realized that she didn't know his name, and cared even less. "Good night."

Andrew settled her and her suitcase in the back of a staff car, then got in next to her. "Whew! You were damned lucky, Caroline, that he knew your father. That could have been very sticky back there."

"Marcus Copeland isn't my father," she said automatically.

"Well, you know that, and I know that, but thank God you had the sense to keep it to yourself. Do you have any idea what the penalties are for flying unannounced into foreign airspace with a war on?"

She was tired and hungry and didn't want to talk about it. "Lecture me tomorrow, Andrew, okay? I can't handle any more just now."

"Right." He didn't say anything else until they pulled up in front of the Savoy Grill. "Here we are."

Caroline looked at the entrance. "I'm not exactly dressed for this," she said awkwardly.

"Never mind. They know me here. It won't be a problem." And, as she still hesitated, he added, "I thought you were hungry!"

"I am," said Caroline, sliding off the seat and getting out of the car.

Andrew ordered for both of them, soup and steaks with grilled tomatoes and russet potatoes, followed by a salad and that particularly English course, the savory—mushrooms on toast. She refused dessert. By then she was too sleepy to care.

As though sensing her mood and responding to it, Andrew kept up the conversation, commenting on the skill of the chef who made do despite the rationing of butter and sugar. He talked about how difficult the blackout was getting in London ("More accidents in the first few months than enemy planes, Caroline, can you imagine?''). He told amusing stories about some of the men in the squadron. And all the while, as she ate and listened to him she felt a warm blanket of contentment creeping up around the edges of her consciousness.

The staff car was waiting outside when they finished. There was no problem checking in to the hotel chosen for her. "It's all been arranged, sir,'' the desk clerk informed Andrew. He carried her suitcase up the narrow staircase to her room, and then, awkwardly, stood with his hat in his hands. "Well, Caroline, I'll come pick you up after breakfast in the morning."

She turned from her survey of the room, the faded chintz on the armchairs, the gleaming mahogany of the armoire, the inviting expanse of the bed, and said, merely, "Stay with me."

Andrew put out his arms, and Caroline stumbled sleepily into them, feeling him hold her close to him, his strong arms around her, his heartbeat familiar. And then, almost as though at a distance, she felt him undressing her and putting on the long flannel nightgown that she had in her bag, felt him carrying her to the bed and sliding her in under the covers. Vaguely, she was aware of him kissing her forehead and murmuring something to her. She didn't know what he said. She was already asleep.

Caroline and Andrew went out to Surrey to the hangars where the RAF airplanes were being kept, and to the small military buildings where operations were being planned.

Caroline had awakened that morning in London with Andrew sleeping next to her. She had remembered little of the previous night; she had been so tired. Andrew had told her that Eddie was safe, and Caroline had gratefully accepted his plan to escort her to him. It felt so good to have Andrew next to her, but that would have to wait. Whatever was going to happen between them would simply have to wait until she had made certain that Eddie would not be a part of the war.

They hitched a ride on a passing convoy of trucks and rode almost all the way with them, the soldiers jovial and joking, passing around packages of American cigarettes, talking about their girlfriends. Caroline watched the passing lush green fields with interest. She had been born in England. Although she had no memories of it, this was her birthplace, and it was exciting to finally be here, even under these conditions.

They walked the last mile together, holding hands, Andrew

carrying her battered suitcase. At the bustling RAF complex, Caroline was shown without ceremony to the small room in the women's quarters where she was to stay. There were few enough women here, secretaries and operations assistants and radio operators, but they all smiled at Caroline in a friendly enough fashion and she returned their greetings with enthusiasm.

They gave her tea in the mess hall, and one of the radio operators, a girl from East Anglia named Gladys, talked with her for a few minutes. "Eddie Carruthers? Our Eddie? Oh, luv, you don't need to worry about him. Saw through him the very first day, the major did." She giggled. "He isn't flying, that's for sure, but it's not for want of trying. They've got him helping us in the radio room. He's a real whiz."

Caroline smiled. "He's a good air controller. It's what he did back home."

"Right you are. Calm. That's a good thing to be around here, what with all the excitement all the time."

Caroline looked out past her through the open door, at the rain-sodden fields. The place seemed almost deserted. "Excitement?"

"Oh, well, we've got our moments of calm here and there. But when the boys are going off, or when the bombers come over, it's good to have somebody with a cool head. We've had to move operations three times already on account of the German reconnaissance planes. Eddie's been a great help."

"I'm just glad he's not flying."

Gladys shook her head. "I don't know. What with the war heating up, sooner or later, they'll be taking whomever they can get, you mark my words. And if he's as good a pilot as everybody seems to think, they might just be using him one of these days. Come to that, they might be using us." She giggled.

"Us?"

"Oh, you know. Women. Pilots. I know that it's against all the rules having women fly during the war, but I should think that they'd be glad of the help."

"Are you a pilot, too?" Caroline asked curiously.

"As ever was, ducky! My father, he used to run one of those little companies—oh, you know, rent a plane for an afternoon, impress your girlfriend. He made a decent living at it, too, before the war. He taught me to fly before I was much older than young Eddie." She grimaced. "So the brilliant bloody RAF has me running the radio room for a bunch of Yanks. I ask you!"

"I see." Caroline sipped her tea. It was scalding hot and too strong, but felt good and warming going down.

"Yes. Well. Got to be off, myself. Go on duty in another fifteen minutes." She stood up, trim and pretty in her uniform. "Thinking of staying long?"

Caroline looked up at her. "I don't know. I haven't thought about it." She felt deflated somehow, her sense of purpose thwarted. She had come to save Eddie, only to discover that he didn't particularly need saving. And now—what? Her sense of purpose removed, she found herself in a familiar position. "I just don't know," she repeated.

"Well, be seeing you around, I suppose. Cheerio!"

Caroline stayed where she was for a long time, turning her teacup around and around in her hands. What *was* she going to do, anyway? Eddie was safe and well. She was going to scold him, of course, when she finally got to see him. He had to know that he couldn't go around frightening people and charging off into the blue without discussing it with anybody, but . . . he was all right.

And Andrew . . . She didn't need her racing heart to remind her of how she was starting to feel, once again, about him. The memories of those early days together in San Francisco seemed very near the surface of her thoughts. She had tried for so long— she had tried for years—to leave those memories behind, to forget Andrew, to love Steven and only Steven. But then Steven had become withdrawn, distant, unreachable, lost in his excitement over Asheford Shipbuilding and angry with her for being who she was. Andrew not only accepted those parts of her that Steven spurned, he loved her for them. Of that she was sure. Despite all the time, despite all the misunderstandings, they still loved each other.

But what was she supposed to do with those feelings? The words of her old psychologist suddenly crept unbidden into her mind: "Feelings, Caroline, are like waves on the surface of the ocean. They come and go. They are influenced by so many things—the wind, the tide, a passing boat. They change, all the time. But deep under the surface is where the real you lies, down where it is deep and dark and peaceful. That part of you isn't influenced by every idea that floats by, by every gust of wind . . . that's the part that you need to focus on. The feelings are just incidental." But were they? Was what she felt for Andrew incidental? Or was Andrew the person who touched that deeper part of her, the real core of Caroline? And how could she tell?

One thing was certain. She would never know if she turned around now and headed back to Newport. She would never discover what any of this meant if she ran away from it. For better or for worse, she was going to have to stay in England for a time. She smiled suddenly. Somehow, she felt as though it was going to be for better.

Justine's eyes searched the doctor's face. He was young and tired, and he didn't want to tell this young woman what he had to tell her. He indicated the chair in the hospital waiting room where she had already been sitting, all these hours. "Please sit down, Mrs. Asheford."

"What is it?" she asked, her throat already constricting with pain. She knew; she knew already. She could read it in his face. It took only his voice to make it real.

"We've done what we can, Mrs. Asheford, but I'm afraid that your baby is dead. It was poliomyelitis. Even if he lived, he would have been crippled." Almost as an afterthought, he added, "I'm sorry."

William drove her home, and all the way back, Justine sat silently, staring in front of her, not listening to the words of comfort he offered her. He had no idea how much they sounded like platitudes to her ears.

She went straight up to her bedroom and closed the door, and later, when William came upstairs with tea and soup and bread on a tray, she refused to look at it. She sat on the edge of the bed, staring into space, not crying, not talking, not doing anything. It was as though her child's death had taken away all the life from her as well, drained her completely of her personality.

Steven had come and taken Nicholas away, to be cared for by Marie at the mansion, and now William called him back. "I don't know what to do," he said. "She won't come out of her room. She won't talk to me. I don't know what she's doing in there."

The big red-bearded man stood in the corridor and rapped on the bedroom door. "Justine? Justine, it's me, Steven. You have to open the door now." There was no response from within, and he knocked harder. "Justine, don't make us break the door. We just want to know if you're all right."

William tried again. "Honey, come open the door. I know how much you're hurting. You have to let me talk to you."

Steven shook his head. "Better give her some time alone," he advised. "Maybe she just needs some time. I'll come back tomorrow, and we can decide what to do then."

But by the next day there was still no sign of movement from the bedroom, and both men were worried. "What should we do?"

"Break down the door, I suppose," Steven said reluctantly. "Come on. We'll do it together."

The two men put their shoulders against the bedroom door and heaved, and on the second try they went crashing into the room. Justine was still sitting in the same position on the bed, staring into space, her eyes blank and empty. "Christ," muttered William, going to her at once and putting his arms around her. "Justine, baby, it's all right. I'm here. It's all right."

Steven grabbed a blanket and put it around her. "Looks like she's gone into shock," he said. "I think we should get her to the hospital."

They put her in the ward for the mentally unbalanced in the same hospital where her baby had died. Justine sat there in the room assigned her, still silent, still focusing her gaze, not on people, but on the middle distance. "You can't stay here all the time," one of the nurses told William, and he reluctantly agreed. "What she needs right now is some time here with us. Some time to rest, and to forget. And, Mr. Asheford, perhaps you're not the best person to come visiting. You may remind her too much of the tragedy. Does she have any friends who can come and see her?"

William looked at Steven. "What about Caroline?"

Steven shrugged. "I haven't seen her in a few days. She's probably out at the airport." He saw his brother's expression, and his own softened. "Don't worry, William. I'll find her. She'll come and visit Justine."

"All right. We should do something about little William's funeral, too. . . ." His voice trailed off uncertainly.

"Caroline can take care of that, too," Steven said. "Leave it to us, Will. We'll take care of everything."

Marie, busy tending both Elizabeth and Nicholas, raised harried eyes to his inquiry. No, she didn't know where Mrs. Asheford had gone. Yes, she thought that she was away for a few days. She had gone off in her airplane.

Steven called the airport, and after some delays, got through
to Bill. "Caroline? Yes, she flew out three days ago. Must be in
California by now. Monday it was that she left, I think . . . let's
see. Yes, Monday. Her flight plan said San Francisco."

Goddamn it, Steven thought. The one time that she was
needed around here, and she had run away again to Eric. Typically thoughtless. She hadn't even bothered to tell him she was
going, which said something about how she was drifting away
from him lately. Well, she was going to have to come back, that
was all that there was to it. Justine needed her. They all needed
her. There was the baby's funeral to arrange and the children to
look after. There was Justine to comfort. Damn it, her place was
here.

He had an even harder time getting through to Eric. No one
answered at his home number, and Intraglobal secretaries with
bored voices urged him to leave a number where Mr. Beaumont
could reach him, when he had time. "I have to speak with him
directly," Steven said explosively. "This isn't business. It's about
his—niece."

It took another fifteen minutes, while Steven held the line, for
Eric to be located and to take the call. "Steven? What's the
problem?"

"I'd like to talk to Caroline."

There was a moment of silence. "Why can't you, exactly?"

God damn it, why were people still playing games with him?
Hadn't he been through enough? "Because she didn't even tell
me she was leaving. Just have her call me, will you? As soon as
possible?"

Eric cleared his throat. "I think that you are mistaken about
something, Steven. Where *is* Caroline?"

"Out there with you! She's run away again, and I'm sick and
tired of it. She's needed here."

"She's not here, Steven."

"But she has to be!" There was a sick feeling in his stomach.
"Listen, Eric. She left Monday. She ordered extra fuel tanks
and filed a flight plan for San Francisco."

Monday, Eric thought. She could be anywhere by now. But
where? San Francisco? But why? He wasn't there, and Starkey
wasn't there anymore. . . . She knew that. She knew that Starkey was in England. And she ordered extra fuel tanks. He took
a deep breath. "Listen, Steven. I'll get back to you. I'll get my
people on this right away. We'll find her. I'll let you know."

"As soon as possible? Eric, there are family problems here. We need her."

"Of course. I'll get right back to you." Eric hung up and immediately buzzed his secretary. "Julie? We've got problems. I want you to cable Beneteau and Giroux and What's-Their-Name, right away. Tell them that there's a problem. Tell them Mrs. Asheford may well be in England now. Got that?"

Julie's voice was calm. "Yes, sir. Mrs. Asheford may be in England."

"Right. Tell them to cancel the other plans, meanwhile. Do that right now, Julie. And then send one of our people from London out to see if she's contacted a Captain Starkey of the RAF. Or just to find her."

"Yes, sir. Right away."

Eric leaned back in his chair, but the expression on his face was far from relaxed. Damn Caroline. The last thing in the world that he wanted to do was endanger her. She was the only family that he had. She was the future of Intraglobal.

And, if they were correct about where she was, she had just flown herself into a collision course with Intraglobal's deadly plans for Andrew Starkey.

Steven hung up the telephone and stared at it for a long moment. Caroline was gone, and she hadn't told anyone where she was going. And their last words together had been spoken in anger. It was easy to regret that now. Harder to see where they had gone wrong, and how they could make it right again.

He sighed and reached for the coffee cup by his elbow. It was cold, but he drank it anyway, suddenly thirsty with his anxiety. He didn't understand Caroline, not anymore. When they had first met, she had seemed . . . different. Needy, somehow. Eager to rely on him, practically forcing him to make all the decisions for her. And now she became angry when he continued to make those same decisions. It didn't make sense.

He loved her. If there was one thing that was certain, it was that he loved her. He had been raised by parents who did not show affection, either to each other or to their children, and Caroline's bright spontaneity had captivated him from the start. She was everything that his dour New England family was not; and she had a depth of caring, too, beneath the bright superficial exterior: That was the side of Caroline that he loved. Not the indecisive, confused little girl that she seemed to have become, but the woman who was capable of more than the little girl would ever allow her to be.

She wanted him to echo her passion, and he couldn't. He didn't have it in him at the moment. She wanted him to go about waving flags and declaring his patriotism, and that was something that he had never felt. He had been raised to believe that it was the family that was important. And Asheford Shipbuilding was the mainstay of the family. Politics was best left to the politicians. As long as you took care of your little corner of the world, then you were doing the right thing. Not that he had ever fully accepted that. After all, during the Depression he had spent several days a week at St. John's helping strangers, the homeless and the indigent. But after he married he had taken on a new role and responsibility, feeling he needed to reserve his caring and his energy for his family and the business. The fact that Caroline's fortune made his business and role as provider incidental did not diminish their importance to him.

It seemed that he was failing at caring for his family as well. Caroline wanted him to take seriously every swoop and dip of her roller-coaster emotional life, and he couldn't keep up with her. She wanted him to feel what she felt, when she felt it, and he didn't know how. And she blamed him for it all.

The truth was that he had been raised with different values and standards. His father had poured every ounce of his energy and emotion into Asheford Shipbuilding and he had raised his sons to do the same. They weren't supposed to question that. They weren't taught to question anything. Caroline, on the other hand, seemed to think that it was her duty to question *everything*. And he was trying so hard to compromise, to come closer to her, to meet her halfway. Sometimes she wasn't even aware of that effort; she thought that he was cold, that he didn't try at all . . .

If only she knew how wrong she was. And now she was gone. Gone, God only knew where. He found suddenly that his hands were trembling: with fear? Had he really lost her this time?

And then, for the first time in a very long time indeed, Steven Asheford put his head down on his hands and wept.

Soizic Aubert frowned at the cable in her hand. ''Caroline Asheford is in England. She is looking for the Eagle Squadron and Captain Starkey.''

"That's right." Rousseau's voice was cold. "So we have to do something about it."

She frowned at him automatically. "I cannot see how our plans for Captain Starkey will hurt Caroline Asheford."

"Don't be stupid, Soizic! Anything can go wrong, at any time! We have to wait until she leaves again. We can wait that long!"

"The point is to keep them apart. If she has sought him out, then I doubt very much that she will be leaving in the near future. She can divorce her husband from Surrey as well as she can in Rhode Island. Or he can become fed up and divorce her. Haven't you heard about all the wartime marriages springing up in England? Do you want Madame Asheford and Captain Starkey to be one of them? Our plan remains imperative."

"And how," asked Françoise, sitting innocently on the sofa, "do you propose to convince Madame Asheford that it is an accident when her lover is killed?"

"Don't be ridiculous, Françoise," Marc Giroux said irritably. "There's a war on, hadn't you noticed? And Captain Starkey is a wartime aviator. They're being killed all the time. He won't be any different. She'll just have to return to America with a broken heart."

Soizic cleared her throat. "The arrangements stand," she said firmly. "We will caution the people involved that Madame Asheford is not to be hurt. I don't think she will be involved anyway. Monsieur Beaumont will be told only that Madame Asheford will remain safe. Are there any more questions?"

Marc Giroux watched Soizic leave the room, and slowly shook his head. She was changing. And he was frightened.

Chapter Sixteen

*E*ddie shrugged. "I didn't think you would find me," he said by way of explanation. "I thought I'd just vanish into the air. I sort of liked the idea." He was annoyed at Caroline for coming after him. "I don't need a nursemaid, you know."

"I'm not a nursemaid. Can't you see that I just care about you? And when I found out how old you are—"

Eddie threw up his hands. "That's great. That's just great. I thought I could trust Margie."

"You can trust Margie to care about you. And, for what it's worth, she didn't tell me. I knew right away. You're not all that mysterious. Eddie Carruthers, even if you like to think of yourself as the dashing wartime aviator—"

"Christ, Caroline, you don't have to make fun of me, too!"

"I don't mean to," she said soberly. "I just want you to understand that it's not a very adult thing to do, tearing off into the blue like that, and worrying people."

"Worrying people? Like who? My parents? That's a laugh. My parents couldn't give a damn. They're too busy with their garden parties and their yachting to worry about *me*."

Caroline frowned. She wasn't approaching this the right way. Instead of convincing him to go home, she was antagonizing him; and the more she said, the less likely he was to hear it. And yet her heart ached for him. His bravado, his swaggering use of obscenities, his entire attitude suggested not so much the RAF pilot as the young boy who wanted so desperately to be one. "Eddie, if I had only known that this was what you wanted—"

"What would you have done, Caroline? Helped me come to England? Lied about my age for me?"

"Talked some sense into you," she said firmly. "What did Andrew say when you got here?"

Eddie looked away. Obviously he had no desire to share Andrew's thoughts with her.

There was a fine rain falling, and Caroline pulled her trench coat closer around her. "Look, Eddie, is there someplace inside where we can go? I'm freezing out here."

"So that everyone can hear you playing nursemaid to me? No, thanks."

She sighed. "All right. All right, Eddie. You win. No more advice. Let's go inside, please?"

He must have realized how sullen he had been sounding, for he made a real effort to accommodate her. "There's usually some tea over in the radio room," he suggested politely. She nodded. "Great idea."

The girl sitting in front of the radio system nodded to them as they came in. "This is where I am most of the time," Eddie explained to Caroline, pouring tea from a kettle on a hot plate. "They won't let me fly, not yet, but they're letting me take shifts on the radio. It's harder here than it was in Newport."

"Why is that?" Caroline was careful to keep her voice neutral. She cradled her hands around the mug of tea. July, and it was still this chilly. . . .

"No radar, for one thing. I didn't know how much I appreciated that until I didn't have it anymore. And we usually don't know what's going on. The squadron keeps radio silence most of the time, so the enemy can't find them." How easily those words fell off his tongue, she thought—*the enemy*. Eddie had already identified himself completely with the squadron.

"Who is she listening for, then?" Caroline gestured toward the girl.

Eddie responded in surprise, "They're up there now, didn't you know?"

"No," Caroline said, feeling her heart lurching suddenly. "When did they go up?"

"Just a while ago. You were still asleep, and Captain Starkey said not to wake you. Reports of Messerschmitts over the Channel."

"None recently," said the girl at the radio. "Mostly it's boring, just sitting here." She smiled at Caroline. "I'm Emma Parkins. Gladys tells me you're a pilot."

Caroline smiled back. "Yes," she admitted.

"I suppose that all of us are. The girls in London, they wouldn't know a propeller from a wheel strut, but we all volunteered for field duty. Half the mechanics are girls, too, and pilots.'' Emma sipped her tea. ''Eddie talks a lot about you,'' she added, almost as an afterthought.

''Sometimes,'' he growled in response to Caroline's look of surprise. ''That was before you came out after me, though.''

Caroline smiled. ''Well, then—'' Caroline was cut off by the radios clattering into life.

Emma seized the headphones. ''Fourteen, what is your position?''

She started writing something and there was a peculiar silence in the radio room, as though everybody were holding his or her breath, living out the combat taking place, even then, miles away up in the sky.

Andrew was up there.

Emma talked quietly into her microphone for several minutes, and then she took off the headset and shook out her short red curls. ''They're on their way back,'' she said calmly.

''What happened?'' There was eagerness in Eddie's voice. Caroline knew, knew with absolute certainty and a terrible cold feeling in her stomach, that if he could have been up there with them, he would have been. ''What happened?''

''Three Messerschmitts. That's strange.'' Emma's voice was puzzled. ''They usually send up more planes than that at a time. Reconnaissance, Captain Starkey thought.''

''Are they all right?'' Caroline's voice had a strangled sound to it.

Emma gave her a quick, bright glance. ''We got two of them. No casualties on our side.''

No casualties. Caroline breathed again, a grateful thought in her mind. Thank God, thank God, thank God. Andrew was still all right. One more battle, one more day that he lived through. She was beginning to see that out here, that was not such a small thing. One more day.

Eddie was enthusiastic. ''Two Messerschmitts! That's terrific! That's great, Caroline, isn't it? At this rate we'll be winning the war in no time.''

''It takes more than two Messerschmitts,'' Emma reminded him, but he was still smiling broadly. Grudgingly, she conceded, ''Every little bit helps.''

Caroline found herself thinking suddenly that those two German pilots would probably not think of themselves as a little bit. For them, the war was over.

"They're coming in," Emma said, and Eddie pulled Caroline to her feet. "Come on! Let's watch!"

Standing together in the fine mist, they watched the squadron land on the short runway. Near-perfect landings, all of them. Only the best American pilots had volunteered and been accepted for this particular duty. Even on the wet tarmac the planes had no trouble landing. One or two of them looked particularly battle scarred, but the bullet holes were probably permanent by now, earned during some earlier encounter. Andrew came in last, and Caroline ran to meet him.

He was striking-looking, she thought. Even in his bulky flying suit he was so handsome. That infectious grin, as though he were coming back from a jaunt at the beach, lifted her spirits. "Hey, Caroline!"

"You didn't tell me you were going up," she said reprovingly, and then threw herself into his arms. "I'm sure glad you're back."

"So am I. Hey, Eddie. You two still friends?"

"More or less," Caroline said, and Eddie nodded.

"Two Messerschmitts!" he said, the hero worship shining in his eyes. "That's great, Captain Starkey!"

"Should have had all three," Andrew said modestly. "The third just ran off, hightailed it north." He sounded surprised.

"Well," said Caroline, walking comfortably beside him, her arm around his waist, "that sounds sensible to me. I'd have done the same thing under the circumstances."

"Probably." But his voice was still puzzled.

"I'll take care of your plane," Eddie offered, and Caroline turned to him, about to speak, when Andrew pressed her shoulders. "It's all right, Caroline. Eddie's been working as a mechanic here, too. He's getting very good at it."

"But—"

"No buts, sweetheart." He kissed her casually, as though they were an old married couple. "Go to it, Eddie," he added, and Eddie grinned again and disappeared.

"Is that such a good idea?" Caroline was still worried.

"Why not? His work is good, Caroline, whatever you think of his age, and I know what you think of his age. Don't worry so much. I'm keeping him grounded, and in the meantime he can make himself useful."

"I still think he should go back home," she said doubtfully.

"He's too young to be out here, Andrew. He's too young for war."

He raised his eyebrows. "And the rest of us aren't? Let me clue you in, Caroline: No one is old enough to die. Not really. Besides, Eddie's not going into combat. He's as safe as anyone in Britain is."

"Somehow," she said thoughtfully, "I don't find that notion particularly comforting."

Farther north up the coast in Scotland, a Messerschmitt fighter landed at a small unused airstrip. The pilot taxied to a stop, but kept the engines running, the propellers spinning. He intended to take off again right away.

A man dressed in a heavy overcoat emerged from the small boarded-up hut by the runway and came walking across the wet tarmac to him. "Well? Do you have the information?"

No polite formalities, the pilot observed. Just as well. He didn't want to stay on this side of the Channel any longer than he had to. "Yes," he said, his voice equally terse. "You were right about the headquarters. That's not the way to do it. They've got tight security and the Asheford woman is definitely there."

"So?"

"So Starkey won't be hard to pick out in the air. He flies the right-wing position in formation, and he's got some sort of design on his fuselage, just below the cockpit cover. It looks like some sort of skyline, and a big gold bridge. Odd design."

"Anything else?"

"He's a good pilot. He's everything you said. But he's reckless, too. When we went after his wingman he went after us, and it was all that I could do to get out of there."

"What about the other two?"

"Shot down." The pilot's voice was grim.

"Very well. And what are your instructions now?"

"Go back to Germany and rejoin my squadron." And that will be a relief, he thought. "I'm not to talk about what happened today. I won't."

"You're so right you won't," agreed the man in the overcoat, pulling a Mauser from an inner pocket. The pilot opened his mouth to say something, and then he couldn't, for the other man had pulled the trigger, two shots rang out, and the pilot slumped forward over the controls.

The man in the overcoat walked away, turned and, taking careful aim, shot a hole in the plane's gas tank. Almost at once a steady stream of fuel began to pour out. He had some difficulty lighting a match, because of the misting rain, but he got it at last and tossed it into the widening puddle below the plane. Then he turned away and began to run.

There was a sound behind him as though somebody had taken in a great breath of air, and then the explosion came, knocking him to the ground with its force. He lay there for a moment, the wind knocked out of him, and then he got up and walked away, replacing the Mauser in the same inner pocket. He got in the Rover that was parked behind the hut and drove away.

On the tarmac, the Messerschmitt was burning. If any of the locals were to come by and see it, they would cheer.

Chantale was in the nursery with the children when the Germans came to the Château de Montclair. She was reading from a battered fairy-tale book, the same stories her mother had read to her when she was a child in Brittany. They held her children's attention as closely as they had once held hers. Catherine was still a baby, and couldn't understand the meaning of the words, but she appeared to like their rhythm, for she always smiled and gurgled contentedly when Chantale read. Jean-Claude listened with rapt attention. He knew all the stories by heart already, and corrected her whenever she missed a word.

Jeannine had come and was standing in the doorway, and with one look at the girl, her white face and trembling hands, Chantale knew. She put aside the book, slowly, reluctantly, as though by spinning out this precious magic time she could make it last forever.

Jean-Claude was immediately indignant. "The story isn't over," he pointed out.

"I know," said Chantale softly, gently. "But Maman has to go downstairs now. Jeannine will stay with you."

"Don't want Jeannine. Want Maman," he said stoutly, his face red, and Chantale opened her arms to him. Holding his small strong body against her, she said, "I have to go, *mon chou*. But if you are good for Jeannine, I will take you out to the stables after lunch." That was a rash promise, she thought guiltily, for who knew where they would be after lunch? But it served its purpose. Jean-Claude's whole world just then revolved around his obsessive desire for a pony of his own. Jeannine walked into the room and picked up the book that Chantale had put down. She still hadn't spoken.

Chantale let go of Jean-Claude and stood up. "You must read clearly," she said to Jeannine steadily. This was what she wanted her children to remember: these magic fairy-tale moments, this sunshine streaming into the nursery, her love, Jeannine's care. She didn't want any fear in that room—not yet. There would be time enough for that later.

"Yes, Countess." The girl's voice quavered, and Chantale put a hand on her arm. "Do this for me," she said, and Jeannine nodded. Jean-Claude, oblivious of their concerns, said, "We left off in the castle of the ogre. Come on, Jeannine!"

Chantale smiled for her and then left. As she went down the corridor, she automatically put a hand to her hair, falling out of its chignon as it always did when she was with the children and their inquisitive, active hands. Not that she wanted to be beautiful for the *sales Boches*, far from that. But she was the Countess de Montclair, and she would show them dignity, if nothing else.

She went halfway down the great sweeping staircase in the front entrance hall, stopping partway down, her hand on the balustrade, to watch what was transpiring below.

It had happened. The barbarians were there.

Pierre stood below her, dressed casually for his morning ride in tweed jacket and jodhpurs and boots, a riding crop in his hand. His dark hair shone in the light from the open door. Across the hallway, immobile against the heavy dark tapestry on the wall, stood Marie-Louise, dressed in black. It wasn't difficult to imagine the servants grouped behind the stained glass and mahogany of the door behind Marie-Louise.

There were two men standing in the doorway, squinting into the gloom of the front hall. Both wore green-gray uniforms, very neat, very smart. So all barbarians aren't Visigoths, thought Chantale. Some even dress well. Their boots were polished and squeaked on the stone floor.

One of them, the taller of the two, was obviously in command. "You are the Count de Montclair?" he asked in French, his accent harsh and guttural to Chantale's ears. "I am Major Hans Werner. I am here to requisition your house." He gestured toward the clipboard in the other man's hands. "Here are my orders. You may examine them if you wish."

From the shadows, Marie-Louise spoke: "We do not question the authenticity of your orders," she said coldly. "We question your right to be in France."

He looked at her for a moment, at the older woman's pinched angry face, and then looked away. Chantale found herself wondering how many women he had looked at like that, women who dared show some pride and dignity in the face of his crass intrusion, who kept their fire and their anger intact. They meant nothing to him.

"We will require the entire estate," Werner was saying to Pierre. "You and your family will be graciously issued travel permits. I am sure that there is some relative with whom you can stay. You will leave the servants, the horses, all vehicles, all household furniture, and so on. You will be reimbursed for any damages incurred during our stay here."

With what? Chantale wondered. Deutsche marks? His promises were meaningless. And how were they expected to travel, with no automobiles?

"You will take what personal items you require and leave at once. We expect to be able to move in here this evening." His voice held contempt. No doubt no one had told him that he was supposed to be talking about peace and cooperation.

Marie-Louise took a step forward. "Our family has lived here for two centuries," she said clearly, her head held high. "You have no right to tell us to leave."

Werner looked at her as though she were as exasperating and harmless as a fly. "You will come back—someday."

"When?" She met his eyes.

"When we decide that we no longer require the premises." He turned away from her, dismissing her, and spoke directly to Pierre. "How many people live here?"

"Do not tell him anything," Marie-Louise said sharply. "He has no right to ask."

"Myself, my mother, my wife, and my two children," Pierre replied. "Mother, it's no good to fight them. We may as well cooperate." His voice was dull and lifeless.

"You are a coward!" She spat out the words. "My son, the coward!"

Major Werner ignored her. "And how many servants?"

Pierre looked blank. "I don't know," he said slowly.

"Let them find out for themselves," Marie-Louise said.

The major smiled. "As you will. We will now make a tour of inspection of the premises, and my clerk will take inventory of the servants we will need. And the other things. You will show us around," he added directly, to Pierre.

Chantale found herself hearing an echo of the voices of the first refugees, the people who had fled Paris before the Germans arrived. We smashed all the china . . . and Grandmother's cabinet . . . better that we should destroy them than leave them for the *sales Boches*. She wondered, belatedly, if they should not have done the same thing. It seemed less of a desecration, somehow. The thought of the Germans sitting at their table, using their silver, riding their horses . . . Everyone said that the Germans had heavy hands; they would surely ruin the horses' mouths. Pierre's father, Philippe, had spent so many years acquiring fine horseflesh. All for nothing. All for the barbarians.

There was the sound of a car engine outside, the slamming of a door, and another man appeared in the doorway. Unlike Werner and his clerk, this man's uniform was black, not familiar in any way, unlike anything that they had ever seen. He was very short, with a neat, dapper mustache, and he seemed quite angry.

"Major Werner!" His voice was raspy. Interesting, Chantale thought, that he should address a fellow German in French. Was this all for their benefit?

Werner was not pleased to see the new arrival. "Major Detweiler," he said coldly, and saluted him. *"Heil Hitler!"*

"Heil Hitler." The short man flapped his hand up in a parody of the gesture. "Major, there has been a mistake. You are not to requisition this estate."

"But, Herr Major—"

Detweiler raised his hand. "Enough. I have said that there has been a mistake. The Château de Montclair is not to be requisitioned. Do I not make myself clear?"

Werner didn't give up very easily. "I have my orders."

There was menace in the other man's voice. "And I have mine. Would you like to compare signatures, Major? I am sure that mine might surprise you. But not pleasantly. Be sensible, Major. There are other estates for you to pillage." He turned to look at Pierre. "You are the Count de Montclair?"

Pierre nodded, wordlessly.

The small man was drawing on his black gloves. "I must then apologize for any inconvenience that the Wehrmacht has caused you. You and your family are free to remain here for as long as you wish. A small gift will be delivered to you later today by way of apology." He clicked his heels together. "If you are quite finished, Major Werner?"

The army officer scowled at Detweiler, scowled at Pierre, and finally scowled at his clerk. "You heard him," he said savagely to the latter. "Get out!"

Detweiler stayed long enough to add one final *"Heil Hitler!"* before departing on their heels. Pierre walked slowly to the door and watched the five staff cars turn around on the expanse of gravel in front of the château and speed away, down the lane between the poplar trees. Only then did he close the door and breathe a sigh of relief.

Chantale walked down the remaining stairs, still holding the balustrade as though for support. "What just happened there?" she asked, frowning.

"By God, I don't know. But I'm certainly glad," Pierre said.

Chantale and Marie-Louise exchanged glances. "Why is it that we are singled out for special consideration by the German Army?" Chantale asked slowly. "What just happened, Pierre?"

"I don't know," he said impatiently, but she could read the truth below his words. Whatever had happened, Pierre wasn't part of it.

He stared at them, but distantly, as though he was performing calculations in his head. Marie-Louise seemed about to say something, and then thought better of it. In the wake of what had just happened, there was nothing, really, to say.

Pierre turned and said shortly, "I'm going out." They watched him go. Somehow, it didn't matter anymore.

Chantale climbed the stairs again, but heavily, feeling exhausted. She went through the motions, putting Catherine down for her nap, taking Jean-Claude out to the stables to sit on one of the horses, and all the while her head was spinning. Why were the Germans letting them be? She felt like a convict, let off by the executioner at the eleventh hour. And she still didn't know why.

Something in the back of her mind said that even exile was better than accepting German favors.

As usual Annie had information but not enough to explain the events of the morning. "The man in black, Countess? He was Gestapo."

"Gestapo?" said Chantale, the unfamiliar word feeling rough on her tongue. "What does that mean?"

"Secret police," said Annie, pounding the crust she was working on. "Hitler's own secret police, Countess."

Chantale sat down. "I don't understand. I don't understand,

Annie." She looked at the cook. "Pierre must have done something. But he doesn't seem to know any more than we do."

Annie shrugged. "Whatever it is, it's good for us," she said.

"What do you mean?"

"I think you know what I mean, Countess."

Chantale drew in her breath. "But surely—with the Germans so close—it's too dangerous to carry on, Annie!"

"Seems to me that that's the first time I hear you talking about danger, Countess."

"This is the first time that I've actually seen them." She could see them again, too, if she only closed her eyes. The rudeness, the total disregard for others, the arrogance. "We will require the entire estate." Perhaps the danger was worth it. She opened her eyes. "We'll carry on," she said, and Annie looked up sharply, surprised by the resolution in Chantale's voice.

Pierre had quickly changed his clothes, not daring to stop or even pause. That would mean having to think, and he wasn't prepared to start thinking about what had just happened. He spent only two minutes in the shower before pulling on slacks and a light shirt and jacket. He took the Citroën from the garage, as it was the only car that had gas in it at the moment, and practically flew all the way into Angers. He didn't want to think. All that he wanted was to see Isabelle. She would make everything all right again. She always did.

He passed two units of Germans on his way in, trucks rumbling along the deserted roads, soldiers goose-stepping behind them, and before long he had broken out into a cold sweat. There but for the grace of God . . . They might have been heading for his house if things had gone differently this morning. No, he told himself: Stop that. Stop thinking about it.

He parked on the rue des Arènes and walked down into the place du Ralliement, scowling at the huge swastika on the theater. He rang the doorbell to Isabelle's apartment, and then, as she didn't come at once, he pounded on it for a few minutes, releasing some of his tensions through a physical act. The fear gripping him intensified. If he couldn't see her . . .

She was at the gallery. That had to be it. It was lunchtime, and she usually came home, but today was different. She would be at the gallery. He practically ran all the way to the rue d'Adam, breathless in the heat, needing her more than he had ever needed her before, not sexually, but in his soul.

Isabelle's assistant, André, materialized out of the shadows. "Ah, Count! A pleasure to see you. How can I help you today?"

Pierre looked around him wildly. "Where is Isabelle?"

André frowned slightly at Pierre's hurry. "Madame Vivier went out for lunch," he said smoothly. "I expect her back around two-thirty. Is there a message that I can give to her for you?"

"No," Pierre said, and turned away. Belatedly, he remembered his manners. "Thank you, Monsieur Chatenay."

André inclined his head. "My pleasure, Count. Come by again."

Pierre walked back to the place du Ralliement. Damn Isabelle. He couldn't really blame her, but her timing was so inconvenient. He had to see her, and she was nowhere to be found. Cursing, he got into the Citroën and started it up, slipping easily into the street. There was so little traffic these days that driving was easy. Gasoline rationing had done much to solve the problem of congestion.

He was rounding the corner to turn back toward the boulevard when, at a red light, he glanced over into a café. There, sitting under the gay awning, was Isabelle. She was laughing, her strange violet eyes happy, her long raven hair causing her to stand out in the crowd. She held a cigarette nonchalantly in her hand, and there had been no cigarettes on the market in Angers for the past eight weeks.

Next to her, also laughing, sharing the joke and the moment of intimacy, was a German officer. The light changed, and the cars behind him were sounding their impatience. Pierre put the car into gear and drove on. It was not what it had seemed, he told himself. The German was a customer, a connoisseur of art. It was all right. Everything was going to be all right.

And, all the while, he knew in his heart that it wasn't going to be, not ever again.

Caroline had a room in town, but she abandoned it after her first night in Surrey in favor of the women's barracks. It made no sense to stay in a hotel, after all, when she could be that much closer to Andrew. Not with him, of course. This was the RAF. But near him, all the same.

The women were, as Emma had said, mostly pilots who had requested field duty in order to be closer to the place where their hearts were already—the sky. They scoffed at the regulations that kept them grounded and asked eager—and sometimes critical—questions of the fliers themselves. Sometimes they made suggestions, which on occasion were accepted.

Caroline fit in after the first day. They were used to the American accent; most of the pilots in the squadron were Yanks anyway, and Caroline's connection to Captain Starkey did not go unnoticed. Already, Andrew was making a name for himself as a brave and compassionate commanding officer. If Caroline had been proud of him before, her heart was close to bursting now.

She was still concerned about her Butterfly, and had—with the benediction of the powers that be—flown it down to Surrey on her own, despite its defective port engine. Eddie had traced the problem within a few minutes. Caroline had been right. The flywheel was gone, and the wires around the magneto were melting. Much longer, and she would have lost the engine altogether.

Even after it was repaired, she didn't take it up, and firmly forbade Eddie to even *think* about such a thing. There would be no secret flights into unsafe territory if she had anything to say about it. "But it's not a military plane, Caroline!"

"You really think that's going to bother anybody? It seems to me that shoot first, ask questions later is more the order of the day around here."

"They'd notice."

"Right. The way that they notice that London is mostly a civilian installation. That hasn't particularly slowed the bombing runs, now has it?"

She wrote a letter to Steven eventually, not knowing exactly what to say. "I had to come to see if Eddie was all right. He is, I'm glad to say, although terribly enthused about the war, as you can well imagine. He's determined to stay here and help in whatever capacity they'll have him, and I'm staying for a while myself, until the plane is repaired and perhaps I can persuade him to return with me. Please don't worry, Steven. We're perfectly safe here, really we are, and I'm in good health. Kiss Elizabeth for me. . . ."

Well, she thought, rereading it, so perhaps she was stretching the truth a little bit. She didn't have much choice, really. The last thing that she wanted was a posse coming after her, and even Steven in his distracted state must have noticed by now that she was gone.

She ate her meals in the canteen along with everybody else, and persuaded the commander to allow her to take turns in the radio room. She went on long walks with Andrew through the wet English July. They talked of everything and of nothing, of flying and of the people who lived in the small world of the Eagle Squadron. They talked of everything but of the feelings that were being nurtured over those rainy summer days, the warmth and the love that was being rekindled again between them as if it had never gone.

Andrew flew several missions a week, sometimes as many as one a day, and every time that he was up Caroline died over and over again, fearful that he wouldn't return. She haunted the radio room, stood for hours gazing out over the runway, waiting for the small specks in the sky that signaled the squadron's return. He would climb down from his Hurricane and smile at her, that heart-stopping smile, and nothing in the world seemed to matter except that he was alive and safe, and they were together.

Two weeks after Caroline arrived in Surrey, Andrew came back with his arm bloody and his fuselage riddled with bullet holes.

She stood waiting, as she did every day, dressed in tan trousers, a white shirt, and a flying jacket, her blond curls tight with the moisture in the air, her dark eyes eagerly scanning the horizon. The planes limped in that day: Two had been shot down over the Channel. Only one pilot had been able to bail out. Caroline had sensed from the beginning that something was wrong—there was anger in those fast landings, those screeching halts. When Andrew came in and she saw his airplane, her stomach knotted inside her. No, she breathed silently, please God, no, please no.

He took a long time climbing out of the cockpit, and by then she was standing next to the Hurricane, helping him. His legs buckled under him for a moment, and Caroline turned and screamed behind her, "Medic! Over here!" before turning back to Andrew. His face was white and pinched with pain, and his entire left arm was a mess, blood and torn flesh mingling together.

They took him into the base hospital and spent more hours stitching him together—and taking out the bullet that had lodged in his shoulder as well. Caroline waited nervously, drinking the cups of tea that they kept bringing to her, biting her lip and praying as she had never known that she could pray. And into the waiting room, belatedly because he had been in London for the day, came Eddie Carruthers.

"Where is he?" Caroline could hear him shouting in the anteroom. "Where's Captain Starkey?"

There were some soothing voices, which apparently he ignored, for the waiting-room door burst open and Eddie ran in. "Caroline! What happened to Captain Starkey?"

"He was shot," she said, as calmly and soberly as she could. "They're operating on him now. Sit down, Eddie, why don't you?"

"Sit down, like hell!" he spat. "Bloody Germans. I'll kill them! I'll kill them all!"

"Stop it, Eddie," Caroline said firmly. "Andrew will be all right. Do you hear me? Andrew will be all right!"

"You don't know that for sure, do you? He's in surgery, isn't he? Goddamn them all. I'll show them!"

"Eddie—" Caroline half rose out of her seat, but he tore away from her and ran out the door. Caroline followed.

In the east, the sky was getting lighter. The surgeons had been working for the better part of the night. There was a chill in the air, that false dawn when everything seems to stop and wait and hold itself suspended in time. Eddie was running down toward the flight line, and muttering a curse Caroline ran after him. "Eddie!"

He wasn't listening to her. He was beyond listening to her, or to anybody. He had lost friends over the Channel, and now he had nearly lost his hero, and it was all too much for him. He ran without hesitation to Andrew's bullet-riddled Hurricane and climbed up.

"No," Caroline breathed. "Oh, God, no." It was like a nightmare. She felt as though her feet were glued to the spot, as though she were moving in slow motion. With all her energy, she cried out, "Eddie!"

He couldn't hear her. The engines were roaring, and he was already taxiing off the flight line and getting in place for the runway. Caroline started running again.

She was too late, reaching the end of the runway even as he lifted the nose of the Hurricane, pointing it to the east, toward the rising sun. All that she could do was stand at the end of that runway and scream his name into the new day.

Chapter Seventeen

Andrew and Caroline sat together in the long mess tent and watched the rain—the endless eternal rain—falling outside. He hadn't flown in the three days since he landed with his Hurricane filled with bullet holes. The surgeon had advised a month's leave. Andrew was compromising with a week's rest. "What do you miss the most?" Caroline asked, yearning to comfort him, trying to think of something heartening to say, looking at him over the rim of her teacup. "Fresh fruit," he responded promptly, without thinking. "I haven't seen an orange or a strawberry in months. I probably don't even remember what they taste like."

"I do," she said. "Oh, Andrew, remember the farm stand we used to go to, just outside of San Jose, on the Salinas road? Remember those strawberries?"

He drank a swallow of tea. "Couldn't forget them," he said. "Sweet, and—"

The tent flap opened and a corporal stood framed in the doorway. He saluted. "Captain Starkey? Message for you."

Andrew stood and saluted in turn before taking the paper the younger man held out to him. How tired he looks, Caroline thought suddenly. There were wrinkles on his face and dark circles under his eyes that hadn't been there the last time she had seen him out in California. California, with its brilliant sun and savage beauty, seemed a lifetime away now.

Andrew sat down again across from her, but his eyes were still on the page he held. "It's Eddie."

All the fear that she had been so carefully holding at bay came flooding back, all the tears yet unshed, all the panic that she had pushed away from her with light banter and the refusal to believe what somehow seemed inevitable. Eddie . . . It was rising inside her, the same way that sickness did when she needed to vomit, the fear clutching at her neck and throat until she couldn't breathe, much less speak.

Andrew's face was ashen. "There's still no word," he said thickly. "He's officially listed as missing, Caroline." His eyes met hers over the page and she saw the same horror reflected there. It was because of him that Eddie had run off, because he hadn't been careful enough, or . . .

He forced down his wild thoughts. He had to be calm, for his men, for Caroline, and he could not allow himself to dwell upon whose fault this was. He had to slow down and think this thing through. First of all, the encounter with the Germans, up over northern France. The Hurricanes had been outnumbered, but Andrew was proud of the men in his section, pilots who knew what they were doing and daring enough to do it. They had been in worse places before.

So what had happened? What had happened that made him forget everything they had taught him about aerial combat? How had he allowed—even for the split second that it had taken—that Messerschmitt to come between himself and the sun?

Or did it matter now? He had caught a round from the machine guns even as Wilson opened up on the German plane and sent it plummeting to earth. Small consolation, when it meant that they had to scrap the rest of the reconnaissance mission, which was what they had been sent there for in the first place. Andrew shook his head. So stupid, so incredibly stupid. None of the men was saying it, of course, but it was stupid all the same.

And now Eddie Carruthers missing, in the squadron leader's own airplane . . . That was really too much. And that *was* his fault. He knew he was not to blame for young Carruthers's stupid stunt, blazing off into the blue like that, to prove something to somebody. In the end, each person was—had to be— accountable for his or her own actions. But Carruthers's presence on a military base *was* his responsibility, and it had been a bad decision to let him stay. A lamentably bad decision. He looked across the table at Caroline's face, at the circles under her eyes, and winced inwardly. She was taking it badly, and that was his fault as well. He should have sent both of them back to the States as soon as they arrived.

Well, if he had failed Carruthers, he sure as hell wasn't going to fail Caroline. Not anymore.

He reached across the table and took her hand. "Caroline,

we have to face the truth. He's probably dead. He's never flown under conditions like this, and going off at first light like that was suicidal. If he didn't hit a barrage balloon he probably ran into some bombers on their way home across the Channel.''

Her hand twitched in his. "It's my fault," she sobbed.

Andrew took a deep breath. "Caroline, listen carefully to me. You've done more than your share. You came here looking for him, and I should have listened to you then. Eddie Carruthers had no place here and I should never have let him stay. I should have sent him back to the States, and I didn't. It was my fault, Caroline.'' He twisted his face into a smile. "If this were a movie, he'd come back, and everybody would find out that it was some plot we cooked up between us, Eddie and me, and we'd both be decorated as heroes. Then you and Steven would get a divorce and we'd live happily ever after. It would make a great movie, Caroline.'' He took another deep, steadying breath. God, but his shoulder was hurting. "But this is real life, and real life is different. And in real life, the people we call heroes are the ones who are too desperate, or too tired, or too angry to care. So Eddie is a hero, and we'll probably never know exactly what happened to him.''

"It's not fair.'' There were tears in her eyes and in her voice, and Andrew squeezed her hand. "No, it isn't. That's the other thing about life. It usually isn't fair.'' He wasn't finished, and wondered if it sounded as though he was lecturing her. "Caroline, you have to go home now.''

"What?'' She sniffed the single word through her tears, distracted for a moment from her thoughts of Eddie.

He stroked her hand with his thumb. "Yes. As soon as we can book you a flight. This was no place for Eddie, and I made the mistake of letting him stay anyway. I'm not going to let anything happen to you.''

"And if I won't go?'' She was aware that she sounded petulant, like a child.

Andrew shrugged. "You can do what you like, Caroline. But you have to leave this base. You're not military, and you have no business being here.''

"But what about *us*?'' Her voice was a wail. "What about us, Andrew?''

This was the hard part. A shiver ran up his backbone, and even though he knew that what he was doing was right—even though he knew that this was the only thing he could do—he felt as though a shadow had passed between him and the sun. Figurative poetic crap, of course. There was no sun, and even if one thought of Caroline as such, he was the one making her move away. "Caroline. I love you. I've loved you for a long time, but we haven't got any business exploiting this situation to work out our personal needs."

"Exploiting what situation?"

He shrugged. "All this. The war. It's dangerous and somehow exciting—I won't deny that, and you shouldn't, either. Being here puts things in a unique perspective, with any moment potentially one's last. . . . Oh, Jesus, you know what I mean, Caroline. It's exciting. It's part of the reason why I'm here, and part of the reason why you're here, and it's ridiculous. It's great stuff for that movie, but it just doesn't work. I love you, I'm not about to deny that, and I do have a fantasy about you divorcing Steven and marrying me instead, like we talked about before. But if that's going to happen it has to happen back home, later. Not here. Not now."

Caroline stared at him. "You couldn't love me. Not if you can say all that."

"You only see it that way because it's not what you want." He shook his head. "Honey, I'm no martyr. I ask for nothing better than you in my bed every night and at my breakfast table every morning. But not now."

"I see." She compressed her lips to keep them from trembling. So he was blaming her for Eddie's disappearance. She was the one who had told Eddie about the RAF, and she hadn't made him go back to America, and she hadn't stopped him from flying off into that deadly sunrise. It was her fault. With that thought, all her childhood experiences and expectations came flooding back. When she did something wrong, she was punished for it. Well, now Andrew was sending her away. Was that God's way of saying that she didn't deserve to be with him? Was God, in some way, punishing her for all these things that were her fault?

Caroline sipped her tea; it was scalding and bitter on her tongue. If Andrew really loved her, he wouldn't send her away. Or was that too simplistic? Perhaps he did love her and thought that she would be safer somewhere else. She narrowed her eyes trying to keep the tears back. Or was it something else? Hadn't she already had this conversation with herself when she came back to Newport from California? Before any of them had ever dreamed of going to England? Hadn't she believed then that Andrew lived in a simplistic world where everything had to be right and everything worked with a minimum of effort? Well, the war was no fairy tale, but Andrew still wanted everything neat and comfortable. No messes. No awkward entanglements. Including her. He wanted her safe somewhere, so that he could deal with one thing at a time. The war now. Caroline later.

But there might not be a "later," and her greatest aspiration in life had never been to simply be put away on a shelf. . . . She wanted more than that—to participate, fully participate, to be loved and needed. Not sent away. Damn it, someone was always sending her away—and always under the guise of its being for her own good.

In his own way, Andrew was doing the same as Eric and Steven had done—keeping her at a distance for their own interests as well as hers. And she knew he loved her—and so did they.

There were tears in her eyes, Caroline realized with a start. Not tears of pain, or even tears of rage—just regret. Regret that she couldn't settle for Andrew's easy way out. Regret that she needed the conflict, the constant living of life in order to survive. And it was a hard realization. It would be easier, so much easier, to simply do as Andrew wanted, wait for the war to end and then—if they were lucky—resume their existence together. So much easier. And so impossible.

She wondered, as she sipped her tea and gazed unseeingly out through the mesh of the mess tent to the rain-sodden fields beyond, how on earth she was ever going to work all this out.

Steven Asheford ran a hand distractedly through his hair and spoke again into the telephone receiver he was holding. "Yes, I'll hold. No, I don't want Mr. Beaumont to call me back. I need to talk with him now."

In front of him, lying open on the desk, was the letter from Caroline. Caroline, his wife, who was off in England doing God only knew what with God only knew whom, and could only say to him things like "Please understand."

Please understand. Steven shook his head and reached for his coffee cup. The coffee was cold and bitter, but he drank it anyway. It paralleled his mood. Please understand—Christ, what the hell did that mean? She had to go spend four months in California, and he was supposed to understand. She had to fly off on her own to England, without even saying good-bye, and he was supposed to understand. One day, Elizabeth was going to come to him and say, "What is my mother like?" and he would say to her, "She needs a lot of understanding."

What was it that he was supposed to understand, what allowances was he being asked to make? Caroline had had a wretched childhood, he knew—with no place to call her home, with her icy grandmother supervising every decision, and her mother absent, both physically and emotionally. Her stepfather had molested her when she was still a child, and then, that terrible incident with the Swiss lawyer on their wedding day. It was all horrible; there was no denying that. But he had tried so hard to change things for her, tried to give her the kind of life that she deserved, that she should have had. He had loved her as none of the people who were supposed to love her ever had or ever would. He had thought, when she married him, that it would be enough.

But it was as though she were a child again, running off whenever the whim struck her, trying to discover this or discover that, telling him that he had to understand. And, each time, Elizabeth became more of a stranger to her. Steven knew that he was closer to their daughter than Caroline, and there was sadness in that knowledge.

He stroked his beard as he continued to wait. Damn Eric for always being so busy, for not having time for the things that mattered. Was he like that, too? Steven asked himself with a start. Had Caroline been asking him for things that he was too busy to give to her?

But she realized that Asheford Shipbuilding was important to him. As a child, his father had always talked about the family business as though it were an altar upon which was sacrificed anything having to do with feelings, or hopes, or dreams. Everything was "for the business," and he had believed that it was the most important thing that there was. Sylvia Asheford had been ineffectual as a parent. It was Aaron, his father, the patriarch, the one who had begun the business and had caused it to prosper, who told the boys what was what in life. And what he told them was law.

For a time, Steven had tried to break loose of it all. That was when he had gone down to the shelter, to look at the old wizened souls cast off by the sea who had nowhere else to turn and no one else to lean on. He had gone there and, feeding them, had fed himself. He had met Caroline there, a precious and fragile soul among precious and fragile souls. But, in the end, he had paid.

After Steven and Caroline were married, William had asked him bluntly where his priorities lay. "Because if they're not with the business, Steven, say so, and I'll buy you out. It's important to me."

"It's important to me, too," Steven had said defensively. To think otherwise was heresy. "But other things can be important as well."

"That's not what Father said."

"Father had to build this business from the ground up. He never had any time for anything else—not for Mother, not for us. We have more leisure, William. Let's not make the same mistakes that Father did."

William had narrowed his eyes. "Mistakes?"

Steven shrugged. "Thinking that Asheford Shipbuilding is the beginning and the end of everything. It's important, but there's more to life than one shipyard in one town in one state, for God's sake!"

"Such as?"

"Such as building a family. Such as caring for people. Such as living, William, not just existing from nine to five!"

"You're very vehement." William couldn't respond, Steven had seen that in the set features and the clenched hands. He felt no passion, no love, not for anything but the business. His marriage to Justine had virtually been arranged, and she had been carefully chosen to complement his way of life. No passion, no danger, no uncertainty. So unlike Caroline . . .

That had been the beginning of the differences between the brothers, and things had gone from bad to worse. The money and contracts flowing in to Asheford Shipbuilding through Steven and Caroline from Eric and Intraglobal had undoubtedly moved the shipyard into the forefront of American defense contracting, but a wedge had thereby been driven between the brothers. William worked as if possessed by some strange demon, as if his brother's contributions compelled him to equal them. As Steven mused, perhaps he, too, had been driven by some need to prove himself.

And now it was William and Justine, and their problems, who were making Steven's own problems come to life again. Sometimes, it was easy for him to do what William did: Lose himself

in the work, forget all the rest, the uncertainty of his life with
Caroline, her evasions and disappearances. When he was working, he was absorbed, possessed by what he did. He didn't have
time to think about Caroline. He didn't feel his hurt.

He smiled at the thought, a twisted smile. Caroline didn't care
how much she hurt him. He was reasonably sure that she was
seeing another man even now, perhaps someone she had met in
California. She would probably deny it if he confronted her, but
he didn't have the energy to confront her. He didn't seem to
have the energy to do much these days. Anyway, she was in
England, living out some romantic fantasy of Life at War, perhaps remembering her mother's stories of Paris during the Great
War. If she thought that that was all that there was to it, then—

Eric's voice broke into his thoughts. "Steven? I'm sorry to
have kept you waiting. I was on another line."

"Have you heard anything from Caroline?"

"Not directly. I understand that she went looking for a young
man to whom she gave flying instruction in Newport, and that
he is temporarily attached to the Eagle Squadron in Surrey. I
have people there now, to persuade her to return to the States as
quickly as possible."

"How quickly?" It wasn't for himself. Steven maintained no
more illusions that Caroline still loved him, even if she ever had.
But his sister-in-law still sat day after day, staring vacantly at a
blank wall, and the children, Nicholas and Elizabeth, grew more
restless, more needy, more demanding with each passing hour.

"As soon as possible." Eric's voice was soothing. "She's in
no danger at the moment, Steven. I promise you that. She'll be
all right."

"Yes," Steven agreed dully. "She'll be all right." The question remained only for the rest of them. Caroline, like her
mother, was a survivor. Steven wondered, for the first time, if—
like her mother—Caroline would leave her path of survival lit-
tered with the corpses of those who had not been as lucky as
she.

The middle-aged man frowned at the paper in his hand. "This
is the complete report? It's not enough to send to Zurich. We
have been well paid for this particular service."

The younger man, wearing the uniform of the German High
Command, shook his head. He had already been having a difficult day, and this Gestapo general was not making things any

easier for him. "That's as conclusive as we can make it, sir. The Hurricane belonging to Captain Starkey was shot down just west of Brest, over the Channel. Our pilots made certain that there was no wreckage and no body recovered."

"How very thorough of you, Herr Major. And yet there is still one thing that puzzles me."

"What is that, General?"

"How is it that Captain Starkey was wounded—by your men, incidentally, who ought really to be off in Bavaria working at target practices—in the evening, and took off alone the following day at dawn? He must have had fantastic recuperative powers, wouldn't you say, Herr Major?"

A shade of uncertainty crept into the other man's voice. "Doubtless, Herr General."

"Ah, yes. So this is the report that I am to send to Zurich. Do you know what we are being paid for this, Herr Major?"

"No, sir." The younger man was beginning to sound very unhappy indeed.

"Ah. Well, I will tell you. In exchange for eliminating Captain Starkey, an objective that can only advance the cause of the Third Reich, as I'm sure that you can appreciate, we are to be given locations for all the radar setups on the eastern coast of England. Exact locations, Major Strausse. The implications of such knowledge do not, I trust, elude you?"

"No, sir."

"So we must be absolutely certain."

"So you want—?"

"So I want you to assure yourself that Captain Starkey is indeed listed as missing and not recuperating, even as we speak, in some RAF hospital. You have contacts in England, Major Strausse. Use them."

"Yes, Herr General." The air in the room was becoming unbreathable.

"Very well. That will be all. Oh, Major Strausse?"

"Yes, Herr General?"

"If you fail, you will die." He paused. "That will be all, Herr Major."

There were fires raging all over.

Fires always flared up in the summer, but they had never been a problem, because the fire stations were so efficient. But now the towns and cities of France belonged to the Germans, who didn't know yet what they were doing, and they didn't give the orders for the fire trucks to respond to civilian calls. Consequently, the conflagrations raged out of control.

The situation would almost be amusing, Chantale thought, if it weren't so very deadly.

She sat for hours in the kitchen with Annie, who pored over the newspapers, the famous—or infamous—column in *Paris-Soir* which recorded the lists of missing people. "They're all going back home, now," Annie observed. "Poor people."

Those who had fled before the German invasion had few choices. They could try to get to England somehow, or they could return home. Sometimes their homes were occupied, and they had to look elsewhere for lodgings. Sometimes they found themselves the uneasy hosts of unwanted and uninvited guests. And always, always, there were the names. Names of those they couldn't find: a child, last seen on the Dieppe road; an uncle, known only to be somewhere in Rouen; a mother, separated from her family during a Stuka attack, whereabouts unknown. The litany of names went on and on, all of them listed in the *Paris-Soir,* and Annie and Chantale read them to each other daily. "We have to remember these people," they told each other.

"Perhaps my mother has heard of them. Perhaps they made their way to the coast," suggested Chantale; but rarely, if ever, did those who started out so bravely make it all the way to England.

"Here's an article," Annie pointed out. "Look, Countess, they're taking us more seriously now."

"What are you talking about?"

"See, here. Death penalty now for anybody caught helping English soldiers to escape from France."

The words blurred in front of Chantale, and she pushed the newspaper away. "I don't want to see it," she said. But she knew, she had known for a long time, that what they were doing was dangerous. After the first time, she had gone to confession.

"I confess that I have broken the law."

The voice on the other side of the confessional grille was gentle. "In what way, my child?"

She had hesitated, but priests, she knew, could not reveal anything told to them here. "I have helped an Englishman to the coast."

"I see." There was a long silence. "Will you do it again?"

"Yes. Father."

"I see. This is not a matter for the confessional, my child. Have you any other sins of which you wish to repent?"

Later, he had invited her to the rectory. "There is no sherry, I'm afraid, in these hard times, nor is there coffee. But I would like to talk with you, Countess."

"Of course, Father."

She had sat on a hard chair with a hand-crocheted doily over its high back, and had listened to him. "Evil things are happening, Countess. It is no sin to break a law when that law is evil." He leaned forward, his benign eyes suddenly piercing. "You have someplace for people to go, Countess?"

"Yes, Father. My old home in Brittany. It's—a castle, there's plenty of room. My mother cares for the travelers. From there there are fishermen, who go across the Channel to fish in Cornwall."

"And, in the meantime, your own home is safe?"

She shrugged. "Who knows? The Germans are not there now. For some reason we are not occupied." In the back of her mind the maddening question persisted: why, why, why? Why had they been spared? Why had the Gestapo chosen to leave them alone? So that they could be watched? "I am very careful," she said.

"I have no doubt that you are, Countess. And your husband? He, also, is very careful?"

"My husband," she said, "knows nothing of what I do. My mother-in-law suspects, but he does not. If she knew, I believe I would have her support. I—I don't know about his."

"Ah." He was quiet for some time. "Countess, I may need to send people to you from time to time. Can you arrange for them to follow your route to the coast—and to England?"

She raised her eyes to meet his. "Yes. Father."

"It is easy to fight a battle as long as shots are still being fired," he said gently. "Your battle, Countess, is far more difficult. I admire you for it."

Annie had been aghast. "You told him?"

"Well, of course, Annie! He's the parish priest!"

"He could have been reporting back to the Germans!"

Chantale shook her head. "You're becoming too suspicious. A *priest,* Annie! Besides, we've known him for years. He christened the children. . . ."

"Happens this time you're right, Countess. But don't think

that they won't go dressing up like priests, or nuns, or whatever else they think will work so that you'll talk to them.'' She shook her head, worry over this potential danger evident in her face. ''Please be careful, Countess. Don't trust anybody. Please don't trust a soul.''

It was after that that Annie read the article out of *Paris-Soir*. ''You see, Countess! Death penalty for us if they ever find out.''

''They won't find out.''

''Only the good God can say that, Countess,'' Annie replied piously, crossing herself. ''Only the good God knows.''

Indeed, thought Chantale. Only the good God knew. Just give us a good run for our money first, she breathed in silent prayer. Just give us a good run first.

That night, two more trapped English fliers crept out of the darkness into her stables, and the following night she sent them on their way. The next night, there were more. And more, and more, until Chantale could scarcely remember a time when they had not been there, when she had not carried their secret wrapped around her like a cloak.

Even the scenery had changed. The Germans had built bunkers in and around Angers, control points, with no guns, just miles and miles of underground caverns, filled with offices and machinery and God only knew what else. ''You must get this information to the coast,'' Father Xavier whispered to her earnestly. ''The British need to know what to bomb.''

''The bunkers?'' Strange and frightening on the landscape as they were, Chantale had not thought of them as presenting any particular danger. ''Why?''

''My child, they're directing all of the German submarine activity out of Brest,'' he said simply. ''Kneel down.''

Recognizing the change in his voice, she obeyed at once, and the passing German soldiers saw nothing but an old priest blessing a devout woman. He intoned the blessing in Latin, making the sign of the cross over her head, before whispering, ''Have you anyone going to the coast tonight? How soon can this message be relayed?''

Chantale crossed herself for added effect. ''Tonight,'' she murmured. ''I will give them the message myself.''

''Splendid,'' he said, helping her to her feet. ''Be careful, my child.''

She rode her horse back across the fields, away from the small church, and took him to the stables herself. Etienne, the stableboy, stood ready to take the reins from her, but she waved him away and led the gelding back to his stall herself. She unsaddled him and slipped a halter on the place of the bridle, rubbing him down all over with straw—the days were hot. Finally, wiping her hands on her jodhpurs and looking around to be sure that no one was about, she climbed up the ladder and into the haylofts.

The lofts were as vast as the stables themselves, room after room filled with straw and hay harvested from the château's own fields. It was here, sleeping by day and traveling by night, that the refugees hid: Frenchmen unwilling to accept the armistice and trying to join the Free French forces of the General de Gaulle; important professors and scientists, people best left undiscovered by the Germans; English pilots still trapped in enemy territory. Today, there were three Frenchmen eager to join whatever forces they could—the Algerians, the Free French, the British—anyone who would let them kill some of the *sales Boches*.

One, a small, swarthy man who had given his name only as Jean, was awake and watching as the trapdoor opened. Chantale could see his hand at his belt, resting lightly but firmly on the handle of a knife. He relaxed when he recognized her and saw that she was alone. She closed the door carefully and trod across the scattered straw on the floor to where they were.

"What is it?" His voice was a whisper. Already he was prodding one of his companions with the toe of his boot, getting ready to flee. "Germans?"

"No," she answered, squatting down in her jodhpurs and riding boots, twisting a piece of straw in her hand. "Where is it that you are going tonight?"

"Who wants to know?" Nothing but dark suspicion in his face.

"I do. I have a message that must get through to England. I want to know if you are the ones to take it."

The other two men were awake now, and watching her. The fair-haired one shook his head. "We'll be in Brest tonight if all goes well. We have to stay there for a few days—we're waiting for some others to join us. We have a boat arranged for Penzance for Monday night."

Chantale considered. "All right. I'll try other channels, but I might as well give it to you first. The RAF needs to be notified that the Germans have been building bunkers here to direct submarine activity out of Brest. Nantes, too, probably, though that's just a guess." A good guess, though, she thought. There were too many bunkers, and that kind of activity needed central processing. Nantes and Brest were being battered by the RAF, as was in fact all of Brittany. But Angers was safe. And Nantes was directly across from them, down the river, on the coast. She reached behind her, into her back pocket. "I've got a drawing for you—here. These are the locations of the bunkers that need to be hit." She looked up at the dark face so close to hers. "Can you see that this gets to the proper authorities once you get to England?"

Jean took the map from her, but again it was his blond companion who spoke. "Don't worry, Countess," he said easily. "We'll see that it gets through." He picked up a piece of straw and stuck it in his mouth. "I guess that what we've heard is true."

"What is that?"

"That the Countess de Montclair is a true patriot. Tell me, Countess, who is your contact in Angers? Who got you this information?"

An uneasy feeling began to settle over her. "That's secret. You know that's secret. And you shouldn't be using my real name," she said sharply, standing up. "Try to get some sleep now. I'll send the cook with bread and wine and soup when it's time for you to leave."

Jean stood up with her. "We only wanted to know," he said, "so that others might be directed to him—or her. In case you're not available."

"I understand," Chantale said. "But please understand why I cannot tell you. Good day, gentlemen."

She slid down the ladder with relief at escaping the oppressive atmosphere, and went at once to find Annie. The kitchen door was open to the sunshine, and Annie sat at the long refectory table, polishing a rifle. Chantale stared at it.

"What is that?"

"A gun, Countess," Annie said comfortably. "Nice to have around sometimes. Reassuring-like."

"Are you mad? All firearms were confiscated last week! Pierre took everything out of the gun room."

"This wasn't in the gun room. It's my own, or was Henri's, God rest his soul, and seeing as I'm his widow it's mine now, and has been these years. It hasn't fired in ages, Countess. I never thought to hand it in. It isn't a gun, not really—just an heirloom." But the way she handled it indicated that she knew more about it than she was willing to let on.

Chantale hesitated, then sat down across from her. "Annie— those men in the stable. Who are they?"

"Just Frenchmen, Countess. On their way to England. Why?"

"They ask too many questions," Chantale said uncomfortably. "They wanted Father Xavier's name."

"Did you tell them?"

"Do me a favor, Annie! I have learned one or two things, haven't I? But it bothered me that they should ask."

"Hmm." Annie finished oiling the firing mechanism and carefully placed the rifle on the bench next to her. "It's easy to get suspicious."

"I know. And it may not mean anything. But I'm worried."

"Hmm. Well, I'll just go and have a chat with my friend the baker's wife, Countess. High time I bought a loaf of bread."

Chantale smiled. "You bake your own bread, Annie."

"Do I, now? Well, everyone deserves a break now and again, Countess. Besides, happens my friend the baker's wife is the second cousin of the nephew of the owner of Pierrot's Restaurant in Tours. And she always has news of her family."

"What about our guests?"

"Well, seeing as they came from Pierrot's before coming here, I just might have some news of them. Be back soon, Countess."

The air in the kitchen was warm, and Chantale felt sleepy. She lowered her head onto her arms, her long red hair spilling out from her barrette onto the table. For a while, she slept.

When the sun was well down on the horizon and Annie had not yet returned, Marie-Louise woke her. "Chantale! Do wake up, won't you, and tell me what is going on?"

Chantale rubbed her eyes. "What time is it?"

"Nearly seven o'clock, and supper won't be on time from the looks of it. Where has Cook gone?"

"She needed to—buy some things," Chantale faltered. "Goodness! That was hours ago."

"Yes, well, we'll have to get Jeannine to fill in. You did say that she cooks, didn't you? I can't imagine what has kept Cook all this time. And on Francie's day off, too."

There was a cold, hollow feeling growing inside Chantale. Annie had gone to talk with the baker's wife, to find out . . .

"I'll be back," she said hastily to Marie-Louise, and ran out the back door and down the path to the stables. Etienne watched, openmouthed, as she tore open the large central door and clawed her way up the ladder.

She needn't have hurried. The loft was empty.

And Annie was nowhere to be found.

Chapter Eighteen

*A*nnie had been arrested by the Germans.

The news came through, a little at a time, piece by piece. It was Father Xavier who told Chantale, three long and horrible days after Annie's disappearance. He said that she was being held in Tours. "What are the charges?" Chantale whispered. He shook his head sadly, hopelessly. "Espionage, I'm afraid, my child."

Espionage. If found guilty by a German tribunal, Annie would be executed.

Chantale rode on horseback into Angers nearly every day. There was precious little gasoline, and she had no real excuse to get any more, not with Pierre watching the gas gauge like a hawk and the German patrols stopping whomever they pleased to ask for identification papers, so she took the horses instead. It wasn't out of the ordinary. In fact, everyone was riding horses these days. You could leave your horse in one of the parks—the Jardin des Plantes or the Jardin des Fleurs—for a nominal fee, and it would be tethered and watched. Meanwhile, you would be free to walk about as you pleased.

Or as free as possible in an occupied city.

On the first day after Annie's arrest, Chantale and Marie-Louise had driven in together to confront the Germans who were presiding over City Hall. Pierre had refused to go, claiming that it would put them in a bad light with the occupying forces—and, after all, Annie was only a servant. Marie-Louise had given her son a withering glance, and put on her best black silks, and called for the car and a driver.

"Ah, Madame la Comtesse." The German officer—one that they didn't know—lifted Marie-Louise's gloved hand perfunctorily to his lips. "And the young countess! To what do I owe the honor of a visit from the gentry? We don't see much of you in town these days." There was sarcasm in his voice.

Marie-Louise answered as though the German had been truly cordial. "We have heard that one of our servants has been arrested in Tours," she said clearly. "We believe the charges to be false and request that you negotiate her release at once." Despite her polite tone, it sounded as though she was issuing an order and not making a request. Chantale winced inwardly.

"Ah. I see." He sat down behind the huge ornate desk that had once belonged to the mayor, indicating that they should sit as well. "I don't know what to say, madame. How was it that you heard so promptly of her . . . detainment?"

"A good employer is ever alert to the needs of his servants," Marie-Louise said, coldly and ambiguously. She had not accepted his invitation to sit down.

"I see. And you, Countess?"

"Yes, Captain?" Chantale met his eyes.

"It seems to me that you ladies would do better with your sympathies than to entrust them to an enemy of the Reich." He riffled through some papers. "I regret to inform you you will need to engage other staff. The person in question goes to trial in the morning, in Tours. There can be little doubt of the verdict. We have it from reliable sources that she was helping English fliers, enemies of the Reich." He raised his eyebrows. "You would know nothing of this—ladies?"

"What my servants see fit to do in their time off is their own business," Marie-Louise said stiffly.

"Unless it is espionage, Madame la Comtesse. Unless it is espionage. However, some do seem to have minds of their own." He put a smile into his voice, making it a sophisticated discussion among equals. "And I know, myself, how independent servants can be these days. Not like the fine old days . . ."

"May we see Annie, Captain?" Chantale interrupted, and he narrowed his eyes as he looked at her.

"Countess. I'm sorry, I cannot grant you that wish at this particular moment. But a few days from now, perhaps. You may of course see her one last time, if you so choose. She is to be brought before a firing squad at the place du Ralliement on Saturday." He smiled again. "Only if she is convicted in Tours, naturally. But we are preparing the site—just in case. Just as a friendly warning, ladies, to other enemies of the Third Reich. We take our duties very seriously. I hope that no other . . .

member of your household . . . will end up meeting such a fate.'' He was looking directly at Chantale as he spoke, and she felt a shiver of fear raking up and down her spine. A friendly warning.

That night Chantale began to have the nightmare. She was sitting on a pebbly beach, much like the one near her old home in Brittany, and was throwing stones into the water. A man in a uniform came and told her that she was forbidden to throw rocks. She stood up and tried to hit him, and he took hold of her wrists, and they struggled. He forced her down to the ocean and her head was underwater and she was drowning, drowning, drowning . . . She awoke, gasping for breath, the room spinning all around her.

The dream came every night after that, the three nights that separated them from the morning of Annie's execution.

The Germans were making a big production of the executions because they wanted to use Annie and the others with her—one woman, three men, all of them unknown to Chantale—as examples. Chantale found her hands trembling as the prisoners were led into the square and paraded before the Opera before mounting the stage created for them. Chantale had to hold a hand over her own mouth to keep herself from crying out.

Annie looked terrible. Gone was the rotund bonhomie, the creases and wrinkles of complacency. There were bruises on Annie's face and on her arms, and one of her eyes was squeezed shut due to a swelling on her brow. Her hands were tied together behind her back, and she walked with great difficulty, as though something was hurting her terribly. But her head was held high, her eyes fixed on a point somewhere over the heads of the crowd, her chin never wavering. Chantale felt a wave of love and pride wash over her. This isn't just Annie going to her death, she thought: This is France. A wronged martyr, still standing tall with everything in tatters but her dignity. Her thoughts were an echo, she realized suddenly, of those she had had the day that she heard about the German invasion: This is France.

Marie-Louise was standing equally tall, almost at attention, beside her daughter-in-law. She was strong, Chantale found herself thinking, almost in surprise, stronger than any of them had ever given her credit for being. Marie-Louise had lived under the same roof as Annie for well over thirty years, and yet here she stood, her eyes bright with unshed tears, her chin high, forcing herself to watch. There was a strength there that was greater than anything Chantale had, herself, ever experienced.

The prisoners were tied to stakes in a line, with a specially constructed wall behind them. The Germans were careful; this contrived execution could easily backfire if any innocent by-standers were hurt or killed by a stray bullet, but no one would be. The *Boche* would see to that.

A young corporal went from prisoner to prisoner, offering blindfolds. Several were accepted, though not by Annie. A priest followed him, speaking in a low private voice to each person. Chantale saw him mark Annie's forehead with the sign of the cross. Again, words drifted back to her. "Only the good God knows, Countess. Only the good God knows."

In the end, it was not Annie who cried the words, but the man standing next to her, with whom she had been arrested. It didn't matter, not really, who actually spoke them. It mattered only, then, that they were spoken. Even as the guns were raised, he cried out, *"Vive la France!"* and then the battery of guns drowned out his voice forever.

Annie was dead, her large brave body slumped heavily against the pole, her eyes still open, still watching her fate. The German Feldkommandatur stood up and read again the new law promising such a penalty to all those who proved themselves enemies of the Third Reich, and exhorting all peaceful French citizens to mark well that such a fate did not befall them and theirs.

"Well, I think that's all."

Caroline straightened and snapped the clasps on her suitcase. Emma, one of the radio girls, stood helpfully by to carry some of Caroline's bags. "I think so," she said.

"Yes," Caroline said vaguely, looking about the narrow barracks as though there were something important that she was forgetting. "That's it, then, I'm off."

Emma followed her through the door. "I do wish that you'd reconsider, Caroline," she said. "Gladys and Margaret are ever so keen to join up with this new outfit, and I heard that there are one or two American girls coming over as well."

"I don't know what I'm going to do yet, Emma," Caroline said tiredly. "I'm going to have to think about it for a while."

"Yes, well, do keep it in mind, then." She glanced out in the driveway and saw the staff car waiting. "Well, I see Captain Starkey's here. I won't hold you up any longer. Cheerio, then, and all the best to you.'' She put down the suitcase on the steps and kissed Caroline's cheek before running across the compound toward the mess tent, with a friendly wave to Andrew as she passed him.

"What was that all about?" He smiled and put an arm around Caroline.

"She wants me to join up with some group they're starting— a women's division of the Air Transport Auxiliary. I told her that I'd think about it."

"Women flying Air Transport?" Andrew smiled. "Great, Caroline. But you're an American. Leave the war to the Brits, why don't you?"

"Leave the war to the Brits, why don't you?" she teased back, and he leaned over to kiss her.

"I'll miss you."

"Tell me to stay," she said seriously. "And I will."

"I can't do that. At which hotel will you be in London?"

"The Regent. Family money might as well be good for something, and all that I can think of now is a long, hot, luxurious bath." She smiled again. "I'll think of you when I'm dining at the Savoy Grill!"

"They've heard of rationing, even at the Savoy."

"I'm sure that they manage anyway." She hugged him fiercely, suddenly feeling swept up by a wave of love, of tenderness, of . . . words failed her. She needed him, and he was making her leave him. Life was so unfair.

"Yes, I'm sure they do." He ruffled her curls in a friendly fashion, and then reached past her for her suitcases. "This all? Nothing to it, my lady . . ."

Caroline followed him down the steps, reluctantly. I won't cry, she told herself. I won't make a scene. It's not as though I don't understand what's going on here. But she could feel the tears welling up, hot and smarting, and she blinked furiously to hold them back.

Andrew was putting her suitcases in the staff car; she busied herself with her rain scarf, belted her raincoat, anything not to have to look at him . . . And then he had straightened and was coming toward her, and she realized, with a sinking feeling in her stomach, that it was now or never. What had the priest said at her wedding? "Speak now, or forever hold your peace." Yes, that was it. She took a deep breath and spoke to him. "You know, we might not see each other again."

Andrew looked uncomfortable. "Caroline, don't be too dramatic. When the war's over, there will be plenty of time—"

She shook her head. "Oh, Andrew, can't you see? You belong to Johnson Industries, just as surely as I belong to Intraglobal. We've never even talked about it. I've lived all my life in that shadow, and I've hated it and I've resented it, but we can't pretend that it doesn't exist. I'm tired of *you* pretending that it doesn't exist."

He wouldn't look at her. "It doesn't have to exist. Not if we don't want it to."

She hadn't liked Steven's response to Eric and Intraglobal, but at least he had been grappling with it, at least he never pretended that it wasn't there. Since she arrived, however, Andrew had never even mentioned the problems that stood between them. "It does, Andrew," she said gently. "And you have to accept that it's part of my life, just as you accept that it's part of yours."

"I don't!" he said suddenly, explosively. "I don't! I can't! I hate it all, Caroline. All the groping, all the manipulation, all the scrounging for money and control and power! I don't want anything to do with it! Not now. Not ever."

She almost felt sorry for him then. "Do you really think that you can make things happen just by wishing for them?" she asked softly.

"What I want," he said through clenched teeth, fighting to keep his voice level, "is peace. Not just in Europe. Peace everywhere. Peace in my heart. I want a family, and a place to live, and enough to live on, and that is all. I don't want to always be arguing, always questioning. I want to know."

"But, Andrew," Caroline said, "no one ever knows. And if you're not questioning, then that means you've stopped thinking."

"Maybe that's not such a bad thing."

She shook her head and moved closer to him. "I have to go," she said gently, and he seized her in his arms and kissed her, again and again, as though he knew already what they had not put into words, but what they both understood.

Andrew released her at last and held the car door open for her. "Call me when you get there," he said, and she nodded, not trusting her voice. He caught her hands on the top of the open door and held them a moment, making her face him. "I'll think about you, Caroline," he said, his voice husky.

"I'll think about you, too, Andrew," she said, tears glittering in her eyes.

He smiled and nodded, as though affirming some decision. "Corporal Kelly?" he said loudly, still watching Caroline.

"Yes, sir?" The voice came from the driver's seat.

"London. The Regent Hotel, if you would, please."

"Very good, sir."

"Good-bye," Caroline whispered.

Andrew touched her lips lightly with the tip of his finger, smiled again, and then stepped back. Caroline swallowed hard and slid into the backseat of the car. Andrew closed the door. Almost immediately, she lowered the window. "When—?"

"Shh," he said. "We'll talk about it. Go now."

She smiled tremulously, nodded again, and then the big car was sliding away down the long driveway and out through the gates and onto the road. The road to London.

She was being followed.

Chantale had thought so, once or twice, but now she was absolutely sure of it. She had tested her suspicions by browsing at two shop windows on the rue des Arènes, and then crossing the street to look into a third. There was always someone there, only a few paces behind, acting as though the windows were as fascinating as she herself was pretending they were. And it was a man, peering into shops of women's clothing.

She went into the bank and watched him through the curtains. He came in a moment later, inquired into the cost of a checking account, but broke off his inquiry when she slipped out the door. He hadn't even glanced her way, but a few minutes later she saw him again, pausing outside a bookstore when she stopped to buy a newspaper at the Tabac.

Well, she said to herself, what did you expect? Your own cook arrested and executed for espionage, and you think that the rest of the household won't be watched for a while?

Let them watch Pierre. Let them watch him make secret rendezvous with his mistress; that should satisfy their need for intrigue. But perhaps they didn't need to watch Pierre. Whatever had been their reason for sparing the Château de Montclair the pain of occupation surely must have something to do with him, after all. Perhaps his mistress was, in fact, Gestapo herself. Chantale almost smiled—almost. The thought was a little too close for comfort, and no laughing matter at all if it was true.

She thought about that as she got back to the Jardin des Fleurs
and reclaimed her horse, a big chestnut gelding that, some years
ago, Marie-Louise had ridden in the local hunt. Not even allowing herself to smile . . . Annie had said, sometimes, that the
countess was a fine lady, but that she certainly hadn't been
around when the good God had handed out a sense of humor to
folks. Am I becoming humorless? Chantale wondered as she set
herself at a slow trot on the road home. Perhaps. Perhaps so.
God knew that there was little enough to laugh at these days.

Still, talking with Annie about it would have been nice.

Chantale knew that she could do nothing in the next few days—
or weeks—or for however long the Germans chose to follow her.
She wondered how they were able to watch Marie-Louise, who
never left the estate. Did they have telescopes trained on the
castle walls and windows night and day? Or was Marie-Louise
too old to be considered a threat?

She might well become more of one soon. Chantale had stood
with her when Annie was shot, and because she couldn't bear
to watch her friend die she had looked at her mother-in-law
instead. Chantale thought that she would never forget the expression on Marie-Louise's face. She was absolutely certain that
some decision had been made right there in the place du Ralliement, some resolution taken.

What remained was for Marie-Louise to share it with her. But
they weren't at that stage in their relationship yet. The icy reserve that had characterized Chantale's first years at the Château
de Montclair was thawing, little by little. But spring had by no
means arrived. A pity, she thought. The war had a way of breaking down the niceties of formal relationships. Things just might
have to be rushed.

She smiled to herself. It wasn't such an unpleasant thought.

Marie-Louise was, in fact, waiting for her in the front hall
when she returned to the château, trying to appear casual, but
straining for news. "Did you buy the newspaper?"

"Yes," Chantale said, putting her packages on the green baize
table in the echoing front hall. Even though the day was hot, the
air was as chilly as ever within these walls. "No sugar, though.
And they say that bread is going to be rationed soon, too. They're
going to issue cards."

"Bread rationed!" Marie-Louise snorted, advancing farther
into the hall. She seemed older today, her small figure slightly
hunched in her eternal black dress and shawl. "What else?"

"Who knows?" Chantale said as lightly as she could. "There are rumors, of course. There are always rumors." She hesitated. "I heard that the Germans have been visiting the library," she said.

The older woman stopped in the act of opening the newspaper on the table. "Not to inform themselves about French culture, I assume?" she asked softly.

"Hardly." She was quick, Chantale had to give her credit. Perhaps she always had been, and Chantale had been too proud— or miserable or martyred—to see it before. "They're burning books. Publicly. At the place du Ralliement." Chantale swallowed quickly; her recent memory of the place du Ralliement was too painful. "They're going to close the library next week. Indefinitely, they said. People ought to have better things to do than to sit around reading, and, if we don't, then the Third Reich will kindly find us something with which to occupy our time. Everyone should work."

"Indeed." The voice was still soft. Marie-Louise turned a page of the newspaper, as though unconcerned. "Some of us feel that we are occupied enough as it is. Would you say that you are sufficiently occupied, Chantale?"

Chantale swallowed. "I think that it is time for me to spend more time with my children and my duties here at the château," she said carefully. "My occupations seem to attract interest that I do not wish."

"Indeed?" There was a different inflection in the voice this time. Marie-Louise still had not looked at her. "A great deal of interest, would you say?"

"I would say that I am never lonely," Chantale replied, stifling a desire to giggle at their way of talking in code. "Even when I walk about in the city, I never feel quite alone."

"This is very interesting," Marie-Louise said. "I'm taking this newspaper with me to my room, Chantale. I will see you at lunch."

And she left Chantale to stare after her and wonder what on earth had prompted Philippe de Montclair to look for a mistress. There was a great deal more to Marie-Louise than met the eye.

Pierre was, as usual, nowhere to be found. The children were delighted that she was back, however, and she took them out to the stables to play with their ponies. Etienne approached her as she stood by the paddock watching Jean-Claude balance himself on the broad back of the pony he most often rode. "Keep your heels down, darling!" she called out to him.

"Countess, may I have a word with you?" He was careful and deferential, but even so Chantale found herself glancing about nervously. "What is it?"

"I wondered . . . some friends of mine might be in the area this evening. I wondered if they might spend the night here." He hesitated. "Usually Annie gave me permission, but as she's not here . . ."

"No," Chantale said, not daring to look at him.

"But, Countess, they're the sort of friends that Annie always wanted to have spend the night!" He sounded anxious, as though she didn't understand his veiled language.

"No," Chantale said again. "I will tell you when you may have friends here again. The accommodations would not be comfortable at the moment. You must tell them that." She risked a glance at him. "Tell them, Etienne, and tell any other friends who wish to come, that it is not comfortable here just now. Perhaps it will be again. I don't know."

He seemed at last to understand, and was surprised. "Is it because of Annie?" he asked baldly.

"Yes," she said again. "That will be all, Etienne."

Chantale was amazed to find, after such a simple exchange, that her heart was beating wildly in her chest. I'm not very good at this, she told herself again. What was it that the first British pilot had called her? A "bloody amateur," that was it. Perhaps that was all she would ever be.

They were following her. They were rationing food, burning books, closing libraries. They had cast a shadow over the land, and she shivered as though it had blocked out the sun.

She took a deep breath to steady herself and watched her children, Jean-Claude happy and unconcerned on his pony, the baby gurgling in her bassinet nearby. No, Chantale thought suddenly, clenching her fists by her side. No. They will not live as I do now. They will not grow up learning to speak German in school and saluting that awful flag and worshiping that hateful man. They are French. I will see to it that they always know that, that they never forget. They are French.

"Jean-Claude!" she called out, her voice sharper than she realized. "Come in to lunch now!"

Father Xavier had been invited. The parish priest dined with them at the château once a week. He didn't look well, she thought as she slipped into her seat across the table from him. Marie-Louise had taken out her good lace tablecloth for the occasion, the one she had brought from her girlhood home in Brissac. The antique silver tea set was waiting on the sideboard as well. Chantale shot her mother-in-law a sharp look, but said nothing.

The priest intoned a blessing over the food—fish, as usual for lunch these days, even though it wasn't a Friday—and ate a few polite bites before beginning the conversation. Even in wartime, there were courtesies to be observed. Patting his mouth lightly with Marie-Louise's fine linen, he took another swallow of wine and said carefully, "Things must have changed for you in the past few days with your cook gone." He himself had presided at her funeral, burying her in the de Montclair plot at Marie-Louise's insistence.

"We've made do," Marie-Louise said smoothly. "Things always change, Father."

"Ah, yes. The only true reality of life. I've quite forgotten who said that." There were circles under his eyes, the same eyes that had twinkled so merrily when he had married Chantale and Pierre, when he had christened their two children. He loved life, and now he lived under a system that spoke only of death. He turned to Chantale. "And you, my dear? How have you been? Dear me, I think it's been over a week since I saw you last. I've quite forgotten what we discussed."

Like hell you have, Chantale thought, smiling politely. "England," she said sweetly. "We talked about England."

"Yes, yes, of course. Tut, tut. I seem to be losing my memory these days."

"It seems," Marie-Louise said acidly, "that most people find it healthier to do so."

"Oh, it is, Countess. It is indeed." His voice was very serious. "I see that you still have fresh vegetables. They've become a rarity at the market."

"We grow our own," Chantale said, wondering where the conversation was leading, and how to tell him that his message hadn't gotten through to England. She glanced at Marie-Louise. Although she had a sense now of where the older woman's loyalties lay, and how sympathetic she was to what Chantale had been doing, it was more than a large step between that and saying, directly, something that would involve her—it was an abyss. Chantale unhappily contemplated the abyss and said nothing.

Father Xavier, however, wasn't finished. "Have you thought of selling some of your produce at market? I remember your husband . . ." he was saying to Marie-Louise. "As if it were only yesterday, I remember him saying to me, before the other war, that people had to work together when there is a common cause, that class distinctions didn't matter, that nothing mattered but one's freedom."

"I remember," Marie-Louise said acidly. "I expect that he was referring to his—friendship—with the farrier's son. He didn't need any excuse as grand as war for that, though." She paused. "If we brought produce to market, the Germans would be there first to buy it. No one else would see any of it. That's how it's been working, Father."

"And they pay in deutsche marks," added Chantale.

He shook his head. "There are some . . . clandestine . . . markets, here and there. We could be sure that at least some of it went to French people, people who haven't had fresh fruits or vegetables on their tables for weeks. Well, it's something for you to think about, anyway." He patted his mouth a final time. "Dear Countess, that was a lovely lunch. And now I must be on my way."

Chantale stood up with him, quickly. "I'll see you to the door," she said before Marie-Louise could respond. "I think I left something in the front hall, anyway."

Her mother-in-law's eyes were watching her as she escorted the priest from the room. If Chantale had looked into them, she would have known that her secrets were safe.

"The message about the bunkers," Chantale said in a low voice in the passageway, wasting no time, "didn't get through. I think the people who were here that day are the ones that betrayed Annie. I can't be sure, but I think so."

"I see. Would you remember them again, my child?"

She thought of the dark blazing eyes in Jean's face, the sardonic amusement of the blond one. "Yes," she whispered.

"Remember them, then. You may be asked to identify them." They had come out into the relative light of the front hall, and Chantale turned to face him. "Whatever are you talking about?"

He shrugged, reaching for his hat and cane. "Vengeance is mine, saith the Lord," he said sorrowfully. "Others like to take it more directly into their own hands. Perhaps these men will live to regret their betrayal. Can you get another message through?''

She shook her head. "I'm being followed. Yesterday, and again today. No one can stay here until they lose interest.''

"I see." The corners of his mouth seemed to droop even farther. "Well, I suppose that it was inevitable." He turned toward the door.

"Father—wait. These other people of whom you spoke—are they friends of Annie's?''

"They are friends of all those who have chosen to fight on," he said with great dignity.

"Then I want to meet them," Chantale spoke quickly.

There was a pause. "That is not prudent, my child. I should not like to see you in any more danger than you are in now.''

Chantale took a deep breath. "Then do you want Annie to have died for nothing, Father?" That was unfair, but she was prepared to be unfair, if it got her what she wanted. "I am one of those who wishes to fight on, Father. And now that she is gone, I am alone here—truly alone. I need other people to help me.''

There was a flicker of amusement in his eye that she didn't understand, and then he nodded. "Give it some time, child," he advised. "You will meet them. I can assure you of that.''

For the moment, she had to be content with that.

Chapter Nineteen

The Eagle Squadron was getting some new airplanes. Not that the Hurricanes weren't performing well. Anything that could hold its own against the superior numbers of the German fighters was a performer, there was no question about that. But, all the same, Andrew Starkey couldn't help feeling a tremor of excitement as he watched the new planes land, delivered gleaming and shiny and new, via the Air Transport Auxiliary from the factories in the north.

They were called Mark I Spitfires, better and stronger and faster than the Supermarine Spitfires of only a few months ago, and, if they did not change the course of the war, at least they were going to buy England a little more time. A little more time, while the Americans refused to commit themselves to a course of action, and the huge ugly Nazi swastika rolled over Europe, threatening the island of Great Britain. A little time, while the British organized themselves and vowed to go on fighting, to the last man, to the last woman, to the last person who would draw breath on English soil and say, with solemn pride, "God save the king!"

Andrew wondered, even as he chided himself for allowing his thoughts to wander so, if the early Britons had felt this way when they saw the Romans invade. That incursion had been in the name of civilization, too. But there had never been anything civilized about invasion, about stealing another person's culture, another person's land, another person's beliefs. That was the reason they had to go on fighting.

And that was the reason for the Spitfires.

Andrew narrowed his eyes against the sun as he watched them land and taxi in. A Rolls-Royce Merlin engine, he knew, would power them to a maximum speed of 416 miles per hour—a good deal faster than the Hurricanes. But the real asset was the ceil-

ing, the ability to fly higher than any airplane in use in either
Great Britain or America—or, as he devoutly hoped, Germany.
They would have to use oxygen, and that might cause a few
problems, but the result would be worth it.

The Spitfires were all down, now—thirty of them, Andrew
was told—and had taxied up the runway and parked themselves
neatly on the flight line, where the Hurricanes had been. Andrew's men had moved the Hurricanes already, earlier that morning: The ATA would be taking off with them later that day, flying
them off to some undisclosed destination. And I hope that whatever poor sucker gets stuck with Fourteen learns about that undercarriage problem before he rolls it over in flames, Andrew
thought grimly. The best to him, wherever he may be.

The Spitfires' formation was perfect. They really did know
what they were doing, he thought, as one after another the Spitfire engines were cut and pilots began making their way out of
cockpits. The ATA, Ancient and Tattered Airmen, they called
themselves, the pilots who, by reason of age or handicap or
unsuitability, couldn't find a place in the RAF and instead delivered airplanes and flew cargo. Good pilots, nevertheless.

According to Caroline, a women's squadron had been formed,
too. Well, the best of luck to them. But not Caroline. Please,
God, not Caroline. All that I want for her is to be home and
safe and off my conscience, at least for the duration. After the
war . . . well, making plans like that was premature. After the
war, they would see.

Andrew turned to the clerk who always seemed to be only a
breath away, ready to take whatever orders Andrew cared to
give. "Corporal, I want the men in Operations in ten minutes.
And see that the ATA people get something to eat before they
leave. I'll hear the commander's report in my office."

"Yes, sir."

The ATA squadron commander was a veteran of the Great
War, and Andrew's interest in him quickened. "Flew the early
planes, then, did you, sir?" he asked, offering sherry.

"No, thank you, Captain. Yes, that's right, back in nineteen-
fifteen it was." He permitted himself a wry smile. "I must say,
piloting these Spits is quite an experience after that. A different
kind of flying, what?"

"I expect so. I gather you're impressed with the Spitfires?"

"Oh, yes, rather. Enormously. High ceiling, and all that. And
a good range, too. I think that you'll find them serviceable."

Andrew sat down. "You're taking the Hurricanes out this afternoon?"

"Right. And then we've got another delivery of the Spitfires to the rest of you Yanks, the other half of this Eagle Squadron of yours. And then some to our chaps over Cornwall way. Yes, enough to keep us quite busy, what?"

He sounded contented.

"I should think so. Anything that I should know?"

"Oh, dear me, no. They fly as the manual says, just now. Haven't seen any action yet, so who knows? But I'd consider myself lucky if I were you, old chap."

"I do." Andrew smiled and offered his hand. "Look out for Number Fourteen, won't you? The undercarriage is sticky, sometimes."

The bushy white eyebrows went up. "Bit of a challenge, what? Never mind, old chap: I'll fly it myself. Could do with some excitement for a change."

Andrew watched him as he rejoined his men in the mess tent, his back ramrod straight. Seeing as the skies over Britain weren't precisely a walk in the park these days, the old man's yearning for challenge seemed like overkill, if anything. Andrew smiled to himself. If half the stories he had heard about those early airplanes were true, then even the German-infested skies must indeed seem like a walk in the park. Bless their worn-out hearts, he found himself thinking as he headed toward Operations. Bless their brave old hearts.

Eric Beaumont had just gotten in to the office, and already the problems were piling up on his desk.

"Call Zurich," several notes said, in Julie's unruffled handwriting. "Call Marc Giroux on his direct line," said another, and all of them within the space of a half hour. "Call Mr. Asheford in Rhode Island."

Eric shook his head and hung up his jacket, fastidiously, on a coat hanger on a rack specially provided for him. He patted his pockets and tossed some coins, two boxes of matches, and a pack of cigarettes on his desk, glancing longingly at the morning newspapers stacked up for his perusal. Zurich would have to come first.

He lit a cigarette while he waited for the call to go through, and tapped the ash impatiently into the ceramic ashtray that Caroline had made for him. "Marc? Is that you? Eric Beaumont here."

"Ah, Monsieur Beaumont. Forgive the early telephone calls, but with the time difference, you see . . ."

"What is happening?"

"Several items, Monsieur Beaumont. Our intelligence sources have been active and have brought to light some interesting information."

"Which is?"

"We are reasonably certain that Japan intends to declare war on the United States. We do not think that they are ready to do so at present, but we are quite sure that within the year there will be some sort of action. We would therefore like to suggest that you direct your defense contracting with that in mind."

Eric raised his eyebrows, staring at his cigarette without really seeing it. So Jeffrey Kellogg was onto something in Tokyo, after all. He would have to get some people there, and soon.

"Monsieur Beaumont?" Giroux was still talking to him. "About the other matter which we discussed . . ."

"Yes?"

"It seems that despite several attempts to eliminate Monsieur Starkey and his influence on Madame Asheford, he is still doing well. Strangely, though, she has decided to leave the military encampment in Surrey, and in fact has taken up temporary residence at the Regent Hotel in London." He cleared his throat. "We think that it would be a good idea for you to encourage her to return to the United States at this time. Information sources inside of Germany indicate that a full-scale aerial attack of Britain is being planned for August. It is impossible under those circumstances for us to be utterly sure of Madame Asheford's safety." An element of steel crept into his voice. "I do not need to remind you, Monsieur Beaumont, that Madame Asheford's safety is paramount both to the firm and to Intraglobal."

"Naturally," Eric said. Personal considerations aside, of course. What the hell kind of game was Caroline playing? And what was this business about not being able to eliminate Starkey? He thought that the firm had enough trained assassins at their beck and call. "What happened with Starkey?" he asked abruptly.

"His airplane was shot down over the English Channel. Unfortunately, he did not happen to be in it at the time."

"How remiss . . . of somebody," Eric murmured.

"Indeed. The situation has been dealt with. It seems that August may well take care of that problem anyway." Giroux cleared his throat delicately. "I am told that it will be . . . a slaughter."

"Just so long as the right lambs are herded in for it." Eric drew in deeply on the cigarette.

"Quite so, Monsieur Beaumont. Quite so." A fraction of a moment's hesitation, and then the lawyer went on. "Finally, there is the matter of the de Montclair family. . . ."

Eric expelled the smoke from his lungs. "Yes?"

"It seems that one of their domestic staff was arrested and executed by the Wehrmacht. There is suspicion among certain circles of the Gestapo that the Countess de Montclair is also involved in some sort of Resistance activity."

"Marie-Louise?" Eric almost choked. "Marie-Louise involved with the Resistance?"

"No, no, Monsieur Beaumont. Forgive me. I meant the younger countess. Chantale de Montclair."

"I see." Eric drew in on the cigarette again. That would be the boy's wife. He had never met her—had scarcely met Pierre, for that matter—but knew of her family. If she was getting politically involved, the situation could be delicate. "What do they know of the firm?" he asked suddenly.

"Only that we are the family retainers. They know nothing of our connection to Intraglobal, or of Intraglobal's interest in their well-being."

"Hmm. And you have managed so far to keep them safe?"

"Of course. By exerting pressure through the Deutsches Bank. The Gestapo will protect them—to a point. If the young countess is really engaged in the movement, then I think there is nothing we can do for her."

"I see. There are two children?"

"Yes, Monsieur Beaumont. A son, Jean-Claude, and a daughter, Catherine."

"I see," Eric said again, grinding out his cigarette. "Well, if there's nothing we can do, then there's nothing we can do. She's made her own choices. She's an adult. If she is really involved, then she knows the risks." He paused. "Just watch the situation, Marc. I don't want anything to happen to those children. They're Philippe's grandchildren. They're the de Montclair line."

"I understand perfectly, Monsieur Beaumont."

"All right. Is that all?"

"Monsieur Beaumont—we'll have to get back to you. We may have another problem. It's not clear yet."

"Right. Keep me apprised."

Julie came in with his coffee when she saw Eric was off the line. "Mr. Asheford called again while you were on the telephone," she said.

"So what else is new?" he asked wearily. "Thanks, Julie. Get him on the phone for me, will you?"

"Sure thing. He's already there. Line four."

"Steven? What's up?"

"I just heard from Caroline!" There was a buoyancy in his voice that Eric hadn't heard in months. "She's in London."

"I know." Eric cradled the telephone on his shoulder and lit another cigarette. "I'm going to call her myself. Convince her to get back here."

"There's no need." There was assurance in Steven's voice. Gone was the depression, the self-deprecation of the last weeks. Eric wondered briefly what had happened. "I'm leaving for London in two hours."

"You're what?" Holy Christ, Eric thought, this is it. I can move multimillion-dollar deals, I can have people killed or saved, I can control the political wind of an entire country, but damned if I can do anything about those closest to me. "Steven, let's think this through," he suggested, his voice sounding far more calm and patient than he actually felt.

"I have. I talked to her already. I'm taking a leave of absence from Asheford Shipbuilding. William can take care of it for a while. I'm going to see my wife."

"Is this a good idea? Look, Steven, what about Elizabeth? You can't be thinking of taking her to England. . . ." August was almost upon them. What was it that Giroux had called the upcoming campaign? A slaughter? "Listen, Steven, it's a better idea just to get Caroline to come home."

"She can't think clearly here. She gets too caught up in Newport—you know, being part of the Lewis family, living on the Lewis estate. She needs to be somewhere where she can be herself. And I need to be with her."

That was something, anyway. "But England? Haven't you heard? They're at war there."

"I know." The voice was untroubled. "It'll be worth it, Eric, if it brings her back to us. I haven't really understood her before. . . . I guess I expected her to fit into my molds, and when she didn't I just got more and more rigid. Well, that's over now, and I'm going to work things out with her. Elizabeth will be fine. I'm leaving her and Nicholas at the estate. There are people there to take care of them. It'll probably only be for a month or so, anyway. . . .''

It was already late July. Eric shook his head. "It's too risky, Steven. Things are happening there that you can't understand."

''I understand that she's my wife. And I want her to stay that way. That's all that matters.''

Damn, Eric though. Damn and damn and damn. He was going to have to do something about this.

But he didn't know, yet, what that was going to be.

Caroline sat on the edge of her hotel bed and cradled the two photographs in her hands. Andrew. And Steven.

The problem was that she loved them both. In different ways, of course.

She shook her head and put the pictures back on the nightstand. She still wasn't clear about why she had written to Steven, why she had asked him to join her in England or why she had spent hours putting thoughts to paper trying to explain what it was about Newport that she kept running away from.

Because that was it. Looking out across the rain-swept fields as the driver took her back to the city, she had realized that she didn't want to go back to Newport, that staying in London—with or without Andrew—was preferable. She knew she didn't want to face the Newport airport, and Margie, and knew that Eddie Carruthers would never be there again, but it was more than that. She didn't want to pace the same small terrace that her mother had paced, and feel the same emptiness and gloom descend upon her.

Her thoughts about Steven, she discovered to her surprise, had little to do with any of that.

Over the last year she had been blaming him for her inability to cope, her inability to focus, to be any of the things that she wanted to be. It wasn't his permission that she was looking for: It was her mother's. Or her grandmother's.

Or her own.

She had never given Steven a chance, never offered him the opportunity. And if they were going to straighten out their lives, they were going to have to do it here, in neutral territory. Not in Newport. Not in California. Here, far from everybody and everything that was familiar.

She was coming to terms with her attraction to Andrew: He offered a hope in happy endings. Andrew promised the moon and the stars, but she wasn't certain he could stand the sun. Andrew wanted the world to be perfect, and if he couldn't have that, he would manufacture his perfect little corner of it and ignore the rest. Which was fine, but Caroline was not certain that such blissful ignorance was permanent.

Steven had taken on an impossible challenge in marrying her. Not only was she an heiress, but she also stood to inherit much more, a corporation that was beginning to rule the world through American firepower. That was no small thing, and Steven was struggling with it, and struggling with her in the process. At least that was honest. And her own struggles, her confusion and insecurity, had less to do with him than they did with her past. She and Steven had both been struggling with the same things, but instead of supporting each other in the conflict, they had turned on each other. And Caroline knew, knew with absolute certainty, that if she went back to Newport now, she would just go on playing out those same tired old scenes, until they really did get a divorce.

So, was it to be Andrew or Steven? Caroline smiled at the photographs and decided to go out.

Sitting on a bench in Kew Gardens, she slowly breathed in a lungful of air. Heady air it was, cool and filled with the strong scent of flowers. She crossed one trousered leg over the other and pulled her leather purse closer to her on the bench. There were two letters in it, and she was taking her time with both of them. Indecision, but not such a bad sort of indecision: The fact of having her affections torn in two directions was a pleasant sort of pain.

She finally closed her eyes and reached into a bag, not looking to see which letter came first. It was postmarked Surrey, and she found herself smiling. Andrew.

July 25, 1940

Dearest Caroline:

We've been grounded more often than not because of the weather. I expect that it's much the same for you in London, and I find myself wondering how you spend your days there. Do you go out for tea, or visit museums, or take in a film when it rains? I heard some Duke Ellington tune on the radio last night and found myself thinking of you.

The Spits are terrific, Caroline, everything that we heard about them is true, and more. We've been having some minor problems with the oxygen, but it's not too bad and it seems to be working itself out. They handle better than the Hurricanes, they're faster and more maneuverable, and they've got a longer range to boot, so the improvement is phenomenal. Now if we can only log some serious airtime! Mostly we sit around and play cards and wait for the skies to clear and the orders to come through.

There was an abortive attack on some of the radar stations on the coast—abortive because we intercepted it, we and the regular RAF squadrons stationed nearby, but it was one hell of a close call. Too close for comfort, if you ask me. We could compensate, I suppose. The radar network's become a lot more sophisticated since the beginning of the war, but it would have been one hell of a blow. Those stations are the first to intercept incoming German planes. The Fighter Command was all in a tizz as the girls here say, and no one's talked about much else for days.

The food's horrible, as usual. How I envy you the Savoy Grill. I'm afraid I can't make it to London in the near future; you know how unpredictable my leaves are. But I'll write again soon, I promise.

Love always,
Andrew

Caroline frowned. There wasn't much in the letter to quicken her pulse—and, after all, Andrew was *supposed* to be the one to quicken her pulse. He was her illicit affair, the man she was seeing behind her husband's back.

After that, she opened the letter from Steven with some trepidation.

Newport, Rhode Island
July 23, 1940

Dear Caroline,
    Yes.
    I suppose that I ought to say more, that I ought to tell you how much I want to see you and talk to you and feel

close to you again. Or else I ought to play Lord of the
Manor and insist that you come home. . . . But I'm not
particularly up to doing either, and I don't suppose that it's
what you're looking for.

So, yes. I'll come to London. I'll be there as soon as I
can arrange a leave of absence and get on a flight.

I'm tired of our playing games with each other, running
away so we don't have to examine any of the hard questions. And I don't expect to resolve all of our differences
all at once either. . . . But, like you, I want a new beginning. Even if ultimately it's the end of things between us,
at least it will be open and honest. We were open and
honest with each other once upon a time, right? I think I
can remember that. Let's do it again, Caroline. Let's stop
playing games.

Yes. I'll be there as soon as I can.

Love,
Steven

Caroline closed her eyes again and sighed. Two men, two very
different men . . . Which one? Which one was her real lover?
Which was the one she would love forever and ever? There was
nothing like walking through a blacked-out city, past fallout
shelters, to give one a perspective on things. She wanted some
peace and some security.

But with whom?

She shook her head and slipped the letters back into her bag.
What struck her, most of all, was how more and more she could
see her mother in herself. Once, she would have stood in judgment on Amanda for adulterous behavior, for flirtations, for using men. And now, here she was, doing the same thing. Had
she inherited this from her mother? Would Elizabeth be the same
way someday? Caroline shook her head. She was doing it, but
she wasn't at all sure that she was enjoying it. . . . And, at least,
she was trying to resolve the situation. That, surely, counted for
something.

She stood up and, with a surreptitious glance around to be
sure that no one was looking, pulled one of the roses from its
stem where it grew, one of dozens bursting forth in heady profusion near the bench on which she had sat. She slid it into the
boutonniere on the simple jacket she wore over her trousers.
People stared at her, she knew, because of the way that she

dressed, but she didn't mind. When there's a war on, you take things like that in your stride.

Besides, she had more important things on her mind for the time being.

Steven hadn't known what to think of Caroline's letter at first. She had been talking about divorce before she left for England. And then, there were Eric's insinuations of another man, an old lover, someone who had something to do with the RAF, and everyone knew that women always fell for uniforms. . . . He had tried not to listen. To concentrate on the problems at hand—the need for new facilities at the shipyard to cover the increases in production that were being asked of them. Elizabeth, turning mysteriously from a baby into a human being with her own distinct personality. William, driven as ever by demons that Steven would never understand. Justine, withdrawn from the people who cared about her into a silent world where she wouldn't feel the pain of her baby's death.

It felt as though he had enough on his plate as it was.

But he loved Caroline. He had always loved Caroline, even when she withdrew from him, even when he didn't understand her, even when she was running away. And when she wrote to him to say, however hesitantly, "Please come," he felt that he had no choice.

They had to make some decisions about their life together, their marriage, their relationship. They had both been running away from those decisions for too long, Caroline to exotic locales, he to his work. If she had finally realized that their problems must be confronted, then it was his responsibility to respond to her. In her own time, in her own place. Not that a bombed-out London would have been *his* first choice.

But he had read more in her letter—the hesitant return of love. Was he imagining things? Was he being played for a fool one more time, because he wanted her to love him and would hear what he needed to hear in her words, whatever their true meanings may be? Even as he packed his suitcase, he found himself remembering Caroline's own mother, and the stories that he had heard about her. How she had used Marcus Copeland to give her child a name. How he had known that it wasn't his own child, but his infatuation with Amanda was such that he could only assert otherwise to the world.

What was it about these women that made otherwise sensible

men love them so blindly? Even when they were coquettish, independent, indecisive? Especially when they were all those things?

Steven shrugged. It didn't matter, not really. Caroline had reached out to him, and he wanted to respond. And all the people whose lives and problems were so closely tied up with his—Elizabeth, Nicholas, William, Justine—well, they would just have to survive without him for a while.

It was a strangely pleasant thought.

Pan Am was still flying into London, and Steven made arrangements to take the train down to New York and fly out that Thursday. He didn't take Elizabeth with him to the train station, but sat with her instead, out on the terrace overlooking the ocean.

"Don't want you to go." Her lower lip was protruding.

"I know, honey. But I'll be home real soon. And Mommy, too." Well, that might be a bit rash, he thought, but what the hell. If he could dream, so could Elizabeth.

He felt guilty about leaving, but he was convinced that he was doing what was right. That working things out with Caroline would be the best for Elizabeth.

Not once did he allow himself to think that other thought, the one lurking dangerously back in the shadowed recesses of his mind: that if things didn't work out now, they never would.

Chapter Twenty

All of a sudden everyone was talking about invasion from the air.

It didn't make much sense, Andrew reflected wearily. All throughout June and July there had been reports of stepped-up activity. But a large-scale strategic offensive? Who knew? Did some gypsy fortune-teller find the answers in her crystal ball or read the future in someone's rejected tea leaves? "Churchill's, no doubt." They all laughed about it in Surrey, but still the reports persisted. Hitler was ready to take England by air.

But England was far from ready to surrender. The effects on the squadron of long-term readiness for combat were worse almost than being a foot soldier on the front lines: At least there you knew precisely where you stood. And, more to the point, where the enemy stood. The pilots, on the other hand, could be torn from sleep and on the flight line inside of ten minutes, winging their way up into a dark sky with little idea of what awaited them beyond. They were brave, but bravery wears thin in the face of that kind of stress. Already, one of them, Jacobs, had been discharged upon the advice of the base doctor, who had shaken his head and said that he would need a long time to recover. A long time before he lost that fixed stare, Andrew thought. And perhaps the only reason there were not more men like Jacobs was because men like him were getting killed.

They had already had upwards of twenty deaths. That meant twenty letters to write to families back home, to talk about bravery and courage and ideals, knowing that the people who would read the letters would have gladly traded all the heroism in the world for having their son, or brother, or husband back safely. Twenty deaths . . . and young Carruthers. They may never know what had become of young Carruthers. Andrew knew that he would carry that particular ache with him forever.

So he let them talk, but as August loomed the talk sharpened, focused, as it was sharpening and focusing all throughout England. Superstitiously, the pilots began looking at the sky, as though expecting the entire Luftwaffe to come sweeping in at any moment.

In July there had been reports of attacks on radar stations, with one completely disabled, and later some bombings of coastal towns, but that was all. Hitler had yet to make his move. It was as though they were all holding their breaths, collectively, going to sleep at night wondering if this would be the one when the attack would come, waking every morning to wonder if this day might be their last.

The tension mounted. The weather had turned hot, the sun shining and the air becoming moist and uncomfortable; the woolen RAF uniforms were warm and scratchy, and the mosquitoes were out. It was not ideal flying weather, either. The Spitfires had developed a tendency to overheat, and the closed cockpits were worse than a Turkish bath, hot and bright and sweltering.

Still the men waited, with the sure knowledge that somewhere over there, just beyond the horizon, the enemy was massing, preparing to attack. . . .

Andrew, for his part, felt frustration. "Don't we have any information?" he cried out during one operational meeting. "Isn't there anybody in France sending us any clues as to what they're doing?"

While the airfields just south of them on the coast in Sussex and Kent were bombed, Andrew's men scrambled, running out to the flight line and revving up the Spitfire engines. They took off with a snarl into the southern sky, but by then it was too late, with time only to play reconnaissance about the damage.

One day they received a radio warning: The radar had picked up incoming Stukas, the horrible screaming dive-bombers, moving toward London with Surrey directly in their path. They were ready when the Germans arrived, and three of the bombers were shot down. Andrew took some men out later to sift through the wreckage of the German planes; and it was there, carelessly moving pieces of cockpit metal out of the way, that he came upon the small hidden inscription: Intraglobal.

One morning, there had been a thunderstorm and the weather

was clearing when a message came through that was a harbinger of the future—the words they had all been waiting for and dreading and fearing. Andrew compressed his lips as Emma deciphered the code for him, and then he called his men to Operations.

"We have the information we've been waiting for," he said, his message terse. "Early this morning, German bomber formations with fighter escorts left bases in Norway and Denmark and proceeded south over northern England." The eyes that weren't watching his face were riveted to the map of England on the wall behind him. He was feeling, suddenly, exhilarated. This was it: This was the beginning. This was what they had trained for, what they had been sent here to do. "RAF Fighter Group Thirteen met them, and—well, gentlemen, suffice it to say that those bombers will never reach their targets now. We have reports of fifteen planes lost from one formation, ten from another, with nearly no English losses."

A ripple passed through the room, a lightening of expressions, a smile here and there. They were off to a good start. Morale, which had been dangerously low these last few weeks, soared. The battle had been joined and it was going in their favor.

Andrew continued, "We've got reports of bombers coming in from France, and they have heavier fighter cover. They've taken off already from fields in Normandy and Brittany, and, gentlemen, they're heading this way." His voice grew grim. "Now it's our turn. Our orders are to engage the fighters, and—when at all possible—take them out. They'll be looking for radar stations, airfields, strategic positions of that kind. It's up to us to see that they don't find them." Again, he scanned the faces of the men in the room with him, and what he saw would not normally inspire confidence: men who had undergone too much stress and enjoyed too little sleep, men with needs that weren't being met, men who hadn't really relaxed in weeks.

And yet they were as ready as they ever would be. There was not one among them who could not count a friend who had been killed with German firepower. Now was their chance to settle the score. Whatever happened in the hours ahead, Andrew knew that he was going to be proud of these men.

"We've got radar positions for two formations heading our way now," he continued quickly, knowing that every moment lost in thought might cost him, or someone else, dearly. "Hurricanes are scrambling from bases on the coast. But we've got to get the Spits up now. We've got a higher ceiling than they have, so we've got a better chance of taking some of the Messerschmitts by surprise. They don't have radar. With surprise on our side they'll never know what hit them. Got it?''

Grave nods all over the operations room. "Okay." Andrew took a deep breath. "I want my formation on the flight line in three minutes. Roger, I'm keeping yours in reserve. We've got to have someone around here rested and ready to take over if we sustain any damages." And a lot of rest they'd get, too, he thought grimly, ready at any moment to scramble. He couldn't help it. He had to assume that there would be casualties.

"Right. Off we go. And, gentlemen—good luck."

Emma had turned on the horn, and the mechanics had finished checking over the aircraft and fueling them, but it was still on, wailing eerily into the afternoon haze, a harbinger of disaster. Andrew didn't have time to ask why, or even to see Emma. Ever since Caroline had left, Emma seemed more and more to fill the void that she had left in his life. She did small things: bringing him tea, laughing when he said something funny, listening when he wanted to talk. They had started taking walks together, too, and telling each other their stories. His were filled with the bright, brilliant California sun and the rugged California coast, hers with the cool mists and full moons of Oxford, where she had been an undergraduate when the war interrupted her studies. "Reading history," she had said, half-apologetically, when he asked. "Not anything useful, I'm afraid."

"There's nothing more useful," he responded. "How else will we learn not to repeat the mistakes of the past?" He was surprised by the look of warmth and gratitude that she flashed his way.

She had learned to fly as a lark, she said. "Well, actually, more of a dare. The chap I was seeing then said I'd be too scared to fly, so I did him one better and learned to pilot." Her father was a landed earl, so the money to fly had been forthcoming, and when the war began she volunteered for the RAF. "And now they have me operating radios!"

"It's a useful thing to do," he said again, but she shook her head. "I'd rather be up there with you."

He was going up there now, and it was with a brief glance of regret toward the base that he climbed up into his Spitfire. He had painted a San Francisco skyline just under his cockpit, and now he patted the picture for good luck. Strapping in quickly—

preflight checks were best abbreviated when enemy aircraft were known to be headed in the direction of the base—he revved up the Rolls Royce Merlin, the horsepower responding smoothly and immediately to his touch. "Good girl." Andrew grinned and put on his headphones.

He watched numbers three and four taking turns on runway 03, then took his place behind them, revved up the Rolls Royce Merlin to maximum output, and glanced around the cockpit one last time. Everything seemed functional. Everything had been functional a scant two hours ago. He would have to go with the odds that everything was still working. One last glance . . . and to hell with it. If it wasn't going to work, it wasn't going to work, and he would end up in flames at the end of the runway anyway. Gladys's South Kensington voice spoke through the static in the earphones. "You are cleared for takeoff, Captain Starkey, anytime."

"Thank you, Tower," he responded automatically. He eased the throttle out and the Spitfire was starting down the runway, gathering speed as it went, faster and faster until the grass on the edge of the runway was nothing but a blur. He eased up, ever so slightly, the nose pointing up, and then he was screaming into the skies. Behind him the next Spitfire would be lining up on the same runway for takeoff. He trimmed back at 500 feet and banked sharply to allow number six enough space to climb behind him, and then he pushed down his transmitter button. "All right, gang. Let's get into formation. Usual groups of three. Visual identification of wingmen. Heading two hundred and forty-five degrees southwest."

His own wingman was coming up on his starboard side: Michaels, his name was. Evan Michaels. Andrew gave him a thumbs-up and caught Evan's grin in return as they moved into the flying pattern they had practiced so often, day after day, until they could do it in their sleep. Andrew pressed his button down again. "Going up to thirty thousand feet," he advised. "Start oxygen." He fitted his own oxygen mask tightly over his face. And pray to God, he added silently, that it doesn't choose this moment to kick out on us.

They flew a steady course, and it was only minutes later that Gladys's cool voice came over his earphones. "You're in luck," she remarked. "I see incoming bogies, range ten miles, dead ahead. You've got your Messerschmitts, laddie."

"Thank you, Tower," Andrew said. "Hear that, guys?"

"Sure did, Andy." The voice from one of the other planes was surprisingly cheerful. "Let's do it!"

"Yes," he said. "Let's do it."

They flew on, waiting for visual contact. When it came at last, the Messerschmitts a good 15,000 feet below them, Andrew spoke again. "All right, guys. Let's show them who owns the skies in this neck of the woods!"

"You got it, Andy."

Andrew banked his plane sharply and entered into the long, curving, graceful dive that would end up on the tail of the leader of the Messerschmitts—the ones that Intraglobal had manufactured, he thought grimly. And it was not just the thought of the German sitting behind the controls that made him hit his machine guns so savagely.

It was going to be a good year for the wine.

That was the report of the head vintner at the de Montclair estate. Chantale had to put a hand over her mouth to keep herself from laughing out loud at the news. Marie-Louise never even looked at her daughter-in-law. She simply received her employee with her usual dignity and listened to his report, dismissing him with a word of thanks and congratulations before she finally turned to Chantale. "Tell me, what is so funny?"

Chantale shrugged, still smiling. "Oh, it's so ironic, isn't it? The world could be coming to an end, but as long as the vineyard holds up, then all is not lost."

"Certainly all is not lost." Marie-Louise replied with a trace of humor not veiled by her indignation. "As long as we can still raise a glass of good wine from our own land, then certainly all is not lost." The older woman paused. "Of course, this year chances are that the vintage won't be allowed to mature. The stupid Germans don't know when to drink wine; they'll open the bottles right away. Barbarians." It was difficult to tell whether she considered them barbarians because of their desecration of fine vintages or because of the occupation in general.

"Barbarians," Chantale agreed, but her tone implied something else altogether.

Marie-Louise looked at her sharply. "Are they still following you?"

"I don't know. I don't think so." Chantale hesitated. "Madame, tell me this—"

The older countess held up a hand. "I shall tell you nothing, my dear. But please take note that the stables are always available, and any time that you should wish to go and visit your father confessor, I will be happy to watch the children for you.''

Chantale looked at her in surprise, but already the icy withdrawal was beginning again. ''And, perhaps, if you could persuade your husband to spend more time at home where he belongs—''

That was an impossible dream, Chantale thought as she saddled her chestnut gelding for a trip to the church to see Father Xavier. To think that anything I could say or do would have any effect whatsoever on Pierre . . . What nonsense. He has people he listens to, and their voices are the only ones that matter to him. Lately, she had noticed, one of the voices that spoke the loudest to her husband was that of the bottles from his cellar; and she doubted very much if, like his mother, he was paying a great deal of attention to the vintage.

The priest had news.

''I'm glad you've come, my child. I was going to have to visit you before long.''

''What is it, Father?'' She was hot and sweaty from the ride and was waiting for him to offer his customary glass of iced water. He used to joke about it. ''The one thing they can't ration or confiscate, seeing as I have the well right outside the church door!''

But today he had his mind on other things. ''We need a safe place to store some things,'' he said.

''People?''

He looked away unhappily. ''Explosives.''

Chantale gasped. She was accustomed to people, the transportation of fugitives away from the hated Germans—but explosives? That was a different matter altogether. ''What are you going to blow up?'' she asked as calmly as she could, but even she could detect the tremor in her own voice.

''The bunkers to the west of the city,'' he said, equally calm, though he wouldn't look at her.

''I see. Because I couldn't get the message through to London to bomb them,'' she said.

Father Xavier shrugged his shoulders. ''Bombing them, or wiring them, it makes little difference in the end, isn't that right, *ma petite*? Unfortunately, some people will die, God rest their souls. But others will be saved, the people who are even now being hunted at sea by the German U-boats. It's an equation that we can't afford to miss, my child."

"I can see that. I can see that." She shivered, even though it was hot, and drew in a deep breath. "I think it's time that I met your friends, Father."

"We don't want you to be too involved. Storing the explosives in your stables will be enough. Don't make yourself into a heroine, my dear. Heroines die young."

"Everybody dies young in a war, Father," Chantale said, thinking of Annie. "I need to meet them, can't you understand?" How could he, she thought, when she herself understood so little? "I can't go on like this . . . feeling so isolated. I must know that others are fighting on the same side."

He raised his eyebrows. "My assurances that that is so are not sufficient?"

"I'm sorry, Father, but no. Not anymore. I need more."

"I see." He pondered for a moment, whistling air in through his teeth. "Got one going bad, I'm afraid. Dentist doesn't have time to see me. Too busy fixing up German mouths at the moment." He paused. "Just as well. I don't think that I could stomach having the same tools in my mouth that had already been in theirs."

"Father—"

He held up a hand, much as Marie-Louise had earlier. "All right, child. Come to late mass tonight, and stay in the Lady Chapel afterward. You may wish to light a candle. We can use all the prayers that we can get."

There was a strange sense of excitement churning inside her. "If I stay long after mass it will be curfew time."

"So it will. So it will. Afraid of breaking a few laws, my child?"

"Not German laws."

"So be it, then." He shook his head, and his voice sounded infinitely sad.

Caroline had imagined their reunion in any number of ways.

Lying awake, alone in the vast hotel bed they had given her, she thought about it. Her favorite version was of Steven stepping out of the cockpit of an airplane, complete with white flying scarf and goggles, and of her running across a field to jump into his arms. She was wearing a long gauzy white dress in this version, and when they ran to each other it was in slow motion.

He picked her up and twirled her around and kissed her hard, and swore never to part from her again.

But Steven wasn't the pilot in Caroline's life, so it seemed that she was getting things more than a little mixed up.

While she waited, she walked the streets of London with an odd feeling of premonition deep in her stomach. What if it didn't work out? What if she was with Steven and decided that it was Andrew she wanted after all? What if Steven acted pompous and arrogant and ruined the whole thing? What if he refused to fit back into her image of him, into her scenario for their relationship?

All the while, the world went on around her. Daily she passed posters urging her to do her part for the war effort. Join the Red Cross. Volunteer for the Home Guard. Work as a nursing sister in an emergency shelter. Become an air warden. Caroline was painfully conscious of not "doing her bit," as they said, but she had other priorities in her life just then. She had come to England for a whole lot of reasons, and none of the issues on her agenda seemed any closer to resolution than they had been when she had come.

Except, of course, for Eddie Carruthers. Even there, she wondered sometimes if she hadn't been fooling herself. If she hadn't hidden behind her proclaimed mission of saving Eddie so that she could come here for other, more devious motives . . . That was nonsense, of course. She had truly believed that she was coming to save him. But she also remembered enough from her sessions with the psychologist to know that her mind could sometimes play tricks on her, and rationalizations are a dime a dozen.

A penny a pound, they would say here.

Caroline looked at the gathering warm-weather storm clouds and shook her head. Hitler wanted Britain, but Hitler was having other problems on other fronts, if the newspapers were correct. Russia, to the east, was sapping German strength. Besides, any day the Americans would formally and officially enter the war, and then Hitler would have to run. Caroline was so sure of that. Everyone was. As soon as the Yanks came, the tide of the war would turn.

But while the rumors of invasion persisted, there was no word from Washington.

And then, stepping quietly and prosaically out of the commercial flight at Heathrow Airport, Steven Asheford arrived.

Caroline hadn't known when to expect Steven, so she wasn't there to meet his flight. He made his own way into the city, which was no small feat. He had never been to England before, and watched with fascination as his taxi driver conveyed him speedily—and none the worse for wear—to the Regent Hotel.

Caroline was in the bar. Steven was directed there by the young man at the front desk, and he paused in the doorway for a moment, gazing at her, feeling as though centuries separated them. In that moment she looked up and met his gaze.

They stared at each other for a long time. He was tired and sweaty from the long trip, hours and hours of flying, which he had never particularly liked in the first place. She had just stepped out of the bath, and was enjoying an early gin and tonic before dinner in the hotel restaurant. He felt older than his years while she looked radiant and young, her short blond curls still moist from the bath and plastered in ringlets over her neck. The blue dress she wore to dinner sparkled with sequins at the shoulder and brought out the color in her cheeks. Steven put his suitcase down and kept looking at her, almost hesitantly, noticing that she hesitated, too.

Their reunion wasn't as she had imagined it would be. He wasn't dashing and handsome; he was just a tall, gentle man with a flaming red beard and hair. He wasn't suave or sophisticated or urbane or witty. He was just Steven, the man she had trusted and loved and married.

Then she saw the light go out of his eyes, and his shoulders slump, as fractionally he turned away. She slid off her bar stool and walked over to him, her legs feeling uncertain under her, as though she had not used them for weeks.

They stood there for a moment, facing each other, not speaking, and then Caroline cleared her throat. "You've got a spot on your collar," she heard herself saying, and just as she was beginning to berate herself for blurting out something that stupid, he put down his suitcase and put his arms around her. She realized to her great surprise that she was crying.

It wasn't at all the way she thought it was going to be. She had conjured up a dashing romantic hero, and instead an ordinary, nice-looking, tired man stood before her. She had imagined still being torn with indecision between Andrew and Steven, and perhaps tomorrow she might be. But not tonight. There was no question in her mind as to whom she wanted to be with tonight.

She laced her fingers through his. "Come on," she said softly, a smile in her voice. "You look exhausted. And do I have a bed for you!"

"What about dinner? You must be starved."

"There's a rumor they've been selling horse meat at the restaurant, and calling it *steak speciale,*" she responded in a stage whisper, with a twinkle in her eye, and more than a little nervousness in her heart. "I can pass that one up, thank you."

He made a face. "Can't say as I blame you," he agreed, and hesitated before asking, "What about registering?"

"What about registering? Are you stalling or something? I'm a guest here already, and you are my lawfully wedded husband. Let them come banging on our door to protest our indecency if they like."

He smiled again. "In that case, Mrs. Asheford, lead me to your bed!"

They undressed in the dark, as though tentative about each other's body, the great half-remembered secrets of their life together sparkling like champagne bubbles in the air all around them. When he leaned over to kiss her, she closed her eyes, waiting for the magic she had sat alone there in that room and imagined. In its place, there was a great peaceful sense of familiarity. She knew his touch; she knew his body; she knew his gestures, just as completely and as surely as she knew her own. He was her husband.

He bent his head to kiss her breasts, and then snuggled his face down between them, and she caressed his hair and smiled as she whispered his name into the darkness. When at length his breathing changed and she realized that he had fallen asleep, she did not respond with blazing insulted aggrievement, but with another tender smile. "There's plenty of time, my love," she whispered. "Plenty of time."

A scant few miles to the south some Spitfires and Hurricanes took on an incoming formation of two hundred German Messerschmitts. The Battle of Britain had begun.

Chapter Twenty-one

Pierre saw Isabelle sometimes, for he couldn't stop himself from going into town, from frequenting the same cafés and restaurants that they had gone to together, for searching for her face among all the faces in the street and under the awnings of the cafés. He was like a drunkard looking for a drink. One look, one glimpse would be enough. . . . Just to see her, he told himself. Even if he couldn't talk with her, or touch her: Just to see her would be enough.

But, of course, it never was.

He did see her, laughing over glasses of champagne in the bars, her strange violet eyes sweeping indifferently by him to light upon some happy Germanic face, her long raven hair being touched and caressed by pale Aryan hands. Sometimes he would see her riding on the outskirts of town, a uniformed German officer sitting tall and straight in the saddle next to her. Once he caught her closing the gallery early, and arms sliding around her even as she flipped the Closed sign in the window. He had to admit it, the truth had bitten him once too often: Isabelle, his darling treasure, the fascinating enticing woman who had sworn always to be his, now belonged to others as well. And not just one other. For all he knew, Isabelle was sleeping with all the occupying garrison of Angers. The pain of it bit through him like a cold wind.

For so long, Pierre had thought of his world only in terms of Isabelle. Chantale and the children were distant and remote figures, possessing none of the fire and the passion that Isabelle had brought into his life. Now came the unhappy thought of living without that fire and that passion. . . . He didn't think that he could bear it.

He wanted to be sure, even when he was past being sure, so he followed her, realizing even as he did how ridiculous he must seem. He watched as she led German officers past the door by the theater, just as she had led him so long ago on his first visit to her apartment. He watched as the curtains at the bedroom twitched, and he stood miserably by, counting the minutes and then the hours that passed before the German emerged again through the door, straightening his tie, whistling gaily to himself. Pierre stood in vigil as she went to parties and receptions, impeccably dressed, escorted by still more Germans. He watched their eyes, and knew from the reflected light that he saw there that she was giving them the fire and the passion that once were his.

Pierre began to drink still more, not just in the evenings, but in the daytime as well, as though the bottles of wine could erase the images that sprang so quickly to his mind, could ease the memories of the places his fingers had caressed, the skin his lips had touched, the marvels that she had shown him.

Chantale watched her husband sink lower into his self-appointed mire, and shook her head. When he began sitting around the château, drinking during the day, she remonstrated with him. "Whatever is so very wrong, you can at least go somewhere else to drink!"

"Why?" he challenged belligerently. "This is my home."

"It is your son's home, also, and I should think that you would prefer he not think of his father as a lazy drunkard!"

Chantale had too many other things on her mind to worry about Pierre. There was a battle raging over the English Channel. Hitler was launching an all-out attack to bring Great Britain under his rule, and there were things—small things, perhaps, but efforts nevertheless—that she could do to impede his progress.

It had started with the explosives. Father Xavier had been as good as his word. When she had waited that day after mass, he drew her back into the sacristy of the church, where a small group of men and women were assembled. They all wore plain black cassocks, and Chantale was asked to don one as well. "That way, Countess, if we're interrupted, we can say that we are planning a religious service."

None of them offered a last name. Many did not have first names, but used nicknames instead, and she was reminded once again of her first pilot, the one who had thought that her title was a secret password. Despite all their mystery, Chantale felt close to them immediately, for they were French, and committed to the cause of France. She recognized only one: Etienne, the stableboy from her own estate. The rest were strangers, but neighbors all the same—small farmers, businesspeople, two nuns from Father Xavier's convent, a blacksmith. They were people who in any other day and age would have been unremarkable, but who had in this day and age agreed upon one thing—that the war must go on. They would continue to fight as long as Germans occupied French soil. Chantale felt her heart swell with pride and patriotism when she met them. She was not alone. There were other people who cared.

The nuns had talked quietly and seriously about the documents that they were forging daily on the small printing press in the convent cellar. An illegal visa to the Free Zone—there were no longer any legal ones—cost thousands of francs. The sisters gave theirs to anyone who needed them for free. The blacksmith had, with some assistance from faceless and nameless comrades, taken apart a stretch of railroad. The next train to pass would certainly be derailed at once—possibly for days, as the ravine was inaccessible by road. A farmer was writing down German movement in his area and he passed on the notes to one of the shopkeepers, who promised to radio the information on that very night. Etienne, with a quick bright glance at Chantale, told of obtaining the explosives to wire the German bunker.

"We can't do it until tomorrow night," he explained. "That's when François and his group hit the power station. Without lights and communications, they'll never know we were there."

"Where are the explosives now?" asked Father Xavier, his voice once again filled with sadness.

"In the stables of the Château de Montclair." Etienne was careful not to look at Chantale.

"They can stay there," she said, surprised that her voice was so clear and steady, "as long as is necessary. And I myself will help to wire the bunker if you need the extra hands."

"It is dangerous, Countess," Father Xavier said after the others left. "Are you sure that you know what you are doing?"

"Do any of us ever really know what we're doing?" she countered. "Probably not. We just muddle through and do what seems right at the time."

The next night she rubbed soot on her hands and face and ventured out after Etienne, a taller shadow after his lithe small one. She stood guard as he and others set the fuses around the bunker and detonated it without so much as a prayer. Together, they watched the night sky turn deadly as it suddenly and horribly lit up in shades of red and orange.

At breakfast two days later Marie-Louise said, conversationally, "I hear that one of the German bunkers in the city burned a few nights ago. A pity that couldn't happen to all of them."

"Indeed." Chantale had felt her stomach lurch at the mention of the bunker. She kept her eyes on her plate and said nothing, but Marie-Louise's bright birdlike eyes missed nothing.

"I heard that it may not have been an accident."

"How could it not have been?" I really must look at her, Chantale thought, and consciously focused her eyes on the older woman's face. Marie-Louise was smiling.

"No reason," she said softly. "No reason at all."

That night they met again, and soon more and more things were going wrong for the Germans around Angers: Staff cars that wouldn't start were found with sugar in their gas tanks. Food items destined for German tables were misplaced. Trains were mysteriously late. And, once in a while, a German officer or enlisted man who had been too daring, who had wandered out into the countryside alone at night, was found dead. No one knew how or by whose hand, but every morning at breakfast Marie-Louise smiled at her daughter-in-law and nodded her silent approval.

The Germans were attacking Britain with a vengeance. And in August they were also dropping their bombs on London.

Caroline heard the screams of the Stukas, the horrible dive-bombers, long before they struck, but the routine was by now so well established that she never had to think twice about it. All it required was going down the stairs of the hotel, out into the street, down one block to the Underground station that served as a shelter from the attacks which were by now almost a daily affair.

At first, Steven didn't understand Caroline's fierce determination to stay in London, but he followed her lead nevertheless, and it was rarely that they were caught outside when the attacks actually came. Other Londoners, that horrible August and September of 1940, were not so fortunate. Entire neighborhoods lay in rubble, and children wandered about the streets, crying for lost parents.

For Andrew, it was one long nightmare.

The English had the advantage of radar stations and of the

Spitfires, but that was all. The German formations were always larger than his squadron. They were rested and fresh, not constantly battered and tired. Just once, he found himself thinking, just once I'd like to have a decent night's sleep, and not go to bed wondering if I'll be awakened by the air-raid siren.

The skies over the Channel were filled with aircraft, and only the most discerning of observers could tell which was which, could tell one side from the other. No wonder they had trouble, Andrew thought grimly, with Intraglobal and Johnson Industries between them manufacturing half the airplanes in the sky.

Andrew came back at night tired and stiff and forced to face the uncomfortable task of writing still another letter to still another family, telling them that a husband or a son or a brother was not coming home. He never got used to that.

And he never grew accustomed to the thought lurking in the back of his mind, the certainty that, somehow, all of this would not be happening if it were not for Intraglobal.

All Caroline's attention, all her energies, were caught up in rediscovering her husband. They stood in line together for bread, and Steven said funny things—silly things, perhaps, but funny nevertheless—about the people waiting in line with them, and she laughed with carefree abandon. They lounged in bed late in the mornings, eating breakfast and talking and laughing together, playing games, snuggling under the thin sheets, making love, long, languorous love, for hours it seemed. Caroline couldn't remember when she had so enjoyed making love with Steven.

They went to Kew Gardens together, and had tea outdoors, and held hands like children as they walked through the streets of the city. And when the sirens began to wail, it was Steven who led Caroline down into the shelters and away from danger. They spent the night there sometimes, huddled underground with masses of other people, old women eating fish and chips from greasy newspapers, children whimpering softly in the shadows, men playing chess together to pass the time. Down there the war seemed both immediate and close and miles away. As long, Caroline thought, as long as we can hold each other, it will be enough.

"I'm sorry," Steven said to her one day as they sat on the banks of the Thames and tossed breadcrumbs to the pigeons. "I'm sorry that I never tried very hard to understand you while we were at home."

Caroline shook her head. "No, it was me," she said. "And I'm sorry. I'm sorry for behaving like a spoiled child, and I'm sorry for not trying to understand you. It must have been awfully hard."

"I just felt that you were . . . slipping away, and I didn't know how to reach you, I didn't know how to get you back. All the things that I thought would make us closer just seemed to drive you away." He tossed a crust on the ground and four or five pigeons immediately congregated around it. "I didn't know how to talk to you anymore, so I guess I just stopped talking altogether."

"And I thought," she said in a shaky voice, "that you were trying to control me, and it was so scary. The way Eric tries to control me, make me into someone who will inherit his company. I don't care about Intraglobal and I don't care about him, and I thought you didn't, either, but then all of a sudden there you were talking with him on the telephone, spending all that time getting Intraglobal contracts for the yard. I thought that maybe I was just a means for you to get close to Eric."

"Oh, God, Caroline." And she could hear the pain in his voice. "Not that. Never that." There was a moment of silence, and then he added, "What do you want to do?"

She felt a heaviness in her stomach at the words. Time to make a decision. "About what?" she asked, keeping her voice carefully casual.

"About us, Caroline." He was not looking at her.

She swallowed. "I want to try again. If you do, that is."

"Oh, my darling!" And then he turned to her and pulled her against his chest. "I want to. I'll try harder, Caroline. I'll try to always understand you. . . ."

"Don't try to understand me," she whispered, uncomfortably aware of the tears in her eyes. "I don't even understand me. Just love me, Steven. Please just love me."

"I will." His voice was a whisper. "For the rest of my life, I swear I will."

By October London was being bombed almost every night.

The concentrated bombing of the city had started with a mistake. The Germans were supposed to be targeting RAF formations and radar installations, and the first London bombing had been an error, but once it started it scarcely stopped. Churchill was incensed, and ordered the RAF to bomb Berlin in retaliation. It was broadcast on the radio that the English squadron had indeed succeeded, but, after that, the Germans abandoned the airfields and radar emplacements entirely and concentrated on London. A grave tactical error, everyone was to call it later—but, for the people living in London, it was the beginning of a season in hell.

It was true that many of the new bombing runs were being intercepted by the RAF before they ever reached the city; if they had not been, nothing of London would have remained at all. But enough planes got through to burn and kill and maim. Buildings were burning wildly out of control, because there simply weren't enough fire trucks to respond to all the alarms. And when they did respond, chances were that the water pressure wouldn't hold out long enough for the hoses to do much good at all. The Underground stations which had originally been shelters for a night or two became crowded with people who lived there all the time—families with small children and pets, old couples huddling together on mattresses on the damp concrete.

Every night when the siren went off Caroline and Steven trudged down to the shelters. Every morning, they came out again to find at least their corner of the world intact. The Regent Hotel still stood.

The Stuka dive-bombers were the worst. Flying high above the city, they would turn and come screaming down before dropping their deadly cargo.

August had given way to September, and the bombing had seemed if anything to get worse. On September 7 the Germans had attacked in the daylight for the first time, and it was then that people began to panic. "It's the invasion," the greengrocer confided to Caroline. "I heard there's landing craft coming up the Thames, even now. You mark my words, duckie, we'll all be speaking German inside of a month."

If Caroline and Steven had ever been able to leave, they could not now. All commercial airlines were giving London as wide a berth as possible, and private aircraft took off at great personal risk. So Steven and Caroline stayed on, moving from the Regent into a small apartment in the city. Early in September Steven had started driving an ambulance. "Reminds me of the shelter," he said to her one night over dinner. "Helpless people. They're the same everywhere."

Caroline shook her head. "Wouldn't you rather be doing something more—productive?" she wondered. "Building something, for example? Wouldn't that be closer to your line of work?''

''My line of work be damned,'' he said calmly. ''What could be more productive than helping people?'' Maybe that's what's been slipping away from me all this time, he thought. Building ships to kill people doesn't amount to much if stacked up next to relieving some of the suffering in the world.

Caroline watched him change with a growing sense of awe. This was what she had missed in Steven—this caring, this compassion. He was, once again, the red-bearded gentle giant she had known during their courtship; and she found herself, more and more frequently, slipping her hand in his when they were out walking together or sitting through a newsreel at the local cinema. She was conscious of looking at him in wonder, unable to remember what it was that had driven her away from him in the first place.

Steven was on the night shift, by far the most active shift, and she slept badly when he was working, tossing and turning with the subconscious worry that gnawed at her heart. When he came stumbling in the next morning, sweaty and tired, more often than not with bloodstains on his clothes, she would feel a rush of love and pride and need. Helping him wash up, she would put him to bed as though he were Elizabeth, and sometimes would stay in the rocking chair beside their bed and watch him sleep. It was a new feeling, this sense of awe at her husband as a person—or was it perhaps so deeply buried that she could no longer recognize it? She didn't know. All that she knew was that she settled into their new routine with joyful acceptance.

But Steven had not so much changed in the last few months as he had become more himself. He had grown more into the person that he had always been, that he was always meant to be. He had grown into himself. And that person was someone whom Caroline could love and respect and feel safe with. Someone who could take all her confused feelings and help her make sense of them. He was a man who had always—and who would always—wait until the storm of her emotions had subsided, and she was able to once again offer something in return for his steadfastness.

The printing press had come in slowly, laboriously hand delivered, piece by piece. Chantale didn't know how to set it up, and she had to wait days until Father Xavier could find an excuse to get someone over to the château to assemble it for her. Those were days of anxiety as she watched the pile of greasy metal and the reams of paper cluttering the stable floor, looking—to say the very least—conspicuous.

The man who came at last was dressed as a priest, but he was not one. Once Father Xavier and Father Dominique, as he was introduced, arrived at the château, the younger man shrugged out of his cassock and pulled a few tools from the hem of the garment where they were hidden. "Where is it?" he asked simply, and Chantale exchanged glances with the priest.

"In the stables," she said in a low voice. "I will show you."

"And I meanwhile," said Father Xavier loudly, rubbing his hands together, "will visit with Madame la Comtesse. Go about your errand, children. Don't let me stand in your way."

Chantale led the man out of the house and down the lane to the stables. There was a fierce north wind—and it seemed colder that fall for all of the deprivations. Father Dominique was tall and walked with a strong, easy stride, the cassock swung over an arm, his much repaired clothing beneath it lending dignity if anything to his appearance. He had green eyes, she had noted in her first glance, and a strong, handsome face. Perhaps a fellow Celt.

Etienne was just inside the doorway, cleaning out the hoof of a horse tethered in the great arching center hallway. He watched them come in, his face devoid of expression, and before Chantale even spoke to him he had unhooked the lead rope and taken the horse away. She took a deep breath and spoke to the visitor. "This way," she said softly, and led him back behind the farthest stalls, where a small trapdoor led to the stable cellars.

Here, had she but known it, had been stored decades ago the bits and pieces of automobiles and airplanes that the farrier's son, young Eric Beaumont, had tinkered with before he interested Philippe de Montclair in his projects, and they brought them above ground—so to speak. Old harnesses and a carriage were stored there now. There was another entrance to the cellars, a vast door, long since overgrown with trees and bushes, out in the orchards. Chantale had cleared it only that fall, had swung the great door open on its rusty hinges. One never knew when it might be needed.

He followed her down the narrow stairs and waited while she lit the lanterns she had placed on the tables and below the tunnel entrance. He nodded when he saw the printing press, as though recognizing an old acquaintance, and immediately spread out his tools on the refectory table.

"I'm sorry that it's so cold here," Chantale apologized. "It seemed the safest place to put it."

He seemed surprised. "Do not apologize, Countess. There's not a one of us that would not prefer safety to comfort these days."

She felt a shiver run down her spine. A tremor of fear, and something else that she didn't quite recognize. Instead of analyzing her feelings, she said quickly, "If you're going to be long I can fetch you a hot drink. There's no coffee, but we have some cider from our own apple orchards that I can heat up, if you'd like some."

He glanced up, his green eyes glinting in the lamplight. "Thank you, Countess. That would be most welcome." He was, she saw, wearing gloves with no fingers in them, and his own fingertips were already blue.

"It's no problem," she said, backing slowly toward the stairs. "I'll be right back."

Here I am, she thought as she stirred the cider over the stove in Annie's vast kitchen—and even now it was really impossible to think of it as belonging to anyone other than Annie—here I am, doing a servant's work, something I would never have thought to do. And wanting to do it, wanting to do anything that will help destroy the Germans, that will help France. My first love, my only priority now is France. How I have changed. And she could almost hear Annie's voice, warm with approval, saying: "Yes, Countess. How you have changed. How you have grown."

Chantale brought him the cider with hands that trembled only a little, and sat, wrapped in a horse blanket she had borrowed from the tack room, watching him as he assembled the machine. "Are you a printer yourself, then?"

He smiled without stopping what he was doing. His eyes were laughing—his eyes, she was to find, always seemed to be laughing, even when he was serious—lights dancing in their dark depths. The hands on the machinery were strong and firm, and the lock of hair that kept falling forward on his forehead was dark, too, a deeper chestnut than her own. His face was thin, far too thin, really, and there were some lines on the forehead even though he was young. All in all, it was perhaps not a face to swoon over, but it was a face that one could like. A face that one could trust. "No, Countess," he said, considering the question. "But it seems that the war makes handymen of us all. I am—I was—a schoolteacher."

"What happened?"

He shrugged. "What happens to us all, Countess? First the Germans told me what books to use, then they told me what to teach. When I ignored them they took my license away. I went on for a time, but then they took my schoolhouse away. The children are now being taught by Germans, and the classes are all in German, and they're being taught that their mothers and fathers are evil for telling them that France is separate from Germany. They've even begun to dream in German, or so I've heard." There was anger in his voice. "There isn't much call for an unemployed schoolteacher here in the glorious realm of the Third Reich, and so I was considerately given work by our mentors. They made me dig ditches for a living, Countess, and paid me very poorly indeed in deutsche marks."

"There are people," Chantale said, "who still contend that German rule is safe and peaceful and inevitable." My husband for one, she thought silently.

"I'll wager those people are generally not out digging ditches because their means of livelihood has been taken away from them." He wiped his hands on a rag and started on another part of the machine. "Do you know how to run this, Countess?"

"No." She was startled. "Should I?"

"Stands to reason, since it's in your barn."

"Oh. I just assumed—that others would be doing it." Her words faded and she felt ashamed of herself. "Will you show me how?"

"Certainly. There's nothing to it really, if you don't mind getting a little dirty. It's always eating paper and you have to keep reaching in to get the whole thing untangled. Come here, I'll give you your first lesson."

Lesson number one, Chantale thought, remembering the first British pilot she had smuggled out of Angers. Lesson number one, Countess. How I have changed, since then.

She slid off her chair and let the blanket fall to the floor. "Yes," she said, her voice stronger and steadier than she had thought that it would be. "Show me."

As the German airplanes screamed over the Channel toward Britain, Hitler vowed that the awful blitzkrieg would reduce the island to rubble. If he could not have it, no one would.

The bombing of London had continued past the point where the people should have rebelled, past the point where their strength should have been sapped, past the point where there was no more common sense in going on. Building after building, block after block was either in ruins or destroyed by fire. Places of business existed no more. People woke in the mornings to find that their homes had been destroyed overnight. There is a point at which the human spirit abandons all hope, beyond which it cannot endure, and the people of London during that fall of 1940 had passed that point and gone beyond it. Their endurance knew no limits. They knew no boundaries, no reasons to stop going on. Political and class differences simply ceased to exist, as they united in their determination to survive.

By the end of October, although the blitz still continued and the Germans continued to drop bombs on English cities, they were saying that the RAF had won the Battle of Britain, saving England from German invasion. Yet the Germans had not given up entirely, and sporadic bombing continued.

Shortly before Christmas 1940 a bomb fell on St. Catherine Street, just as an ambulance rounded the corner. The ambulance was driving in the dark because of the blackout, taking wounded children to a nearby shelter. For one brief moment the scene was illuminated in bright stark black and white as the bomb exploded, and then all the street seemed to catch fire instantly, and the ambulance was lost in the conflagration.

Chapter Twenty-two

The voice was low, but it filled the small church. "I am the resurrection and the life, saith the Lord; he that believeth in Me, though he were dead, yet shall he live; and whosoever liveth and believeth in Me shall never die."

Caroline sat still in the first pew, staring straight ahead, willing herself not to cry. He that believeth in Me . . . One of the many things that she and Steven had never had time for, it seemed. She wondered if his faith had been something more real and alive and vibrant than the solid Anglican heritage that she had had, something that had found an outlet not in words but in actions. That's what everyone said, anyway. That Steven had died in the best way possible, serving others.

She shook her head. There wasn't a good way to die, not really. Death was the enemy, and whenever anybody died, death had won.

People were kneeling. The woman next to Caroline nudged her with an elbow and Caroline slid obediently down to the stiff kneeler in front of her pew. "Grant," the priest was intoning, "to all who mourn a sure confidence in Thy fatherly care that, casting all their grief on Thee, they may know the consolation of Thy love." Everyone around Caroline murmured a low amen, but her eyes were blurring with tears again and she found that her lips wouldn't move. "Grant," he went on, oblivious of her misery, "us to entrust Thy servant Steven to Thy never-failing love; receive him into the arms of Thy mercy, and remember him according to the favor which Thou bearest unto Thy people."

How could she entrust Steven to anyone's love, when she had taken so long to entrust him with her own? He had been her husband, but for the most part she had used their relationship for everything else under the sun. She had made him into her father, her brother, her confidant, her enemy. For a time they had been lovers, but a couple? A true married couple, the kind that you read about in books, the kind the priest was talking about as Steven was buried? Hardly. Only for a scant few months. And she realized with a start that she was mourning their marriage as much as she was mourning Steven's death. The two, it seemed, had died together. But the man had lived much longer, and it seemed he had much more to show for himself than the marriage ever did.

The organ was playing, and she stumbled to her feet, feeling the music wash over her like the ocean, beauty heaped upon beauty, and all that she could feel was the bitterness of betrayal. She hadn't done what Steven needed, hadn't been what Steven needed, and now it was too late. Once more Caroline was struck with the bitter knowledge that no one—not even Steven—was governor of his own life.

They buried Steven in London Cemetery, and his wife was his only family member there to mourn him. But Caroline was so immersed in her own thoughts that she never even properly mourned, never properly said good-bye, never did any of the things that, later, she would regret. All that she could think as she stood numbly by, with the snow fluttering down all around her and the wind cutting through her thin black coat, was that once more she had failed. Just as she had failed as a daughter, just as she was failing Elizabeth as a mother, so, too, had she failed Steven as a wife.

There seemed little sense really in going on, heaping failure upon failure, disappointment upon disappointment, bitterness upon bitterness. She went back to the cold, dark flat that she had shared with Steven and sat on a kitchen chair and stared at the gas oven and dared herself to turn it on. Or not to turn it on. Turning it on, after all, was the easier of the two alternatives.

The dusk settled in around her, and still she sat, staring at the oven without really seeing it, hearing all the voices in her head. Steven's, from before they were married: the night at the shelter when she decided that she needed him more than anything in the world, the night that the old man had died and they had sat there together, sole witnesses to his passing. "He needed someone here, someone to love him." Her mother's, blurred by years and distance: "But, darling, of course I love you! But there are just so many other interesting things in life, aren't there, and one simply can't have it all, can one?" The steady voice of the psychologist, wearing his tweeds and smoking his pipe: "Feelings are on the surface, Caroline. Come to know what's under the surface."

Well, she had done that, hadn't she? She had come to know what was under the surface, and she didn't like it. She had found out she wasn't capable of loving the way that Steven had, without reservation or strings attached. If Steven had lived she would have been able to test their newfound love, but as it was she couldn't be sure. She had married Steven because she thought that she loved him, but she had abandoned him when he disappointed her. She had thought that she loved Andrew, but she had found that he was nothing other than her romantic thoughts of what a lover should be. And Elizabeth? How could she in all honesty say that she loved her child, when the girl had always taken second place to flying in Caroline's life?

She sniffed loudly, and then, shattering the silence of the apartment, the telephone rang.

Go away, Caroline thought. Just go away. Leave me alone. It rang, shrill, insistent, destroying the melancholy peace that she had woven around her, until with an exclamation of impatience she got up and yanked the receiver to her ear. "What is it?"

"Caroline? It's Eric. I just heard about Steven. I'm terribly sorry, my dear."

"Oh." She sat down, wrapping her free arm around her slender body, suddenly aware of how cold it was in the apartment. "Thank you." Even to her own ears, the words seemed lifeless, dull, and devoid of feeling.

The same awareness was in Eric's voice. "You sound terrible. Is there anyone there with you?"

"Of course not." She could feel a bubble of hysteria rising inside of her. "The only one here was Steven, and he's not here anymore."

"Look, Caroline, get a grip on yourself. This isn't doing any good. You have to come home now, right away." His was the voice of authority, of one accustomed to instantaneous obedience. "I've made all the arrangements. You can come to San Jose."

"No one is flying out of England," she said automatically. No one but the Germans, who dropped their bombs on the cities and then flew home to supper with their wives and children.

"I've arranged it. It's not a problem. Just stay where you are, and someone will be there within twenty-four hours. I promise.

And I'll make sure that you're happy here. You can bring Elizabeth out with you. You can stay for as long as you'd like."

"No," she said again, but he wasn't listening. She could hear the faint hiss as he lit a match, and she imagined him sitting at his desk, lighting a cigarette, the first long inhale. "Caroline, I know how difficult this is for you. I really understand. When Sarah was killed, I wanted to die. But you have to go on." He sucked some more smoke into his lungs. "You have to go on because Elizabeth needs you."

"No," Caroline said. What did Eric know, anyway? How could he ever equate his grief with hers? He and Sarah had been happy together. Every story that had been told her about them reflected the same picture: of a young couple immersed in each other, contented, loving. Surely when Sarah died his only regrets were for the life that they might have had—whereas her regrets ran far deeper. She not only grieved for the life she and Steven might have had, but for the life that they *could* have had, the one that she had squandered. "No," she said. "I need to stay here. It's where he died."

"You'll always remember him, Caroline. You don't have to stay in the same place to remember him."

"You don't understand," she said, and suddenly the tears were there, the tears she had so successfully kept at bay all day and evening. "I—oh, Eric, it's all my fault . . . I didn't know . . ." She couldn't talk, her tears were choking her, and then her shoulders were hunched over and wrenching with sobs that racked her body, the grief that finally poured out of her.

Eric was talking. "Caroline—oh, Caroline, do get a hold of yourself. Caroline! Stop saying that it's your fault. It's not your fault. Do you hear me? It's not your fault. You had nothing to do with it."

"I did. . . . I did," she sobbed. "I didn't . . . care . . . until it was . . . too late . . . and now . . . it's always going to be too late."

His voice held authority. "Caroline, listen to me. Don't talk. Just listen. Are you listening? Can you hear me? This is not your fault. We all make mistakes. We all say things we wish we hadn't, we all do things we wish we hadn't done—or else it's the other way around, and we leave out the things we should have said and done. This isn't your unique experience, dear girl. Everyone feels the same way. I felt the same way when Philippe died and when Sarah died. There were so many things I should have said to your father, and sometimes I still lie awake at night thinking about them and regretting them. Do you hear me, Caroline? Sitting around blaming yourself and thinking about suicide isn't going to help you, and it isn't going to help Elizabeth, and it sure as hell at this point isn't going to help Steven."

"How did you . . . know . . . I was thinking . . . ?"

"Because I know you. It would be a dramatic gesture, Caroline, but a self-indulgent one, too. A lot easier than facing the world, and facing life if that's what you want to do . . . but you'd disappoint me. And you know that it would disappoint Steven."

"So what else is new?" she asked miserably. The sobs were subsiding now as she listened to his steady voice. "I've always disappointed him."

"If you continue to do so you'll make his life meaningless. Do yourself a favor, Caroline. Stop the dramatics. Stop blaming yourself; it's too conceited. There are other people in the world besides you and Steven and your own little universe. You have a daughter, for starters. A responsibility."

"Now you sound like Justine."

"Another responsibility. Do you know that Justine's very ill? Do you know that her son is living at your house in Newport because she can't care for him anymore? It's time you stopped feeling sorry for yourself, Caroline, and faced reality. I'll have you home soon."

The old resentment flared up again. "No. I'm not coming home."

He sighed. "Caroline, don't be difficult—"

"Then don't treat me like a child!" she fairly shrieked into the phone. "I'm an adult! I've gotten myself into this situation, and I'll get myself out of it. I know you're probably right, but you have to understand I can't hear that from you right now. I need some time to decide what I want to do. I need you to give me some time, Eric."

"You may not have much time. London's still being bombed."

"I am," she said sarcastically, "aware of that fact. Oh, Eric, I love you. And I appreciate what you're trying to do . . . but please let me work through this my way."

There was a long pause at the other end of the line. "I care about you," he said at length, as though only just then discovering it.

"I know." She said it quietly. "I'll take care of myself, Eric. I promise. And I won't turn on the gas."

Even as she replaced the telephone receiver in its cradle, she wondered how she could ever keep that particular promise.

The church bells were ringing, all of them at once, just as they did on every New Year's Eve, as though this year were no different from any other.

Soizic Aubert held her champagne glass in her hand and smiled at all the people around her, at the confetti and the streamers and the songs. Only dimly, through the closed windows, could she hear the church bells. And it was only her imagination, she told herself, that heard them tolling for death and not life this particular year. Sometimes Soizic let herself think about the war, and she didn't like it. She couldn't bear to ponder the fact that people were suffering and dying, and she didn't like the thought of her own country being occupied by foreigners. Sometimes she wasn't sure if she could live with the knowledge of her own involvement, her distanced contribution to the whole thing.

It was 1941.

Marc Giroux was, as ever, working. Even in the midst of the fashionable New Year's Eve party, he sat apart from the others, leaning slightly forward in his seat, his heavy face flushed with the drink and the excitement, talking with—whom? Soizic didn't recognize the man who sat so stiffly across from Marc, but their conversation was deep and quiet and brooked no interruptions.

Raphael Marchand put his arm around Soizic's shoulders. "New Year's Eve prerogative," he said, and kissed her cheek. "Happy nineteen forty-one, Soizic." His speech was faintly slurred, and she realized with sudden surprise that she had never seen any of her colleagues drinking before. She had always been too shy, felt too inadequate, to attend parties, and even though Marc had insisted that they go to this one, she still felt out of place.

"Happy New Year, Raphael," she responded automatically, and smiled, lifting her champagne glass to his. "Let's drink to peace."

"Peace? When has peace done us any good?" He laughed. "Drink instead to war, Mademoiselle Aubert, the war that is making us all so very rich." He nodded toward Marc Giroux, still intent on his serious conversation. "Don't think that he's not pulling strings toward that end now, even as we speak."

"Who is that man?" she asked, her voice low. "I don't recognize him."

"Ha! And so you shouldn't!" He lurched a little on his feet and put a hand on her shoulder for support. "Just the most important—"

"The most important what, Raphael, dear?" It was Françoise Duroc, cigarette in hand, slipping easily into their conversation. "If it's gossip, have I got some for you! They say that Hitler's been taking rejuvenation pills! I ask you!"

Raphael turned to her, sidetracked. "I'll do you one better," he said. "A joke. Hitler called Mussolini the other day and asked him why he wasn't in North Africa yet. And Mussolini said, 'Excuse me? The connection is very bad. I take it you're calling from London?' "

Everyone laughed. Soizic stole another glance toward Marc, but she wasn't going to learn anything more from Raphael, not with Françoise there. "Excuse me," she said softly, smiling to take the edge off her rudeness, and slipped away from them. Robert Beneteau was sitting on a velvet-covered sofa, dignified and distant from all, a very young very blond woman sitting on a chair at right angles to him, sipping champagne in silence. He caught sight of Soizic and patted the seat next to him.

"Ah, Mademoiselle Aubert, do spare a moment for an old man, won't you?"

"Only if you'll stop reproaching yourself with your age. I'd wear it as a badge of honor, myself!" She sat down, smiling politely for the girl, and accepted a refill of champagne from one of the white-coated waiters hired for the occasion. "Happy New Year, Monsieur Beneteau."

"And the same to you, Mademoiselle Aubert. May it bring us all happiness."

"I would have said peace, but that doesn't seem to be such a popular opinion this evening."

He raised his eyebrows. "Is it not? An error, mademoiselle, mark my words. We must always strive for peace."

"Even," she said carefully, "when war shows itself to be more profitable?"

"Ah, but you are confusing business with real life. They are very different, Mademoiselle Aubert. Very different. Not everything which is good for business is good for people."

"I wouldn't let some people hear you say that. It sounds like heresy to me."

He shook his head. "Even at the firm, we seem to have lost track of some of the principles that I would have liked to see us build upon. . . . Don't be too eager, Mademoiselle Aubert. If fame and fortune are to come, they are to come, and fate will not listen to your pleas one way or the other. But to play with people's lives . . ." His voice drifted off and his blond companion watched him with a curious lack of response in her face.

Soizic frowned. "I always thought . . . I've been given the impression that playing with people's lives is what it's all about. Manipulating them so that we are in control. Isn't that what counts?"

"It did, once. Playing the game was all that mattered once. But these days, my dear, I wonder. I truly wonder if it is worth it at all." He smiled, and there was tiredness in his smile. "Forgive me. Late parties no longer agree with me. Enjoy yourself, my dear, and leave the philosophy to your golden years. By then it will be easier for you. Philosophy only makes sense when formulated by those who no longer have the power to do anything about it anyway. And now I think that Brigitte and I will retire." He rose slowly to his feet, the blond girl instantly beside him, supporting him. Soizic rose as well, worry in her eyes. "Are you all right?"

"I'm as all right as I'm ever likely to be, my dear. Good night."

"Good night, Monsieur Beneteau." She watched him with troubled eyes, watched as he stiffly walked out the door, the young girl supporting every step. Who was she—child, lover, mistress, nurse? Perhaps a little of each—one of the requirements of advanced age.

Raphael was again by her side, still laughing. "Why so serious, Soizic? Come on . . . we're about to start a round of singing."

She didn't turn, still watching Beneteau's disappearing back. "And what will you sing, Raphael?" she asked softly. "Will it be the *Marseillaise* tonight . . . or *Lili Marlene*?"

"What are you talking about?" He followed her gaze, and then nodded in comprehension. "Ah, yes, the old man. He gets that way when he's had something to drink. And sometimes people who have also had something to drink listen to him. I wouldn't recommend it, Soizic. I really wouldn't." He gripped her elbow suddenly, forcefully. "Don't listen, Soizic. You're going somewhere. You've been promoted over all of us, and you ought to look at that. You're young and bright and going places. Don't let a little sentimentality stand in your way."

"Is that what it is?"

He shrugged. "Looks like it to me. Don't listen to him, Soizic. Developing a conscience at this late stage in the game could be hazardous to your health."

She finally looked at him. "Meaning what, Raphael?"

He shook his head. "Ask your lover," he said, jerking his head toward Marc. "Don't ask me. There are certain times when it is more . . . expedient . . . to know nothing, hear nothing, see nothing. And stay healthy. My preference, in any case. And now I'm going to sing."

He let go of her arm and turned away, and she looked down past the bright blue silken dress which matched her eyes so perfectly to the darkening bruise that his fingers had left there. She stared at it for quite some while.

It hadn't been too difficult for Chantale to learn how to run the printing press.

Dominique had shown her that first day. Later, Father Xavier gave her a dog-eared manual for it. God alone knew where it had come from. Chantale carefully studied the leaflet at night in her room, and when she was sure that she knew what she was doing, she had asked Father Xavier what needed to be printed.

This press was not intended for the false visas which could convey a person to the Free Zone—or, better still, to England. The Sisters of Charity printed those in the basement of their convent on the rue des Arènes, and the Germans hadn't thought yet to search there. "Give them time," Sister Aurelie said to Chantale one night. "When they finally figure out we're people as well as nuns, they won't hesitate."

"Then I'll do them for you," Chantale responded.

Father Xavier wanted Chantale to print pamphlets. "We'll write them," he told Chantale. "And then we'll distribute them at night, when nobody is around to see us, after curfew."

"Pamphlets about what?"

He shrugged. "Freedom. Resistance. How the fight has to go on. We all believe that. Now we have to spread the word. People must know that there are some of us who didn't surrender at that farce at Compiègne." He pulled a book from his cassock, a

Bible or missal, and handed it to Chantale. "Go on, look inside."

She opened it hesitantly, only to find that the gold-embossed pages hid a hollow interior. She looked up and met the priest's eyes.

"This is how I will convey the information to you. You have only to print it up. I will have others come to the stables to fetch and deliver it. I already have several articles written by Dominique."

"Is that his real name?"

He shrugged. "Who knows, Countess? And what does it matter, except that he is pledged to fight the Germans?" He smiled. "There was a time, Countess, when what would have mattered to me was whether or not someone was a good Catholic. Now all that I care about is whether or not he or she hates the Germans."

"Times change, Father."

"Indeed they do, my dear. Indeed they do. I'll be by tomorrow with some materials for you to try out—or perhaps I'll send Dominique. He's living with me now, posing as my curate." He smiled again. "What the Pope doesn't know . . ."

"Or the Archbishop of Angers?"

"The Archbishop of Angers has far more on his mind these days than clergy deployment in his diocese. My best to your mother-in-law, Countess."

"Until tomorrow, Father."

It was in fact Dominique who came the following day, dressed in his cassock, with the addition of spectacles . . . and a missal. He stood outside the château on the sweeping gravel drive and announced, as he might to the world, "Some prayers for you, Countess."

Chantale smiled in amusement. "There's no one here to hear you," she said. "My husband is in town and most of the servants are as well. It's market day." Or what used to be market day, she thought. Nowadays there were those who called it fasting day. With all the restrictions and shortages and rationing, it was difficult to come home with more in one's basket than when one had set out. That winter they had begun rationing cheese, eggs, and oil. Butter, coffee, bread, and sugar had already all but disappeared. Now fish and chocolate had been added to the lists. Bread not only became rare, it became black, as white flour was unobtainable.

The de Montclairs were fortunate. Not only did they have chickens, but they also had produce from their orchards, wine

from their vineyards. More often than not, the servants going
into town for market brought items in with them to give away,
or barter for something that was needed in the kitchen. Marie-
Louise suspected that a great deal of it ended up on the black
market, but there was no way to prove her suspicions and she
did not wish to accuse any of the servants.

Dominique glanced around him. "Still, it's safer not to talk
here," he said.

Chantale shrugged. "As you wish. Let's walk out to the stables."

He walked silently beside her, his strides long and assured,
the spectacles and book making him look like a timid young
cleric. She had some hot cider waiting in the cellar, and he drank
it gratefully while she lit the lanterns. "I have some articles,"
he said. "And some identification papers."

Chantale looked up sharply. "I thought that the Sisters—"

"The Sisters have enough work for three convents. We've been
trying to get the Jews out of Angers. That's a great deal of pa-
perwork."

Chantale frowned. "The Jews? Why on earth?" And then, in
the next breath, "I didn't know that there were any here."

"The Germans don't like Jews," Dominique said matter-of-
factly.

"The Germans don't particularly like us, either, but we're not
running away," Chantale answered.

Dominique started preparing the papers for the press. "It's
not the same, Countess. We have a chance—a slim one, perhaps—but a chance at survival. They don't. When I say the Germans don't like them, that's a gross understatement." He
straightened up. "Give me that rag, will you?" He wiped the
grease off his hands and put the crank onto the press. "I might
as well start this, since I'm here."

She couldn't speak for several minutes above the noise of the
press and retreated back to her corner where the horse blanket
still waited, wishing that she had brought more cider down. Finally he straightened and stopped turning the hand crank.
"Whew! That's all for now."

"Tell me about the Jews." Chantale had, to the best of her
knowledge, never met a Jew, but she had read the Old Testa-
ment.

"Hitler wants to kill them." The words were stark and simple
and, in that cold cellar, vaguely obscene.

"What do you mean, wants to kill them?"

"Just that." He came and sat next to her. "Oh, Countess, you're so protected here. You don't know about what goes on in the world."

"I know a little," she said, thinking of Annie. "And my name is Chantale."

"Chantale, then. Hitler doesn't like Jews. Don't ask me why; there's a different reason every week. But he wants to wipe out their race. We think that, in time, he might even try it. So we don't want to take any chances. We're giving them false papers and sending them—as many of them as we can—to England. They'll be safe there, for now."

"For now," Chantale echoed. She was suddenly uncomfortably aware of how close to her he was sitting. "How could he kill a whole—a whole race of people?"

"How could he invade Poland? And Belgium? And France? Who knows what goes on in his mind?" He shook his head. "I sure as hell don't, Chantale." He wiped some sweat from his brow. "I'd better be going. I'm taking the identity papers and leaving you the leaflet to get out. Either Father Xavier or I will be by on Wednesday to pick it up."

Chantale shivered. "Dominique—"

He turned to her, his green eyes burning brightly. "Yes?"

She was suddenly confused. "Nothing."

"Nothing?"

"No," she said, and then as he moved to leave, "Yes."

He turned back to her and reached down with his hand, putting his fingers under her chin, tilting her face up to his. "Yes," he said softly as he bent to kiss her.

Just one more letter, Andrew Starkey told himself. Just one more letter like this one, and I'm not going to be able to stand it any longer.

He wondered if other people had been in a position like his, this conscious determination of his own ability to remain sane, this sure knowledge that he was teetering on some sort of brink and a deep fear of the abyss beyond. It was late, and he was tired, and his mind was undoubtedly playing tricks with him, but, still, he wondered. Was he being fanciful or was he simply more aware than others of being shoved against the wall?

He shook his head and reread what he had just written.

Surrey, England
January 30, 1941
Mr. and Mrs. Charles Smith
14 Bromfield Street
Boston, Massachusetts, U.S.A.

Dear Mr. and Mrs. Smith,

It is with deep regret that I write to inform you of the death of your son, Charles Jr.

As Charlie's commanding officer, I have had many occasions to watch his work and to witness his bravery. Charlie was a real patriot, Mr. and Mrs. Smith, one who cared about the well-being not only of his own country but of the world, and that was why he volunteered to come to England and fly for the Royal Air Force.

You'll know by now that he distinguished himself this past summer and fall during the period that they're now calling the Battle of Britain, but which for us pilots was pure hell. Charlie flew the tightest formation of any pilot I have under my command, and he never once wavered. His wingman was shot down twice and Charlie went after the German fighter, both times, and got him, both times. I wish that I had had the time to write you and tell you about that then. It's very sad that the only time we have contact is when one of the pilots doesn't come back.

We were flying cover for an RAF bombing run into Germany—over the Ruhr Valley, where a lot of their aircraft production goes on—when we were attacked by some German fighters. Charlie's plane was hit almost immediately, and it exploded before he hit the ground. I think that I can assure you that he didn't feel anything. It all happened too fast for that.

Words are not enough to tell you how deeply I regret this loss, both for my squadron and for your family. Please know that he will be missed here in Surrey. If there is anything that I can do, please do not hesitate to contact me.

Yours sincerely,
Andrew Starkey
Captain, Eagle Squadron
Royal Air Force

He shook his head. Yes, Charlie would be missed in Surrey, and not least of all by the pretty village girl who worked behind

the bar at the Hawk and Boar. What was her name? He should
remember. Charlie talked about her all the time. Something out
of Dickens . . . Dora. Yes, that was it: Dora.

Andrew sighed and shook his head again. It not only didn't
get any easier, it got harder, every time. It got more difficult as
he got to know his men better, heard them talking about their
homes and their families, their dreams and their hopes. It got
harder as he found himself pulled into the tangled web of their
lives, as he found himself liking them and needing them. He
would miss Charlie, too, the slow Boston Brahmin drawl, the
beers they had consumed while Dora polished the glasses behind
the bar, Charlie's stories about life at a New England prep school.

He didn't know if he could write any more letters like that.

It wouldn't be so very bad, he realized, if the only enemy was
the one that goose-stepped its way across Europe and barked its
idolatrous salute to the small man with the big ego. . . . War
was something that he could understand. Country X invades
Country Z and Country Z retaliates. It even made sense if Country Y decided to come and help out Country Z.

But what didn't make sense were the people who didn't care
who fought and who died as long as there was money in the
coffers when the dust settled. The people who sat in the boardrooms, with their faces in the shadows, and who directed the
scenarios as though they were Covent Garden plays. The people
who, to the knowledge of most of the world, did not even exist.

But Andrew knew that they existed. Andrew knew their faces
and their names. And he knew, with a sickening certainty, that
when this was all over he was going to get them back for what
they had done.

Intraglobal—or, more accurately, a subsidiary of a subsidiary—
was still working on aircraft for the war, and that winter a new
fighter plane came into existence—the Mosquito. It was to be
used by the English and whoever cared to assist them.

It was developed thanks to the profits from another subsidiary's aircraft—the Junkers Stuka, the fantastically accurate and
frightening German dive-bomber.

Eric Beaumont heard the annual reports from both subsidiaries and smiled with satisfaction. Things were running smoothly
and he could relax his constant care, constant attention. He loved
the airplanes, and he loved seeing what new innovations he could
add to all of them. They were his first and his last and his con-

stant love, but another issue was nagging at him, fluttering in the back of his mind, haunting his sleep. And it was high time that he got on with it.

He appointed people to oversee the development and construction of airplanes, and indeed of all future defense contracting, for the Pentagon was getting more and more involved every day. He placed a call to New Mexico. "Julie? Get me Oppenheimer on the line, please."

The future was being developed. And he was going to be a part of it.

Chapter Twenty-three

"More tea, my dear?"

Caroline shook her head. "No, thank you. It was delicious. Thank you."

Lady Everard smiled. "I like to see you girls eating something. You're nothing but skin and bones, all of you."

Caroline shook her head again, and watched as the offer of more tea moved around the table. It was five weeks since she had come here, and still it seemed more like a dream than reality.

Three months since Steven had died and she had decided that she couldn't go back to the States, not with the war still on and America so reluctant to become part of it. Steven had died because he cared, and she wasn't going to betray that caring further by acting as though nothing had happened and going home. He had been killed by the Germans, and now it was up to her to do what she could to end the war so that no more innocent people had to die. It was too late for Steven. Perhaps it would not be too late for others.

So she had volunteered for the Air Transport Auxiliary. She had passed the test with only minor problems—she was to fly in a Tiger Moth and had been unfamiliar with it when she took off for the qualification. But she had earned herself a place with the Ferry Pool.

Emma had been right: There was no shortage of women pilots, qualified and experienced and willing to do their part, and if the RAF wouldn't have them, the ATA most certainly would. By 1941, when Caroline joined, there were already two women's pools, with more women driving ambulances while they waited their turn to qualify. Twenty-five of the women were Americans. Caroline brought the number that winter to twenty-six.

The American women were from all over the country, women

who for all sorts of reasons had decided to become part of the defense of Britain. One was married to an Englishman. Another had been a lifelong Anglophile and could think of nothing she would rather do than be part of England in time of need. Several saw the moral imperative underlying Roosevelt's pronouncements: If America was bound to supply defense matériel, then it followed that people would also be useful. "After all," one of them said to Caroline when they first met, "if Hitler takes England, then Long Island is next." They came from all walks of life as well, from the mechanic's sister who had learned to fly on a rebuilt Blériot biplane to heiresses as wealthy as Caroline, devotees of the tennis and yacht circles.

The Englishwomen were a disparate group as well, from daughters of baronets to shopgirls who had learned to fly just before the war when the Civil Air Guard offered subsidized flying lessons to men and women alike. And they all graduated from the ATA headquarters at White Waltham moving on either to Hambledon or to the manorial home of Sir Lindsay Everard at Hatfield.

Sir Lindsay Everard was an enigma. A member of Parliament, he was also chairman of the Royal Aero Club, but he rarely flew at all anymore. He was an accomplished pilot who had flown against the Germans in the First War, and—like others—he was frustrated by the strict requirements of the RAF for its fighter and bomber pilots. Unlike others, however, he had some say in government and could do something about it. He turned to the ATA. He might never have gotten involved with the women pilots had it not been for his wife, who had learned to fly and had in fact only recently obtained her license. It was she who pointed out that not using the women pilots was a terrible waste of potential, and it was she who reflected that if the American girls were willing to come over and fly, then they had a right to a comfortable home, some decent hospitality, and a place to lay their heads at night. Sir Lindsay's objections, if he had any, were quickly overruled, and their manorial home—complete with private airstrip—soon became Number Six Ferry Pool of the ATA.

Caroline became part of it.

The drill was simple. "We move airplanes, girls." Their commander was an English woman, Pauline Gower, well known in England for what was still called pioneering efforts to get women more involved in aviation. It was she who had begun the women's divisions of the ATA in December of 1939. Sir Lindsay was nominally in charge, but it was really Pauline who ran the pool. "We have all of the disadvantages of the RAF and none of their advantages."

Caroline leaned back in her chair and watched Pauline as she spoke. This, she thought, is someone I can trust—someone I can admire. Pauline reminded her, in so many ways, of Sarah Martin Beaumont. Brave, daring, not unwilling to do stunts to get what she wanted, Pauline lived for the moment. That was how Eric had described Sarah, and that was how Caroline would describe Pauline Gower. She was a woman who loved life, and lived it as completely and intensely as possible. Caroline was not only in awe of that ability, but certain it was one she herself would never possess.

Physically, Pauline was small and dark, a handsome woman with quick birdlike movements and bright inquisitive eyes. She laughed a lot, showing a row of nearly perfect white teeth, and when she looked sad or pensive her whole face clouded over. She was older than most of them—in her late thirties—and she had more stories to tell than anyone Caroline had ever known.

"If we're shot at, the best thing that we can do is take evasive action," Pauline told Caroline her first night at Everard Manor. "We haven't got any guns, so it doesn't make any sense to stand and fight. Even the fighters we deliver are unarmed for the trip."

"But why?" Caroline was bewildered. "It doesn't make sense. If we ever *are* attacked . . ." She let her voice trail off uncertainly.

"If we ever are attacked," Pauline said briskly, "we are still women. And women are not fighter pilots. And that, my dear, is the bottom line. Look for cloud cover or outrun them or out-maneuver them if you can. Ditch the plane as a last resort if you have to. That's all we can do."

"It's not fair," Caroline protested.

"Of course it's not fair," Pauline said unsympathetically. "War isn't particularly fair now, is it?"

"No," Caroline said miserably, thinking of Steven.

"Right. So we practice. Every chance we get, every time we have airplanes, we practice. I'll expect you out with the rest of the Ferry Pool in the morning."

In the morning meant, Caroline learned, at first light. It was early and freezing cold—the manor had no central heating, and her hot-water bottle had given up any semblance of warmth hours before it was time to get up. Caroline bathed by splashing cold water over her shivering body, and dressed quickly, pulling on long underwear beneath her trousers and her flying suit. The flying suits they wore were facsimiles of the ones worn by RAF pilots. Heavy and bulky with the all-important parachutes strapped on the back, they were drafty in open cockpits. Caroline pulled up the mock-fur collar so that it swathed her neck and blew on her hands to warm them. A vacation it wasn't.

But then, it had never started out as one.

And she couldn't complain that she wasn't able to log enough flying hours. Sir Lindsay had some old airplanes of his own which he made available to the Ferry Pool—two old Aeroméchanique biplanes, wonderfully preserved, a Tiger Moth, a Blériot biplane, and a temperamental Curtiss machine that started up only in good weather, which effectively kept it grounded for most of that winter and spring. They practiced continually, going up in pairs and simulating attacking each other. They practiced parachuting—this maneuver with more than one pilot in the airplane—and they practiced landing in the huge swimming pool attached to the estate. Caroline found every day exhausting—and exhilarating.

It was mostly the cold that registered in her memory. None of the practice planes—and precious few of the "real" ones she eventually flew—had closed cockpits, and the wind was vicious, finding every opening in the flying suit, reducing toes and fingers to numbness. The noise, too, was deafening. Caroline learned early on to wear earplugs under her flying helmet.

Radio contact was prohibited. After all, as Pauline pointed out, there was absolutely nothing to keep the Germans from listening in on their radio channels.

"But they won't understand, will they?" asked Juliet Francis, the youngest pilot in the pool, not long out of school when the war started.

Pauline looked at her in exasperation. "There's no law that says they can't learn English, Juliet." Juliet blushed, and everybody laughed.

Laughter was their most common antidote to the cold and the fear—and, sometimes, the despair. It was the only release that they had. Flying in bad weather and the obstacles of barrage balloons as well as the very real possibility of German aircraft made the flying itself treacherous, and, as Caroline soon learned, completely unpredictable.

"I never flew a Moth before," Caroline told Pauline one evening, laughing over her qualifying test. "I really didn't know what I was doing."

Pauline raised her eyebrows. "Well, then, you might as well get used to it," she said.

"What do you mean?"

"Do you think that they give us lessons on these crates we're flying? Hardly. We're lucky if we get a peep at the manuals before we take off."

Caroline stared. "I don't understand."

Pauline sighed and poured out more coffee. Lady Everard always left some out on the sideboard, so that insomniacs could help themselves. "Look. We fly everything—well, that's not quite right, is it? Everything except seaplanes." She made a face. "They think we might be embarrassed if we had to ditch in the drink and stay overnight with a male crew. Imagine! Daft ideas they have in Whitehall. Anyway, we fly everything else. They've divided them up into five groups, and we have to qualify separately for each group."

"I thought I had already qualified."

"For the ATA, right. And for Group One, I should think— that's the Moth. More difficult airplanes, heavier ones, bigger ones are in higher groups." She smiled. "If you want to set yourself a goal, no woman's yet qualified for Group Five."

Caroline smiled and shook her head. "Not just now, thanks. Maybe tomorrow." She hesitated. "And then what?"

"Well, once you qualify, we put your name on the rota. And when some aircraft need delivering you take them by turns, so at any time the manor here might be full, or empty, depending on who's qualified to fly which run, and what airplanes need moving." Pauline took a deep breath. "Bob Morgan down at White Waltham—he's the chief technical officer—he's written up a sort of manual for each plane. Really they're more like notes. And if there's time they give you the notes ahead of time, so you can see the layout of the cockpit, and if there's anything special or quirky you have to know about the airplane. But sometimes there isn't time, the bloody high and mighty RAF wants something right away so you just pray a lot." She gave Caroline a sideways smile. "Twice now, I've been reading the Ferry Pilot's notes while I taxied the airplane out."

Caroline shuddered. "That sounds dangerous!"

"Well, of course it is. War isn't exactly a holiday." Pauline smiled.

No. It was no holiday.

Emma arrived during Caroline's second week at Hatfield. She was smiling and as pretty as ever, having finally gotten her transfer approved from the RAF to the ATA, and pleased that she was finally going to be doing something useful.

To Caroline it didn't feel particularly useful, not at first. Caroline hadn't yet made a delivery and what with the arctic wind blowing about and the difficult maneuvers and the practice jumps out of the Aeroméchanique airplanes, she was beginning to feel very frustrated. Caroline found herself looking at the planes with less curiosity than she would have once. She was beginning to see that making airplanes was perhaps not the best way to strive for peace, but her thoughts were far too occupied with other things to philosophize about her inheritance. She had pushed Eric—and Intraglobal—so far to the back of her mind that, most days, it was easy to forget all about them altogether. What she was doing was far more important.

Caroline didn't see much of Emma at first, because Emma was sent right out with seven other women to deliver a unit of Tiger Moths to Scotland. "Why not me?" Caroline asked.

Pauline shook her head. "When you're ready, Caroline, I'll send you. You still have some work to do here."

Caroline fumed, wondering even as she did whether her irritation had more to do with her frustration at not actually flying any assignments yet, or with the fact that it was Emma who had been chosen to go. There was an unspoken, almost unrecognized rivalry between the two of them. Caroline refused to acknowledge it. She was, after all, still mourning the loss of her husband, and Emma did not refer to it, but it was there all the same.

On Emma's first night at Hatfield, Caroline asked her, her casual tone belying her feelings, "And how is Andrew? I haven't heard from him in months."

Emma turned the porcelain milk-and-honey complexion toward her. "Andrew? Oh, he's well, thanks."

Caroline was confused.

Emma, a faint blush on her cheeks, spoke up again. "I may as well tell you, Caroline, he's asked me to marry him."

"I see," Caroline said again, feeling her stomach turn to lead inside of her. "And what did you answer?"

Emma's eyes widened. "Well, yes, of course! If we both live through the war, there's nothing I'd rather do than marry him."

"And move to California?" Caroline couldn't resist asking.

"Oh, I don't know about that. He's been talking about settling in England, Andrew has become . . . a bit disillusioned with the States, I daresay, and he's contented enough here. We'll see. It's all well in the future, of course."

"Of course. I had no idea that you were so . . . close."

"Yes, well, neither did I. I wasn't sure for the longest time." Emma turned around to face Caroline. "You know, when you were there in Surrey, I'd have said that it was the most impossible thing in the world. But once he told me you'd split up . . ."

"He told you that?"

"Oh, yes, Caroline. Right away, in fact. Just after you left, I should think. He said, 'Caroline needed me for a time, but that's over now.' "

So Andrew had already given up on her before she had ever begun to give up on him. It was very interesting. And it hurt. She smiled cheerfully for Emma instead of acknowledging what was in her heart and said, "Well, it's all water under the bridge now. Have you made arrangements to see him?"

"Oh, yes. We'll take leaves together, that sort of thing, and when we can't I'll just hop down to Surrey or he'll come up here. It's not as though there's not enough room at the manor."

No, thought Caroline. There's enough room here. The only question was whether there would be room for the three of them.

She went up the next morning for a simulation attack. Helen Ferris flew the Aeroméchanique airplane they had dubbed the Messerschmitt, and Caroline flying a Spitfire was supposed to try to avoid her. The weather was, as usual, cold and blustery and terrible, and Caroline wasn't in the mood for it. She had stayed up far too late the night before with a glass of sherry, trying very hard not to think about Andrew and Emma.

Helen almost had her twice before Caroline finally woke up enough to play out some of the maneuvers Pauline had been teaching her, using the flaps to drift up in front of Helen so she was forced to swerve off her attack. If done correctly, it placed the other airplane into a stall, if it had been coming at her with any significant speed. But Helen looped gracefully out and came after her again, and Caroline gritted her teeth and gained some altitude to get Helen off her tail. Caroline reached for the oxygen mask, climbing until she was sure that the Aeroméchanique plane couldn't follow. It was cheating, and they both knew it, but

Caroline was bad tempered enough that morning to do it anyway.

"What kind of nonsense was that?" Despite the cold, Pauline was waiting on the tarmac, not even giving Caroline and Helen a chance to get inside where tea and fruitcake would be waiting. "I've never seen anything so silly in my life."

"I couldn't help it," Caroline said stiffly. "I didn't know what to do."

"I have something to say to you," Pauline responded, motioning Helen to leave. "You came here with quite a reputation and with a number of feats to your credit—notably that night landing you made in London last year in the blackout. I must say I was impressed. But I haven't been particularly impressed with your performance since you've been here. Wake up, Caroline." Pauline's face showed her concern, although her words were harsh. "I think that you can become an excellent pilot. You might even become an outstanding human being, come to that. But you'll need to do a lot of work on your attitude. This isn't Newport, Rhode Island, and who you are doesn't matter in the least to us. What you can *do* is what matters. If you don't learn anything else here, then I hope that you'll learn that."

Caroline sniffed in the wind, her nose running with the cold. "What does any of that have to do with my flying?"

"Ah, well, that's rather the point, isn't it, Caroline? You can't divorce what you do from who you are. You're one person, one whole, marvelous, complicated human being. There's no Caroline the woman, Caroline the pilot, and Caroline' the mother. There's just you, my dear, and what happens to you in any of those spheres is going to affect everything. You need to see that. Life isn't neat, Caroline. Life is messy, and real, and terrible, and bloody exciting." Pauline leaned forward and shook Caroline's shoulder gently. "I want my Ferry Pool to be the best, Caroline. And I hope you'll be a part of it. But you've got to commit yourself to it and you've got a long way to go before you're ready."

"I want to be ready," Caroline said numbly. "I want to be a good pilot. And I want to make a difference, here in England, against the Germans."

"Then wake up, Caroline. Wake up and reach for it. Are you so afraid of success you can't even try?"

Caroline stared at her. Afraid of success? Was that what it was? Did she really undermine everything she did well just so she wouldn't have to test her ability to succeed? ''I don't know,'' she whispered.

''Well, there you are, then. When you do know, you'll be able to fly for me.''

Caroline went in then, to tea and fruitcake and the blessed warmth of a huge fire banked in the dining room. But her thoughts were far from the cheery room. And there were other things to think about as well. Like why she was so afraid to see Andrew again. Especially Andrew with Emma.

Caroline had finally come around to believing in her relationship with Steven, to accepting his love and tentatively to extending him hers when he was killed. It was useless to pretend that that left behind no void, no emptiness, no craving for warmth. Could she have settled back into a relationship with Andrew— Andrew whom she knew so well, whom she had loved, whom she could still love? It would be so easy to bury her grief for Steven in another love.

Perhaps that was what her mother had done, all those years ago. After Philippe was killed, and Amanda left so quickly— Eric told her that it was a matter of weeks before she was gone. Perhaps she had been so overcome and so unable to face her feelings and deal with them that she had had to run away. And she'd run straight into someone else's arms. Marcus Copeland had been that man. Was Caroline now trying to make Andrew into another Marcus Copeland?

She shook her head. Whatever she might believe when she was in a dark mood, she knew she was not her mother. She might have to spend the rest of her life trying to prove it to herself, but she was not her mother. All the things that she had hated about Amanda, despised about her, seemed to be cropping up, one after the other, in her own personality. But I know better, Caroline told herself fiercely. I know better.

Knowing better didn't seem to be of much help in changing her patterns, however. And Caroline realized, as she stretched out her frozen toes to the fire, that changing her patterns was what everybody was talking about. Doing the job she had set out to do. Taking responsibility. Growing up. Excising the selfish, demanding part of her that seemed to come directly from her mother, who had always had what she wanted.

Well, wasn't that true of Caroline, too? Why blame it on Amanda? Every time that something had gone wrong in her life, somebody had been there to rescue her, to patch things up. First

Eric, then Steven. And when she had been emotionally unable to cope with her past and her present, a priest and a psychologist were assigned by her grandmother to rescue her. When things had gone awry in her marriage to Steven, she had run to Andrew. She had never, she realized suddenly, dealt with anything by herself. She had never had to wrestle with any of life's demons on her own. There was always someone there to do it for her. "That's because we're watching over you," Eric would have said, but now she realized that that wasn't what she wanted. That's why she hadn't gone back—after Steven's death. She didn't want Eric and Intraglobal and those Swiss lawyers always there to break her fall. It was time, as Pauline had said, for her to stand on her own and grow up. The thought frightened her a bit, but she was ready.

The first step was to come to terms with her feelings for Steven. Her feelings for him alive, and her feelings about his death. Only then could she look at Andrew with any kind of objectivity. One thing was for certain: She wasn't going to play her mother's game. She wasn't going to go running to Andrew so that he could save her, could keep her from facing her thoughts and feelings about Steven. If there were monsters here, then she had to face them alone. Then—and only then—could she face Andrew. And flying for the Air Transport. God knew if she couldn't deal with her feelings, then she sure as hell wasn't going to be able to deal with any Germans.

Caroline took a deep breath and put down her teacup. At least she had identified the problem. That, as her shrink would have said, was the first step.

For the first time in weeks, she slept soundly that night.

"What we have to do, gentlemen, is work harder on this project. You have all read the material. Our concern is that within the next year or so the German scientific community may well have developed a bomb that would be capable of eliminating an entire city."

One of the men at the long conference table in Intraglobal's Manhattan offices shook his head and looked up at Eric Beaumont. "But *we're* not at war with Germany! What do we care if they do?"

There was a murmur of protest around the table, and Eric held up his hand. "Mr. Schreiber, it is true that we are not at war with Germany, but Japan has signed a mutual-assistance pact with Germany. And I think that we are all aware that it's only a matter of time before the official declaration comes through.''

Still standing, Eric placed his hands on the table and leaned over, speaking softly. ''In the past eighteen months defense contracting—via the Pentagon and with Congress's approval—has increased by two hundred percent. Government contracts for major warships—aircraft carriers, battleships, destroyers, submarines, you name it—have increased by three hundred percent. The Navy shipyards are so backlogged that the government is privately contracting with every available major shipyard in this country. And that's just the beginning, gentlemen. I could say the same thing for airplanes—fighters, bombers, transport planes. I could say the same thing for ground units—tanks, troop transports, amphibious vehicles. And that's not even going into the weapons themselves.'' He straightened up. ''No, gentlemen, there's no question in my mind—nor should there be in yours. We will be going to war with Germany—and soon.''

A portly man sitting near Eric and smoking a cigar shifted uncomfortably in his chair. ''But can such a weapon really exist? Propaganda is a major wartime tactic, let's not forget that. A bomb that could destroy an entire city? Let's be reasonable.''

''I am being reasonable,'' Eric said calmly. ''And I would hardly make such a suggestion on the basis of my own research, gentlemen.'' He took a deep breath. ''Dr. Einstein has drafted a letter which is on its way to the White House, even as we speak. He—and others in the scientific community, Szilard and Teller and Oppenheimer—is terrifically concerned. Germany may be as far as two years ahead of the United States in terms of research and development. Intraglobal has been financing some pioneering efforts, but it's hardly enough.'' He looked around the table. ''Gentlemen, you're not politicians. I appreciate that. You're not scientists. You are members of the business community, and as such I appeal to you. We need to begin a major effort to secure government financing for this project. And we will all benefit from it.''

The men seated around the table were looking dazed. ''I had no idea that this was even going on,'' someone said. Another added, ''A bomb? A bomb to wipe out a whole city?''

The portly man looked at Eric and said simply, ''How?''

Eric rubbed his forehead. ''The principle of the bomb is simple enough.'' He paused long enough to light a cigarette. ''If

matter can be made to disappear, then an equivalent energy
would become available. And more energy, gentlemen, than you
or I can imagine. Billions of times more energy than that released by any other known method. It's called nuclear fission.
They're breaking atoms to release this energy and using uranium
atoms to do it. If it can be held together long enough, and released at precisely the correct moment—"

"Good-bye, New York," said one of the men around the table.

Eric nodded. "Good-bye, New York," he echoed. "Dr. Einstein says that the Germans have stopped the sale of uranium
from the Czechoslovakian mines. The implications are clear,
gentlemen."

"What can we do about it?"

Eric sat down and leaned forward, almost confidentially.
"There is a way to appropriate more money," he said. "President Roosevelt has approved and Congress has created a vehi-
cle—the National Defense Research Committee. They're
researching all kinds of weapons, naturally, but for my money
this"—he jabbed at his paper with his fingers—"is the one to
concentrate on. Intraglobal is one hundred percent behind it."
He paused, letting the implications of that statement sink in.
"And as you all subcontract from Intraglobal, it's in your interests, as well, to lobby for more funding for atomic research via
the NDRC. Especially now."

"Why especially now?"

He stood up again, restless. "Because, like it or not, the Brits
are coming aboard. The President wants them to, and frankly I
can't think of any way of blocking it. Their scientists have been
working on the question, and I must say have made some significant progress. An alliance between our scientific community
and theirs would make great sense just now. Some of their technical know-how, with our financing . . . We could get ahead of
Germany. And, believe me, gentlemen, that *is* the goal. We have
to get ahead of Germany, and when we officially declare war
we'll be able to exercise far superior firepower."

"We'll be in alliance with Great Britain?"

"For the moment, yes. Perhaps only for the moment. We
shall have to wait and see. As I said, this alliance is very important to President Roosevelt, and it does make some sense."
He sounded grudging. "An atomic energy partnership, in view

of perfecting an atomic weapon. It will be satisfactory all around."

He had convinced them. There was some more talk and opinions were aired, but he had convinced them. He could see it in their faces, hear it in their voices. They were his subsidiaries and subcontractors, each powerful and important in his own right. They would raise the voices that Eric needed raised.

Jeffrey Kellogg alone remained behind after the others had left. He took off his glasses with great care, polished them, and replaced them again. "Well," he said finally, "for someone who has had no training whatsoever, I should say that your thespian talents are truly remarkable."

The comment irritated Eric, and he shuffled needlessly through some papers. "What do you mean?"

"You almost had *me* convinced that Roosevelt *talked* you into this alliance business. Sob stuff, there. Stiff upper lip and all— Well, I'm really only doing this because my President wants me to," he parodied. "You sounded just the suitable patriotic note. I was impressed."

"There was no need to be."

"Hmm. Well, just out of curiosity—and since we, too, have our own form of alliance, you and I—why exactly are you pushing so hard for this to go through?"

Eric stopped riffling through his papers and looked up. "You mean you haven't figured it out yet? Good God . . . This is a gold mine we're sitting on, Kellogg. A veritable gold mine. And I want Intraglobal to have a piece of it."

"The lion's share, you mean."

Eric shrugged. "Whatever. The British are ahead of us, and it would be expedient to use their people along with ours. And as long as we have the presidential blessing in the NDRC, we've got to seize the moment."

"An atomic bomb," drawled Jeffrey, "might end the war sooner than it would otherwise. That cuts into profits, you know."

"Those profits are puny compared with what we might be getting into. Wake up, Kellogg! This energy we're talking about—sure it will make bombs. Deadly bombs. Efficient bombs. But I don't particularly care about that. What I care about is what else it can do. Atomic power, Kellogg! Power plants running on splitting atoms." He smiled, a little crookedly. "All in our name, of course."

"Of course. But the stuff sounds pretty unstable to me, Beaumont. Would it be a safe power source?"

"It's unstable as hell. But it's also cheap. It will be in demand." Eric thrust the papers into a folder and stood up. "Maybe it will be safe. Maybe it won't. It *will* make money. And isn't that what matters? Sorry, Kellogg. I have an appointment."

"But—" He was talking to the air. Eric had already left.

"Caroline needs to leave England."

Marc Giroux stood up and walked over to the window, staring out at the busy street below. He had once had a habit of stating the obvious; now he despised it in others. "We've been saying that for months, Eugene. Are we any closer to a solution?"

Eugene Rousseau shook his head. "Monsieur Beaumont has tried to apply pressure. It hasn't worked. Even with her husband killed . . ."

"Madame Asheford," said Soizic softly from the sofa where she sat, "has a very stubborn streak in her. Nothing will get her to do what she does not want to do. She has to make up her own mind."

"Well, it's about time that she did. Hitler's got a revised invasion date," said Rousseau.

"Hitler," said Giroux from the window, "has had revised invasion dates since last July. That was supposed to be the big one, remember? The British, however, didn't cooperate. It seems that Madame Asheford is not the only stubborn person in England."

"What of Captain Starkey?" asked Robert Beneteau. It was the first time he had spoken.

Rousseau shrugged. "We thought he might be killed in the fall, but it didn't happen. A lot of his squadron have been shot down, so there's still a possibility. However, since he's now engaged to Emma Harrington"—Rousseau paused and smiled—"he seems no longer to pose a threat to Madame Asheford."

"But Madame Asheford's continued health is vital." Beneteau caught Giroux's look and shook his head. "No, Marc, I have no illusions about her. She'll never be able to run Intraglobal—it's too massive, and she hasn't got the sense. But Monsieur Beaumont isn't ready for a successor yet. And if Elizabeth Asheford is ever to take over—or better yet, Caroline remarries and bears a son—we need to watch over that family very carefully. If that whole estate goes into proctorship because Madame Asheford meets an untimely death—''

They all sat and gloomily contemplated that possibility. ''It can't happen,'' said Rousseau quietly at last.

''Of course it can't. So let's see if we can get Madame Asheford out of there before the whole country explodes under her, shall we?''

Chapter Twenty-four

Amanda was bored. She still loved Africa, and she still loved her new husband, and she enjoyed being an enigma to everyone who had known her in her past, but the war was making life tiresome, and she was fed up with it all.

There was no relief in sight.

There were no more safaris because the rich people who could afford them before the war were all either fighting it or busy thinking of ways to avoid fighting it. And safaris had become Julian Thackery's life, so he sat around too much, uninterested in the farm, and drank a great deal of gin. There was no question of his being called up, and that was an added blow. If only he could be useful. . . . But even that was denied him, even the possibility of defending his country was out of his reach, so he sat on the wide front porch and drank.

The gin made him bad tempered, and Amanda had never been one to patiently soothe anybody's moods away.

She could go to Newport, of course, except that she had surrendered the mansion on Ocean Avenue to Caroline, and it would never do to go, hat in hand, to her daughter. It was quite out of the question, really. And she ought to stop thinking about it.

Paris was equally out of the question. Where once it had been delightful, it was now occupied by the Germans with their hideous uniforms and terrible manners. Amanda had met quite a few of them, though they had confined themselves mostly to North Africa. Still, there were enough of them interested in the mines to make further forays south, and they considered the Belgian Congo as much theirs as Belgium itself. They had loud voices, and the language they spoke was harsh to the ears, and Amanda avoided them as much as possible. They'd make terrible lovers, she thought, stiff and regimented and humorless.

And so Amanda sat out the rainy season on the veranda with

her husband and his gin and arguments. The letter from Celia came as manna from heaven.

London, England
19 March, 1941

Dearest Amanda,

Well, darling, I do wish that I had some charming things to tell you about London in the springtime, but I really don't. It's so dreary, what with the war still on and all the shortages. You've simply no idea. We haven't seen coffee in so long that I can't remember what it tastes like, and the tea is terrible, though when that goes the whole country will be up in arms, you mark my words. Bread is scarce, butter never seen, and sugar unheard of. Really, darling, it's more that I can bear. And half the time we have to sleep in hideous shelters. I fully expect that one morning I shall wake up next to a rat.

Still, there's a remarkable esprit de corps. It's amazing to see. David was remarking on it, and I thought, well, I shall have to tell Amanda, she'll find it amusing. All of us crowded together all the time. It really starts to make no difference whose father is an earl and whose mother is a charwoman, which is rather a change for stuffy old London, don't you think? I slept next to a priest a few nights ago. He smelled like peppermint, and he blessed me the next morning, even when I told him that I'm an agnostic. "Then I shall bless you twice, my dear lady," he said. "You need it more than the rest of us." Can you imagine? I'll swear there was a twinkle in his eye. That's a new one—priests with a sense of humor.

Well, here I am rattling on, and I still haven't come to the point. Is that a result of age, do you suppose, darling? What a dreary thought. David says that I'm better at fifty than I was at twenty, but he always gets this nervous tic in his cheek when he's lying, so there you are. Anyway, your daughter is here, isn't that extraordinary? I only found out by accident, at Women's Auxiliary. (We're *supposed* to be knitting socks for the troops, but we talk more than we knit, I'm very much afraid.) Pamela Stickland was talking— you remember her, darling, she's the one who wore that frightful gown at her coming-out party, we thought the Yacht Club would never book any of us again, and then she

upped and married a Member of Parliament, so she had to
have more taste than we gave her credit for. She was complaining about this and that, you know how one does, especially with the war on and all, and she said that it would
be all right if one didn't feel so isolated, what with there
being hardly any mail from the States anymore, and no one
really from home to talk to. And then Marjorie Heath-
Bennet chimed in—you don't know her, darling, she's one
of those frightfully serious Englishwomen who always wears
tweeds, but good ones, and probably played hockey for her
school—and she said, oh, there are American girls at Hatfield. And I said, whatever for, and Marjorie said, why,
they're pilots, flying for the Air Transport Auxiliary. That's
a group that delivers airplanes all over the place, darling. I
didn't know about them either until that very moment. She
rattled off some names—I think that she's friendly with Lady
Everard, and they're based at her manor house, or so I'm
told—and I was thinking, ho-hum, don't you know, when
she said Caroline Asheford. Well, as you can imagine, I
perked right up when she said that, and I said, Caroline
Asheford from Newport? And she said whoever else?
Amanda Osbourne's daughter. They hadn't heard about your
latest marriage, darling, in fact some of them thought that
you were still Mrs. Copeland, they're *that* out of date, so I
had to do quite some explaining.

Well, darling, as you can imagine, I didn't just take Marjorie at her word, but I had David do a little investigating.
It's so convenient to be married to him, with all his government connections. And what do you know, it *is* Caroline! Her husband got killed this winter in one of the air
raids in London, but I imagine you know that, and now
she flies for the ATA. Everybody in the world is trying to
get her to leave—that uncle of hers, well, *you* know, Eric
Beaumont, has been sending telegram after telegram telling
her to give it all up and go home, and she won't.

Well, I thought that you'd be frantically interested in all
of that, so I thought I'd just dash off a letter to you, and let
you know. But now, darling, I've got to run—hairdresser's
appointment. Can't let the war interfere with life's neces-
sities, can we?

Do give my love to dear Julian.

                                        Celia Montfort-Hayes

Amanda shook her head over the letter. She smiled, and then shook her head, and then smiled again.

She glanced out to the porch where Julian was sitting, drink in hand. London was his home, after all. It might do him good to go back for a while. It might even, she reflected, give him something to do with his time besides drink.

Amanda looked back at the letter. So Eric wanted Caroline back in the States. She wondered why. And, at the same time, she wondered what she could do to thwart his plans.

Over the winter, they had flown fewer missions.

At the height of the Battle of Britain, in late summer and fall, they had been up four and five times a week—as many times as they could, getting their Spitfires serviced while they ate and slept. Some fellow had come in from General Headquarters, saying something pious about the amount of rest and relaxation necessary in order to maintain one's psychological equilibrium during wartime, but most of the pilots ignored him. If there had been rest and recreation to spare, they would have taken it.

The winter weather had often kept missions grounded, and the horrible intense onslaught of German planes had diminished to a more manageable level. The Germans, after all, had to contend with the same weather conditions as did the British, with the added disadvantage of not flying over home soil. So they flew out now once or twice a week, sometimes even less than that, and for many of them the afternoons on the ground melded in their collective memories into one long gray twilight. It was a twilight of waiting, of countless hands of cards, of gallons of the nondescript ersatz coffee, not knowing at any time when another mission would be scheduled—or another one scrubbed. When any of them looked back on that time, the one thing that they could *not* remember was sunshine. It was as though it had vanished from their lives for the duration.

Andrew's major problem during those winter months was to keep up some sort of morale. He pleaded with headquarters for films, for a change in the food that they ate, anything to give a lift to the routine, but more often than not he was informed, rather coldly, that "Britain is going through a time of shortages, Captain. We can, however, let you have some woolen socks for the men." Whatever shortages England was going through, it was not in the nimble fingers of women who knitted for the troops. Andrew could picture them—a maiden aunt, a gentle nun, the newsstand dealer's wife, all of them adding to the piles and piles of warm woolen clothing for the troops. He smiled. Thank God for maiden aunts.

He knew that Caroline Asheford was flying for the ATA, and he wasn't sure he was so pleased with the idea. Naturally, he worried about Emma. During the winter, it hadn't seemed to matter. The ATA couldn't, after all, be flying in the horrible weather that was keeping British and German pilots alike grounded, and so he relaxed, even wrote letters to Emma complaining about the lack of rations and movies, confident that she must be thinking about the same things.

What he didn't know—and what Emma didn't tell him—was that even when fighter pilots were grounded, the ATA went on. The feeling in upper management was that there were no Germans around, so the skies were relatively empty, and it made sense to deliver airplanes to their destinations in time for them to take off when the weather cleared. They didn't fly when the wind was hurricane force, or when it was snowing, but that was about all. All through those gray twilight days of winter, when the RAF sat around and played cards, the ATA was up delivering planes.

By spring the number of RAF missions increased again.

They were hell. It didn't matter how many times they had trained, or how mentally prepared they were for flying into a battle situation, or even the knowledge that their entire *raison d'étre* involved flying fighter planes. It still was hell. The fear, the horrible grinding fear left them feeling sweaty and nauseated, and then, immediately after takeoff, the internal lift, the exhilaration which told them better than any radar screen that they were, indeed, about to engage. During the fight itself, instinct took over and their thought processes were left far behind. There was simply no time to think. There was time only for each pilot to fly and to shoot, to evade—and to pray with the back of his mind that he wasn't going to die.

Andrew came to know those feelings well. He lived with the fear, and the excitement, and the sickness. And he, who had never seriously prayed about anything in his life, found himself addressing whatever Maker he had on a far more regular basis.

It was easier, Andrew realized, for his men. For them it was a simple matter of good versus bad, us versus them. The Nazis were evil people doing evil things, and they had a moral obligation to stop them. He had felt that way, himself, once. In those days patriotism shone like a star, and getting up there and getting another Jerry was all that counted. But he had gone beyond that. . . . He had begun to understand more, to lift a mere corner of a very large curtain he had never even known existed, and what he was finding out was tarnishing that patriotic pride.

More and more, he found himself wondering if he and his men—and his German opposite and *his* men—were anything more than marionettes in a game that was bigger than any of them could imagine. If decisions he made held anything other than momentary importance. More and more, he questioned whether the war was being fought for freedom—or for another, more ominous reason.

The answers were not to be found in England, that much he knew. They were to be found in California, in the formal boardrooms frequented by his uncle, the massive corporate worlds of Johnson Industries and Intraglobal. That was where the real decisions were being made and the outcome of the war was being determined. Andrew was more than ever certain of his facts. He had written some letters home: personal letters, which Jeffrey Kellogg would never have occasion to read, but which asked pointed questions. He didn't like the answers.

But he had a job, an obligation and responsibility to his squadron, and to the dream that hadn't quite died inside of him. It was here that he was destined to fulfill his role in the drama that was being played out.

Caroline Asheford was part of that murky corporate world, and he knew now that that was one of the reasons he had let her return to her husband. He hadn't fully understood his thoughts when he had sent her away. Then he had still held on to the hope of a future together. But soon after, he had come to see that Caroline had been right when she said they couldn't ignore their respective positions with Intraglobal and Johnson Industries. She had wanted no part of Intraglobal; she had always been clear about that. He had to grant her honesty. But . . . things changed, and people with them. He wasn't certain he could trust her to remain free of that world, and in any case Caroline would forever remind him of it all, simply by virtue of who she was. Because of who she was, he would never be able to forget who *he* was.

Thank God Emma was different. She was simple and straightforward, innocent of all of those dangerous undercurrents in his world. Andrew smiled to himself. When this was all over, they would marry and retire to some quiet corner in the English countryside and take up sheep farming. Or something.

In the meantime, though, it was enough to simply know that she, alone perhaps in his not-so-innocent world, could be trusted.

He thought about that all the time, as the spring ripened into another rainy English summer, and his squadron reached farther out over Europe for the elusive German fighter planes.

In June they were serving almost primarily as escorts, as Churchill ordered out the bombers to fly missions into Germany itself. The Germans had radar—it was nowhere near as sophisticated or accurate as the British installations on the coast, but even the few rudimentary dishes that did exist would pick up something as large as a bomber formation, and so there was fighter escort provided, even on the night runs.

Mostly the expeditions were uneventful. The Germans didn't have time to scramble a unit before the British were on their way out again, although Andrew did see one bomber hit and go down in flames. At that moment he felt a cold shiver of fear down his spine, just as if somebody were pouring ice water down his back. He knew how people died in bombers; the gun turrets became a kind of inferno and screaming agony was the gunner's last taste of life, and he counted it as a personal failure, a personal responsibility.

"You can't carry too much weight around with you," Emma said on the telephone later that night when he called her. "Other people have shoulders, too, you know."

But Emma's words were not enough. He got drunk that night in the small operations room, drinking neat Rannoch whiskey and hearing those screams in his mind, over and over again. He had begun to hate not only what he did, but who he was becoming.

In late June they were returning from a bombing run to Nuremberg. They'd been successful, and the pilots all had had a chance to catch their breath and relax on the return trip. With relaxation came the inevitable gallows humor. "Mick, I thought he had you there!"

"Him? Nobody would have him but his mother!"

Andrew depressed his transmitter button. "All right, guys, calm down. We're not over friendly territory yet."

"Friendly territory? How friendly can you get? Captain, I

could tell you stories about how friendly those French girls were before the war—"

Appreciative chuckles came from some of the men in the formation. "I had a girl in Paris once. . . ."

"Get that, guys? Even Smith had a girl in Paris!"

"That's nothing. *Everyone's* had a girl in Paris once."

Andrew frowned, but he wasn't seriously worried. They had to blow off steam, and there were few enough German fighter bases in France. Someday, he was thinking, we'll all get together and talk about all these fictitious girls we once had, and—

There was a shadow flickering fast over his left wingtip and the thump of his air current being disrupted, and then a Junkers fighter pulled out fast, climbing. One of Andrew's men was screaming into the radio, "Jesus Christ! Where did they come from?"

"Stay calm," Andrew ordered tersely, looking around quickly. A whole formation, God damn it. "You know what to do, guys."

"Yeah . . . Watch out, Carter, you've got one on your tail!"

Another voice: "I've got him in my sights, it's all right. . . ." And then the German plane was spiraling down and down and down, with black smoke pouring out of it. "Yeah, Gleason!"

"Catch that one, Captain?"

Andrew didn't bother to reply. He was too busy diving out of the way of the Junkers that he had turned and was trying to get him in his sights.

He looped away to the left—there wasn't any sun to contend with—and came back under the plane, counting on the Spitfire's maneuverability to win the day. But he was tired; he hadn't slept in over twenty-eight hours and even the best of pilots loses an edge when he's been in command for that long with so little sleep. Andrew was a good commanding officer and a good pilot. He wasn't a miracle worker.

There was another Junkers, above, waiting for him.

He hadn't seen it. It was the one fundamental thing that he had been taught, and that he himself taught to his recruits: Keep looking around you. Never assume that just because you have somebody in your sights it doesn't mean that somebody else might have you in their sights. He had made that fatal assumption because he was tired, because he was heartsick, because he had begun to ask the questions that a military man must never ask, the terrible questions of why and wherefore. Those questions distracted him from the task at hand. They make the possible seem impossible, and that is no way to win a war. To win a war, to be the kind of fighting machine that is needed in order to score victories, you must not think, must not question, must not dream up hypotheses. You must simply command and obey, and leave the historians to sort all the rest out later. Andrew Starkey had begun to think, and when he did he lost his edge. In a sense, in that sense, his destruction was inevitable.

He hadn't seen the Junkers, and then it was too late, because it was curling in behind him in a long graceful dive that would land it on his tail. Even as he desperately rolled the Spitfire out in an attempt to escape, he knew that it was over, that there was no time for a last message, no time even for a last thought—time only for regrets.

The Spit shuddered as the cannon fire reached it, and the controls on the instrument panel went wild. The stick was nearly wrenched out of his hands as the plane staggered across the sky.

He waited to die.

For some reason, the Junkers wasn't coming in for the kill. The explosion that Andrew was waiting for never happened, and he realized, with a dawning of hope, that he might still have a chance. A fuel line had been hit, and the motor was dead. The Spitfire didn't have a chance. But he still did.

He reached for the cockpit canopy release. It seemed jammed, and the panic mounted inside of him as the Spitfire started to dive, straight down toward the ground which was approaching faster and faster and faster. Then the cockpit cover slid back, and he was fighting the wind and the air pressure to get out. His beloved plane was going to be his coffin if he didn't get out.

And then he had pushed himself free of the cockpit and was falling alone through the night sky. He couldn't see anything under him. He had no idea how far up he still was. He pulled on the chute cord and felt the inevitable moment of panic when he was sure that it wouldn't open, that it couldn't possibly open, and then suddenly it was open and dragging him back up into the night sky.

Away to his right there was a tongue of flame. Good-bye, Spitfire, Andrew thought sadly. We had some good times together. And someone will write you off as a number on a column of numbers.

Below him, there were patches of blackness darker than the blackness around them, and he started to peer around. Someplace to land. Someplace, preferably, where there was a nice soft field and . . .

Trees. He cursed and desperately pulled at the parachute lines, but it was too late to guide it much of anywhere and there didn't seem to be anywhere to guide it. All of France spread out under me, Andrew thought, and I have to come down in the middle of a damned forest. The branches were rushing up at him now, and he bent his knees and brought his hands up to protect his face, and then the branches came up under him, scraping his body, grabbing at his chute. He was dragged down through the tree until the chute snagged and caught and held. Andrew took a deep breath and pulled his gloved hands away from his face. Great. Just great. Dashing Captain Starkey, swinging high in a tree.

He couldn't stay there long. Someone would see the bonfire made by his Spitfire, and they would come looking. Chances were, in occupied France, that it wouldn't be anyone too friendly.

He winced. That was the problem with being a pilot. The pilot felt invincible up there in the sky, spreading death and destruction from afar, but the people he had been shooting at didn't take too kindly to that kind of treatment and tended to be less than hospitable when the pilot dropped out of the sky. Whoever was here on the ground, he didn't particularly want to meet up with them.

Every muscle in his body was aching, and a gash on his arm was throbbing with fiery pain. He reached up to the chute lines above him, and pulled himself up by sheer force of his arm muscles until he could reach one of the branches above his head. It snapped as soon as he put some weight on it, and he winced in pain as his other arm took all of the force of his body. The second branch was better, stronger, and he pulled himself up and onto it.

Reaching into his belt, his fingers closed around the knife that he kept sheathed there and, still perched like a monkey on his branch, he hacked and sawed away at the chute lines. They were strong. A few minutes ago, he had been profoundly grateful for that fact. Now he mumbled and swore as he wasted precious seconds, precious minutes cutting those lines.

Getting free of the parachute wasn't enough. It might be dark now, but the sun would eventually rise, and his parachute would still be hanging there—signaling to the Germans that a pilot had dropped to safety. He pulled at it, trying to move it down into his reach, thinking that he could bury it somewhere and then be on his way, but it defied him. He couldn't see the damned thing, which was awkward, and every twig and branch seemed to have conspired to keep it stuck up where it was. It was no good. He wasn't going to be able to bring it down.

He switched his attention to the tree itself, a strong poplar. Here at least he could do something. He worked his way over to the trunk and as gently as possible let himself slide down, from branch to branch, hands and feet scrabbling for a hold. He jumped the last eight feet, landing at last on the nice soft ground that he had fantasized about on the way down. It was tempting to just sit there, take a nap, wait until morning to see where he was and where he should be going, but waiting could be deadly. Wearily he got to his feet and started feeling his way out of the copse.

It was only about eight hundred yards long, but it felt like eight thousand, with hidden branches reaching out to scratch his face and grab at his arms, with roots rising up to trip him, with strange noises at his back, mocking his steps.

And then he was free of the trees and out into a field, an orchard of some sort. He narrowed his eyes until he had it. Grapes. A vineyard. Well, that placed him somewhere in northwestern France. If he was right about where they had been when the Junkers attacked, probably somewhere just past Paris. That wouldn't be so bad. He could probably work his way west to Le Havre, and then find somebody on the coast to ferry him across to England. For a price, naturally. But he would work that out when the time came.

A pale moon was emerging from behind some clouds, and Andrew reached into a pocket of his flying suit for the map and compass that were part of the standard survival kit for RAF flyers. The map wasn't going to do him much good, not until he had a bearing on where he was, but he wanted to be sure that they were there. A security blanket.

Andrew took a bearing with the compass and started skirting the vineyard, stopping when the moon grew brighter, flattening his body against the small dwarflike trees, blending his shadow with theirs. He wasn't good at this. He hadn't been trained by the OSS; he wasn't Special Services—just a pilot. He didn't see anyone watching him, but he didn't know if that was only because he didn't know what to look for, what to listen for. As silently and inconspicuously as possible, he kept heading west, hoping to reach a village that was identifiable on his map, from which he could take a bearing.

Whenever he stopped he was aware, acutely aware, of the exhaustion he was beginning to feel. It was sapping his strength and making him careless. He had been exhausted after the bombing run to Nuremberg, that was why he had been hit by the Junkers in the first place, and the parachute jump, the fear of being seen, the miles he was slowly and steadily creeping across the countryside were robbing him of any inner resource he thought that he might possess. His enemy was not the foreign countryside. His enemy was not even the unseen German patrols which would put an end to his military career in one fell swoop. His enemy was the tiredness that urged him, in a voice that was becoming more and more seductive, to simply stop, to find a thicket or a tree and lie down, to let his weary limbs and aching muscles rest. To sleep . . . finally sleep . . .

Andrew shook his head, as though he could dislodge the thoughts. He had to reach a village. He had to figure out where he was and find someplace safe before he could even think of stopping. He was by a road, unmarked but showing signs of being well traveled, lined with the ubiquitous poplar trees. It ran west, and west he went with it, staying by the edge, ready to fling himself into the ditch at any moment. For the first hour he saw no one, stumbling along, pacing himself, shrinking into the shadow of a tree whenever the moon broke free of the clouds. The cold was starting to get to him, too. June nights could be deceptively chilly, and his flying suit had been ripped by the fall and the tree. He was shivering almost constantly, and his steps were getting shorter and more erratic.

By the time the false dawn was lightening the sky he really felt ill. Twice he had had to duck into the ditch when he had heard airplanes, although he had never seen the planes themselves. Once he had nearly hurt himself clinging to a tree at the last moment when a German patrol car sped by, going east. He sat for a moment after that, waiting for his eyes to readjust to the darkness after the glare of the headlights, and then he forced himself wearily to his feet and trudged on. Several times he saw scattered farmhouses, none of them with lights on, but that made sense, the German government had imposed a curfew, with fines and punishments for lights found on after eleven.

The sky darkened again after that, and then in an instant, dawn was really upon him. The birds all around burst out into a cacophony of song, and the sky behind him lightened in riotous shades of pink and blue. Andrew looked around him, panicking. He crept away from the road, to a wall and hedgerow defining the fields that ran by the road.

Then, finally, when he was just giving up hope, he saw a sign. He was twenty-three kilometers away from Rouen. Andrew had never seen a more welcome sight in his life. To know where he was, to not be proceeding in a blind nightmare world, was more of a relief than anything he could ever have calculated.

He knew where he was. Now all that he had to do was to figure out how to get to Le Havre. How to reach the coast, and from there to England. . . .

He stopped for a few minutes, hidden from the road by a boundary wall, and took his last chocolate bar from his pocket. He ought to conserve it, he knew, but he was too tired, too hungry, too overwhelmed to think very far ahead. As the sun crept around to the wall where he sat, he tipped his head back to rest . . . just for a moment . . . just to close his eyes . . .

Caroline banked the Mosquito fighter to the left and peered through her goggles. Farnsworth Field, just where it was supposed to be, and she was even on time. That was unusual these days. More often than not, bad weather or the long trips that were often lengthened to avoid enemy aircraft made the ATA pilots late with their cargos. But today she was on time. It was exciting to be flying the brand-new Mosquito, to be the first pilot to deliver one, and absurdly exciting to be delivering it precisely when and where she was supposed to.

She landed almost perfectly. She liked the Mosquito, it handled well, tight and neat and somehow reminiscent of her own Butterfly, still languishing in a hangar outside of London. It was the first of the line, a prototype, the beginning of what people were claiming would change the tide of the war.

Three men in overcoats and military boots were waiting for her, and they rapidly strode out across the field to greet her. They were polite as only the English can be, but she could see that they were eager to spend time with the Mosquito, not with her.

"Well, then, Mrs. Asheford . . ."

She smiled. "It's everything that they said it was, Wing Commander. You'll enjoy flying it."

"Thank you so very much. And we have more arriving?"

"Tomorrow. Thirty of them, I think."

"Right. Right." He rubbed his hands together. "Well, then, if there isn't anything else . . ."

She flushed slightly. "Well, actually, if you could arrange a ride for me to the nearest railroad station, it would be helpful. I need to get back to Hatfield."

"Of course. Of course." The wing commander turned to one of the other men. "Johnson?"

"Yes, sir?"

"Arrange tea for Mrs. Asheford, and have her driven to the station, won't you?"

"Yes, sir."

Caroline picked up her gear and followed him, feeling bulky and awkward in her flying suit. She carried everything with her—parachute, overnight and emergency items, helmet. Lugging so much gear around made sense, but it was dreadfully awkward as far as practical implementation was concerned.

Caroline accepted the tea gratefully and drank thirstily, nibbling on fruitcake and scones and telling Flying Officer Johnson, between mouthfuls, about the Mosquito's performance. Finally he had her driven to yet another dreary railroad station to await a train. She had grown, in the past four months, wearily accustomed to trains.

The ATA delivered planes. What its pilots did in order to get back to their ferry pools depended entirely on their own resources.

Caroline fell asleep on the train, lulled by the hypnotic click-click of the wheels on the tracks, and dreamed once again of the house on the beach. She walked up to it slowly, aware as she walked of the wind blowing sand around on the dunes, bending the scrubby bushes with its force. She walked slowly up to the house, a small single-story structure. The windows were all open, but there was nothing but darkness within them. Lace curtains were blowing around each window.

She went around to the front of the house, to the open front door, and stepped hesitantly over the threshold. There was a room on her left, the only furnished room in the house, with a thick Oriental carpet in red tones. The walls were lined with bookcases. Caroline walked into the room.

There was a large oaken desk, and a very large, very fat man sitting behind the desk. He stood up as Caroline entered and walked slowly around the desk, putting out his pudgy hand for hers. As though hypnotized, unable to resist, Caroline gave him her hand. He looked at the large ruby ring on her finger and, taking a knife in his other hand, cut off her finger in order to remove the ring.

She must have cried out, for the next thing she knew she was back in the railway carriage, with the conductor bending anxiously over her. "Miss! Miss, wake up!"

"What is it?" Caroline looked around her, startled.

"Nightmare, sounds like," he said. "No wonder. We've all got nightmares these days, miss." He held out a glass of water. "Here, drink this, it'll put you right side up."

She drank it obediently, and smiled for him. "Thank you so much. I'm all right now."

He wobbled down the narrow corridor, and she watched him go. It was months—no, years now since she had had that dream. It had started when she was a child, just after her stepfather had raped her. She had had it frequently after that, but as the years passed the dream receded. She couldn't remember the last time she had dreamed it. The colors were as vivid, the feelings the same—fear, nausea, the sense of being so heavy that she could not control her own movements.

Her psychologist had had a lot to say about that dream. He had been fascinated with it, with the symbolism he saw entwined in her childish imaginings. He had spoken to her of her passivity, of her need to go back into the womb but finding that there was nothing for her there. She had listened to him carefully, but it had made no difference. For Caroline, the dream was sheer terror. And she believed that every time she dreamed it something terrible happened to her.

Or to someone she knew.

The train clattered on, and she sat staring out of the window without seeing anything. It had begun to rain—part of her mind, detached, noted that the other girls were going to have a hard time delivering the rest of the Mosquitos if the weather held— and the water ran in long flowing rivulets down the window-panes. Caroline stared past them out to the sodden fields and darkened horizon, the occasional cow or house flicking past as though in a newsreel film. Her heart was keeping pace with the clatter of the wheels on the tracks.

Something terrible was going to happen. And, with the war on, there was no shortage of possibilities for disaster, of recipes of doom.

Finally the train pulled into the station and Caroline, still dazed, gathered up her gear and slid down the steps, feeling awkward and bulky and miserable.

From somewhere off to her left, she heard a voice.

"Good God, there she is. Caroline, darling, I never thought I'd have to say this to you, but you look simply ghastly, dear. Why on earth can't they design something for you to wear that's more attractive? Even Sarah found that she could look lovely and still fly, and I can't see why on earth you can't too."

Caroline stopped, not turning, her heart pounding. She didn't need to look around in order to identify the voice. It was, quite simply, unforgettable. And to come straight out of the blue, and coupled with her dream like that . . . Something awful *was* going to happen. She was sure of it now. She turned slowly to face the harbinger of disaster.

"Hello, Mother," she said very quietly. And then burst into tears.

Chapter Twenty-five

At the German Air Command Station outside of Paris, the Junkers had all landed safely. All that were there to land, that is. Two were lost: Rolf Detweiler and Jurgen Hoffmann. They would be hard to replace.

The commander, still wearing his flying suit, the imprint of his goggles marking his face, strode directly from his airplane into the command center, where he knew that the *Feldkommandatur* would be waiting.

The *Feldkommandatur* was sitting at his desk, looking at a map of northern France. He glanced up sharply when the commandant entered. "Well?"

"We got him, sir," he said, his voice level, his back ramrod stiff.

The *Feldkommandatur* glanced at the other person in the room, a portly man in civilian clothes. "You are sure that it was Captain Starkey?"

"Yes, sir. We made sure afterwards by listening to the exchanges between the other pilots in the unit. It definitely was him, sir."

"Good." Again the glance at the man in the corner, and now the young pilot began to feel nervous, too. Whoever he was, he carried weight. Gestapo? God, I hope not, he prayed fervently.

The man stirred, as though feeling all of the thoughts aimed his way. "Did his airplane explode?" he asked.

"Not in the air." He didn't know whether or not to add "sir," and waited a moment too long. "It went into a dive and exploded on impact."

"Was there time for him to bail out?" His accent was very precise, almost too formal. He spoke the German of one who had rigorously studied the rules at school, not grown up speaking the language. Some local authority?

"Possibly." He was now feeling exceedingly uncomfortable. What if, after all, he had botched the whole thing?

The gentleman in civilian clothes turned to the *Feldkommandatur.* "May I suggest a search of the area? Just to make sure?"

"Of course." The *Feldkommandatur* was cooperation itself. "I will have it ordered immediately." He glanced up and dismissed the young commandant. "Well done, Strasser. You may go now."

The pilot clicked his heels together and turned for the door, none the wiser. But such was life in the Luftwaffe, he thought philosophically. As he closed the door, he could hear the *Feldkommandatur* saying, "We will search within a fifty-mile radius of the crash site, Monsieur Giroux. Rest assured, if there is something to find, we will find it. . . ."

They had located a site.

Eric had initially indicated a preference for California. He liked to have everything under his nose, under his control. But the scientists had talked him out of it. They wanted the desert.

They needed to farm out the various stages of the project, and Eric, with Jeffrey Kellogg practically breathing over his shoulder, had assured himself that the various companies chosen were either already Intraglobal subsidiaries, or were susceptible to buyout. There had been a great many cries of protest by small companies during that spring of 1941, but Eric got his way. Directly or indirectly, he was going to both control and profit by the manufacturing of an atomic bomb.

There were two places, initially, that he had in mind: Oak Ridge, Tennessee, as a site for a uranium separation plant; and Los Alamos, New Mexico, for the bomb laboratory itself.

The law firm was resisting the idea of Intraglobal's concentration on this nuclear experiment. Rousseau was dispatched from Zurich to remonstrate with Eric: Was this really necessary? The money that was coming in from manufacturing airplanes was steady and, in fact, quite overwhelming. Intraglobal had come up with some interesting new designs, and Eugene Rousseau was confident that if Eric continued to concentrate his efforts in this direction there would be many more aviation breakthroughs. Why should Eric diversify to such an extent? And why take such a personal interest in this particular diversification?

Eric listened patiently to all of Rousseau's complaints, then took him to lunch in Berkeley, where he introduced the lawyer to the young professor whose career Eric had been following with such interest. Rousseau listened to Oppenheimer, and later he listened to Szilard, and he came back to San Jose almost convinced.

Eric spoke with some passion about the project.

"Don't you see, Eugene? All of this is beyond my grasp. I understand what's happening here, but I could never in a thousand years have originated any of this myself. That is why I am so enthralled with it." Eric lit a cigarette and began to pace the office, making Rousseau, who was sitting down, swivel around to watch him. "When I started, all of my work was original. Oh, I collaborated here and there, with Hugo Junkers, for instance, but mostly it's been original. I felt as though there was nothing that I couldn't do, nothing I couldn't create. Do you remember when I first moved out here what they called me? What Edward called me? The 'French wonder-boy,' everyone said. And I believed them. I thought that I could do it all."

"Well," Rousseau said drily, "you have done quite a bit, haven't you? Intraglobal is as close to owning the worldwide corporate state as anyone is ever likely to come."

"Owning, yes. God, I own more than I keep up with! And the power, and the control . . . It's heady stuff, Eugene. But do you think for a moment that I wouldn't exchange it all for those days when I could create? When I could make ideas happen?" He paused at the desk and ground out his cigarette in the ashtray, leaning against the edge of the desk as he faced Rousseau. "We've just come out with a new fighter plane in England—well, one of our subsidiaries has."

"Right," Rousseau said warmly. "The Mosquito."

"Yes. Do you think, Eugene, that I designed it? That I had anything to do with designing it? Or that I worked personally on the Messerschmitt, or the Stuka, or the Spitfire? They all have my name on them in one way or another. But I didn't design them. I didn't even have final approval on the designs, for God's sake, not because it wasn't offered, but because I knew that it wouldn't make any difference. They aren't mine! I've lost my touch, Eugene. I've lost it."

"You're very busy. It's a busy time. Perhaps if—"

"Don't patronize me, for Christ's sake. Please don't patronize me. We've known each other too long and too well for you to start doing that." Eric took a deep breath. "I've gotten away from the fundamentals, from what Aeroméchanique once was.

Well, that's all right: We're not Aeroméchanique or even A.R.M.
anymore, and I'm not the same person I was twenty years ago,
either." He shook another cigarette out of his pack and lit it.
"But now—for the first time in years—I feel *excited* about something, Eugene. I feel the same way that I did back in the stables
of the Château de Montclair when Philippe and I used to experiment with motorcars. On the edge, Eugene. We're on the brink
of something so important that the world will sit up and take
notice. And I love that feeling. God, I *need* that feeling. That's
why I have to keep working on this."

"But it sounds as though the scientists have it covered. . . ."

"Of course they do." Eric's voice was impatient. "Do you
honestly think that I can compete with these people? With Einstein? Don't be ridiculous." He strode over to the window and
stood with his back to Rousseau, drawing in on his cigarette. "I
didn't even go to college, Eugene. You know that. Everything I
know, I've learned on my own, taught myself. It's gotten me this
far, and don't think that I'm not grateful to be here. Me, the
farrier's son." He permitted himself a smile that Rousseau
couldn't see. "I don't even begin to measure up to their expertise, their knowledge, their creativity. But to be part of it all,
Eugene! Just to be part of this kind of work! A year of it is worth
ten spent in this office."

"Not to the firm," Rousseau said drily.

"Intraglobal will take care of the firm. I need to do this for
myself." He turned back to face the lawyer. "Besides, I have a
feeling about this atomic energy. There are a lot more possibilities than just a bomb at stake."

Rousseau raised an eyebrow. "Lucrative possibilities?"

Eric smiled. "What other kind are there?"

Andrew awoke with a start just before noon. The sun was up
and shining almost directly down on him. With a sudden plung-
ing feeling in his stomach he remembered where he was.

He looked around him sharply, but he could see nothing out
of place. He was leaning against a weathered stone wall, broken
here and there, the gaps filled in with trailing lilac bushes. There
was a field in front of him, with cattle and sheep grazing together
at some anemic tufts of grass. Andrew wondered fuzzily why, in
occupied France, there were so many of them, and looking
so sleek. But he had more important things on his mind first.

Such as finding his way home.

He pulled himself to his feet, cautiously looking around him before climbing over the low wall and back onto the road. He was heading for Rouen, and after Rouen for Le Havre, and after Le Havre . . . next stop, London, Andrew thought. London and the Savoy Grill. London and Emma. London and . . .

These thoughts were getting him nowhere. He scowled at the road, and at the sun, and at the road again, before setting off.

The first car drove by after about fifteen minutes. Sleek and black, it came from the west, traveling fast. Andrew flattened himself against a tree, but the precaution was unnecessary. At that speed, no one would have noticed him. The second came from behind him, approaching slowly and with the unmistakable noise of a diesel truck engine. Andrew dove for the stone wall, and the truck passed by.

Three hours later, he was still trudging along. The tiredness had seeped from his muscles into his bones, the incredible weariness that spoke only of stopping, never of going on. All that mattered was to find something to eat, a bed with clean sheets . . .

Stop it, he told himself again. Stop it, right now. You'll have all that and more, but you've got to keep your wits about you now. But it had been hours since he had eaten, and the nap in the shadow of the wall had done nothing to relieve the bone-deep weariness that he was feeling. He was going to have to restore his strength, or he wasn't going on at all.

Another hour, and he knew that he must be approaching the outskirts of Rouen. Best to find something to eat, and then a safe place to sleep for a while. He would go on once it turned dark. He knew that traveling by day was not only dangerous, it was in all probability suicidal. There were German patrols everywhere. It was sheer luck that he hadn't been picked up by one yet.

There was a café up ahead. He could see it now, the French he had learned long ago in high school coming to the surface. Café du Chemin. *Chemin*—road. Well, he was on the road, wasn't he? It seemed appropriate. And he had some money in his pocket—English money, but surely worth as much as the deutsche marks that the Germans around here would be using for payment.

It was dangerous. He knew that. Stopping to lean against a tree, he considered the possibilities. There was still no sign of life, which was odd. Surely there should be people about at this hour, doing their shopping, children going to school? The open door of the café beckoned. And now he could smell something: the odor of fresh bread, and of something frying, wafting over the still air. His stomach rumbled in response.

He had to eat. It was that simple. In order to go on, he had to eat. It was dangerous, but he would have to take the risk. He didn't know anything about living on the run in a foreign country. They had taught pilots survival techniques earlier on, but that was in the regular RAF. Andrew's squadron had formed later. He had no idea what he was doing. He could only listen to his intuition, and it was telling him, now, that he had to eat.

Taking a deep breath, he crossed the street and paused for only a moment before he walked into the Café du Chemin.

It was dark inside, particularly after the brightness of the sun, and for a few moments, Andrew stood by the door waiting for his eyes to adjust to the gloom inside. A long bar of dark oak ran the length of the room, the usual collection of bottles behind it, a polished espresso machine taking pride of place at the end. There were only a few tables, the small round ones which were customary in French cafés—he remembered that from his old French classes, too; it was amazing the things that one stored away in one's mind—and only two of them were occupied. Over by the window sat two old men, berets on their heads, wearing heavy cardigans despite the warmth of the weather. One of them was smoking a pipe. At another table sat a lone man, younger, more rotund, concentrating exclusively on the omelet in front of him. That was what Andrew had smelled from the street. Behind the bar stood a girl, polishing glasses. She couldn't have been over twenty. Pretty, Andrew thought, with a worried look on his face.

No one had jumped when he came in. No one had shouted for the police. No one, in fact, seemed to be paying much attention to him. He let out a long breath of relief. Until that moment, he hadn't realized that he had been holding it in.

He walked over to the bar, smiled his most winning smile for the girl, and asked, "Sandwich?" hoping that the word was the same in French, or at least comprehensible to her. She had dark blue eyes, almost violet, and porcelain-white skin, he noticed even while he worried about what her response would be.

The eyes widened and she said, almost under her breath, "*Anglais?*"

Andrew nodded. "I'm hungry," he said, keeping his voice low, hoping again that she would understand what he was asking for.

She didn't, but she seemed to have other things on her mind. *"Attendez,"* she said in a low voice. *"Attendez ici."*

"What?" Andrew asked. "I don't understand." But she was gone, ducking behind a curtain at the rear of the bar.

He turned around slowly, his back to the bar, and looked at the other people in the room. They were still not showing any interest in him, an almost studied indifference, he thought. He compressed his lips. Maybe this had been a mistake. Maybe . . .

"Monsieur?" said a voice behind him, and he turned to see that the girl was back. Next to her stood a middle-aged man, slightly swarthy of complexion, with gray hair and eyebrows, and in his hand was a gun, an ancient fowling piece that looked as though it had not seen service in years.

Andrew looked from it to the girl. "I meant nothing," he said. "I'm only hungry."

"Your name, please?" It was the man speaking. His English, though heavily accented, was impeccable.

Andrew couldn't decide what to do. Surely, he thought, a man who spoke English so well wouldn't turn him in. France might be an occupied country, but its citizens weren't Germans.

Finally, he spoke. "Captain Andrew Starkey of the Royal Air Force," he said. "My airplane was shot down—"

Both the girl and the man began showing signs of alarm, and the man gestured quickly with the gun toward the curtained doorway. "You must get out of sight. Go in here, please."

Andrew hesitated. Was it his imagination, or had all of this been a little too easy, too simple? The first roadhouse he came to and someone who spoke English was eager to shelter him, to hide him from sight? And why on a day when there should have been people about, soldiers on patrol, was there no one to be seen?

The man was impatient. "Quickly!" he insisted. "There are Germans about! Come in here, you will be safe."

The girl was watching him, biting her lower lip, twisting her apron in her hands. Andrew took a deep breath. He had little enough choice in the matter: Take his chances here, or surely die out there when his strength was finally sapped. He chose to take his chances.

He ducked in through the doorway, and the curtain fell closed behind him.

There had been people staying in the stables for more than three nights in a row.

Chantale was concerned because they should not have been there for so long. The courier who was to escort them to the coast was two days late. It could mean anything; there were many reasons for delays these days, but she feared the worst.

The people in her stables were Jews.

They had been sent by Dominique. "Terrible things are going to happen to them, Chantale," he told her, passion burning in his face like a flame. "Already they are being told to wear a yellow Star of David on their sleeves so that the Germans know who are the Jews. And worse things are coming for them. They have to be our priority, Chantale. They have to be!"

Chantale watched his eyes in puzzlement. "Everybody wants to get out of France. Why are these people so special?"

"Because Hitler seems to think so."

She had never met a Jew before, and when the first group of them came—an extended family of father, mother, children, an uncle, a grandmother—she herself took them supper in the loft where they huddled together for warmth. Their blessing over the food was in a strange, guttural language that she had never heard, but their conversation was as ordinary as anyone else's. Chantale listened for a while before leaving them. Later, she said to Dominique, "I can't imagine why he wants them in particular. They're just like everybody else."

After that family came another, and then an eminent professor who was very much in demand. The courier always arrived on time for them all. He was expensive—it was worth 60,000 francs to get people out of France—but there were always means to pay. Families sold all their belongings, and Chantale almost always made up the difference.

"Household expenses have risen," observed Marie-Louise at dinner one night, and Chantale shrugged.

"Prices have, too."

"Hmm," said her mother-in-law. "Well, see that it stays within reason."

It didn't, but Marie-Louise never mentioned the money again. Pierre didn't notice. He had always left the running of the household up to his mother and his wife, and was less interested than ever in domestic concerns.

Pierre's love for Isabelle Vivier had grown in the shadow of her rejection into something sick and obsessive. He still went into Angers, daily, following her around, from rendezvous to rendezvous. He watched her as she closed her studio—early these days—and left on the arm of a uniformed German, a major or a colonel. She was always conscious of rank. He followed them from restaurant to café, from bar to movie theater, and finally, back to her apartment. He stood shivering on the corner of the place du Ralliement and the rue des Arènes, lighting a cigarette, watching.

He tried to stop. He tried to interest himself in his family, in his children, but he found Isabelle's face floating up between his and theirs, her dark violet eyes laughing at him, her lips caressing his cheek. He needed her, and the fact that he could no longer have her did nothing to lessen his desire or longing.

Chantale didn't notice Pierre's absences anymore. She had come to expect nothing of him, and her own time was too taken up with other things, more important things. There were the children, and her determination to keep whatever family ties that still existed alive. The rest of her time was devoted to the refugees, communications with the courier, and the underground press. And then, in the last eight months, there had been Dominique.

She couldn't have said at what point it was that she realized she was falling in love with him. It could have been the afternoon when he came by unexpectedly to find her in the stables with Jean-Claude and Catherine. She had held the baby while Dominique lifted Jean-Claude onto his pony, and had jogged around the paddock, taking the time to play with a small boy whose own father had no time for him. She had felt a strange warmth in her chest then.

Or it might have been one of the nights, one of the many nights, when they worked late over the printing press and had stopped to drink cider—they were always drinking cider, hot in the winter and cold in summer—and he told her how he dreamed of Europe at peace. "I'll go back to teaching, then. Perhaps even your children, Chantale," and her heart had lifted at the thought of seeing him again and again, a part of her future.

It didn't matter when she first realized her feelings. It mattered only that she was slowly aware of a love she had never known before, certainly not with Pierre. An eager anticipation when she thought about him coming by, daydreaming about him when he was away. Her pulse quickened when she saw him, the sparkling eyes that always looked amused, the long hands with delicate sensitive fingers, the voice that she could have listened to for hours. It didn't matter that he still wore the priest's cassock which Father Xavier insisted upon. Chantale was carefully respectful whenever they were around other people. When they were alone . . . she almost blushed at the thought. Those were feelings that she must never, never act upon. Marriage was a sacred institution, blessed by God. And no matter who her husband was or what he did, she had to retain her sense of dignity, or worth, of who she was. It could well be all that she had left.

Dominique, for his part, treated her with friendliness and courtesy, as an equal in what they were doing. He probably, she realized, would never have even spoken to her if they had met under different circumstances. The difference between their classes was too pronounced.

And now the—what? fifth?—group of Jews was hiding in her stables, and the courier was late.

She waited all day and finally, in time for vespers, walked over to the church. Father Xavier was lighting the candles on the altar when she arrived, but she couldn't wait through the service. She was too impatient, and she walked quickly down the aisle to the vestry.

Father Xavier closed the door behind him and frowned at her. "This is not a good idea, Countess," he said in a low voice. "Religious fervor, I am sorry to say, does not become you. More importantly, changes incite gossip." Then he looked more closely at her face and touched her arm gently, awkwardly. "Chantale—I am sorry. What is the matter?"

"It's the courier," she said. She didn't know the man's name. "He was supposed to be here on Monday. He's never been this late before."

"Good God," he muttered. "I thought that they had reached the coast by now."

"My mother says that she's had no—visitors—for over three weeks. What are we going to do, Father? He must have been arrested. And I have people now, waiting."

"Don't panic," he said automatically. "We'll just make other arrangements. Dominique will have to take them to the coast instead, that's all.''

"Dominique?" she said, then lowered her voice, afraid of what Father Xavier might hear in it. "Dominique doesn't know the route. He doesn't know the area, the Bretons. He's an Angevin." She said it as though speaking of a foreign country, as, for a Breton, perhaps it was.

"We have no choice," he whispered harshly. "There is no one else. I have to go in to vespers now, child. Go home. We'll make arrangements for your people. Try to reassure them if you can.''

"When, Father?"

"In a day or so. I need Dominique to deliver some papers tomorrow. If he can manage to get some sleep in the afternoon, then tomorrow night. Don't make any rash promises, child. Just tell them that help is on the way." He went back into the church as quickly and quietly as he had come, and Chantale walked back over the fields to the château, her mind spinning and whirling.

What she had told Father Xavier was true. The Bretons co-operated with other Bretons; that was what made the channel operation so successful. They had far more in common with their Celtic neighbors from Wales and Cornwall than they did with French people from Normandy or La Manche. Chantale had been able to make the vital connection in Anjou not because of her status as the Countess de Montclair, but because she was a Breton.

Dominique, she feared, would never survive the trip.

That left only one alternative. There was only one person who could take the Jews safely to her mother's house.

Once she made up her mind, she acted quickly, too afraid that given time she might change it. She had to do the unthinkable— go to her mother-in-law.

Marie-Louise was sitting in her drawing room reading a book, a cup of cider on the table beside her. "I saw you," she said clearly as Chantale opened the door, "going across the field. Have you become religious?"

Chantale walked swiftly over to the mullioned window, looked out, and then turned to face the older woman. "I have been helping the Underground, the Resistance," she said clearly. "I have to leave tonight to bring some people to the coast. People who are wanted by the Gestapo." She took a deep breath. "I'll be gone for a few days. I just wanted you to know—in case. In case anything happens. I . . ." She turned back to the window. More clearly, she said, "I want the children to know. I want them to be proud of France."

"And of their mother." There was no acidity in Marie-Louise's voice. Chantale looked at her again and saw two tracks of tears running down the older woman's cheeks. "I wish—" Marie-Louise smiled and shook her head, and more tears squeezed themselves out of her eyes. "I knew, of course. I've known all along. I just . . ."

"I know." Chantale walked over and knelt next to Marie-Louise's chair. "I know. It's all right. It will all work out."

She shook her head again. "You and Pierre in the same family—it doesn't make sense."

"It makes all the sense in the world," Chantale said. "Balance, madame."

"And you—you must go tonight, in person?"

"There is no one else."

"There is no one else. The lament of all the saints." Marie-Louise sighed. "God go with you, then, my child."

Chantale smiled and stood up. "Father Xavier will make sure that he does," she said. She walked to the door, and then, with her fingers on the handle, hesitated. Turning back, she went quickly to where Marie-Louise still sat, immobile. Chantale leaned over and, very quickly, kissed the dry parchment cheek.

Three hours later she was on the road to the coast, driving the old farm truck filled with people.

Andrew had eaten well and slept rather too well. It was to a world tinged with the gray of twilight that he awoke.

The room where he lay was empty—an unused storage room by the look of it, with a bed built into the wall in the Breton style—but he could dimly hear voices somewhere off in another room. The girl had given him some soup and fresh bread, with cider to drink. The man had urged him to go to sleep. "We wake you later, yes?" he said, nodding encouragingly. "You sleep now."

Andrew had hesitated, but only for the length of time that it took him to put his head down on the feather-filled pillow. Then, once again, sleep crept around the edges of his consciousness.

He had slept too long. He awoke with the heaviness that spoke of too much, not too little, sleep. He sat up slowly, and then, cautiously, pushed back the sheets. It was then that he realized he was wearing no clothes.

His own clothes had been neither too dirty nor too wet to warrant their being cleaned. Moreover, he had been wearing them when he came into this room. The only reason he could imagine for removing his clothes was to keep him here, perhaps longer than he chose to stay. The little voice that had been crying warnings inside his head ever since he had come to the village was speaking louder, and Andrew finally decided to listen to it.

He had waited too long.

Even as he stood up, the door opened, and the girl from the bar stood silhouetted in the doorway. Behind her, ominous in their green-and-gray uniforms, were two German soldiers.

Chapter Twenty-six

Caroline was almost surprised when the letter from the RAF came addressed to Emma and not her. Emma held it in the palm of her hand, arms outstretched, as though it were a snake that might bite her. "I don't want to look."

"Don't be silly," Pauline said briskly. "Get on with it and get it over with, that's what I always say. Go on, Emma, do it now."

So Emma had opened the letter with several of them looking on, and they all watched her face turn paler than it was already. She looked up and gazed around vaguely. "It's Andrew," she said unnecessarily.

"Is he dead?" Caroline steeled herself to hear the worst. It could only be that. Why else such beautiful stationery, such careful attention to detail? It was one of those letters that Andrew himself hated to write, the letters to the people who cared only about the person involved, not about the kind of hero the letter made him out to be. Emma didn't reply, and Caroline took a deep breath. "He's dead, isn't he?" she asked again, as though repeating the words could somehow take some of the horror out of them for her.

Emma looked around as though dazed. "No," she said slowly. "He's alive. He's been taken to a prisoner-of-war camp inside Germany. He was shot down over France and arrested somewhere near Rennes." And then she burst into tears.

Caroline had taken the news inside her, and later she had taken it with her when she went to Scotland to pick up a Mosquito fighter to be delivered to some RAF unit in Kent.

"Are you sure you should go?" Pauline asked her, just as she was strapping her parachute on over her flying suit.

"Of course," Caroline said, keeping her voice level and as innocent-sounding as possible. "Why not?"

"You tell me," Pauline said, but Caroline shook her head.

"I'm fine, Pauline," she said at last. "He's Emma's fiancé, not mine. You should be looking after her."

"I already have. I've grounded her for a week, and I've got an idea that it might be the best thing to do with you, as well."

Caroline shook her head, her fingers finding the accustomed buckles. "Don't be silly, Pauline," she said. "Andrew's an old friend, nothing more. I'm relieved that he's still alive, and I'm really quite all right."

Pauline let her go, but still with that expression of worry on her face, and Caroline purposely did a low fly-by over the manor so that Pauline could see how controlled her flying was. She was taking one of the earl's old planes, a creaky old de Havialland, up to Scotland with her, and was leaving it there. One of the girls from the Ferry Pool was on leave not far away and had agreed to fly it back, solving transportation problems for both of them. The cockpit was open and gusty, and as it was unusually cold for October, Caroline was grateful for the hot-water bottle that Lady Everard had thought of at the last minute. "There you are, just tuck that in your suit and you'll be in Scotland before you know it."

Well, not quite, but it helped. It was not an atmosphere conducive to musing, Caroline thought. The news of Andrew's arrest had jarred her more than she cared to admit. She had thought, for a while, that they were invincible, she and Andrew. Tied together by an invisible wire, woven of past experiences together, she had thought that they were charmed. They had both had so many close calls with the weather and the enemy and the ever-unpredictable flying machines they so loved, and they had both emerged unscathed. Until now. Now Andrew had been shot down, and Caroline was no longer as sure of her own flying ability as she once had been.

There had been another moment of uncertainty when she had come back from delivering another Mosquito. She had returned on the train and found her mother at the station. Then, too, she had been sure that something terrible was about to happen, and— oh God, Caroline thought, that was it. She had known that something terrible was going to happen, and Andrew was shot down. The two events were not so unrelated as she had thought.

Her mother. Caroline was still not sure why Amanda had come all the way from the Congo to see her. The gesture was so dramatic and so pointless. They had talked together of noth-

ing, of the war, of the airplanes that Caroline was flying: Not
of Steven, not of Eric, not even of Newport. Amanda had been
cold, shivering violently the entire time that she was there. Her
blood, she explained, was more suited to Africa these days.
Caroline wasn't sure what that meant and wasn't particularly
interested enough to ask. Their meeting had been stilted, awkward. Caroline had invited Amanda to return to the manor with
her, but Amanda said no, she and her husband—a quiet, almost
likable sort—had other plans. She had stood and looked helplessly at Caroline and finally, taking her daughter's face in her
gloved and perfumed hands, she had lightly kissed her cheeks.

"Why did you come, Mother?" Caroline asked, her voice
tired and helpless-sounding.

Amanda only shook her head. "You wouldn't understand,"
she finally said.

"You always assume that I can't understand!" Caroline burst
out. "Look at me, Mother! Look at me! I've grown! I've
changed! I'm not someone you need to protect, or ignore, or
even love. I'm a mature adult woman, and for once—for *once,*
Mother!—I'd like to be treated as one!"

Her mother's husband took his pipe out of his mouth then and
said, rather feebly, "I say."

Amanda was staring at her. "You're so like Philippe," she
said slowly. "How could I ever treat you as an adult? You remind me too much of him. It would . . . hurt . . . too much."

Caroline reached over and touched her mother's hand gently,
hesitantly. "Don't go on punishing me for the rest of my life for
who my father was," she said, struggling to keep her voice even.
"Don't do that to me, Mother."

Amanda herself seemed close to tears. "I never loved you,"
she said helplessly. "I've wished—lately—that I did. That I
had." She took a deep, shaking breath. "That I could."

"I don't mind," said Caroline, realizing with sudden surprise
that she didn't. All her life she had minded, had minded desperately, but that time was past. She no longer needed the same
things from her mother. "I don't even need you to like me,
Mother. Just treat me as a person. Just look at me and see who
I am and deal with me from there. That's all that I ask."

Amanda shook her head. "There's so much lost time," she
said doubtfully. Then she looked up and caught Caroline's eye.
"I came because I wanted to see you. Because I do care, I truly

do, about what happens to you. To see if you were . . . surviving. I'm afraid that I gave you a great deal to contend with.''

"I don't understand."

Amanda shrugged. "Oh, you know. That blasted company. And that blasted house. You don't have much room to maneuver between them, do you?''

Caroline smiled and reached for her hand again. "Only the skies, Mother," she said. "Only the skies."

Amanda had long since gone back to the Congo, and now Caroline knew that it had been months since Andrew had been captured. News traveled slowly in wartime.

Caroline banked the Mosquito to the left, around the barrage balloon whose position she was beginning to know so well, and then moved back on course, her altimeter and compass steadying as she resumed her heading. God, it was cold.

She wondered for a moment what Andrew's life was like. Surely the Germans must treat their prisoners with honor and dignity! They were, after all, doing the same thing, only on different sides. . . . But she knew better. In her heart, she knew better. He was suffering, she knew. He was probably cold and miserable, and they would have put him on some horrible work detail. She shivered at the thought. There was nothing that she could do; the only person who could possibly do anything for Andrew was Eric, and Eric would never help him. Caroline remembered Eric's anger when he confronted her years ago about her love affair with Andrew. "He's Johnson Industries, Caroline," Eric had said coldly.

You couldn't trust Johnson, he had told Caroline. They were devious. They used people like Andrew, and they would use Caroline, too. The world was filled with men she could fall in love with. Andrew Starkey was not one of them. Andrew Starkey was off limits. No matter who he was personally, what he did, what he believed, for Eric he would always be part of Johnson Industries. And, in those days, it was clear that Johnson Industries was the enemy.

Caroline wondered if that still was the case. Surely, with the war on, they had better things to do than to bare their fangs at each other? And then again, perhaps not. Eric didn't seem to think that the war was as important as she made it out to be, or so it seemed to her from his frequent letters and telegrams, urging her to give up the fight and return home. "You've done your part, Caroline. You've assuaged your conscience. Now please come to your senses.''

It was an odd thing to say: You've assuaged your conscience. Did Eric really think she was flying Air Transport because of Eddie? Because of Steven? Or did he think that she had some strong patriotic urge to fight on on the side of the righteous? Well, perhaps that was part of the reason she stayed on in England despite Eric's pronouncements, despite the childish letters, scrawled in crayon he forwarded which showed her that her daughter was beginning to grow up without her. But it was more than that, too: It was Caroline's chance, perhaps her only chance to prove something to herself. That when things got rough, she didn't run back home or to Eric. She was facing life on her own. More than that, she was proving she was strong enough, not only to withstand the terrible physical stress of flying Air Transport, but also strong enough to find herself in it as well.

Pauline had been right: Caroline had come to her as a child. She was trying very hard to become an adult before she left.

Soizic Aubert sighed and tossed the file folders on the conference table. ''Perhaps,'' she said softly, ''things are getting a little out of hand.''

Eugene Rousseau glared at her. ''Things are getting very much out of hand,'' he said acidly. He stood up and paced around the table for a moment, glaring indiscriminately at the assembled lawyers. ''First,'' he said, ticking items off on his fingers, ''we have Monsieur Beaumont paying more attention to a possible laboratory in some godforsaken desert than he does to the war effort in general.''

''Slow down,'' Marc Giroux said softly. ''I don't know that that's such a bad idea.''

''Secondly,'' Rousseau went on, ''there is the small matter of Captain Starkey being interned in a prisoner-of-war camp.''

Françoise Duroc didn't even look at him. ''That sounds like a good interim solution to the Starkey problem,'' she purred. ''Certainly nothing to get upset about.''

''I disagree,'' interjected Raphael Marchand. ''We've vacillated too much already on that question.''

''Continuing on,'' said Rousseau. ''Thirdly, we have Madame Asheford continuing to fly airplanes in and out of places which are questionable, to say the least, in terms of safety.''

''We have someone watching her,'' Soizic said mildly.

Rousseau glared at her again. "Well, that sounds to me like enough protection," he said sarcastically. "Finally, there is the young Countess de Montclair who is now providing a personal escort service to any Jew who wants to get out of France. It's only a matter of time before they pick her up."

"Yes," said Soizic. "That is a problem."

"I thought we'd agreed that we can't protect her any longer. Some people simply must suffer the consequences of their actions," said Françoise.

"She ought to be warned at least," Soizic objected.

"And be told what?" snorted Françoise. "That what she's doing is dangerous? I have a sneaking suspicion that she knows that, Soizic, dear."

"All of this," Rousseau said pontifically, ignoring their interchange, "is not including the latest news from the political front."

He paused significantly. There was no need to elaborate; they had all been following the news. The Japanese had attacked the United States naval base at Pearl Harbor, in Hawaii, on December seventh. Within a few days, the U.S. found itself officially at war with both Japan and Germany. Business, they knew, would be booming for Intraglobal, but America's entry into the war left several questions unanswered and various courses of action open.

"Did Monsieur Beaumont know?"

Marc Giroux glanced around. "Suffice it to say that Monsieur Beaumont was aware—as were others—that there was going to be a Japanese attack, yes. He did not know precisely where or when, although I am given to understand that in making an educated guess he was accurate in his projections. It would have made no difference for him to have shared this information with anyone, as the government of the United States was not likely to believe him. They did not, after all, believe their own ambassador to Japan when he made a similar suggestion earlier this year."

"So America joins the fray." Françoise shrugged. "All the more business, I should think. He should be pleased."

"And should we be pleased, Françoise? Do we have any contacts in Japan? I must confess to a feeling we've been somewhat insular in our preparations, focusing as we have almost exclusively in Europe," said Giroux.

"We're living up to our mandate," said Raphael mildly, smoothing his bristling mustache, "to look after the fortunes of the de Montclair family and lineage, and to protect the interests of Intraglobal and of that side of the lineage. I should think that we're managing.''

"Managing?'' asked Rousseau. "Then why all these loose ends? Why these problems? I've said it before, and I'll say it again, it's time to act on all of this.''

"I'm not sure what you're proposing, Eugene,'' said Giroux, his voice weary. He was feeling his age these days, the more so since Robert Beneteau was not well and unable to attend all the meetings and conferences on his agenda. Giroux had been deputizing for him for weeks now. "I do think Soizic is correct, that a friendly warning to the Countess de Montclair would not be amiss. Then, duty done. If she chooses to seek her own destruction—well, that will be her affair.'' He cleared his throat. "And, Soizic, I think that you're the person to do it. You're both from Brittany. She'll trust you. Are you willing to try?''

It would be the first time Soizic had visited France since the occupation. She suppressed a sudden vision of towns and villages like her own taken over by people who spoke a foreign language and had different ways, an occupation that she had helped to bring about. All in the name of Intraglobal and partnership in a prestigious law firm. She sighed. "Yes, I'll go.''

"Good.'' Giroux's voice was brisk. "We'll be sure that you have all the papers you need. There won't be any problems getting through. There isn't a great deal we can do to help Madame Asheford when not even her own mother was able to intervene on our behalf. And we need to keep these things in perspective. It is not Madame Asheford who will one day run Intraglobal, it is her daughter, Elizabeth. If Madame Asheford dies, it will be regrettable, no doubt. It will not, however, be the end of the world.''

"It would leave Elizabeth Asheford without parents,'' observed Françoise.

"And with enough money—and Monsieur Beaumont as conservator—to be raised quite properly without them. I don't think that we need to worry about that.'' Giroux cleared his throat. "Does that cover all of your problems, Eugene? We no longer need to worry about Caroline Asheford. Times change; circumstances change; and our policies, too, must change in order to keep up with them. All in all, I think, we should be congratulating ourselves. Intraglobal is doing very, very well indeed.''

"And that," said Françoise, "is all that matters, *n'est-ce pas*?"

Soizic went to visit Chantale that January.

Chantale was not expecting a visit, not from anybody. During the last year, her life had fallen into the kind of routine that would have seemed madness to her before the war but which now made perfect sense. Time spent with her children, time spent with her mother-in-law, and time spent with Dominique, working on the printing press, attending clandestine meetings, and in the last several months as courier between Angers and the coast.

It was the last activity that Dominique had been the most angered about. That first time she had decided to venture out alone had nearly turned to disaster. Even with the forged papers that she herself had printed in haste only moments before departing, she had been stopped and questioned at every roadblock, every sentry station. The papers noted her passengers were farm workers being transported to an estate in Brittany. Once or twice she had been sure that discovery was inevitable. But she had gotten through.

"Beginner's luck," said Dominique angrily. "Don't expect to have it so easy again."

But Chantale had told Father Xavier that she would do it again. "They're using their life savings to bribe their way to the coast," she said. "My mother and I—we won't charge them anything. It makes more sense, Father!"

"Not for you, Countess. Not for a woman."

Tears stung her eyes. "That's ridiculous. You'd let one of your precious nuns do it!"

"My precious nuns, as you put it, do not have two small children at home who depend upon them."

"So they're more expendable? That's a curious set of ethics you have, Father."

He had relented, but only on the condition that Dominique was to accompany her. "It will excite less suspicion, Countess. A woman, driving a truck, at night? I think not. But a priest— ah, that is another thing. Even the *sales Boches,* from time to time, they respect the Church."

So Dominique traveled with her, and in the long weary nights they talked and ate and sometimes she fell asleep in the truck, her cheek pillowed against his shoulder, her even breathing measured with his, and the same thought had to be in both their minds. But they never spoke of the feelings that were between them, as though by tacit agreement it had been decided that they must not. And despite the danger and the constrictions on their actions, the times she spent with Dominique were filled with a curious kind of peace and contentment.

Now into this unusual sort of order came the woman lawyer from Zurich. She came not to see Pierre, as one might have expected, or even Marie-Louise. It was Chantale that she sought.

Chantale, summoned from the stables, came into the library with her outdoors clothes still on—a heavy tweed coat, boots, scarf and hat, mittens. January was moist and cold in Anjou, and one had to dress accordingly. The contrast to the cool and efficient figure sitting on the velvet sofa was immediate. The lawyer was wearing a tailored wool suit in some indeterminate shade between gray and blue, a white shirt, gray stockings, and smart black shoes. Chantale found herself wondering, irrelevantly, how she had managed to walk through the snow—they had recently had a dusting—without ruining those shoes. She had short black hair now cut in a fashionable bob and vivid blue eyes, and it was the eyes that gave her away. She wants to see me because she's from Brittany, Chantale thought. With those eyes, there was no question.

She rose when Chantale came into the room. "Countess? I am Soizic Aubert, from the law firm of Beneteau, Giroux and Aubert in Zurich."

Chantale automatically shook her hand. "I am enchanted, madame," she said, the words on her lips before she could even think them. "Please sit down. Have you been offered something to drink? There is no coffee, but we have our own cider. Or perhaps a glass of wine?"

"No, thank you," Soizic said quickly. The de Montclairs had no coffee, but she had had some before she left the office, a rich blend of java beans. She had no business taking anything from these people. "You know that we are the firm representing the de Montclair estate?"

"Yes," Chantale said uncertainly. "I have often wondered why a firm in Switzerland did so, but I gather that the firm has had a long relationship with the family."

"Oh, yes, indeed," Soizic said. "For several generations. And the move to Switzerland was recent—just before the last war."

"I see," said Chantale, who really didn't, but also didn't particularly care. "Forgive me, Madame Aubert, but wouldn't you prefer to speak with my husband or mother-in-law? They know more about the family affairs than I do."

"No." Soizic was emphatic. "It is you, Countess, I came to see. This is not strictly a business meeting."

Chantale raised her eyebrows. "Indeed? Pray continue, Madame Aubert."

"Well, we have been following the family affairs, and we are aware of the fact that you have been involved with the Resistance movement, both here in Anjou and in Brittany." She saw Chantale's look of surprise. "Please do not waste your time, Countess, or mine in denying it. We have records of meetings. We know of your liaison with Father Xavier Humbert and with Dominique Pointeau. We know that you have hidden various people here at the estate, that you maintain a printing press, that in the last six months you have been serving as a courier between here and the Château de Kerenec, where your mother is also involved in Resistance work." She took a deep breath. "All of this activity, Countess, is distressing to the firm."

Chantale stared at her for a moment before replying. "And what business is it of yours?" She asked at length, her voice cold. "I see no reason why I should have to answer to you, or to your firm."

"Of course you need not answer to us." Soizic leaned forward, lowering her voice. "Countess, please understand. I know I have no authority to tell you what you may and may not do. You must not think that I am here to judge you in any way. In my own heart, I applaud what you are doing. I am a Bretonne, as you are, and it hurts me to think of the *sales Boches* in my village, presiding over my town hall, burning books in my library. In my own heart, I know that you have searched your conscience and that is why you do what you do." She leaned back again.

"In a more official capacity, I am here to warn you. The Germans have stepped up counterespionage procedures, Countess. There has been too steady a stream of people crossing the channel to serve with the Free French under De Gaulle. This is rapidly becoming a major concern for them, particularly now that the Americans have entered the war. They are spreading nets, Countess, all up and down the coast. It is our fear that you will be caught in one of them."

Chantale listened to Soizic with growing concern, but she refused to give in to it. "And if I am?"

Soizic shrugged. "Then there is no hope, Countess. The Gestapo has very unpleasant ways of making people confess—and die. There is nothing that anyone will be able to do for you."

Chantale sat still for a moment. She had finally taken off her mittens and scarf, and now she plucked at them on her lap. "Madame Aubert," she said, looking up, "do you not think that I am aware of all these things? Do you not think that all the time I wonder if I am going to deprive my children of their mother? My husband would hardly miss me, but I daresay that they would. And I would bring down suspicion on a house that has had little to worry about from the Germans, for reasons that are perhaps better known to you than to me." That much was not clear to Chantale. If the law firm knew so much about her activities and those of the Germans, then perhaps they had something to do with the estate's being spared. The thought sickened her. "I cannot stop what I am doing. It is the only possible response to what is happening in France now."

Soizic said, "There are other ways to resist. You can stay home and teach your children of freedom, so that they can change the world."

"How can I teach them of freedom and ask them to change the world when I am not willing to stand up for it myself? That would make me a very poor teacher, Madame Aubert." She held up her hand as Soizic started to speak again. "No. Say no more. You were told to give me a warning, and you have risked much to come here and do so. Thank you. But you will never persuade me to stop doing what I know in my heart to be right." She paused. "You are the lawyers of the de Montclair estate. If anything does happen to me, please see that it is passed intact to my children. My husband is not very competent in business matters. And they are, after all, your concern. They are de Montclairs by birth, not marriage." She permitted herself a smile.

Soizic shrugged uneasily. "I have warned you, Countess."

"Yes," Chantale agreed. "You have done that." She stood up. "Good-bye, Madame Aubert."

"Countess—"

"Good-bye, madame. A safe journey back to Switzerland."

Soizic shrugged and left. Behind her, Chantale stood staring at the door for a very long time.

Eric had heard the U.S.'s declaration of war with equanimity, for he had known that it was going to happen. He spoke almost daily on the telephone with President Roosevelt and could picture the man on the other end, cigarette holder in his hand, face perpetually in a frown. He spoke less and less with Jeffrey Kellogg, for while theirs was a wartime alliance, Eric was beginning to work on things that would long outlive the war—and Johnson's usefulness.

The nuclear bomb was becoming, more and more, an obsession.

He had recovered the uranium ore from Staten Island, where it had been stored after being removed from the Belgian Congo, and he had had it transported to the sites being established in Tennessee and New Mexico. He consulted constantly with the scientists who were beginning to work on the project. He once again renewed his correspondence with Joliot-Curie; he lunched with Robert J. Oppenheimer at Cal Tech. And, all the while, his own establishment spread out over the fields outside of San Jose. Already, other industries were beginning to settle there, as well, just to be close to Intraglobal.

He no longer had any real hopes of Caroline's returning to the States—and, less and less, saw the necessity for her to do so. Caroline, he finally realized, had made her own decisions about her life. He had other things to attend to. The dream of nuclear fission grew and glowed in his mind.

Elizabeth's tutor's name was Laura Tilling. The children were instructed, always, to call her Miss Tilling.

She wrote the letters to Caroline in England, listening patiently as Elizabeth told her long stories. ''. . . and tell her that I went with Rosemary to the party and we ate ice cream and I got some on my party dress and I had scallops for supper and Nicholas keeps pulling my hair . . .'' Miss Tilling condensed it as best she could, and always enclosed some of Elizabeth's artistic efforts. Elizabeth carefully printed her name across the bottom in large block letters that ran together: "Love, Elizabeth-Erica-Asheford."

Miss Tilling had her own thoughts about mothers who weren't around to look at those pictures in person, but she kept them to herself. She was being paid handsomely to look after the early education of Elizabeth and Nicholas Asheford, and any judgments that she made about their families, she made in the secret places of her heart.

Besides, rich people did things differently. Everyone knew that.

Chapter Twenty-seven

Chantale and Dominique had spent the night at her mother's house. The weather was warm for the first time that spring, and they had gone walking together on the headland above the ocean. It was as though there were no war, no occupation, no dreadful purpose to their visit. Their being there felt, of all things, both natural and normal, and Chantale found herself, against all odds, relaxing. There was a strong wind, and something, some strange plankton or sea organism, was making the water below glow phosphorescently. Chantale pulled her shawl more tightly around herself.

They talked about the war, and they talked about her children, and finally, they talked about him.

He told her he had decided to enter the priesthood.

Chantale stood still, not knowing what to say. Over the last year she had had so many happy daydreams. She had finally allowed herself to consider divorcing Pierre and she had imagined days after the occupation when she and Dominique could be together all the time. She had thought of herself in his embrace, touching the brown tanned muscles of his arms, feeling his lips on hers . . . She had thought of all those things and believed that someday they would happen. Now he was telling her that they never could.

"I suppose that it came from acting the role of a priest all this time," he said reflectively, looking out across the cliffs to the darkness of the sea beyond. "From talking with Father Xavier about the war, about why the war is happening."

"Why does he say that the war is happening?" She had her own views on the subject, but she was interested in listening to his. Right now she needed to talk about something, anything to keep herself from thinking about the divide that had just opened up between her and Dominique.

He shrugged. "That God has given us free will. And sometimes we abuse it, and the balance between good and evil gets upset. Father Xavier says that everything in the world is a matter of balance. When it is working right, it is as God intended. When the balance gets upset then we have to do something to change it, to put things back into proportion again. That's why he's working with the Resistance. It all makes sense to me, Chantale. And that's what I want to do with the rest of my life."

"When?"

"After this is all over, I suppose. It will end sometime, Chantale. I know that it will. The Americans are fighting the Germans now. One day, you'll see, they'll be landing on these very beaches; they'll come and the Free French will join them and we'll all rise up. Together we'll drive the *sales Boches* out of France. And there will be peace. There's no time to attend seminary now, there's too much work to be done. There will be time enough later when the Americans have come and gone and it's all over. Meanwhile I'll stay on with Father Xavier and learn what I can from him while we work in Angers."

"I see." She was quiet, looking out to sea, the wind stinging her cheeks. So she had been wrong about him after all. She had imagined that he had feelings like hers, feelings of affection—of desire, even—for her. It looked as though she had been mistaken, that it had all been a product of her fevered imagination, of her foolish fantasy. She felt an emptiness, a sense of loss, that was overwhelming. And she felt foolish. After all, the man was not her lover, perhaps not even her friend. He was only a close co-worker in a cause that was important to both of them. That was all.

"About us, Chantale," Dominique said suddenly, as though he had been reading her thoughts. His voice was shaky. "I won't deny—I can't deny—that I have feelings for you. They've been strong feelings. But we both know that there is no future in that—you are a real countess; I am a schoolteacher. It's best this way. We can stay friends. Perhaps one day I will marry your children for you." She caught a glimmer of a sad smile in the darkness. "I won't say that I haven't thought a lot about you in making this decision."

"I had hoped," she said in a low voice, "that things might have ended differently between us."

"I know." Without looking at her, Dominique reached over and took her hand. "I know. I have had these thoughts, too. But you must believe me when I say that this, truly, is best. For both of us.''

"Hardly for both of us," Chantale said, feeling the tears constricting the back of her throat. "You have your God, who can never disappoint you, and I have my husband, who cannot fail to disappoint me. You can't say that that's a fair exchange."

"But it is the only one." He squeezed her hand in his. "It's the only one that can work, Chantale."

"I know," she said to make him feel better, but there was misery in her voice and in her heart. "I know, and I hate it." She took a deep ragged breath. "And I hate you for being so good, and so attractive, and for making me love you."

"I didn't make you love me. Not any more than I've made myself love you. It just happened, Chantale."

Chantale's heart skipped with those words. He did love her. "I thought that one ought to respect God's hand working in fate."

"God," Dominique said, "is never behind adulterous desires."

Chantale shook her head. "That's too easy. Now you sound like a seminary textbook. Don't let the priesthood take away your humanity, Dominique."

"Perhaps," he said quietly, half to himself, "it can't take away something that I no longer have to give."

And then he had walked her back to her mother's house, through the huge front doors that she had known so well as a child, past the suit of armor in the front hall, and up the stairs to the corridor where the bedrooms were located. They paused outside her door, and Chantale turned to face him. "Can a priest," she whispered hesitantly, "kiss me good night?"

"I'm not a priest yet," he said. They stood quietly for a long moment and then his arms were around her. He drew her tightly to him, and was kissing her face, her mouth, her neck, her hands, and all of it with a reckless abandon she had never experienced with Pierre.

Dominique carried her into her room, and stretched her out on the bed, still kissing her, still touching her, and she found herself responding, the passion inside of her burning brighter and hotter than she had ever known it could. As though Dominique had touched something, awakened something that had long lain dormant, and she knew, suddenly and with absolute cer-

tainty, that no matter what the future held she could never be
the same again.

He was undressing her, slowly, and then faster and faster as
though the flames were licking at his fingers, too. Her shirt was
off, so, too, was the silky white brassiere she wore beneath it,
and he had bent and was kissing her breasts. Chantale clung to
his head and half sobbed with desire, her fingers entwined in
his curls, her breath coming in ragged mouthfuls. He slid the
skirt from her, and the petticoat, and was unfastening her stockings from her garters with fingers that trembled. She could hear
his breathing, and she wanted to urge him to hurry, to hurry . . .
They had only the night together, she thought, and his God only
knew what the dawn would bring.

He took her with the same gentle passion she had believed
was in him throughout all the time she had known him. The
same kindness and tenderness. The same passion and commitment. His rhythm became the rhythm of the sea, became her
rhythm, as they loved in the house on the cliffs and the waves
pounded the rocks below them.

Later, Dominique fell asleep in her arms as quickly as Jean-
Claude or Catherine would, his breathing regular and even and
a little shallow. She cradled him and smiled into the darkness.
Who knew what the future held? He might well become a priest,
and, then again, he might not. No one knew, not now, not with
the occupation all around them and so few people that one could
trust. Later, there would be time to make decisions about their
lives. Later. For now, loving was enough.

Was this, Chantale wondered, what Pierre found with his mistress in Angers? This happiness? Was this why he went off to
her, time and time again, willing to risk everything—even hurting his family—for time stolen in her arms? If this was what he
found, then at last she understood. She had never been this happy
with Pierre. It followed that perhaps he could never be this happy
with her.

But Dominique . . . Dominique was something else altogether. Dominique was strong and bright, intelligent and committed, and loving him was loving all those things in him.
Perhaps her fantasy could yet come true. De Montclairs had
never divorced, no matter what happened, but certainly the time
had come for them to awake to the realities of life.

She was feeling drowsy. Soon she, too, would be asleep.
Strangely enough, it was Marie-Louise who she was sure would

understand, would see that this man could give Chantale so much
more than her son ever would. Chantale had fulfilled her role in
Pierre's life, giving him a son, a future Count de Montclair.
Surely that was all that was necessary! Surely now she had a
right to some happiness?

She kissed Dominique's forehead gently, tenderly. Whatever
happened, she told herself, whatever decision any of them
reached, tonight had been worth it. She knew love, real love,
love with a man who wanted her as much as she wanted him.
Whatever happened, she could face it now. Because she had
known this love, had known Dominique.

She didn't remember falling asleep. All that she remembered
later was a sense of drifting, drifting and smiling, and when the
sun came streaming into the room Dominique was laughing at
her.

"Do you always smile in your sleep?"

Chantale purred and stretched. "Only when I've spent the
night with the man I love."

He raised his eyebrows, but he was smiling. As the day wound
on, they filled it with themselves and with each other, with long
walks on the beach and a quick trip into the village for provi-
sions, with conversations with Chantale's mother which they
filled with double-entendres for each other's ears alone, with
good food and another hour spent in Chantale's old bedroom,
exploring each other's bodies even as they were exploring each
other's minds. Chantale was still smiling when evening came
and they set out to return to Angers.

Her mother stood in the doorway, looking worried. "Be careful," she warned them. "Please be careful."

Dominique went back to her and unexpectedly kissed her
cheek. "Don't worry," he said. "I'd rather die a million deaths
than let anything happen to her."

"I worry," she said. "I always worry. About all of us."

"Good night, Maman," Chantale said, kissing her. "We're
going to be all right." She looked at Dominique, and he smiled
and reached out his hand for hers. "We're going to be just fine,"
he said, and they were off.

Chantale and Dominique stopped at a railway station in Nantes.
When they had traveled with only a few refugees, they took
the trains which ran erratically from the coast through Angers
on their way to Paris. The Germans were trying to make the
train service more efficient, but there were always delays, pieces

of track being blown up, trains mysteriously rerouted. None of those things happened when Chantale and Dominique used them. The Underground had strong connections with the people who ran the rails.

The trains were safe, had always been safe. Chantale relaxed, sitting on a bench, while she waited for Dominique to make arrangements with Henri, the old stationmaster. Henri always smiled at them, told them what a fine couple they looked together, the gap in his teeth making the smile seem lopsided. Chantale wondered what he would think if he knew of Dominique's decision to enter the priesthood.

She hardly noticed the man sitting down on the bench a few feet away from her, the man in the dark belted raincoat who was engrossed in his newspaper. She didn't see the two other men, one of them lighting a cigarette, who paused nearby to consult the train schedules. She was thinking about Dominique and the wonderful feelings he had awoken in her body.

"Countess de Montclair?" The voice was Teutonic in its guttural precision. She looked up, focusing hazily on the man in front of her, a man in a neat black uniform. A German. She steadied her gaze on him, forcing herself not to look around for Dominique, not to give him away if they were watching her for her reactions. The Germans had arrested priests before.

"Yes?" It was useless to deny who she was. They would have had a good idea before they even approached her. "Yes? I am the Countess de Montclair. What is it that you want?"

He pulled out a wallet with an identity card. "I am Captain Berndt Schlimmer of the Gestapo, Countess. I am afraid that I must ask you to accompany me."

The man on the bench was watching her now, as were the two who had been looking at the train schedules. Behind Captain Schlimmer were several more men, all in the same dark uniform, and she suddenly thought of the woman lawyer from Zurich. "We won't be able to protect you . . . they will kill you."

So they will, she thought, her legs shaking as she contemplated standing, getting up from the bench and walking away from Dominique. She had prayed for a good long run, and she had had it. Now Dominique's God was demanding an accounting. She had been prepared for this possibility for a long time. Only recently had she come to believe it wouldn't happen. It had been Dominique and her own fantasies about him that had kept her believing in a future beyond the war. For her, there would probably be none. She would end up like Annie, in front of a firing squad.

Fighting back panic and a desire to look once more in Dominique's direction, she tried to clear her mind. If her information about the Gestapo was at all correct, she was going to have a difficult few hours ahead of her. The important thing, the primary thing, was to be sure that she didn't take anyone with her.

So it began now.

She straightened her spine. She was the Countess de Montclair, and they were going to know it. "Why," she asked coldly, "should I do that, Captain?"

"Because we need to talk, Countess. I would prefer to do it at my office. We can go there now and make this pleasant, or you can choose to refuse, in which case the gentlemen behind me can show themselves to be very unpleasant indeed. The choice is yours."

Chantale shrugged. "You occupy us. We have no choices." She stood up and, with as much dignity as she could muster, followed them to the waiting car. Out of the corner of her eye, she saw the figure of a priest reaching for a telephone, and she knew that Dominique saw her, and would stay away. That was the most important thing. She was probably going to die anyway, but at least Dominique could live. With some help from that God of his, he might well live to preside over the marriages of her children.

She was sure that she would not live to see them.

Time had stood still.

Dominique Pointeau had read his share of novels back in the not-so-distant past, when reading was still something that one had time for, could indulge in, and he had always smiled when that line appeared: "time stood still." What nonsense, he had always thought.

And then, for him, time did stand still.

Or perhaps it was like a movie, a movie in the old days, when the film was still rough and uneven. What had happened in the railway station had seemed so disjointed, had seemed to move so slowly, that he could have sworn it was in a book or a film. But not in real life.

Not in his real life, anyway. And, God, not in *her* real life, please no.

He had watched the Gestapo take Chantale and he had noticed, of course, how careful she was not to betray his presence to them. He had wanted to run to her, but even in the short period of time it took for them to lead her away, he had had time to think.

Now, as he sat on the train heading for Angers, Dominique ran a hand quickly through his rough hair. The clenched feeling of panic in his stomach had not gone away, but if he was going to help her, if he was going to get her out of there, then he had to think. And act. But with a clear mind.

He had to leave her in order to help her, though his first reaction would have been to follow her downtown to Gestapo headquarters, anything to be near her. But he didn't know many of the people in Nantes, and Angers wasn't so far away—not for a free man. And in Angers there were people who could help her. The countryside rushed past, and the wheels on the tracks seemed to mock his thoughts: They have her, they have her, they have her.

It was the risk that they all ran. Every day, every member of the Resistance knew that his or her life could come to a sudden and unpleasant end; and Dominique knew, too. His own life he had been willing to offer as a sacrifice to his country—but hers? He had never stopped to consider in these confused days and nights of working with her, respecting her, falling in love with her, that his might be the ultimate sacrifice: giving up not himself, but the woman he loved.

He found himself biting his fingernails, as he hadn't done in years, not since he himself had been a pupil sitting at an ink-scarred desk and wondering what response to give to the teacher. Not since he had transgressed some family rule and found himself in front of his father, eyes downcast, knowing that no matter what he said there would be a whipping for it. The gesture was automatic, the old response to anxiety, and Dominique bit his nails and stared out the train window at the country which she might, even at this moment, be dying for. . . .

Stop it, he told himself. Get a hold of things. You can't help her if you don't start thinking rationally. He leaned back against the seat and closed his eyes. He thought of Chantale, allowed himself finally to think of her, and it was as though a torrent of feelings had been unleashed, like a waterfall, to wash over him. Chantale. He had never known anyone like her, no one with that combination of sweetness and strength, that need to see the good in everyone and that ability to discern and combat evil when she

saw it. So filled with contradictions . . . Pierre de Montclair
didn't know what he had, didn't realize that the treasure wasn't
somewhere out in the city, but at home. Dominique felt a sudden
surge of anger. If Pierre had had more moral strength, more
character, then it would be he who would have taken the difficult
midnight passages, and it would be he being held by the Gestapo. Not Chantale.

It was useless to think about that. Useless to imagine what
could have been. Father Xavier had once told him, "The most
empty words in the language, I've always felt, are 'if only.' We
could build a thousand churches, and fill them, too, with 'if
onlys,' my son. But the world is a different kind of place, and
we would do well to work on a more positive vocabulary." Well,
that was easy enough for Father Xavier to say: He had gone
straight from school into seminary. Surely no woman had ever
tempted him to renounce—or not take—his vows; surely he had
never loved as Dominique was beginning to love Chantale. There
could be no "if onlys" in Father Xavier's staid life.

But for him, it was different. And even if their paths were
indeed going to part, even if one day she had to return to her
castle and he had to go to his studies, still he could do this for
her. He was going to save her.

Father Xavier was waiting as the train pulled into the Angers
station, his face grave and troubled. "I have heard," he said
immediately, as soon as Dominique joined him. "I received a
call on the telephone. From Nantes. We know where they've
taken her, and there's a rumor that she won't be there for long.
Hurry, there's much work to be done."

Dominique hurried. He set his hat on his head with a movement of decision, and his brisk steps echoed in the large, vaulted
hall of the station. He would save her. He would save her. He
would save her.

Soizic Aubert slammed the street door and ran up the stairs to
the office. Marc Giroux was on the telephone when she burst
into the room, and he waved at her to sit down, but she ignored
him and pulled out a cigarette and paced around while she waited
for him.

The call had come on her day off. She had gotten up and had
spent most of the morning sitting on the terrace with her croissants and coffee, looking out over the lake, feeling the sun

warming her face and shoulders. The first real spring day, and she had it all to herself to enjoy.

She had started writing again, a hobby she had taken up in school, and had never thought of very seriously. She always hid it from Marc, afraid that he would laugh at her. It wasn't very good, she told herself, but it was fun to do.

Perhaps it was the lake that had inspired her. Marc had told her once, when she had first moved in with him, that this was where some of the greatest horror fiction had been written, as a result of a dare at a summer party. A group of writers, he told her, had been drinking together when one of them proposed that they each write the most horrible story that they could think of. Mary Shelley had gone back to her room and written *Frankenstein,* while Bram Stoker had begun *Dracula.* Soizic flushed: What was she doing, beginning to compare her work to theirs? There was obviously nothing in common, only a lake and a desire to do something more, something beyond the everyday workaday world . . .

She closed her eyes and waited for the next lines of her poem to come to her, and it was then that the telephone rang.

"Soizic? *Ici,* Marc," he said crisply. "Can you come to the office? I know it's your day off, but there's been some trouble."

"What kind of trouble?"

"Chantale de Montclair. She's been arrested by the Gestapo in Nantes."

Soizic broke all the speed limits driving into the city, and now she paced nervously, waiting for Marc to get off the telephone, to tell her what had happened so that she could start thinking about what they could do. She was aware that her affection and respect for Chantale were standing in the way of her objectivity. She knew that they had little enough in common, only the place they had once come from, but, for Bretons, that was enough.

Marc Giroux hung up the telephone and looked at her. "Are you all right?" he asked automatically.

"Of course not. Tell me what happened."

He shrugged. "We know little enough about it, Soizic. Only that there was a leak somewhere along her chain of operations. Someone turned her in. She was arrested at the railway station on her way back to Angers, and she's being held at Gestapo headquarters in Nantes. They'll be transferring her to Angers, I expect. If there's going to be a trial and execution, they like to do it around the people who are most likely to be affected by it.''

"Will they execute her?"

"Of course they will, Soizic. What do you think? Unless they question her too closely. I hear that a lot of resistance workers die during questioning.''

"You mean torture.''

"I mean torture. It's quite commonly used. If she betrays anyone, it won't last as long, it'll give them other people to work on.''

"She won't," said Soizic with conviction.

"Then we must hope that she dies quickly. It won't be pleasant for her.''

There was a feeling of panic in her chest. "I have to go there, Marc.''

He frowned. "There's nothing you can do. Aren't you a little too involved, Soizic? You warned her. That's the extent of our responsibility.''

"I don't care about our responsibility. I can help her.''

"How?''

Soizic took a deep breath. "I can help her die, Marc. There are tablets one can take—if I could get it to her—''

He shook his head. "It's too risky, Soizic. I won't allow it.''

Soizic indulged in a rare flash of temper. "Speaking as my partner or as my lover?''

"As both. Please don't try, Soizic. You've done all that you can. Leave her. She knew what she was doing.''

Her chin up, Soizic walked to the door. "Responsibility is a relative term, Marc. Pray that you're never in need of something that it wasn't someone else's responsibility to provide.''

Chapter Twenty-eight

It was the fourth day.

Or that was what Chantale thought. It was hard to tell. She hadn't seen daylight since she had been arrested, and her sense of time was distorted. It didn't matter, not really: What possible difference could it make whether it was Monday or Tuesday or Wednesday? All the days were the same; all the nights were the same. Time made no difference.

The interview in Nantes had been short enough. The Gestapo was very much afraid that the Countess de Montclair had been illicitly smuggling people out of France. If true, the consequences would indeed be regrettable for her. But she could help herself. If she would just tell him who was helping her, who was the head of her organization . . . Such a pretty young woman was surely not operating alone. She could make things easier for herself if she cooperated.

Chantale had listened to him in silence, and said finally, "I take full responsibility for my acts, Captain. There is one else involved."

Schlimmer shook his head. "I was afraid that you might say that, Countess. I am very sorry to hear it." He stood up, riffled through some papers on his desk. "You will be transported to Angers this afternoon, and detained there until you change your mind. Please understand that your family will have no influence in this matter. It is extremely regrettable that this had to happen, Countess. I am sorry."

"Of course you are," she said coldly. "Good day, Captain."

They had taken her in a closed staff car all the way to Angers, with no stops, no pauses along the way. She didn't bother telling them that they needn't have worried. She was not about to try to escape. To what? For what? They would always know where to find her, and she didn't want her children seeing her led away by the Germans. Pierre she didn't care about; Jean-Claude and Catherine, she cared about a great deal.

Once in Angers she was taken to the city hall. That was where the Germans had established their headquarters, with the troops stationed on the other side of town, at the railway station. Down in the cellars there were some cells—Chantale thought that the Germans had probably had them built. They didn't seem to be the kind of place that the French police would have used for drunks. She was unceremoniously pushed into one of them, the door slammed, and that was that.

Later that night—she wasn't sure how much time had passed—the door creaked open and a strong light came shining into her face. No one was polite this time; no one called her Countess. There were three men, all of them in the same dark uniforms, and they didn't waste any time talking to her. One of them pushed her onto the floor, and then they all started kicking her at the same time. At first she tried not to cry out with the pain, not to give them that satisfaction, but when one of the kicks landed on her breasts she gasped. After that, with blows on her back and legs and arms, she cried out again and again . . . and then, finally, gratefully, she lapsed into unconsciousness.

When she woke up, she felt as though every part of her body was aching. Tentatively, she tried to move, and almost immediately cried out again as her whole body was wracked with pain. That wasn't going to work.

She lay a while longer on the hard wood floor, and gradually her bruises and injuries settled themselves into individual aches and pains and she could sort them out. One or two cracked ribs, she was sure. Bad bruising on her chest. Something wrong with one of her legs. And the throbbing in her head wouldn't go away.

On the third attempt, she managed to crawl over to the wall where she sat, leaning against it, her heart thudding quickly with the effort. There was something sticky all over the floor. It was impossible to see in the darkness, but she thought that it must be her own blood. Still more or less whole, she told herself grimly. Not bad. They would come back, and she'd have to see, then, but it was a good feeling still to be alive.

What was Dominique thinking now? And Marie-Louise? She surely knew why her daughter-in-law had been arrested. Chantale thought of her mother-in-law, stern and commanding, going downtown to lodge a formal complaint, just as they had when Annie was arrested. Perhaps, even now, Marie-Louise was standing just a few feet over Chantale's head, talking to the commander of Angers, informing him that arresting a countess was really intolerable. Chantale smiled. Marie-Louise would be perfect in the role—and she wouldn't get anywhere at all.

She leaned her head back against the wall and drifted in and out of consciousness for a while. At one point she dreamed, rather vividly, that she and Dominique and the children were on a picnic of some sort, but she moved a little and the pain woke her again.

Some time later—she had no way of knowing when—the door opened again and a light came shining into the room. Chantale looked up groggily. Her cell, she saw, was much smaller than she had realized. It had seemed miles across when she had had to crawl over to the wall, but it was in reality very small. There was no furniture, only the door, and the door promised no escape.

This time it was a man alone. He said several things to her in German, words that she didn't understand, and then to her horror he was kneeling next to her on the floor and pulling at her skirt. She said no several times, but she could smell alcohol on his breath, and he didn't stop. Oh, God, she thought, there's nothing that I can do to stop him. . . . The German was fumbling with her panties when she started screaming. He said something sharp and angry under his breath, and put a hand over her mouth. Whatever this was, it was not standard Gestapo questioning techniques, and Chantale bit his hand hard, screaming again when he moved it.

There were voices and the sound of boots running outside in the passageway, and then several men were crowding into the cell. The man was pulled off her, and immediately punched in the stomach before being dragged away. It was Captain Schlimmer who stood there, out of breath, looking from the young soldier to Chantale in distaste. "Countess," he said formally, his face red, "please accept my apologies. This man will be dealt with appropriately."

Chantale smoothed her skirt down and struggled to sit up straighter, wincing against the pain of the movements. "Captain," she said in a low voice, "tell me why it is acceptable for me to be beaten but not to be raped?"

He seemed to notice for the first time the bruises and gashes on her body. "Countess," he said, "you must be questioned. As a member of the Resistance, you are a danger to the Third

Reich. But my title was Baron before it was Captain, and we are of similar backgrounds. You may be questioned; you may even be tortured. But I will not see you abused.''

He clicked his heels together and strode out of the cell, calling to the others to follow him. Chantale watched the light fade down the corridor, listened to the last footstep, and sighed when they were gone and the darkness descended once more completely around her. So there was honor sometimes, even with the Nazis. It was an interesting concept.

She slept after that and was awakened twice more for a session of what was presumably questioning. No one spoke to her, and each time there were three soldiers, who spent all of their time kicking her around the cell. By their third visit, she blacked out quickly, so that she didn't feel the blows until she awakened to their aftermath.

Finally they came to take her somewhere. ''Where?'' she asked, but the soldier shook his head.

''*Nicht verstehen,*'' he said, and she focused her energies on walking instead of asking questions.

It was quite disconcerting to find that she couldn't

One of her legs was probably broken. She had suspected that it might be, but here was positive proof—her inability to put any weight on it at all. They had to half lead, half carry her up the stairs, and all the time she moaned with the pain shooting through her leg. She was brought to one of the offices upstairs and lowered into a chair. Captain Schlimmer was sitting behind the desk, a large ornate affair. Chantale studiously didn't look at him, gazing instead at a painting of Napoleon which was hanging over the fireplace. She had no idea what she looked like, but she knew that the term pretty would never again be used when describing her.

He didn't waste time. ''Countess, it pains me to see you suffering like this. I'd like to give you another chance to put an end to it.'' He clasped his hands together and leaned forward. ''Tell me, Countess. Tell me some names. Give me some meeting places. I promise you as a gentleman that all of this''—he gestured toward her, almost distastefully—''will stop. A firing squad at dawn. We could even arrange for it to be private. Please, Countess, for your own sake, tell me what I need to know.''

Chantale stared at him for a long moment. Finally, she said, ''Do you have a cigarette?''

"Of course, Countess." He shook one out of a package on his desk, leaned over to give it to her and to light it.

"Thank you, Captain." She inhaled deeply and blew it out as slowly as she could. "Tell me—Baron—in my place, what would you do?"

"I would do the sensible thing, naturally."

She raised her eyebrows. "Indeed? You are a poor liar. I would have thought that a baron would do the honorable thing."

The captain's brow contracted. "What I would do is irrelevant, Countess," he said, his irritation evident. "It is what *you* choose to do that makes a difference." He took a deep breath. "Your mother-in-law has been to see me."

Chantale felt some comfort just by hearing the words spoken. "Somehow I thought she might."

"I have decided to allow you to see her. She has persuaded me. She has agreed that the best thing is to help you understand the reality of the situation, help you change your mind. For the sake of your children."

She looked at him through the plume of smoke from her cigarette. "She would never say such a thing," she said angrily. "My mother-in-law is a woman of principle."

"She is also a woman, Countess. And your children are, I believe, very young? And it is perhaps questionable as to whether your husband will be the best possible influence on them?"

Chantale didn't answer, and after a moment he pressed a button on his desk. The door opened and a young corporal appeared. "Captain?"

"Send Madame la Comtesse in, please."

Chantale narrowed her eyes. It had to be a trick. Surely they wouldn't let Marie-Louise talk to her? It was so unexpected, she had no idea how to respond. And then the slow dignified footsteps were behind her and Marie-Louise's voice, regal as ever, was saying, "Please leave us, Captain. My daughter-in-law and I need some time together."

"Not long, madame," he warned, and then clicked his heels and was gone.

Marie-Louise walked slowly into Chantale's line of vision. She looked older, grayer somehow, the lines around her eyes and mouth more deeply etched. Marie-Louise lowered herself into the chair opposite Chantale, looking at her with shock and concern. Her voice, when she spoke, was barely a whisper. "What in God's name have they done to you?"

"I'm all right," Chantale managed to say. "Why did they let you come?"

"To persuade you to confess," Marie-Louise said. She looked around the room. "I expect they have some of those wretched listening devices somewhere here. Our friend Captain Schlimmer was too happy to leave us alone."

"What does it matter?" Chantale asked wearily. "I won't say anything. It's not worth it."

"Not worth . . . this?" Marie-Louise gestured at Chantale's body. "It couldn't have been pleasant."

"No," Chantale agreed. "But if I talk to them now, it will negate everything that I've ever done. I can't tell them anything." She looked at Marie-Louise. "What will you tell the children?"

"That their mother died a patriot, a true daughter of France," Marie-Louise said austerely. "And I will look after them. Their father is hardly competent to look after his own shoelaces. Have you any messages for them?"

Chantale shook her head. "Just tell them," she said helplessly, "that I love them. That I did this for them, so that they can live in a free France . . ." She couldn't continue talking.

Marie-Louise nodded and stood up. "Then I will leave you to your fate, my dear," she said clearly, and put out her hand as though to shake Chantale's hand. Chantale looked at her in amazement, and then reached up her hand. Marie-Louise pressed something into it, something small and hard. She leaned over to kiss Chantale's cheek, and whispered quickly, "It is from the woman lawyer in Zurich. If you bite down on it hard, you will die quickly. It is some kind of poison." Aloud she said, "*Adieu*, Chantale, my dear. We all do what we have to do. I will look after the children for you."

"Thank you," said Chantale, feeling that the words were inadequate, her hand closing over the pill in her palm. Soizic had brought this for her? "Tell the children . . ."

"Yes," Marie-Louise said, straightening up as the door opened and Captain Schlimmer walked in. "And I'll tell Pierre as well." She looked at the officer. "I regret, Captain, to tell you that my daughter-in-law will not change her mind. It is something that we will all have to live with." She gave Chantale a ghost of a smile, fleeting and sad. "Good-bye, my dear child. May we meet again in happier times."

"Good-bye . . . Mother."

"It is unfortunate," Captain Schlimmer said, "that your family could not make you see sense. I'm very much afraid that this afternoon we will be compelled to . . . question you, Countess."

Chantale's hand tightened around the pill. "And I will not answer you."

"We shall see," he said, shaking his head sadly. "We shall see."

She still couldn't walk, and they helped her to follow the soldiers down the stairs again and back to her cell. It was illuminated this time, with bright arc lights, and there was a chair set in the center of it. They dumped her onto the chair and tied her securely to it with ropes. Captain Schlimmer walked in, standing behind the lamp. She could smell his cigarette. "Now, Countess, I must ask you again. Who were you working with in Angers?"

Chantale shook her head.

She didn't see his gesture, but there was a whistling sound and suddenly her blouse was ripped open and a whip was lashing across her breasts. She cried out and slumped sideways on the chair, straining against the ropes. Her tongue searched for the pill which she had slipped between her gum and her teeth, but she told herself, not yet. Not until it looks as though they did it. They can't know that Marie-Louise helped me. I won't let them suspect that Marie-Louise gave me a pill. She said to herself that she might not even use it today, but wait until later so there would be no suspicion.

"It will be easier for you, Countess, if you would just help us," the voice droned on behind the lamp. It was polite, gentle, soothing. She was supposed to trust this voice, with its easy assurances. She was supposed to confide in him, tell him what he wanted to know, so that she could die with peace and dignity. That was the promise. And if I didn't have this capsule in my mouth, she thought suddenly, the idea would be attractive. Very attractive, indeed. "No," she said again, and almost immediately the whip descended again, this time on her back.

She gasped and the room began to tilt around her. Someone poured cold water over her head, and someone else moved the light closer so that it was glaring in her eyes, blinding her. "Please, Countess," Schlimmer's voice said. "Save yourself. Your comrades don't care about you. No one cares about you. There have been no rescue attempts. Save yourself. Tell us."

"They care," she protested automatically.

Schlimmer laughed. "Don't keep fooling yourself, Countess. You're alone. We're the only ones who can help you now. Tell us, and we'll take away the light. We'll loosen the ropes. We'll even give you something to drink and a nice soft bed to sleep in. Imagine that, Countess. We care about you. They don't. Tell us their names."

"No," she said, her tongue working the pill around so that it was between her teeth. "Never!" she added. *Vive la France!* she thought, and this time as the whip descended she bit down as hard as she could.

For a moment she was sure that it hadn't worked. The pain was there, searing her body, red-hot and alive, and she knew that it must have been a trick, a terrible Nazi trick to make her feel invulnerable. But then, slowly, she could feel herself falling over, toppling down, down, down, to where there was darkness and calm and, ultimately, relief.

Chapter Twenty-nine

*I*t wasn't for a long time after Chantale's death that Dominique began to acknowledge that sometimes resolution is not enough. That sometimes even the greatest of would-be heroes can fail.

He and Father Xavier had considered every prospect, every plan, only to come up against the rock-solid wall of impossibility. The Gestapo quarters were considered impenetrable, and in the long run, they—the Resistance—could not risk everything for only one. Not even for Chantale.

It took Dominique a long time to accept that, and an even greater time to live with the pain of Chantale's death. It was a searing wound, inflicted anew it seemed with every breath he took—and no matter what Father Xavier said, he felt it separating him from his God. Perhaps forever.

Pierre had begun gambling after Chantale died.

It was nothing at first—someplace to go, something to do. Anything was better than sitting at home with his mother's silent accusations raining down on him like hail. It was she who had told him one night when he stumbled in, drunk, that Chantale had been killed by the Gestapo. He had looked around him stupidly, as though his wife would appear at any moment and prove his mother wrong. He hadn't even known that she had been arrested.

"What would the Germans want with Chantale?" he questioned disbelievingly.

Marie-Louise shook her head angrily. "You never knew her, did you? You never took the time to try to know her. She was worth a hundred of your dirty little mistresses."

"What was there to know?" he asked. "She was a wife."

"She was a great deal more than that, my son, and I am proud of her as I could never be proud of you. You are weak, weak! And blind. She was working for the Resistance right under your nose, and you never even saw. How could you see? You were never here to see anything! Your children could have grown up and been on their way, and you would never know."

Pierre shrugged, unconcerned. "I will pay attention to what I want to pay attention to," he said with all the drunken dignity that he could muster. "If she was really working for the Resistance then she deserved to die. But I don't believe she was."

There were storm clouds in his mother's face, but her voice was even when she asked, "And why should you not believe it?"

"She wasn't that intelligent," he said casually, indifferently. Not like Isabelle, he thought with a pang. Chantale never talked about art or politics, or any of the important things in life. She filled her conversations as she filled her days, with small details and unimportant concerns: the children—and he was so *tired* of hearing about the children!—and the household; a peach she had picked that morning from a tree in the orchard and how beautiful it had been; a star she had wished on the night before. And she never seemed to understand how boring she was.

Chantale in the Resistance? For a brief moment he considered it. Everyone knew that the Resistance movement was filled with Communists, and Chantale was too fastidious to spend time with Communists. Everyone knew that Communists didn't wash very often. That was what the Germans said, anyway, and Pierre saw no reason to disbelieve them. So that ruled that out. Unless there had been a man . . . That was something that he could understand, that he could relate to. Some man getting her involved. Some man whom she was sleeping with . . .

He almost laughed at the thought. His frigid wife, sleeping with someone else? The thought defied imagination. No, his mother was wrong. Whatever had happened to Chantale, she hadn't been working for the Resistance.

He scowled at Marie-Louise, who was watching him, silently, the anger draining the color from her face.

"Where did you get your information, anyway? She probably just went crying off to that mother of hers. I knew that the Bretons couldn't be trusted. I knew it. But no, you had to have your way, you had to have me marry one. . . ." His voice trailed off and he shook his head. "There's no reason to go on talking."

He was halfway across the front hall when she began to speak.

"Your wife," she said, her voice quavering just a little, "was the strongest, bravest woman I have ever seen. If that is how the Bretons are, then we need a whole country full of them, we might not have been so quick to surrender to the *sales Boches*. She put up with all your insults and infidelities with dignity, and she did all the things that most of us do not even dare to think about in order to help her country."

Pierre stopped and turned to look at her. "Don't be so melodramatic, Mother. It doesn't suit you." He was pleased with that sentence. It was something that Isabelle might have said.

"It is not melodramatic," Marie-Louise said coldly, "to acknowledge heroism when one sees it. It is sheer stupidity to do otherwise. Your wife was tortured and killed by the Gestapo, and the only mistake that she made in her life was marrying you."

He shrugged again. "Whatever you say, Mother. Will there be a funeral? I don't think that my black suit fits anymore."

After that, there was not a moment of peace at the Château de Montclair. Every night the same complaints were raised: You don't spend any time with your children; you don't respect your wife's memory; she was a far better person than you could ever be. Night after night it went on, and in the daytime, too, whenever Marie-Louise could corner Pierre. On and on and on, until his head was reeling with the sound of her voice and he couldn't stand it any longer.

It was then that he saw Isabelle again.

She was the one to seek him out and he responded to her reemergence in his life as a man in the desert responds to an oasis, with desperate and aching need. She found him in one of the bars that he frequented, drinking the cheap wine that was all that they served anymore, hunched over his glass as though it alone could offer him any salvation. He didn't notice the appreciative ripple that passed through the room, the male space being invaded by something lilting, feminine, and extraordinary. He didn't even respond to her scent, rich and lush and heavy. The first he knew was when she was sitting on the barstool next to him, and her long fingers had reached over and were taking the glass from his hand. "Pierre, darling," she said.

It was as if all his dreams and all his nightmares were coming true at the same time.

She was wearing purple, a deep purple silk sheath dress which followed the contours of her perfect body. Her fingernails and lips were scarlet. Her long, raven-black hair was tied up in some intricate style rarely seen in Angers. So she had a Parisian coiffeur. Her eyes, the same extraordinary violet eyes that had haunted him for so long, were fixed on him at last. At long last.

"Isabelle," he said indistinctly, his voice slightly slurred by the drink. "Isabelle. You've come back."

She glanced behind her, quickly, almost apprehensively, and he looked over her shoulder to see a uniformed German standing there. "Pierre, darling," she said, "I want you to meet Major Hans Werner. Hans, this is the Count de Montclair."

The German clicked his heels together. He was making an effort not to indicate how distasteful he found Pierre, and the effort showed. "Enchanted, Count," he said in correct if heavily accented French. "Isabelle speaks fondly of your friendship."

"Does she, now?" Pierre looked at Isabelle. "Why don't you get rid of him so that we can be together?"

She still looked nervous. "Pierre, darling. Let's leave this place. It's so—masculine." She gave a delicate little shudder. "Hans has offered a late supper. Wouldn't that be lovely? Pâté and duck and champagne."

"And where did Hans find such delicacies? On the black market? No restaurant in Angers is serving them."

"My staff," Hans said, "works miracles for me. Would you do me the honor, Count, of joining us?"

Pierre shrugged. "Why not?" he asked rhetorically, draining his glass before he stood up. "Lead on."

A Wehrmacht staff car was waiting outside for them, and they were conveyed to the Hôtel de la Gare. Hans had a suite, and at a table bedecked with fine linen and spotless silver they were served the promised feast.

"This is *much* better," sighed Isabelle, sipping from her fluted glass. "I do so adore champagne."

"I know that you do, my dear," the major replied, and they smiled at each other over their glasses.

Pierre cleared his throat. "Is this a new game?" he inquired. "Having an old lover watch a flirtation with a new one?"

"Pierre!" Isabelle gasped. "Don't be so gauche, darling. Hans is merely being kind." She gave the German another one of her secretive, breathtaking smiles, and then turned back to Pierre. "Actually, darling, this is business. Hans asked me if I knew anyone like you, and so you came to mind."

Pierre hadn't yet touched his pâté. "What precisely do you mean by someone like me?"

"An investor," Hans said smoothly. "Isabelle, my love, don't you need to powder your nose?"

"But I'm hungry!" she protested.

He glared at her. "Go now, Isabelle, please."

She got up meekly enough after that and went through the double doors to the bedroom, shutting them gently behind her. Pierre watched her go with amazement. "I don't know how you did that," he said. "But you have my admiration. Isabelle never was obedient with me."

"It's a matter of knowing how to dominate a woman," the German said blandly, as casually and conversationally as if they were discussing the market value of radishes. "Here, Count, have some more champagne, and I'll tell you why you're here."

Pierre accepted the refill and broke a crust of bread. Spreading the pâté on it, he said, "Well, then, go on."

"Very well. Recently, some fellow officers and myself decided to try a little business venture—on the side, as it were. Not officially sanctioned. We opened a casino—oh, very small, very discreet. We thought to attract some of the other officers, and it seems to be working. A few Frenchmen even, those whose consciences don't forbid them from trafficking in deutsche marks. Even when a country is occupied, there are ways to make money. You follow me?"

"Avidly," Pierre replied. "More champagne, please."

"What we require at this time is a good Vichy citizen like yourself to join us in this venture. We feel certain that we could attract even more good Vichy citizens if we had someone to set an example. Someone with money and from a good family. I believe that you call it 'of the nobility'?"

"That's what we call it," Pierre said grimly. "What do I get in return?"

"Ah, well, Count, there we have it. We have nothing to give you. But then again, you are not particularly in a position to make demands on us." He leaned forward, elbows on the table. "We understand that your wife the countess recently met with a rather tragic death."

"News," said Pierre, "travels fast."

"In certain circles, it does, yes. The countess died tragically, I believe, while being questioned by the Gestapo." He shook his head sadly. "My condolences, Count. And yet her death leaves many questions unanswered. Did she indeed work for the Underground? Was her family involved as well? What secrets are hidden out at the Château de Montclair? And, perhaps most interestingly, why did she die so suddenly, when the blow she sustained was hardly enough to kill a rodent? There are many questions, Count. Questions that we at the Wehrmacht ask ourselves."

Pierre shrugged. "I wasn't involved, if that's what you're getting at."

"No, we think that you were not, Count. But your mother possibly was. Perhaps even your son was used as a courier, who knows? It would be unfortunate if we had to question them as well. And we could also question you, if we felt the need."

Pierre was starting to get frightened. He had seen Chantale's body before they closed the coffin. He had an idea—a small idea—of what her last moments were like. He had no wish to submit himself to similar treatment. "What do you want me to do?"

Hans leaned back again, relaxed. "Very little, Count. As I said, become a fellow investor in our little enterprise. A visible fellow investor. That is not asking so very much, is it?"

"No," Pierre said faintly. "No, I suppose not."

Hans smiled. "And I'll make it worth your while," he said. "Agree, here and now, to do this for us, and Isabelle is yours for tonight."

"Isabelle?" Pierre gasped. "She would do that?"

"She will do as I wish," Hans said, the smile never leaving his face. "What will it be, Count?"

Pierre was lost, and he knew it. He would do anything for Isabelle. Even for only one night. There was nothing that he would not do for her.

"Yes," he said fervently. "Yes."

After that, Pierre kept his promise. He became part of the illicit casino, and he did more even than Hans had asked of him: He started to gamble.

It was innocent, at first. He risked a little here, a little there. But Marie-Louise knew that the estate funds were rapidly being depleted, and she confronted him. "It's de Montclair money, Pierre," she said, trying to reason with him. "Think of your son, for God's sake."

"I don't care," Pierre mumbled, and when she said something again, he turned and hit her across the face. Marie-Louise stumbled back against the wall. "Leave me *alone,* damn you!" Pierre howled. "Just leave me alone!"

She watched him go, a cold cloth on her cheek, and when he was gone, she went into her sitting room and turned to the one person in the world that she thought could do anything for her. Slowly drawing her engraved writing paper from her desk, she wrote a long letter to the woman lawyer in Zurich who had cared enough about Chantale to help her die.

For once Caroline wasn't flying a Mosquito fighter. She had been excited about this particular transport, because it was a new classification for her. She had proven herself to Pauline's satisfaction on the small, light fighter planes, and had been permitted to test on something larger. "It's not your flying skills that I've ever particularly questioned, you see," Pauline said after Caroline landed and went over to her supervisor, questions in her eyes. "It's always been your judgment, your maturity that was in doubt."

"Well, then," said Caroline, trying to keep her voice casual, "how did I do?"

"Not badly at all," Pauline said, making a mark on the clipboard she always carried. "You'll do."

Caroline smiled. It was the highest praise she had yet earned, and from somebody she had learned to respect.

She was finally flying multiengined airplanes, and this was her first official delivery. It was a bomber, a Handley-Page Halifax, fresh out of the factory with only test miles on it and the brand-new Bristol Hercules engines—the ones that were slowly taking over from the water-cooled Merlins—powering it. She had felt a shiver of excitement as she stood on the tarmac looking at it: four engines, with power turrets mounted fore and aft on the fuselage and twin vertical stabilizers. They said that the new Halifaxes were going to be able to carry thirteen thousand pounds of bombs in their wings and fuselage. Caroline smiled to herself. At least she wasn't going to have to deal with that kind of drag. All airplanes were disarmed when in transit.

She had on this first run a passenger: Lord Dugannon, down from Scotland to London for diplomatic talks of some sort. Pauline hadn't liked the idea. "We're not a passenger service," she complained to White Waltham. "Send the RAF to pick him up if it's all that important."

"Churchill has asked us to do it, particularly when we start picking up the new Halifaxes. He had something to do with appropriating funds for them to work on that new engine, and he wants to see how well it flies,'' she said later to Caroline. "I don't like it, and I don't approve of flying passengers, but you'll have to—just this once.''

"That's all right,'' Caroline said breezily. "I'll take it up to ceiling and freeze him to death. He'll never want to fly again!''

"Just be careful,'' Pauline said, a frown on her face. "I don't like it.''

Caroline had checked Lord Dugannon's gear carefully, ascertaining that his parachute was outside and not inside his flying suit, that he was well strapped into the copilot's seat. Then she went through her preflight check. The engines were roaring in her ears. She put on the radio headset even though there would be no signals, and gestured to him to do the same. At least they could talk to each other.

They took off into a bright dawn, with the spring air chilly all around them and the sun beginning to rise on their left. Lord Dugannon was much taken with the sunrise. "We don't see them like this on the ground,'' he said in contentment, watching it for some time with a childlike pleasure.

The Halifax was flying like a dream. Although it was heavier and more sluggish than anything Caroline had flown before, it moved with a sort of ponderous grace. Once she got used to the reaction time, she relaxed. The sun had come up nicely and the trip ought to be uneventful.

And then a Messerschmitt came on her from high on her left, right in the sun, just where he was supposed to be. *If* Caroline had been looking. But she wasn't looking. The forecast had called for a sunny day and there had not been any radar reports of German activity when she left the manor. The first knowledge that she had of the German plane was a spatter of machine-gun fire that riddled the fuselage and caused the Halifax to shudder under her hands.

Lord Dugannon immediately began shouting and Caroline looked around her desperately, seeing for the first time the fighter that had materialized out of nowhere, cursing the fact that she wasn't flying the faster, more maneuverable Mosquito and that the plane was unarmed. They were going to be shot out of the sky because someone had decided that women shouldn't fly armed planes.

And what were you going to do with an armed Halifax anyway? she asked herself sourly. Send the Scottish lord back to man the gun turret? Or drop a bomb on the Messerschmitt?

She was going to have to do something—and quickly. The fighter was circling, and she was going to be in his sights again any minute. Banking to the right, she started climbing, looking around her for cloud cover. For once, the weather report had been correct. There were no clouds to be seen.

The Halifax had a ceiling of thirteen thousand five hundred feet. She was approaching that fast, and the Messerschmitt was keeping up with her. He wasn't in any hurry to send her down; it was as though he was playing with her, delaying the kill for some devious reason of his own.

Lord Dugannon was fumbling with his safety belt and still shouting something. As he hadn't pressed his transmitter button down, she couldn't hear him, but his intentions were obvious. Caroline's hand shot across and grabbed his wrist.

"Stop!" she shouted. "Stop! You can't jump at this height!"

He ignored her, struggling to free his hand from hers, and the Halifax started going down. Caroline wasn't sure what was worse, the Messerschmitt still circling around them, waiting for her to straighten out so it could come in behind her and blow her out of the sky, or the man next to her who had suddenly become mad, grabbing at controls instead of sitting quietly.

She pressed her button so he could hear her. "Lord Dugannon! We have to get lower before you can jump. Please wait."

He turned toward her then, and she saw the ashen look on his face. He said something, and she gestured toward his transmitter button. He fumbled and found it and said, "I've never parachuted before."

Oh, God, Caroline thought. This is all I need. She forced herself to smile at him. "It's all right. We may not need to. And if we do, I'll help you. But it's important to stay calm."

"Calm?" He had pressed his transmitter button before screaming, and she flinched at the volume. "Calm? We're going to die, young lady! We're going to die! And you want me to stay calm!"

"We're not doing to die," she said forcefully. "Please just sit still for a moment."

It was about time to pay attention to the German behind her. If there was any way of avoiding it, she wasn't going to send this beautiful expensive big machine to the scrap heap, though it would almost be a blessing to see Lord Dugannon depart. Still, there were some options. Not many, but a few.

She banked again sharply, this time to the left, so that she could stay out of his sights for a few more minutes. Next to her, Lord Dugannon was sobbing into his hands. Caroline pressed her lips together and made a decision.

"Here," she said. "Look here. I need your help."

He looked up, his face streaked with tears. "We're going to die," he whined.

"We're not going to die," she said again. "And you can help. Give me your hand."

"My—"

"Give me your hand!" she shouted and, surprisingly, he obeyed.

She took it and put it on the flaps lever and made sure that he was grasping it tightly enough. "Don't do anything now. Don't move. Just keep your hand there. When I say 'flaps,' I want you to push it all the way down, as hard as you can. No," she added, seeing his muscles tense, "not now. Don't practice. Just when I tell you to. Do you understand?"

"Yes." His face was chalk-white.

"Good. Don't move your hand. Keep it there." And now, she thought, let's see if the Germans are as smart as they want us to think they are.

She straightened out finally from the wild turns she had been making—straightened out and kept a course, as though she had decided to try to outrun the Messerschmitt. She couldn't, and he knew that. If he wanted her, he was going to come for her now.

He came.

He moved into the long, graceful dive that was going to set him directly behind her, ready to shoot. She watched him as he began the dive, and counted under her breath. She had no idea how fast he was going; she could only estimate, and if she was wrong she was going to kill them both.

Just before the Halifax would surely be in his sights, she screamed to Dugannon, "Flaps!"

He put them down, immediately causing the Halifax to bounce upward, pillow soft. The Messerschmitt was coming in too fast and was suddenly on top of them, banking fast to the right in a desperate attempt to avoid a midair collision, banking too fast and going into a spin. Caroline shut her eyes for a moment. She might well have deliberately caused what was happening to the pilot in the other plane, but she couldn't help in that moment feeling some empathy with him. She knew what he was experiencing: the world spinning around and around out of control, with no way to tell which direction was up and which was down. If he was lucky he would gather his senses long enough to pop the cockpit cover and bail out. She opened her eyes and banked the Halifax so she could see where the Messerschmitt was going down. There was a plume of smoke from somewhere below her, but no sign of a parachute. She shook her head and felt her stomach move a little.

It was time to get going. There may have been other Germans around—he must have gotten lost from a unit somewhere. No one ever flew over enemy territory alone and in bright sunlight, and she didn't want to stay and see if she could duplicate her efforts. Adjusting the flaps, she returned to their original course, and it was only then that she realized that Lord Dugannon was leaning over and throwing up between his legs.

"Julie!" Eric Beaumont's voice was more forceful than she had ever heard it. "Julie!"

She hurried to his office door and looked in. He had a telegram in his hand and an ashen look on his face. "Julie. For God's sake, get me Roosevelt on the telephone, and now. I want to send a telegram to Churchill. I want Caroline Asheford out of England tomorrow!"

"I don't understand." Caroline's voice was bewildered. "I did the best that I could under the circumstances. Why am I being punished for it?"

"Well," the tall thin man said judiciously, "not exactly punished, my dear. We're writing up all sorts of good things about you, and it's an honorable discharge."

She looked across at Pauline, sitting quite still at another table in the operations room at the manor. "What's going on, Pauline?"

"Oh, for heaven's sake!" It was the tall man again. He wasn't wearing a uniform, but he was connected somehow with the military, or so Pauline had said. "My dear Mrs. Asheford. You did indeed do your best. No one here is questioning that. You managed to save the life of an important member of Parliament, and not incidentally a bomber that cost a great deal of money. And I gather you did so rather cleverly?''

He looked at Pauline as though for confirmation, and after a moment she nodded. ''Oh, yes. The old flaps trick.''

''Right.'' He obviously had no idea what she was talking about. ''But what you did is also seen as—er—inconvenient in certain circles.''

''Inconvenient?'' Caroline was perplexed. ''What does that mean?''

''Well, here we have an unarmed plane being flown by an ATA girl pilot''—he spoke the last two words as though he were mentioning an unspeakable disease—''downing a Messerschmitt. It won't do. We're trying to recruit women for ATA, damn it. And there's some feeling about your being American, as well.''

''What he is saying,'' said Pauline directly, ''is that it's politically expedient to ignore the whole thing. And they can't ignore it if you're still around. That's what makes you persona non grata now.''

''Well, er, we can't precisely ignore the whole thing. No, it's most unsatisfactory. We must bolster the spirit of the people, what? And a Jerry down is a Jerry down after all.''

Caroline thought that she knew what was coming now. ''So someone else was flying the plane,'' she said too loudly.

''Er, well, that's right. And Lord Dugannon—''

''Lord Dugannon?'' Caroline burst out. ''Lord Dugannon? He was either screaming or getting sick the whole time!''

''He is offering to take responsibility for the action,'' the man said mildly.

''I don't believe this!'' Caroline appealed to Pauline. ''The man was an idiot! I was lucky to get us down in one piece!''

''And that is greatly appreciated, never fear,'' the tall man assured her quickly. ''But, officially, Lord Dugannon was flying that airplane.''

''He can't!'' Caroline spluttered. ''He can't even fly! He can't even—''

''Caroline, forget it. It's all over,'' Pauline said suddenly, tiredness in her voice. ''It's all over now. They've made their decisions.''

''They can't force me to go,'' Caroline said, her voice strained with the force of holding back the tears which were suddenly in her eyes and blocking her throat.

"I'm afraid that we can, Mrs. Asheford. You're being discharged from the ATA. That's step one. You're also being asked to leave Britain. If you do not do so, the government will be forced to deport you."

She looked at him, the thin, pleasant face studiously neutral. She looked at Pauline, who surprisingly had tears shimmering in her own eyes, and then she stood up. "God damn you all," she said thickly. "I've done everything I can to help you, even when my own country wasn't doing anything, and this is the thanks I get. Well, God damn you all. You don't deserve to win this war!" She was being unreasonable and she knew it, but the hot sudden pain was too much to bear. The pain of losing the easy camaraderie of the ATA, the pain of losing England itself, the place where Steven had died. Flying would never be the same, not ever again. She stalked to the door, tore off her flying helmet, and sent it spinning to the ground. "God damn you," she said again, and slammed the door behind her.

And the next day she left for America. For Caroline Asheford, in the spring of 1942, the war was over.

Chapter Thirty

May 1943.

"I know we're years behind the British in radar development. Frankly, I don't particularly care. It's a simple enough problem. We're allies, for God's sake. Haven't we been shipping them war matériel for years? Just get some of their people over here to work on the radar project. No sense in duplicating each other's efforts. And for God's sake, get out to New Mexico. We need you on this project!"

Eric Beaumont slammed down the telephone receiver. It was maddening, truly maddening. All the most brilliant scientific minds were at the Massachusetts Institute of Technology working on radar, for Christ's sake. Whereas they should be out at Los Alamos. Radar was important, of course, but it was old hat by now. They were doing something far more essential out in the desert.

Eric was waiting for a visitor, but he never wasted his time. Back in the days when he had first come to San Jose, when he had lived with his mother-in-law, she had said something to him that he had never forgotten: "Don't wait to have time to take on a new challenge, because time will never come. You have to make time. Remember, most important tasks get done in the odd five or ten minutes between other projects."

He remembered Anna's words now, just as he reminded himself of them nearly every day, and immediately sat down to look over some other designs that Julie had placed on his desk only that morning—designs for the jet-propulsion engine that the Intraglobal laboratories were working on. Already they had fitted one into a Messerschmitt, though the damned pilots apparently didn't know what to do with the extra speed yet, and were using the thing as a bomber. He scrawled a suggestion or two in the margin and was about to sign it when Julie knocked on the door. "Mr. Beaumont? President Roosevelt is here to see you."

The President looked tired. He was supposed to be inspecting some of the naval training bases and had spent most of the morning doing just that. He looked as though he was carrying the weight of their collective responsibility squarely on his shoulders. Refusing Eric's offer of refreshment, he instead fitted a cigarette into the long holder he used. "So what is the problem, Mr. Beaumont?"

Eric sat down across from him, not behind his desk, and lit his own cigarette. "It's Los Alamos," he said briefly.

Roosevelt's eyebrows went up. "Los Alamos? I thought that things were progressing well there. You told me so yourself last month. You sounded moderately pleased with yourself, I must say."

"I was. The work is progressing well. Dr. Oppenheimer is director of the laboratory now, and we're continuing to work on recruitment. You see some of the finest physicists in this country are still working on radar."

"And?"

"Well, we're getting more and more interference from the military. The Army is demanding to inspect the laboratory on a weekly basis, to have everyone stop what he's doing to explain it to the Joint Chiefs of Staff, that sort of stuff. The scientific mind is a very delicate thing, Mr. President. They are not going to continue to work under that kind of constant pressure."

"I see." The President drew in on his cigarette. "And it is a bomb that is being manufactured at Los Alamos?"

"Of course it's a bomb. That's the whole point, isn't it? You need isolation to work on a bomb, not truckloads of tourists every other day. Not to mention the sociological aspects of the question. There's a whole community living there, a compound not unlike this one. Families, stores, a dance hall. It's the scientists' home, as well as their laboratory. They need some privacy."

"Of course it is a bomb," Roosevelt repeated, almost musingly. "A weapon. Wouldn't you say that weapons should come under military jurisdiction, Mr. Beaumont?"

Eric saw where his train of thought was leading now, and he didn't like it. "There is more than one point of view on that issue," he said evenly. "The weapon in question doesn't yet exist in reality—only in theory. Surely the military has more interest in the deployment of real weapons against the real enemies that we have than in supervising what may ultimately be a dream?''

''You don't believe that it's just a dream.''

''Of course I don't,'' said Eric impatiently. ''I see it in my mind just as clearly as I once saw airplanes, just as clearly as I once saw rockets, just as clearly as I'm now looking at jet propulsion. It's going to happen, Mr. President. Someday. It's going to happen much more quickly if the military keep their noses out of it. If you want to use it in this current war, then you're interested in speed. Let us develop the damned thing in peace, then your people can have it, can use it to their heart's content.''

''Develop a death bomb in peace. That's an interesting concept, Mr. Beaumont.'' The President ground out his cigarette. ''I will see what I can do to quiet some of our overeager personnel. No promises. I'll see what I can do.''

Eric walked him to the door. ''That's all I ask.''

Roosevelt paused at the door, looking at the calendar on the wall. ''May fourteenth, nineteen forty-three,'' he read aloud. ''Well, here's a bit of good news for you. In less than two weeks I meet with Churchill.''

Eric could feel his heart leap. ''Yes?''

''You know that the British are working on this atomic energy deal as well. Not that they have the people that we do. Well, we're signing an agreement to resume the exchange of information on tube alloys. Your cooperation is assumed.''

''Of course.''

''Splendid. I'll make sure that it's properly worded. What I want is their cooperation, but I also plan to make it clear that we're the ones running the show. Postwar production. Wartime makes strange bedfellows, and I don't want us to be harnessed with the English forever. We'll just get that in writing. It ought to please you.''

''We already have a policy of cooperation.''

''So we do. This isn't cooperation, Mr. Beaumont. I'm not negotiating anything. I want to be perfectly clear that the U.S. is going to have the upper hand on atomic-energy development both now and later.'' He hesitated. ''You've been keeping up, I assume?''

''I bought out a company last year,'' Eric said blandly, ''that was doing alloy experimentation. There are a lot of possibilities that I'm looking into. But I'll own them all, one way or the other.''

''What kinds of possibilities?''

Eric shrugged. ''Rocketry. X-ray equipment. Communications. And naturally nuclear weapons.''

The President put on his hat. ''Keep me informed.''

''Of course.'' But Eric knew that he wouldn't.

For some time, they had worried about whether any of the de Montclair estate would be left to pass on to the children. Pierre was drawing his family down with him into his self-appointed vortex of destruction.

Months had gone by, months filled with the horrors and preoccupations of war, and none of it touched Pierre de Montclair. Only his own drama was of any interest to him; only his own loss—the loss, it should be noted, not of his wife but of his mistress—was the occasion for any sorrow. He lived his new obsession, drinking and gambling at the roulette table until he went home with nothing.

It was Soizic who first learned about it, and who tried to remonstrate with the count. For a time he seemed better; for a time, Marie-Louise reported nothing out of the ordinary. He still went in to Angers, but the drain on the family account had stopped. And then he started again, in as feverish and dedicated a fashion as if he had never stopped. They all agreed. Either it had to stop, or new means had to be found to supplement the family income. The situation was clearly intolerable.

Marc Giroux stopped it by writing a letter to the vice-president of the Deutsches Bank. Once again, blackmail and pressure were brought to bear in order to protect the Château de Montclair.

Soizic, reading the letter, grimaced. ''Must you be so— blatant?'' she asked distastefully.

''There isn't much time to be otherwise, my dear. The Countess Marie-Louise was thinking of selling the château because of Pierre's debts.''

He glanced at her as she sealed the letter. Such passion . . . she was still so young. The same passion had sent her to France in order to save the Countess Chantale from Nazi torture; the same passion made her feel, more than he ever could, what the ravages of war and occupation had done to Europe. He loved her more than ever, seeing the differences between them as interesting, not realizing that she viewed herself, next to him, as pathetic.

Perhaps when this was all over he might actually get up enough courage to ask her to marry him. Strange how he hadn't thought of it until now. His wife had died so very long ago, and he had always taken it for granted that he would never marry again. And yet there was a youthfulness and vulnerability about Soizic that made him want her, not just sexually, but forever.

She would probably say no. She was too young. She was too clever. She would want, soon, to be moving on to other things, to other men. But he would never know if he didn't try. . . .

"Lock the door, Soizic," he said suddenly, his voice low. "I've forgotten what it's like to make love in the office."

She turned to him with a delighted smile. "But the work?"

"Damn the work," he said heavily, getting up from behind the desk and walking around it toward her. "For twenty minutes, damn the work. . . ."

Caroline sat herself in the cockpit and reached over to strap her daughter in the copilot's seat. "There. Is that tight enough?"

Elizabeth nodded. "Yes, Mommy."

Caroline still hadn't gotten over her anger—not yet. It was going to be a long time before she stopped raging about not being able to fly for the ATA and being dismissed like a schoolgirl for an institutional infraction. But, despite herself, she was enjoying her time with Elizabeth. She had forgotten what it was like to sing her to sleep, to watch her playing, to take her up flying. She hadn't realized that Elizabeth at five years of age would no longer be a baby, but a little girl with a definite personality—a real person.

It had been hard telling her daughter about Steven, almost as hard as it had been talking to William about his brother. William blamed her. If she hadn't run away, Steven wouldn't have had to go after her, would still be safely building ships in Newport. William blamed Caroline, but not enough to stop relying on her to take care of Nicholas. And Caroline had learned to stop blaming herself.

Justine had been transferred to a smaller hospital that specialized in treating psychiatric illnesses, and the people there were guardedly encouraging. With the proper treatment, she might speak again—someday. In the meantime, she was being given cold baths and other forms of hydrotherapy to stimulate her. She received shock treatments, which often showed encouraging results in similar patients. She was being given psychiatric therapy. Eventually, with a lot of help . . .

Everyone at the hospital was pleased that Caroline had returned. She was someone for their social workers to talk to, for William had closed himself off to them, as though the pain of dealing with Justine was more than he could bear. The trauma of seeing her mute and helpless was too much for him. He had stopped seeing his wife, had stopped talking to her doctors, despite their protests that she still, in her own way, needed him.

Caroline had gone to visit Justine at once, and had immediately requested a private room and special services. "The money doesn't matter, don't you see?" she said. "I'll take care of it. I'll take care of her." And so it was to Caroline that they telephoned their reports and made cautious assessments of her progress.

And it was Caroline who came back to look after Nicholas.

He had been staying at the estate and been taken care of along with Elizabeth, but he was over a year older than his cousin, and something had to be done about his education. Here William refused to let Caroline assume the finances, as he had done at first with Justine's hospitalization. Nicholas would go to public school, he said firmly, and that was that. He could live at the estate, but he would go to public school. William Asheford was not going to be dependent upon his sister-in-law for his son's education.

So it was that Elizabeth had tutors, and Nicholas was driven to school every morning by Edwards, the chauffeur who in his day had escorted Margaret Lewis and Amanda Lewis and Caroline Copeland, and now found himself with a little boy in the backseat making faces in the driving mirror.

And still, Caroline flew.

She had been in her Butterfly when the news came about the Battle of Midway, and later when they got the news about the Bataan Death March, and it was while flying her Butterfly one day off Block Island that she saw a German U-boat surfacing and she called Civil Defense to send somebody after it.

Often Elizabeth would accompany her. She was still too young to be afraid, and so Caroline took her up frequently, practicing the acrobatics that had been forbidden in the ATA—not that there weren't ATA pilots who disregarded the ban, but Caroline had been practicing being less rebellious. She indulged herself now, looping the loop, turning and twisting this way and that, gaining height only to dive down, fast, laughing all the way. Elizabeth caught her spirit and laughed, too, clapping her hands in delight. Her mother had been gone, and had now come back. Anything that they did together was fine with her.

Caroline listened to the news of the war—she couldn't not listen, it was in all the media around her—but there were other things in her world now, things that Steven had once urged her to pay attention to. Gradually, they were becoming more and more important to her: Elizabeth starting to read and write, looking at a globe to learn about the world, memorizing poetry that she recited at night after dinner; Nicholas, leaving every morning for school, getting into mischief on the beach or in the stables, laughing and playful and always hungry; Justine, distant and fearful, looking at Caroline as though she were a stranger, polite to her doctors and nurses at the psychiatric hospital. And the estate: Caroline had never realized how difficult it was to run a large household; there were always problems to cope with.

Slowly, hesitantly, Caroline had been returning to St. John's, finding solace in the old remembered words of the Book of Common Prayer. Insisting that the children accompany her, she who had never had any strong personal faith was surprised at her need for it now.

Eric telephoned frequently, wrote occasionally, and always with questions about Elizabeth's education. How was she doing? Would she be going off to school soon? What subjects interested her most?

"You only want her for your damned company," Caroline accused him.

He laughed. "My dear, I'm not ready to abdicate the throne yet."

"Good," she replied in earnest. "I'm not sure that I want her to have it anyway. Wouldn't it be nice for one of us to have a normal life for a change?"

"Some people weren't born to have normal lives," he said.

"Elizabeth was," Caroline said fiercely. "Elizabeth was."

Intraglobal had never brought her anything but grief, and she was determined to shield Elizabeth from all of that. The Lewis fortune was enough. Elizabeth would inherit that. But that was all. For once, someone was going to be able to make her own decisions abut her life.

Sometimes she wished that that person could have been she.

* * *

Andrew Starkey frowned as he buttoned his shirt. It was looser than ever; that meant that he had lost more weight. Dysentery, probably. It was hard to remember a time when he hadn't been sick.

It was hard to remember any time before he came to the prison camp, and harder still to visualize any future outside of it. It could be worse, he supposed. They had cigarettes on occasion, when they could bribe the guards. There was bread and soup. They didn't starve. They heard horror stories about the other camps, the concentration camps that the Germans had filled with Jews on their way to Hitler's famous "final solution." When you thought about that, Andrew realized grimly, you understood just how much worse things could be. At least in the prisoner-of-war camp no one was killed. Not deliberately, anyway.

He had been assigned to a work detail. At first it was digging ditches; the Germans seemed to have an inordinate fondness for ditches. They were always moving the latrines even when they had just moved them the day before. At first Andrew thought that the guards were suspicious that the prisoners might tunnel out of the camp, but soon enough, when he came to know them better, he realized that it was just the literal simplicity of the Aryan mind. The prisoners were to work, so they worked, even when there was no work to be done.

Later, they gave him more sophisticated tasks to perform, helping out the German mechanic at the motor pool. Andrew had one day cried out in frustration, "Why am I doing this? I don't know anything about fixing engines."

"What do you know, then?" asked the corporal, as frustrated as Andrew about his prisoner's lack of ability.

"I can fly airplanes. And I can cook," Andrew responded, thinking back to the faraway days in San Francisco, and the restaurant he had once owned. Not much, in the end, to say for himself. He could fly airplanes, and he could cook.

But cooking, it transpired, was what they needed the most, and Andrew spent the remainder of his incarceration in the vast prison kitchens. Gourmet food it was not, but working there was a damned sight better than the motor pool.

Most of all, there was time to think. Time to relive that horrible encounter with the Messerschmitt; time to wonder how things would have been different if he had made other choices. Life was like that, he realized. Fate took so many different guises and disguises, and left one wondering if one had any choices to make at all. A step to the left or to the right, a word spoken or left unspoken, a glance in one direction or another, a voice that cried of death in the night. Everything and nothing contributed to what finally happened to a human being. Perhaps, if he had not been shot down then, he would have been shot down later. Perhaps it was just in the hand he had been dealt.

But thinking about that was nonsense, because Andrew, of all people, knew better. He knew what the face of Fate looked like. He knew that the puppeteers were casually pulling strings from the safety of their offices and boardrooms and golf courses. Nothing violent had ever touched them. They never had to look at the results of their work, not the *real* results. They were only interested in their charts and their statistics. They would never have to dig ditches, or carry guns, or feel the hot sick breath of death on their necks as their airplanes burst into flames around them. No, they drank their martinis and drove about in their limousines and talked about the art of puppeteering, never about the puppets.

Their names were Jeffrey Kellogg and Eric Beaumont.

They kept their faces in the shadows; they hid behind corporations behind corporations behind corporations; they influenced the politicians who put their names to the acts, but the acts were still theirs. They needed to grow, and in order for them to prosper, others had to die.

There were animals, Andrew thought, which ate their own offspring. Fish . . . some fish did. And maybe some birds, and some spiders. None of them were exactly higher forms of life. But humans did, too, only they disguised what they were doing so it wouldn't seem so primitive. Jeffrey Kellogg was consuming his own, not just his family, but everyone who got in his way. Andrew wondered what the death toll was, for them, now. At least when Hitler killed, he knew that that was what he was doing. He didn't hide behind other people, other names. He was clear about his priorities.

All through the long months Andrew shivered in the kitchen, shivered with the illness that never quite left him, that sent him heaving to the latrine once or twice a day, every day. All through the long months he shivered, and worked, and thought about his uncle, and about Caroline's uncle, and all the evil that they had brought with them into the war. That was a joke, he thought sourly. Maybe there wouldn't have been a war if it hadn't been for them.

And then, early in the summer of 1943, the letter came.

London
July 15, 1943

Dearest Andrew,

This is such a hateful letter to write, but I'd best just get on with it, shouldn't I? That was what you always said, when you had to write one of those horrid letters to the families of one of the boys who had gotten killed. . . .

Andrew, I'm writing to tell you that I'm breaking off our engagement. I'm getting married to someone else. I'm sure that you'll understand. There's a little something on the way to speed up our plans. Otherwise I would have waited. I'm going back to New Zealand with him, once the war's off.

I've left the ATA altogether. There wasn't much point in staying, not after Caroline Asheford left. I need to tell you something else, Andrew. I was supposed to be watching her—and you. People were concerned about what might happen if you and Caroline were to actually get serious. I must say that I wasn't altogether displeased with the assignment. We *did* have some jolly times together, didn't we, poppet? But it's time now for me to be getting on with my own life, so I've resigned.

You're a sweet and sensitive man, and I know that when the war is off you'll be able to find someone who will be a fine wife to you.

All the best,
Emma Harrington

Andrew stopped talking after that.

The prison officials grew concerned and a parade of doctors examined him, but he had destroyed the letter and no one understood what had happened. He went about his work as usual, but there was a blank stare where his eyes had once been lively, and then, slowly, the gaze grew black with hatred. He became frightening in a way that no other prisoner had been frightening before. Prison guards asked to be transferred from his cell block, and the chief cook pleaded with the commandant to put Andrew someplace else. The change in him was eerie, and they were taking no chances. Prisoners who give up have nothing left to lose.

Sweet Emma. Sweet, innocent Emma. The one bright, shining light in his existence. His pretty English rose. Sweet Emma, with her laughter and her candor, her naïveté and her childlike confidences.

Sweet Emma, who all the time had been working for Them.

Which? Johnson Industries? Or Intraglobal? Or did it matter? It was all the same. He couldn't even have a woman in his life without it being someone—what was it she had said?—"assigned" to him?

Emma had made him believe in a world away from the war, outside of corporate intrigue, a world where two people could find peace and happiness, a place where simple values and a simpler life-style were possible. With Emma he thought he could disengage from all the horror, retreat from all the indecencies, turn his back on all the evil. She had made him believe in a world where they could find a corner of lush green grass, a field or two, a cottage with a thatched roof, children playing by a fireplace.

She had made him believe in a world that she didn't even believe in herself.

Or perhaps she did. Perhaps she was going off to find it in New Zealand. Perhaps she knew that it would never be hers as long as she was with him, with a man who carried the shadow of Johnson Industries looming over him like the specter of death itself.

That was naive thinking, he reminded himself. Emma had never seriously believed in a relationship between them. She had said that she loved him, but it was never true. He was her assignment. A pleasant one, perhaps. She did acknowledge that they had shared jolly times together, but an assignment nevertheless.

Eric Beaumont had said that he must never marry Caroline Asheford. And Eric Beaumont had done everything in his power to make sure that he wouldn't. He had succeeded—both times. People like Eric Beaumont and Jeffrey Kellogg always got what they wanted.

Night after night, Andrew lay sleepless on his bunk, his hands crossed under his head, staring out into the darkness and thinking. The thoughts eventually became obsessional.

Andrew had decided what he must do. The world could no longer be controlled by power-hungry megaliths. No one else knew, not even Caroline fully understood what was happening. He was the only one who knew. He was the only one who understood.

And he was the only one who could do anything about it.

Chapter Thirty-one

*F*or Caroline, the passing of time was defined not so much by the seasons—she had seen far too many of them come and go, anyway—but by the songs on the radio, by the films at the movie theater. Nineteen forty-three was "I'll be Seeing You," with its plaintive melody and sad refrain: "I'll be looking at the moon, but I'll be seeing you . . ." The memory of Steven and her feelings about him tugged at her consciousness every time the song was played. Nineteen forty-three was *Casablanca,* too, which she took Elizabeth and Nicholas to see, sitting in the darkened theater on a Saturday afternoon with the children on either side of her, absorbed in the drama which, in all probability, was going on in Europe even as they watched. Elizabeth was five, too young to understand, but Nicholas was vociferous about his opinion on the way back to Ocean Avenue.

"I'd like to kill Germans!" he announced happily.

"What makes you say that?" asked Caroline.

"They're bad people," he said seriously. "They close down parties."

Caroline smiled to herself, tightening her hands slightly on the steering wheel, her eyes on the road. "Yes, Nicholas," she murmured, "they certainly do that."

"Did Uncle Steven kill Germans?" he wanted to know.

"No," she said. "Your Uncle Steven believed more in life than in death." I only wish that I could have kept up with him, she added, unhappily, to herself.

"Daddy makes ships that kill Germans," Nicholas said proudly.

"What are Germans?" asked Elizabeth.

"Germans are people who live far away from Newport," Caroline responded. "Their leader is a little bit crazy, and he's making them hurt other people. That's why there's a war going on, honey. So that we can stop them from hurting more people.''

"Nicholas hurt me this morning," announced Elizabeth. "He hit me."

"Did not!" he retorted.

"Did, too!" she answered in the age-old childish exchange, and Caroline sighed. So, too, it seemed to be with countries. Did not, did too, did not, until one of them got fed up with the diplomatic exchanges and struck the first blow. Political life seemed to be filled with childish nonsense like that. Not that Hitler was nonsensical, of course, and not that the bombing of Pearl Harbor was childish play. But, in the end, it would all just fade into the past, like the things she knew about the First War when her father died.

She glanced into the backseat at Elizabeth. Caroline's father killed in one war, Elizabeth's father in another. It didn't seem very fair, somehow. And it was always the women who were left behind to pick up the pieces.

Well, her own mother hadn't been very good at picking up pieces. She just went from one shattered relationship, one shattered dream, to another, and let the pieces stay where they had fallen. But Caroline had learned that broken glass had to be cleaned up. Even if the men did the breaking and the women did the cleaning up.

And now there was Nicholas, one more generation of males ready to go and shed blood on the flimsiest of pretexts. Like his father, who obsessively drew designs for battleships whose guns would kill people he had never seen, would never know. Nicholas would probably have his war someday, too.

The thought reminded her. William. She had to go and see William. The school term was starting soon, and Nicholas needed things. He was seven years old, going into the second grade already. And Caroline knew better than to pay for anything for Nicholas herself, knew the rage that his father would fly into.

There was more to that rage, though, than William's anger with Caroline for her part in Steven's death. There was something there, something dark, lurking just below the surface. It made Caroline afraid. It was something to do with the business, with Asheford Shipbuilding. They were doing well; that was what everyone said. And, with Steven's death, William was now the sole owner, reaping the profits of a profitable industry. And yet he couldn't afford a private school for his son, could barely buy him clothes. Something was terribly, terribly wrong.

She was almost afraid to find out what it was.

In 1944 the song on the radio was "Swinging on a Star," and Caroline hummed it to herself all the time. "Would you like to swing on a star, carry moonbeams home in a jar, and be better off than you are . . ." She sang it to Elizabeth at night to help her sleep, and Elizabeth's memories were laced with dreams of catching moonbeams in a jar and carrying them home to her mother.

Elizabeth was six years old, and Caroline was beginning to teach her how to fly. Nothing significant, nothing important, just letting her feel the stick in her hands from time to time, the same way that other parents set their children behind the wheel of a car and allowed them to steer for a few moments. Elizabeth loved it, loved every moment of it, laughing in delight with her tiny parachute strapped to her back and her aviator's goggles obscuring her view. "Can we fly today, Mommy?" was her most frequent request at the breakfast table, and more often than not, Caroline said yes.

Nicholas was not as happy. He was being teased at school for living in a great mansion. He was certainly the only child from Ocean Avenue to attend public school, and his classmates let him know precisely what they thought of it. He came home, day after day, week after week, with bruises on his cheeks and black eyes. Caroline fussed over him as if he were her own child, but even she couldn't overlook the anger that glared back at her.

Nicholas had to defend himself on a daily basis in the school-yard, while Elizabeth had lessons at home. Nicholas was teased and made fun of by the other children, while Elizabeth had a tutor who called her "Miss Elizabeth." Nicholas had nothing; Elizabeth had everything.

That was how he saw it. Elizabeth even had a mother, a real mother, while his had disappeared. He was eight years old, and had finally been taken to visit his mother at the hospital. Caroline had asked William for permission, and he had looked at her with vacant eyes and shrugged his shoulders. She took Nicholas, on his eighth birthday, just the two of them. First they went out to lunch at the White Horse Tavern, where she let him eat all the ice cream that he wanted, and then they took the Rover that she had borrowed from the estate up into the green rolling hills and to the hospital. Somewhere she had read that all psychiatric hospitals were on pretty grounds; it helped people feel better. Justine's hospital was no exception. The green lawns were dotted here and there with nurses and attendants in white uniforms, with people wearing dressing gowns and pajamas. The lucky ones. Justine was rarely permitted on the grounds because once she had tried to drown herself in the stream when they had let her out.

Justine spoke on occasion, but her conversations were those of a child. "It sometimes happens, with the shock therapy," the social worker had told Caroline. "It makes them better, but it does destroy some brain cells."

"That doesn't sound like a cure to me," Caroline said cautiously.

"Oh, but Mrs. Asheford, it's worth it, believe me. Why, just to hear her talking! She's made such progress!"

Justine had been in the hydrotherapy room when Caroline and Nicholas arrived, and they waited while she was sponged down and dried off. Caroline had visited the room where it took place, and had had nightmares about it for a week afterward. It was like a scene out of Dante, a scene from hell. All the tubs were sunken into the floor, two rows of them, so that the patients' heads were level with the attendants' feet. Fourteen people at a time went in for therapy; fourteen people were put into the tubs, and then the canvas tops were lowered over them, so that just their necks and heads were visible. Sometimes they were tied down, so that they would not hurt themselves. And then ice-cold water was spurted into the tubs, and the patients all began screaming with pain, and a terrible banging noise, the drumming of their hands and heels on the interiors of the tubs, filled the room. Sometimes they lost consciousness. Caroline couldn't help thinking that the ones who blacked out were the lucky ones.

"It seems hard to believe, Mrs. Asheford," the director had said that day, escorting her out, "but it really helps them a great deal. Purges the body. Quite an effective treatment." But now, as Justine was brought into the room, Caroline looked at the bluish circles around her friend's eyes and the bandages around her hands and ached for her. Perhaps, she thought, the illness was more humane than the cure.

Justine smiled at them vaguely, and allowed herself to be lowered into a chair. The nurse, smiling encouragingly at Justine, put a crocheted afghan across her knees, as she would for an elderly lady, even though the day was warm. "There you go, Justine," she said brightly. "Some nice visitors for you. And later we'll have milk and cake in the solarium."

"I want milk and cake now," said Nicholas.

The nurse gave him a bright, superficial smile and said, to Caroline, "Don't tire her too much, Mrs. Asheford, please." Caroline nodded, wondering what it was that made the nurse call Justine by her first name while according Caroline the dignity of her family name. The nurse left, again scattering the artificial smile over them. Like confetti. Like a benediction.

Caroline leaned forward. "Justine," she said softly. "Nicholas is here to see you."

Justine looked at her blankly, her fingers playing nervously with the blanket on her lap.

Caroline was used to this. "Nicholas," she said again. "Your son, Justine. It's his birthday today." She looked at Nicholas. "Say hello to Mommy, Nicky," she suggested.

He looked at Justine warily. "Isn't Mommy," he said stoutly, lapsing back into baby talk. "Can we go now?"

"This is your Mommy," Caroline said patiently. "She's sick. We've told you that before. Mommy is sick and that's why you live with Elizabeth and me."

"Sick," said Justine helpfully.

Nicholas was looking at her with distaste. "No," he said again. "Mommy's nice. Mommy lives in a house, a pretty house, with flowers in the garden." He looked at Caroline accusingly, "You're trying to trick me!"

"Nicholas, I'm not," Caroline said. "I just thought that you ought to meet her. She is your mother."

"Pretty blanket," said Justine musingly.

Nicholas was on his feet. "You're a bad person," he said to Caroline. "You're mean, and I hate you. I hate you!"

"Nicholas—" Caroline said imploringly, but he was gone. She could hear his footsteps echoing down the long, polished hallway. Someone would catch him, she thought. She looked back at Justine, feeling suddenly exhausted.

Justine looked back at her and smiled brightly. "Bad person," she said.

Nicholas was silent all the way home, and after that Caroline rarely talked to him about either of his parents. He fought on in the schoolyard, and became tough, and she watched the changes in him with a mixture of sorrow and tenderness. There was nothing that she could do for him.

In the early summer of 1944, everyone in France was suddenly talking about liberation.

There had been rumors for months, and Marie-Louise de Montclair listened carefully to every one of them. But as summer approached the talk became more animated. The Americans had landed on the beaches of Normandy just to the west of them, and De Gaulle himself was rumored to be in France. The Maréchal Pétain, old fox that he was, had been arrested and was imprisoned at the fortress in Belfort, over in the east. If there was any justice in the world, he would be executed.

Every day, there were reports of heavy armored tanks moving in and out of Angers.

There had been nights of terror in the springtime, when the Americans had started their bombing runs over Nazi installations in France. Marie-Louise had heard that the convent over on the rue de l'Esviere had been partially demolished, because the Americans were aiming at the railway station, and missed. She heard the news with sadness, partly because it would be so difficult for the sisters to rebuild, and also because their school was where she had already decided that Catherine should go. It was a good school, a proper boarding school for young ladies of good families. She hoped that they would rebuild by the time Catherine was old enough to be sent there.

Change was in the air. The bombings increased in a steady crescendo, but now the sound of airplanes winging by in the night air brought not terror but joy. People ran out of their houses to cheer them on. They were American planes, and their presence in the skies of France could mean only one thing: liberation. Liberation was at hand. It was nearly over. Soon, they all told each other; soon the Americans would be in Angers.

The Germans, typically, said nothing, going about their business as usual. But beneath their cold countenances one sensed an undercurrent of fear, almost of despair. The children knew it first, as children always do, and little boys in the streets started throwing stones at the German staff cars as they drove by.

Father Xavier, who came often these days to visit Marie-Louise, shook his head. "They should go soon," he said. "Before they lose face."

"Why be concerned about that?" she asked.

He shrugged. "They are human beings, too," he said softly. "Perhaps I have lost sight of that."

There was a shriek and Jean-Claude ran across the courtyard, directly in front of them, chasing one of the stable cats. "And how will the children do with no mother?" the priest asked, sadness in his voice.

"They will carry on," she said with dignity.

"Easier to talk of than to do. At least they have their father."

"For what that is worth," she said grimly. The word hovered in the air between them, the word that neither of them dared to utter, because it was so final, so irrevocable: traitor. "Personally, I prefer for them to cherish the memory of one who has been brave. Pierre will interfere with them as little as possible."

And then, finally, the Germans admitted what everyone had known: They were leaving. They announced it in much the same fashion that they had announced their occupation of the city: down at the place du Ralliement, with loudspeakers and a trumpet. There were no apologies, no regrets, no feeling of sorrow on their part. It might as well have been an interesting military maneuver that they were talking about, rather than the abandonment of a city they had once held to so tightly. "There is to be no interference!" the voice in the loudspeaker boomed. "Troublemakers will be severely punished!"

"And why would we want to interefere?" muttered an old woman in the crowd. "Godspeed, that's what I say."

Marie-Louise did not go downtown to hear the German speeches, but Dominique had been there, and he told her about what had transpired. They sat together in her quiet sitting room, drinking cold cider. He was trying to give up smoking.

"So," Marie-Louise said at length, "soon you will be free to enter the seminary."

"Yes," he said. "Soon I'll begin my studies. I'll be going to Paris." He hesitated for a moment, looking down at his glass of cider, and then, almost desperately, at her face. "I want you to know," he said with some difficulty, "that I loved your daughter-in-law. You may have had your ideas about what was going on between us, and I want to set the record straight. It wasn't—it wasn't just lust, Countess. I loved her."

"Thank you for telling me," she said steadily, not looking at him but off, somewhere over his shoulder. "You have no need to do so."

"But I do," Dominique hesitated, searching for the right

words. "It was hard work, what we did together. It would have been easy to take advantage of someone. I never did."

"I wonder," she said softly, "if it is I that you are trying to explain this to—or yourself."

He flushed. "A woman should stay faithful to her husband," he said. "Chantale was not, and you are her husband's mother. You deserve an explanation."

"I have seen nothing in my son's conduct that warranted faithfulness on his wife's part," Marie-Louise said, looking directly at him.

"I was with her," he said, "that last night that we were at Kerenec. I very nearly wasn't. I thought that we might both live to regret it." He looked up, and she could see the tears glinting in his eyes. "It seems that I need not have worried. And I shall have a lifetime to regret it after all."

She responded to the thought and not the words. "You can come here," she said, "whenever you would like. You will always be welcome. The children will like seeing you, I think."

"I'd like that," he said. "I'd like to see them, too."

When General de Gaulle entered Paris, just on the heels of the Americans, Marie-Louise experienced a sense of sadness, sadness at the end of things, which made no sense at all. The Germans had left. Life could get back to normal. But, as she walked about her orchards, she wondered what going through the everyday paces of her life meant. How could things ever be normal again? Which one of them would be able to forget the conquerors, their arrogance, their cruelty? Who in all of Anjou had not lost someone because of the occupation? How could life possibly go on as it had before? She had thought that they had all lost their innocence with the First War, but she had been wrong. That had been a war fought by gentlemen. This had been a war declared by madmen.

Even in the midst of triumph, the feeling of sadness persisted. Now is the time, she thought. Now is the time to mourn. Who could grieve properly when the Germans were still there? How was it possible to find the words while always listening for the step in the night, the knock on the door that might be the signal of doom? No, it was not possible to mourn, not then. All human feelings had been outlawed.

But now they could. She went to the cemetery to place flowers on the graves, and Marie-Louise was only one among those who grieved. She had lost a daughter-in-law just as she had finally come to know what a great gift a daughter-in-law could be. And she had lost a son. Pierre might well live on, but she knew him now. She knew, and she would gladly have given ten years of her own life not to know what he had become.

When Marie-Louise heard the Americans were coming, she instructed Father Xavier to offer them the Château de Montclair as barracks. Green trucks, this time, rumbled up the long winding gravel road, between the poplar trees, and the colonel who hopped out of the first one was ridiculously young, ridiculously childlike-looking, with piercing blue eyes and a shock of red hair. Celtic ancestry, she diagnosed at once. Breton eyes.

"I am the Countess de Montclair," she said with dignity, extending her hand to him. He took it, gave her a boyish smile, and then—to everyone's amazement, and a few guffaws from his troops—bent down to kiss her wedding band. "Colonel Philip Ryan, at your service," he said formally. "Thank you for your hospitality."

He signaled to a young corpsman, who jumped out of one of the jeeps carrying a large carton with him. "We've heard of your shortages," Ryan said, "and we thought you might not refuse a few gifts." He took the box and opened it, and Marie-Louise's eyes filled with tears at the contents. Soap, real Ivory soap. She hadn't seen soap in years. Coffee. Chocolate. And oranges.

Jean-Claude and Catherine were standing on the steps behind her, watching the uniformed men with wide eyes. Ryan took an orange in each hand and advanced toward them. "Like one?" he offered. Catherine shrank back behind her brother, frightened, but Jean-Claude boldly put out his hand for the orange, which he inspected with great seriousness before attempting to bounce it on the front steps.

Marie-Louise turned to face Ryan. "I am sorry," she said. "They have not seen oranges. The little one was born during the war. They think it's a ball."

His eyes were filled with tears, too. "We have a PX," he said, though the name meant nothing to her. "They'll have so many oranges they'll be sick of them, you'll see."

She smiled in return. "Thank you," she said simply. "Thank you for your kindness. For . . . everything." And how inadequate are those words, she thought. For our lives. How do you thank this child-colonel for our lives? She reached over and, very lightly, kissed his cheek. "And now come inside. Your men will want baths, I imagine.'' She linked her arm through his and led him up the steps. ''My husband's name was Philippe, too,'' she said as they walked. ''You are welcome here. There is a certain symmetry in that, don't you think?'' Their voices faded as they disappeared into the front hall, which was, as ever, cold.

In Angers, more Americans were driving through town, down the boulevard de Roi René and past the castle, over to the boulevard du Maréchal Foch. They were laughing and waving to the people who lined the streets. A girl darted out from time to time, to bestow a flower or a French flag upon one of them. Most often the soldiers grabbed the girls in response and kissed them as well. Somewhere, a band was playing. The mood was one of drunken euphoria. All the church bells, silent these four years long, were ringing out their exultation.

Coming from the rue Saint Dénis, however, a procession emerged out into the sunlight of the place du Ralliement. Pierre de Montclair was the first to notice it—Pierre who had been standing vigil outside of Isabelle's apartment all these days, hoping to see her, to comfort her, perhaps even—in his wildest dreams—to get her back, now that her German lovers were gone. He saw them, a few men and women prodding these bedraggled-looking creatures along with canes and sticks, shouting obscenities: a group of women, ten of them perhaps, dressed in skirts and blouses and raincoats, one or two of them barefoot. All their heads had been completely shaven.

Pierre gasped, and then narrowed his eyes as he heard what the shouting was about. ''German whore,'' one man was saying. ''You cuckolded your whole country!'' cried a woman. No, Pierre prayed silently. Not her. His goddess could not be here, among these freakish-looking women with no hair, these pitiful souls who did not even look like women, who stumbled so haltingly along. Please, no . . . But they were ugly. No wonder they had slept with the Germans. Isabelle was different. Isabelle was beautiful. Isabelle was perfect.

Isabelle was fourth in the line of women being paraded around the streets of Angers.

Where the razor had missed them, there were still a few tufts of black hair here and there on her otherwise bald head, making her look like some sort of molting bird. Her violet eyes were as strange and beautiful as ever, but her hands were tied loosely in front of her and there was a rip in the crimson dress that she was wearing. Red, thought Pierre: her best color. Why couldn't they respect her? She was only doing what she needed to do in order to survive. She stumbled, and one of the women turned toward her. "Walk for us now," she sneered, spitting in Isabelle's face. "You sure paraded around for your German lovers!"

Pierre stepped forward, his heart bursting with pity and pain. "Isabelle!" he called out. "Isabelle! I'm here!"

The violet eyes looked over in his direction, and she paused for just a moment. "Go away, Pierre," she said, her voice tired.

"No!" he cried. "I must know where they're taking you! Isabelle! I love you!"

One of the men turned toward him, with narrowed eyes. "Ha!" he exclaimed. "It's the high and mighty Count de Montclair. You have a taste for German whores, Count?"

Pierre swung his arm up, almost reflexively, as though to hit the man, but there were other people blocking his way. Then, just as it seemed that there might be violence in the place du Ralliement after all, the cavalcade of American trucks and jeeps swept into the square, out of the rue des Arènes. People scattered, and the women with shorn heads were prodded to go on.

"I still love you!" Pierre shouted desperately, and Isabelle shook her head.

"You're pathetic, Pierre," she said. "That's all you ever were, and all you ever will be. Pathetic." And then she walked on.

He fell back after that, and went to sit on the steps of the opera house, watching the Americans drive around in formation. What was so great about the damned Americans, anyway? At least the Germans had looked neat, had had some precision to their formation. These men were grubby and dirty and tired. Some exchange. Just above him, to his left, was her empty apartment. He wondered how long it would be before she was released, before she could come back home.

One thing was certain. He would be waiting. He would always be waiting. What was that Oscar Wilde line he had heard, back in the days when his tutor still was at the château? "If you don't take too long I will wait for you for the rest of my life."

He would wait. He was the only man who had ever really loved her at all.

Chapter Thirty-two

June 1945.

Captain Andrew Starkey, Eagle Squadron, Royal Air Force, was released from his prisoner-of-war camp three weeks after Hitler committed suicide.

There was no pomp and no circumstance, no waving of banners, no people concerned or even moderately pleased. There was not even any transportation out. "If you go west," they all said, "you'll get to France."

So they walked west, a ragged cortege of misfits, and Andrew trudged along with them. Still silent, still nourishing thoughts of revenge. There were trains for part of the distance, and occasionally a truck stopped to pick up one or two of them. Andrew was not a popular passenger.

"Gone round the bend, he has, sir," volunteered a young British corporal to one driver. "Place will make you nutty, that's for sure. Trying to get to bloody America, he is."

Miles across Germany, a Germany he had never seen before. He had flown over these towns and these fields, but they meant nothing to him, nameless, faceless, just like the people he shot at. They came out to watch him trudge by, and sometimes yelled something to him in German. Nothing, he deduced, very flattering. But he didn't listen and even if he had, he wouldn't have understood.

It was miles across France, a France dimly remembered. Gaiety here, laughter, a liberated country with a flourishing black market, its economy just stumbling along as he was, trying to recover, its new president the famous war hero, General de Gaulle. They smiled at him, beckoned to him, but all he could remember was that betrayal behind the worn curtain at the Café du Chemin. He heard that they were shaving the women's heads,

429

the women who had slept with the Germans. He hoped that they had gotten that girl at the café.

Waiting at Dieppe for a boat, he shivered with the fever that was racking his body, shivering despite the summer heat. He waited with the silence shrouding him like a cloak, and the demons inside of him providing him with enough energy, just enough, to get back and do what he had to do.

Someone had to do it. And no one else knew. Oh, some people had small pieces of the picture, bits of a jigsaw puzzle that had been scattered on the veranda in a fit of pique on a summer day, but that was all. He alone knew what the picture looked like when it was all pieced together. He knew and, in knowing, had lost any pretensions that he had ever had to free will. He couldn't live his own life, not any longer. They had taken that away from him. Very well, but let them learn that there were consequences. Let them learn that someone, somewhere, had to take responsibility for all the killings, for all the deaths, for all the cries of grief and sorrow. He, Andrew, would show them.

On the boat to England, he was sick all the way, vomiting over the side until there was nothing left to throw up. The sudden summer storm over the channel had sapped him of the strength his long march had started to build up inside of him. London seemed strange, foreign. Once London had been his delight. Now it held only ghosts, the ghosts of past conversations, past events. Emma laughed at him from every pub. Caroline, serious and earnest, pointed out the gutted buildings and crater holes made by the bombs. He waited until his demobilization papers were completed and ready, and then he booked himself on a commercial flight to New York. The Air Force had offered transport to returning prisoners of war, but he had had enough of the military. In his last few hours, he visited London Cemetery and stood for a time looking at the gravestone, which read in neat engraved letters: "Steven Harrison Asheford." No dates; no inscription; just the name. Perhaps Caroline had been in a hurry. Or perhaps the name was enough: This man was here, and he died.

Andrew sighed, rubbing his gritty eyes and trying to pull the strength from inside of himself. One more death to add to the list. One more death to hold them responsible for.

He arrived in New York in July and booked himself a room in a hotel, intending to rest for a week or two, see a doctor, take care of himself, gather strength. California was gleaming and glistening ahead of him, holding its sweet promises of revenge. But California would have to wait.

Eric Beaumont never forgot what he saw that day. Even Eric, who had become accustomed to power, accustomed to grandeur, and to dreaming and seeing his dreams take shape and form, was awed by the test run in Alamogordo, New Mexico. Even Eric never forgot that grandeur, that power, and that terror. The exploding bomb produced a great sense of nothingness, an absence of matter, the ultimate silence. Eric never forgot the great mushroom cloud billowing out over the desert. Or Jeffrey Kellogg, standing next to him, swearing under his breath, "Holy shit. Holy shit."

Kellogg's presence there was the part of the experiment that worried him the most.

They all shared champagne when it was finally all over, Eric and Jeffrey and all the scientists and technicians, the generals with their flimsy paper passes clipped to their uniforms. Dr. Oppenheimer kept repeating, over and over, "We did it. We did it," much as though trying to convince himself.

"Ready for the real thing?" Eric inquired.

The tall scientist turned to face him. "The real thing? That's up to the politicians, surely," he said, puzzled. "We were hoping that it wouldn't come to that."

"It might not," Eric said. "Don't worry until it's time to worry. It might not." But Germany had surrendered in May, and yet three months later Japan still showed no sign of even thinking about giving up. People were tired of war. They wanted it to be over. If those weren't reasons enough, he didn't know what were.

Roosevelt was no longer President. Eric hadn't reckoned with that happening. Only last year, he had been elected for another term. He was brave; he was patriotic; and he was also human. Like other humans, there were limits to what he could do, and he died when he least wished to do so. Before, even, the Germans had surrendered.

So Harry Truman was living in the White House and Eric was trying very hard to mend fences with him. They had never seen eye to eye. But wartime is the best of all possible times to put aside personal considerations, and Eric was working night and day to bring Truman around to his point of view. On the whole, he thought, it had chances of working.

He flew back to San Jose from Alamogordo a pensive man. It was as though things were speeding up suddenly and he no longer could control them. Not as tightly as he once had. Perhaps he was just tired. The war had dragged on unaccountably, and although business was thriving he was beginning to get tired. Very tired. He started thinking about a sailboat and the Greek Islands at sunset. . . . He had never been to Greece. Perhaps, if they had had any money, he might have taken Sarah there for a honeymoon. But it was too late for that now. She would never see the Greek Islands. Still, it didn't mean that he couldn't do so alone.

Back in his office, he immediately reached first for a cigarette and second for Sarah's picture on his desk. Strange how it sat there, day in, day out, and he looked at it without really seeing it. He inhaled on the cigarette, held the smoke in his lungs for a long delicious moment, and looked at her. Sarah . . . She was laughing in the photograph, her eyes bright and crinkled up in merriment, her auburn curls covered with her leather flying helmet. There was a white scarf around her neck. Sarah had been the one to start that trend back in 1911, even before the war when all pilots wore them. Sarah had always been fashion conscious. She dressed perfectly for every occasion. Even for her own death.

That was morbid thinking. They had had good times together, before she fell out of the sky. . . . They had had wonderful times.

Funny, he thought, replacing the picture on his desk. Funny how I can go for months and months, not thinking about her, not aching for her; and then, suddenly, it's as though she's in the next room. As though I can smell her perfume. Always, when I'm tired . . .

That was it, of course. Tiredness. Weariness brought on thoughts of opportunities lost, dreams forgotten . . . thoughts of Caroline, the girl he had tried to raise as his own daughter, and who had suffered so much, and survived so much. The war had hurt her, especially losing Steven. But she had found strengths inside herself that he hadn't even guessed that she possessed. It would have been easy for her to go back to America, but instead she had joined that flying outfit and done whatever it was that she felt that she had to do. Eric hadn't understood any of that, but he knew that it was important to her—and had changed her.

She was coming out for a visit shortly, sometime in early

August. And she had met somebody recently, some fellow she ran into at the symphony . . . What was his name? Robert Stoddard, that was it. Eric had had him investigated—everyone who came in contact with Caroline was investigated—and he had to admit that he seemed a good choice. Stoddard had his own money, so he wasn't after hers. He was a musician, and absorbed enough in his world that he wasn't going to want any problems to interfere with it. He would be good for Caroline, Eric thought. It would be nice if the two of them got married. He glanced again at Sarah's picture on the desk. He had loved only her, and he had been lonely . . . incredibly, insufferably lonely. He didn't wish that for Caroline.

He shook his head and shrugged himself out of his suit jacket.

There was one important issue that needed to be solved right away. Eric grimaced in distaste. He didn't like what he had to do, but it was inevitable. He had to protect himself and Intraglobal. He wasn't going to take any risks. He had been watching Jeffrey Kellogg's face out at the test site. He had seen the awe, and the wonder and the amazement. But he had seen more than that, too. Kellogg's brain had been ticking away behind those steel-rimmed glasses. The war was going to end soon, and, with it, his unholy alliance with Johnson Industries. And it seemed to him that Johnson Industries was getting a little too greedy. The atomic project was Eric's and his alone, but he had a feeling that Jeffrey Kellogg didn't quite see it that way.

Eric pushed the button on his intercom. "Julie? Have Gunther Anderson stop in, will you, please?"

"Yes, sir." Cool and unruffled as usual. Eric shook his head. Julie knew in what capacity Gunther was employed by Intraglobal, but Eric had long ago given up trying to analyze his assistant. If she had any life at all outside of work, she disguised it cleverly. He had had her investigated, once, twice, periodically, and every time came up with nothing. She lived for Intraglobal. He had given up wondering why.

Gunther came in a half hour later, cheerful, unconcerned. "How you doing, Mr. Beaumont?" he asked. "You have any of those fancy French cigarettes for me today?"

"Help yourself." Eric gestured toward his package. "I've been thinking about taking a vacation," he said.

Gunther sniffed the air, as though trying to determine the direction of the wind. He looked like what a Californian was supposed to look like, muscular and tan, with bleached-blond hair and bright blue eyes. A lifeguard on his day off from the beach. He lit one of Eric's cigarettes and inhaled rapidly. "Nice time of the year for a vacation," he observed.

"It's hard to go," Eric continued, "with so many things on my mind. Pressures."

"I can understand that," the younger man acknowledged. "Anything I can help you with, Mr. Beaumont?"

Eric cleared his throat. "Do you know Mr. Kellogg?" he asked. "He's the chief executive officer of Johnson Industries."

"Mr. Jeffrey Kellogg? Portly gent, wears glasses? Yeah, I know him. Not to speak to, of course. We move in different circles."

"That sounds like him." Eric leaned back and made a steeple of his fingers, looking intently at Gunther over them. "Mr. Kellogg is starting to worry me, Gunther," he said.

The younger man shook his head sorrowfully. "He shouldn't do that, Mr. Beaumont. Especially seeing as you want to be going on vacation, and all."

"My thoughts exactly." Eric leaned forward abruptly. "Can you take care of him for me?" he asked.

Gunther shrugged. "Why not? How permanent do you want it to be?"

Eric narrowed his eyes. "I could find time for a funeral before I go on vacation," he said. "It would be only proper to pay my last respects to a valued friend and trusted colleague."

Gunther ground out the cigarette. "It can be arranged, Mr. Beaumont."

"Good. Soon, if you can. And I'll have Julie arrange a bonus in your paycheck, Gunther."

"Don't bother, Mr. Beaumont. I don't have enough time to spend what you pay me now, anyway." He brightened. "Recognize that? It was a line from *Casablanca*. I've been thinking about how to use it."

Eric, who hadn't seen a film in over ten years, nodded encouragingly. "Well done, Gunther. And now you're on your way."

With satisfaction he watched the muscular back leave. So the Jeffrey Kellogg problem was resolved. Kellogg would be replaced, of course, but no one could replace the wealth of information and ideas inside his brain. No one would know what Kellogg knew; no one would know what verbal agreements he had had with Eric. Killing Kellogg was effectively going to dissolve the tenuous partnership they had so precariously shared during the war.

The game was about to start again. Eric smiled. He wasn't convinced that it had ever really stopped.

Caroline and Elizabeth Asheford arrived in San Jose three hours after the news of the bombing of Hiroshima was broadcast.

They had taken their time getting to California. Caroline hadn't flown cross-country in years, and had found that having her daughter as a passenger made her more careful, taking fewer risks. Especially with the weather. Whereas before she might have gaily assumed that she could outfly any thunderstorm, now she shook her head owlishly. "We'll stay here another day. It's not worth the risk."

Elizabeth was seven years old, and already a pilot in her heart. "Let me try, Mommy!" she begged endlessly, and sometimes Caroline handed over the controls to her. Navigation bored her ("I just look out the window and see the mountains, silly Mommy"), but the act of flying itself was her chief passion in life. "It's like writing a poem," she explained to a puzzled Caroline. Years later, when the psychologists explained that flying was a right-hemisphere activity, Caroline understood her daughter's intuition: Even then, Elizabeth knew.

It took them a month in all to fly from Newport to San Jose, and the airport was buzzing when they landed. "What is it?" Caroline asked anxiously. God damn it, she thought. If the Japanese have chosen this moment to attack the coast . . . But it turned out it was the Japanese who had the most to fear.

Hiroshima had been bombed, with the new wonder bomb, the atomic bomb. Everyone, they were saying, had been killed.

"That's not possible," protested Caroline, but the newsstand operator nodded vigorously.

"It's true, miss. Been a secret project all these years out in the desert. New Mexico, I hear. It burns everything: buildings, people, cows—you name it." He turned from her and raised his voice. "Evening *Chronicle*!" he yelled. "Get your *Chronicle* here! Atom bomb flattens Hiroshima! Japs close to surrender!"

Caroline, feeling nauseated, bundled Elizabeth into a taxi and headed out for Western Avenue. No, she was thinking, not that. Not Eric. He had talked about some experimental laboratory out in the desert. . . . It had to be something else, someone else.

He made airplanes that participated in wars. But this was something different altogether. This was something . . .

Evil.

She shivered at the very word. It couldn't be. Eric would never do that. Eric couldn't do something that monstrous. A whole city, filled with people. He would explain it all to her, she reasoned. Tell her that he had nothing to do with it. It was someone else. It had to be someone else.

Eric wasn't home.

Caroline should have stopped there, she realized later. She should have stopped there and waited for him to come home. If she hadn't gone to his office that day things might have turned out differently. It was another "if only" to add to a long list of recriminations with which she would have to live.

But she needed to see Eric immediately. All that Caroline could feel, in her tiredness and disillusionment, was horror. A city full of people. One minute they were there, going about their business, and the next moment they were gone, burned out of existence. Their children's children wouldn't even have the buildings left to remind them. They were Japanese people, and the Japanese had bombed Pearl Harbor. But surely this was unnecessary retaliation for a few battleships, a few aircraft carriers?

She wasn't thinking very clearly. She put Elizabeth's sweater back on her and called another taxi. "I'm sorry, darling, but we have to go see Uncle Eric."

"Why, Mommy?"

Caroline said, as evenly as she could, "I have some questions to ask him."

She stared out the window all the way to the Intraglobal compound. She could see only the charred bodies, and the cloud, the bomb-cloud exploding overhead. How could something so small do such damage? She leaned forward and addressed herself to the driver. "Did you hear the news? About Hiroshima?"

"Yeah, sure did," he said, his voice cheerful. "I always said Truman would make a better President, and look. Just a few months in office, and he's going to have us out of this war in no time. Roosevelt, him, would have had us fighting on for another four years."

Caroline sat back in her seat, confused. Elizabeth said, "What's Hiroshima?"

"It's a city in Japan." Dear God, how does one tell a child

about an atomic bomb? "The American Air Force dropped a bomb on it today."

"Were they bad people, Mommy?"

Caroline squeezed her hand. "No, sweetie. No, they weren't bad people." How bad does one have to be, she wondered, to deserve annihilation? Most of all, worst of all, they weren't even in the army, or the navy, or the air force. . . . They were ordinary people. Librarians and doctors, housewives and children, and now they were all dead because their emperor was being stubborn.

Because Eric Beaumont had built a bomb.

She rushed Elizabeth through security at the compound, and almost ran up the stairs in the main building to Eric's office. His assistant, Julie, was out of her chair and barring the entrance to his office as soon as she saw Caroline. "I'm sorry, Mrs. Asheford. We weren't expecting you."

Caroline hesitated. She wondered what Julie saw: tousled blond curls, a simple white dress with a belt hugging her slender waist, high-heeled sandals. Elizabeth was pretty, her long chestnut hair in two braids, her brown eyes wide with lack of sleep. They were presentable, from a strictly fashion point of view. But there was something in her face that had moved Julie out of her chair that fast. "Hello, Julie. It's all right. Eric is expecting me."

"I'm sorry, Mrs. Asheford. I don't have your appointment noted. If you'll just take a seat, I'll see if Mr. Beaumont is free just now."

Caroline waited until Julie had turned to reach for the intercom, and then she walked through the door.

If she had thought to find Eric in some illicit act, she was disappointed. He was sitting behind his desk, talking on the telephone. When Caroline and Elizabeth entered, he showed no surprise, just motioned them in and continued with his conversation. "Well, Mr. President, all that I can say is that we do have something slightly larger . . . it's a bit different, actually, but should produce satisfactory results. No, I have no doubt that the military will be able to define a target area. Yes, the capabilities are there. Very good, Mr. President. And the same to you, sir."

He hung up the phone and looked at them consideringly. "I would say welcome, only it looks as though that's not what you're here for."

Caroline said, "We just heard about Hiroshima."

He wasn't disconcerted in the least. "As I imagine the world has. How was your trip? I expected you last Tuesday."

"It doesn't even bother you, does it?"

Eric shrugged and reached for his cigarettes. "Should it? I've been working on this project for four years, Caroline. It's a little late to develop niceties like a conscience."

Glancing at Elizabeth, Caroline said, "Some of them were children, Eric."

"I didn't choose Hiroshima. You can blame the Joint Chiefs of Staff for that one."

The telephone buzzed before she could reply, and he picked it up, his eyes still fixed on her. "Yes, Julie? He is? Hmmm. All right. I can see him. No, he doesn't need to go through Security, I'll vouch for him." He replaced the receiver and looked at her quizzically. "Another unexpected visitor. Captain Andrew Starkey, lately of the RAF. Do you know anything about this, Caroline?"

It was as though Eric had punched her in the stomach. She gasped, and Elizabeth tightened her hand in her mother's. "Andrew! Here? Why?"

"I imagine we're about to find out."

There was a knock on the door and Julie opened it, standing aside as she announced, "Mr. Starkey." Andrew strode into the room, past Caroline, as though she didn't exist. The door closed behind him with a whisper.

Andrew had changed, Caroline thought, and her heart went out to him. Those years in the prisoner-of-war camp hadn't done him any good. She felt guilty, suddenly, for her own years of comparative ease. He was gaunt; even the good suit which he had obviously recently purchased hung on his frame, as though he had bought it too big, hoping to someday grow into it. His eyes were sunken, and although it was surely her imagination which made his hair gleam gray in the light, it certainly looked lank and, somehow, dead.

He glanced at her indifferently, as though she were a casual acquaintance, and then he turned to Eric. "I went to see my uncle," Andrew said in a low voice. "He wasn't there. He was dead."

"I know," Eric said comfortably. "A terrible accident. I attended his funeral. I'm sorry that no one told you."

"How could they? I was crawling across Europe. You should see Europe now, Mr. Beaumont. It isn't a pretty sight."

Eric frowned, less at the words themselves than at the tone in which they were delivered. "Is there something that I can do for you, Andrew?"

"Yes," Andrew said thoughtfully. "Yes, I rather think that there is." He reached into an inner pocket of his jacket and in one fluid movement withdrew a gun and pointed it at Eric's chest.

Caroline screamed, and shoved Elizabeth behind her.

"Stop making that noise," Andrew said sharply, and the buzzer on Eric's desk started ringing.

No one moved. Caroline found that she was shaking, physically shaking, and all of them were looking at the intercom and its insistent buzzing sound. Only Eric, still relaxed, was looking at Andrew. "What would you like me to do?"

"Tell her that everything's all right," Andrew said, encouragingly, pointing to the buzzer with the gun. Eric pressed the intercom button. "Yes, Julie?"

"Are you all right, Mr. Beaumont? I heard a scream."

"Everything is fine, Julie. Thank you. That will be all." He pulled his hand away from the intercom and looked at Andrew. "Satisfactory?"

"You're very cool about this whole thing, aren't you?" Andrew asked. "Me, I don't understand that. If I had an instrument of death pointed at me, I might sweat a little. Wouldn't you, Caroline?"

She jumped when he said her name. "Probably."

Andrew laughed. "Probably. Well, that's a pretty standard human response, Miss Probably. But we're forgetting that Mr. Beaumont here doesn't share too many responses with the rest of humanity. He's above all that."

Eric said, "What do you want, Starkey?"

"Oh, it's Starkey now? I was Andrew just a few minutes ago. But never mind. That's part of your technique, isn't it? Your way of distancing yourself? It makes sense." He paused. "I went to see my uncle so that I could kill him. But somebody already took care of that for me. It was very convenient. Did you have anything to do with his death, Mr. Beaumont?"

"Don't be absurd."

"Pity. If I killed you, and you had killed him, it would be the proverbial two birds with one stone, wouldn't it? Are you starting to sweat now, Beaumont? Starting to think about the possibility that you might not make it out of here alive?''

"Andrew, please!" Caroline's voice was pleading. "Please don't do this.''

Andrew looked at her briefly, but she wasn't sure what he saw. He certainly didn't look at her as if he saw Caroline. His eyes were curiously opaque, and Caroline shuddered with fear and pity.

"You're part of it, too, Caroline. You say that you're not, but you are. And Emma. Sweet lovely Emma. She worked for you, Beaumont, didn't she?''

"I don't know what you're talking about," Eric said calmly.

"Of course not. Of course not. Have you ever thought, Beaumont, about how many people you've killed in your lifetime? Just you alone?''

Oh, no, thought Caroline. He knows about Hiroshima, and that's why he's here. After the prison camp, he probably can't stand violence anymore. She could feel Elizabeth shaking behind her.

Eric said, "If you have a point, please get on with it."

"Oh, I will. I will." He smiled again. "I haven't calculated the exact number yet, but I think that we could do with millions, for a starter. And that's excluding your little escapade this morning. Millions, Beaumont. First you supply one side, then you supply the other. First you're one of the Allies, then you're a Nazi. Playing both sides, huh, Beaumont? Predictable. And very profitable.'' His voice hardened. "I flew your planes, Beaumont. And so did the guy who shot me down.''

"That's business," said Eric calmly. "I haven't actually killed anyone, myself. And you surely can't blame me for being an astute businessman.''

"Of course not. Well, it seemed to me, just sitting and thinking about it all this time, that part of your education is sorely lacking. You see, you deal in violence every day. You deal it out, like a pack of cards. But you never have to *see* it, Beaumont. You never have to be around afterwards to pick up the pieces.''

Eric was looking at him intently. Caroline could feel her heart hammering in her chest. The ticking of a clock was suddenly unnaturally loud in the room. No one said anything for a moment, and then Andrew continued.

"Well, I thought I'd help you out, Mr. Eric Bloody Beaumont. Make you look at death. Make you see it, and smell it, and hear it. I want violence to haunt your dreams for the rest of your life, Beaumont.''

Caroline said, ''Andrew, no!'' but he was already raising his gun. Slowly, gracefully almost, hypnotically, he put it into his mouth and pulled the trigger, and a moment later he fell forward, spilling all of his brains and a good deal of his skull out over Eric Beaumont's desk.

Caroline's gaze met Eric's for one brief moment, and then the room was spinning all around her, and she fainted.

Chapter Thirty-three

*J*une 1956.

There was no band playing, but Holbrooke Academy had never, in its hundred years of existence, felt any need for bands. They were plebeian at best, garish at worst, and the graduates of Holbrooke Academy were anything but plebeian. They were the daughters of people with money, who presumably would go on to become the wives of people with money—unless they took time out to play for a while first. That was one of the accepted things abut Holbrooke Academy, that its students had the time and leisure to do as they pleased, just as it was accepted that the nouveau riche were not considered "people with money." Money meant family money, and at Holbrooke Academy the daughters of the families with the money were given proper educations as befitted their positions. And now they were being sent out into the world, with a few appropriate speeches, a benediction by the school chaplain, a muted a cappella chorus of "America the Beautiful," but not with a band.

The graduates were dressed in simple white gowns, slightly academic in tailoring, utterly unsuitable for the day which had turned out, after a few morning rumblings to the west, to be clear and hot. The teachers were wearing black academic gowns, some with Master's hoods, all with mortarboards, and they looked, if anything, more uncomfortable than the students. Only the visitors had been permitted any choice in their costumes—if, indeed, there was choice within the narrow confines of their social sphere. The men all wore suits, for to do otherwise would be unthinkable. The women, for the most part, looked as though they had dressed for a lawn tea party, with flowered dresses and wide-brimmed hats and short white gloves.

There were several pairs of eyes scanning the first row of graduates, looking for Elizabeth to see what she would look like

442

on this her first official day as an adult. They were not disappointed; for if Elizabeth Asheford had done anything while she was in high school at Holbrooke Academy, she had become beautiful. Her hair, in contrast to her mother's blond curls, was very dark and very thick, almost black, one would have thought, except for the slight glimmer of red when it caught the sun. She normally wore it loose down her back, and tied back from her face with the aid of a wide bandeau. But today, for her graduation, she had pinned it up in an elaborate and elegant chignon. Her eyes, too, were dark, a deep brown, enigmatic at times, open and innocent when she chose for them to be, always curious and alive. She was thin, not through any effort on her part, with slightly rounded breasts and hips. People were constantly telling her that she was pretty, and she smiled when they did, because it was proper to do so, but she knew what she saw in the mirror. She looked too intelligent. Men were afraid of women who looked too intelligent, and that was why she had begun to cultivate the wide-eyed naive look. It didn't eliminate the intelligence, but it gave people something else to think about.

At school, they had tried to call her names like Eliza and Liz and Beth, but she had smiled that gentle unemphatic smile and said, softly, "My name is Elizabeth." Her father had chosen that name, and her father was dead. It was, she always thought, the least that she could do, to honor him.

It was all that she could do. She had been too young when he died to do anything else for him. She remembered him vaguely, but it was a distorted memory, soiled like a photograph that had been handled too much. She wondered sometimes if it was her father that she remembered, or only her own fantasy of what he had been like. She had been three years old when he died.

He had been replaced since then. Her mother was too young, too pretty, and too wealthy to remain a widow for very long, although she had gone through a most proper period of mourning. It wasn't until two years after the war was over that she had married Robert Stoddard. Elizabeth had been nine years old then, and had carried the wedding rings into the church for them. She didn't blame her mother for remarrying, and in any case the estate on Ocean Avenue in Newport was too big, too lonely for one person, especially now that both Nicholas and Elizabeth were gone. And Uncle Bob was a nice person. He was a concert pianist, and when he wasn't traveling he filled the estate with beautiful sounds. He had the most wonderful hands, with long, graceful fingers, but he didn't mind using his hands for other things, too, like playing softball out on the lawn or putting swings in trees when she was still a little girl. No, there was nothing wrong with her mother's choice of a second husband, and Elizabeth had heard stories at school of how terrible stepfathers could be. All in all, she was fortunate in Uncle Bob. But it didn't keep her from wishing that her own father had lived just a little longer so that she could have known him better.

Well, that was water under the bridge, as they liked to say. Now she needed to concentrate on what was happening here: The speeches weren't exactly riveting, but that wasn't old Dr. MacKenzie's fault. He hadn't had much to say since around the First World War, and evidently had been saying the same thing, over and over, at every graduation ceremony ever since. Elizabeth stifled a yawn. All her friends had been saying how much they were going to miss Holbrooke, how they were going to miss one another, how they absolutely must stay in touch. Stay in touch. It was an odd expression. Elizabeth couldn't think of a time when she had used it herself.

Miss Holbrooke Academy? Well, perhaps. She had learned a great deal here, even when the teachers had thought that it was more important for her to learn manners than academics. Her name might have been Asheford, but they all knew where she came from; the house on Ocean Avenue wasn't still called the Lewis estate for nothing. That was what they chose to focus on— the old Newport family, the money, the estate. Not Asheford Shipbuilding; not the scandal. Uncle William imprisoned for embezzlement and Aunt Justine still and probably forever shut up in that place that they all euphemistically called a rest home for difficult patients . . . No. Holbrooke Academy despised scandal. But Elizabeth's grandmother had been a Lewis before she married, and eventually they all came back to the Lewis estate. With husbands and children in tow, with different last names, but they all came back. That was what mattered.

Uncle Bob had taken to his new life easily enough. He came from old Newport money, too, and it was the sheer bad luck of being the third son, and not the first, that had kept him from living in his family estate by the water. He had made up for it over the years by talent and recognition, and people had approved of the match with Caroline Asheford. Everyone admired Bob and Caroline Stoddard.

Except Nicholas.

Elizabeth frowned. Her cousin Nicholas was becoming more and more like a character out of a dime-store novel. He wasn't here today. He wouldn't come within a mile of Holbrooke Academy. "A place," he had called it once, "where the young and silly become older and sillier." He had gone to public schools in Newport, and he never let her forget that, even though they lived under the same roof. He was the poor relation. "Some of us, dear cousin, are going to have to go out and work for a living."

She had thought his distinctions foolish, and then charming. It was only recently that she had begun to detect the slightest edge of menace behind the light, bantering tones and the frequent alcoholic scenes. "To my charming cousin!" he had toasted at her sixteenth birthday party. "May she live to a ripe old age to enjoy what she has coming to her!"

He didn't live on the estate, not since he had graduated from high school two years ago and enrolled at City College in Providence. "Thank you, but I think that I can just about scrape by on my own," he had said. "It will mean an adjustment in the style of living to which I have become accustomed, but I think that I can manage that."

Elizabeth's mother had said in that tone of frustration and helplessness that she always used when she addressed Nicholas, "But you know that you're welcome to stay here. We could buy you a car, and you could drive to the city."

He took the car, and a modest living allowance, and went to live in an apartment in Providence anyway. Elizabeth had visited him there, just once, last year when she had been in the city for some shopping. Sitting in the backseat of the estate Rover with the chauffeur scanning the numbers on the houses, she searched out his address with some difficulty. "That must be it, Miss Elizabeth."

Nicholas had answered the door wearing only a pair of overalls and with a bottle of beer in his hand. He wasn't pleased to see her, standing grudgingly aside to let her enter. The apartment was small, and felt damp, and there were clothes strewn everywhere. The radio was on, playing music that seemed excessively loud. Nicholas made no excuses, or any move to clear a place for her to sit. "Did your mother send you to spy on me? To make sure that I eat all my green vegetables?"

"Don't be silly, Nicholas. She doesn't even know that I'm here. I just wanted to see you."

"Well, you've seen me. Don't bother coming again."

Elizabeth's temper had flared. "You might bother coming down to Newport from time to time. Mom misses you, and since it's her money that's underwriting this whole venture, it's the least you can do."

"Ah, yes. Dear Elizabeth, never missing an opportunity to push my nose into the fact that her side of the family is rich and mine isn't."

"That's not the point. You just could come around sometimes. You have a car."

"Ah, but gasoline is hardly cheap. And I need what I have to go on my monthly visits to my parents in their respective institutions of incarceration. I don't forget them, cousin dearest, even though you may choose to."

"That's not fair, Nicholas! My mother—"

"Ah, yes, your mother, the saint, pays for my mother, the loonie, to live in comfort. I know. She even goes and sits and makes what passes for conversation between them, probably more frequently than I do. I confess that I have never really taken to that particular exercise in masochism. So what am I supposed to do, Elizabeth? Play the prodigal son? I find myself ill suited to that role. Repentance means accepting that you're wrong, and I'm not about to do that."

Elizabeth hadn't gone back again.

The President was talking now about shining futures. He was comparing the graduates to ships sailing out of the protective harbor of Holbrooke Academy and into the sea of life. Ho-hum. Much better to think about this afternoon, and the graduation present that was waiting for her.

She knew about it already, because Mom and Uncle Bob had wanted her to help pick it out. They had spent many happy evenings together, the three of them, poring over catalogs, until they found it. Elizabeth hadn't been allowed to see it, not yet, but she knew that it was waiting for her, shiny and polished and new, on the tarmac of the airfield.

A Piper Cub. Her very first, very own airplane.

She had her pilot's license before she had her driver's license, and she could fly long before that, before she qualified for her "ticket." If it came down to that, she couldn't remember a time when she couldn't fly, not really. That was Mom's doing. Mom was a great pilot; she had done any number of solo cross-countries and had even, just as the war started, flown alone across the Atlantic and landed during a blackout in London. That was something. Elizabeth talked about it a lot. When she was very small, they had flown to California together a few times, but then something happened and they stopped going out to California. Elizabeth didn't know exactly what had happened, and Mom wouldn't talk about it, but Mom did teach her to fly and that was the main thing.

There was nothing more wonderful in the world than flying.

Elizabeth closed her eyes and smiled to herself. Three, at most four hours from now, she would be up there. Alone. In the world that she loved the most, the world where nothing mattered but the sky and the sun and the clouds. Her own special world, surrounded by that intangible substance that, like the water of the ocean, could be calm and gentle and then turn wild and stormy. Up where she could look down and all the people and all their problems just faded into insignificance.

Graduation was all well and good, but what mattered, what really mattered, was flying.

Four rows back, Caroline Asheford Stoddard surreptitiously wiped the perspiration from her brow. It was a silly ceremony and she was wearing a silly hat, but certain conventions and certain rites had to be observed, and she was willing to do what was expected of her.

She glanced at her husband sitting next to her. Certainly, in his light gray suit, Bob looked as comfortable as ever, but then again, he never minded the heat. Sometimes she thought that he just didn't notice. Bob was one of those people who were acutely aware of the important things in life, and blessedly obtuse about the rest. She slipped her hand into his and was rewarded with a brief squeeze.

Well: Elizabeth was graduating from high school. That was something, anyway. For someone who had had such a tumultuous early life, she had grown into a remarkably stable person, so Caroline must have done something right, though she couldn't think of what it was. Marrying Bob had helped. He was such a decent, sure, loving person. Maybe it was Bob who had helped erase those early memories, of parents who took turns at never being around, of that last horrible trip to California and what her daughter had seen there . . .

Caroline flinched at the thought, an unconscious response, and Bob immediately looked at her questioningly, concern on his face. She smiled brightly and shook her head reassuringly and returned to her thoughts. Eric . . . It was so very hard to love someone and realize that he could no longer be part of one's life. She had thought so much about it, back when it happened, had remembered the years living with him on Western Avenue, thought about how he had rescued her and cared for her when no one else would. He had taken the place of her father, and then she had rejected him.

That was what he had said. "You can't just walk out of my life, Caroline. We've been too close."

"I don't know you anymore!" she had burst out. "You're doing things I don't like. I can't be part of that world anymore, Eric. I can't do it."

His face was very pale. "Caroline, don't do this to me now."

She could see the pain in his face, and she hated herself for what she was doing to him. "It's not you, Eric, don't you see? It's what you've become. It's all these things that you're doing. Andrew was right, you know, but it didn't make any difference to you. You'll just go on as you always did. Because Intraglobal is the only thing in the world that matters to you."

"You matter to me. Elizabeth matters to me."

"Not enough to change what you're doing." Caroline took a deep breath. "From now on, we're on opposite sides of the fence."

He frowned. "What are you talking about, Caroline?"

She bit her lip. "I can't just hate what you're doing, Eric. I have to do something about it, or else feel that I'm participating by my silence."

"Caroline—"

"I've been thinking about this, Eric. I'm going to start a group back home, a group to tell people about what is happening. About the flip side of what you're doing. About the dangers of atomic weapons. The dangers of putting too much trust in American corporations." She had stood up and walked over to the window, her back to him, because she couldn't stand watching his face. Despite everything he had done, she still loved him like a father. "I have to live with my conscience, Eric. And if I've learned anything, it's that there are terrible realities in the world. Horrible things happen to people, and if we can justify having survived the war at all we have to do something positive to balance those horrible things." She drew in a deep breath. "I can't justify what you do. And I can't justify my participation in it."

"You're part of Intraglobal, Caroline."

"Not if I choose not to be." She turned to face him. "That would have worked with me once, Eric. There was a time in my life when I would have gone along with that, you know. Let you tell me what to do, and done it because I felt guilty. And I *do* feel guilty, telling you this. But I'm not going to let my past determine my future. You all tried: Grandmother, and you, and Mother, and your lawyers, and even my father. You tried to make me into the person that you wanted me to be. For Intraglobal. I'm not a sacrificial lamb, Eric. I don't like what you're doing, and I don't believe in what you're doing and I'm going to fight it."

"But we're family," Eric protested. "You have to stand behind me."

"No," Caroline. "I don't. What I have to do is live my own life. Go back to Newport and make a decent life for my daughter. Maybe become a flight instructor at the airport; I liked teaching once. And give people information about the corporations that rule their lives. They might not be ready to hear it yet. But that doesn't mean that I don't have an obligation to try."

His face had gone hard. "It won't do you any good, Caroline. We're too powerful for you to make any difference."

"It will make a difference," Caroline said. "It will make a difference in my life. Trying is what makes the difference. I'm not going to just live with it. If I don't try, I'll be as guilty as you are."

"Who are you," Eric asked suddenly, anger in his voice, "to pass judgment on me? Who are you to say that I'm guilty? Your father helped start this company."

"I am not my father," she said with dignity.

But he shook his head. "You'll see, Caroline. You'll see."

"I'll see," she agreed, and she hadn't gone back since then, and over the years Eric had stopped telephoning, stopped writing, stopped imploring her to understand.

Caroline understood. She had even come to understand Andrew, and why he had done what he did, though she couldn't understand the forces that had driven him to do it in front of a child. She understood what the catharsis had meant to him, the absolute need to make Eric confront the violence that he had engendered all those long years.

And continued to engender. Caroline didn't need to be in contact with Eric to read the newspaper, to understand what she heard on the radio. She could almost sense Eric's hand in so many things, always behind the scenes, never named by name, but there nevertheless. She knew intuitively how important Intraglobal had become, even if the name itself was unfamiliar to most people; that was how Eric wanted it. Power, not fame, had always been his goal.

She listened to Senator Joseph McCarthy on the radio, and she knew whose words he was using, who gave him his direction, his information. She read about the escalation of the Cold War between the United States and Russia, and in her mind she raised a glass to Eric: "Starting another profitable scare?" And she had fought him every step of the way.

She saw a country that had lost its innocence when two clouds appeared over Hiroshima and Nagasaki, and she still had nightmares about the children that had died, and she still hated Eric for what he had engineered.

Yet she had found love and a certain kind of peace. She had learned how to rid herself of the guilt. She taught young people how to fly and she took care of Justine's family as well as her own. She wrote letters to public officials and met with other women to warn them of what was happening to their world.

She knew that Eric still watched her, and she knew that he was watching Elizabeth, but she continued to live her life with determination, as though he weren't there, as though he had never existed. His name was never spoken on Ocean Avenue, and if Elizabeth had blurred memories of some distant relative in California, that was just what they remained.

"You'll have to tell her someday," Bob remarked, and Caroline nodded. "Someday. Not now." She wouldn't even buy Elizabeth an airplane that she knew to be an Intraglobal product. The Piper was safe. Eric didn't have anything to do with Piper.

Nevertheless, there were hints that he—or one of his lawyers—was around. The scholarship to Radcliffe that had come through for Elizabeth before she had even completed her application forms; that was surely their doing, grooming Elizabeth to someday take Eric's place. But she never could, Caroline thought; Elizabeth was a good person, gentle, kind. She would never, thank God, have any of Eric's ruthlessness.

She had even tried to dissuade her daughter from attending Radcliffe. The Rhode Island School of Design was so close. "You've always said that you wanted to study art."

"There are a lot of things that I want to study, Mom. Art's just one of them. And I can't wait to see Cambridge!"

Bob had put a reassuring hand over Caroline's. "It's all right," he said gently. "It's a good school, not a center for indoctrination. She'll be all right."

But would she? Caroline bit her lip and worried as she watched her daughter stand up to receive her diploma. Would she really be all right? Her daughter didn't feel the shadow of the megalith that was towering over her, not yet, but one day she would.

And then what would happen to her?

Standing off by himself, shielded from most of the spectators by a sturdy elm tree, Eric Beaumont watched the graduation ceremony with ill-concealed irritation and fought an impulse to light a cigarette. This was a peculiarly American custom, lending such pomp and circumstance to a mere high school graduation—in France the students just learned by mail whether or not they had passed the formidable baccalaureate examination. Moreover, it was too hot. New England heat, he was discovering, was far worse than California heat: moist, humid, heavy. He could feel the sweat forming on his back and dripping down beneath his shirt. He was getting too old for this sort of thing. Once one had passed sixty, one should be able to at least expect a reasonable degree of comfort, *n'est-ce pas*?

Still, he hadn't wanted to miss this. Elizabeth Erica. Caroline couldn't take that away from him, the name that he shared with the child, even though she had taken God only knew everything else away. There had been no opportunity to play surrogate grandfather, as he had expected; no Christmases around a family tree, watching Elizabeth open her presents and squeal with delight; no outings and treats; no chance to inspect her first boyfriend. Eric wanted to see her grow and become intelligent and educated, but mostly he wanted to be part of it all. As the years went by that had become more important to him than the future of Intraglobal. Philippe's granddaughter. He hardly knew her at all.

Well, it was understandable. Caroline had delicate sensibilities, and the stunt that young Starkey had pulled was too much, really. Understandable, but painful nonetheless. It wasn't his fault, after all, that the boy had become deranged. It happened often enough in prison. And to exclude him so firmly and so completely . . .

He risked a glance in Caroline's direction. She was looking good; he had to say that for her. Still slim and pretty, with the rebellious Amelia Earhart curls tucked neatly under a flower-bedecked straw hat, and a flowered print dress over spectator pumps. She still looked young and innocent and carefree. And that man, her husband . . . well, for once Caroline had shown a great deal of sense. Good Yankee stock; old New England money. Even though he wasn't heir to the family estate they had left him quite a respectable wad anyway, and he did well for himself with his records and concert performances. Never married; married to his work, they said, until he met Caroline Ashe-ford, the war widow who loved to fly. Eric knew that he flew with her now, studying his scores in the copilot's seat on their way to concert engagements, surfacing only when she prodded him on the shoulder to say that they were landing.

Elizabeth was a pilot now, too. She looked so different from her mother, it was hard to compare her with Caroline when Caroline was her age. There was more of Philippe to this child. The dark eyes, the dimple, the widow's peak: Those were all Philippe. And Elizabeth gestured with her hands when she talked. That habit had not come to her from a cold Newport mansion—that was straight from Angers. Someday, perhaps, she would learn about her grandfather.

But not from his friend. Caroline had made that clear. Eric was not welcome. There would be no trespassing on their lives. He narrowed his eyes as he watched Elizabeth walking up to receive her diploma—his sight was going, but he refused to wear glasses—and then, duty done, he sighed and turned away. He walked down the sunny grass lawn to the driveway, where the limousine was waiting, and a moment later it was as though he had never been there. He had an appointment in Washington, a meeting with the House Committee on Un-American Activities, and he couldn't afford to be late.

Soizic Aubert-Giroux frowned at the program in her hands. Her English, though fluent, did not run to the valedictory flourishes that accompany graduation ceremonies in the finer New England preparatory schools, and she had lost where they were. Not that it mattered. She was here for the duration anyway. She had made the mistake of sitting on a chair that was next to a tree, and her very fat neighbor on the other side ensured that no early exit would be possible. She might as well, she told herself, relax and try to enjoy this, though how anybody could enjoy anything in this heat was beyond her comprehension.

Elizabeth was eighteen years old now, a child. She had yet to make any kind of imprint in the world. And it was desperately important that Elizabeth do so. No one could control the megalith unless they had first learned to control other companies, learn for themselves the ins and outs of business—and of life. With some luck, Eric Beaumont would need no help for another ten or fifteen years. Elizabeth had time.

But, all the same, Elizabeth was being watched. Groomed and prepared, without her knowing it, without anyone knowing it. She was going to gain the experience that *they* wanted her to have, become the kind of person that they wanted her to be. That was their mandate.

Soizic was not usually deputized to be the presence in question. She preferred to stay in Europe, partly through natural timidity ("People will think that I'm gauche. I don't know the customs. They will laugh at me.") and partly through a desire to stay close to her husband. She had married Marc Giroux a month to the day after Japan surrendered to United States ("An easy anniversary to remember!" Marc had laughed) and was still insecure enough to detest long separations.

No, Elizabeth's scrutiny was usually assigned to Eugene Rousseau, who after all had a longer experience of America and its ways. Soizic was happy enough to leave it to him, but as it turned out, Elizabeth's graduation coincided with the funeral for Robert Beneteau, and although Soizic was a full partner in the firm which now also included Rousseau on the letterhead, she felt that she had known him the least of anyone, and would be the least missed. So she had volunteered. Sitting in the heat of a Rhode Island summer, she was beginning to wonder why.

Everything was going well—better than well. She knew what her report would be: They could relax. As long as Elizabeth Asheford didn't come crashing out of the sky in that new Piper Cub her mother had bought her for graduation, they could relax. Everything was going to work out.

Perfectly.

Two hours later, Elizabeth was flying out over Block Island, the sun cascading into the cockpit of her airplane and her joy sparkling like champagne bubbles all around her.

About the Author

Jeannette Angell is the author of *Wings,* and is currently writing the third novel in this aviation saga. She lives in Georgetown, Massachusetts.